THE KING'S HIGHWAY

G.P.R. JAMES ESQ

Contents

CHAPTER I. 7
CHAPTER II. 13
CHAPTER III. 21
CHAPTER IV. 25
CHAPTER V. 36
CHAPTER VI. 41
CHAPTER VII. 46
CHAPTER VIII. 53
CHAPTER IX. 64
CHAPTER X. 73
CHAPTER XI. 84
CHAPTER XII. 93
CHAPTER XIII. 100
CHAPTER XIV. 113
CHAPTER XV. 126
CHAPTER XVI. 135
CHAPTER XVII. 147
CHAPTER XVIII. 154
CHAPTER XIX. 166
CHAPTER XX. 178
CHAPTER XXI. 192
CHAPTER XXII. 205
CHAPTER XXIII. 211
CHAPTER XXIV. 226
CHAPTER XXV. 236
CHAPTER XXVI. 244
CHAPTER XXVII. 258
CHAPTER XXVIII. 268
CHAPTER XXIX. 276
CHAPTER XXX. 283
CHAPTER XXXI. 297
CHAPTER XXXII. 308
CHAPTER XXXIII. 317
CHAPTER XXXIV. 325
CHAPTER XXXV. 333
CHAPTER XXXVI. 343
CHAPTER XXXVII. 351
CHAPTER XXXVIII. 361
CHAPTER XXXIX. 372
CHAPTER XL. 381
CHAPTER XLI. 392
CHAPTER XLII. 401
CHAPTER XLIII. 409
CHAPTER XLIV. 418
CHAPTER XLV. 425
CHAPTER XLVI. 433

THE KING'S HIGHWAY

BY

G.P.R. JAMES ESQ

CHAPTER I.

Though the weather was hot and sultry, and the summer was at its height, yet the evening was gloomy, and low, angry clouds hung over the distant line of the sea, when, under the shelter of some low-browed cliffs upon the Irish coast, three persons stood together, two of whom were talking earnestly. About four or five miles from the shore, looking like a spectre upon the misty background of clouds, appeared a small brig with her canvas closely reefed, though there was little wind stirring, and nothing announced the approach of a gale, unless it were a long, heavy swell that heaved up the bosom of the ocean as if with a suppressed sob. The three persons we have mentioned were standing together close at the foot of the rocks; and, though there was nothing in their demeanour which would imply that they were seeking concealment by the points and angles of the cliff,--for they spoke loud, and one of them laughed more than once with the short but jocund laugh of a heart whose careless gaiety no circumstances can repress,--yet the spot was well calculated to hide them from any eye, unless it were one gazing down from the cliffs above, or one looking towards the shore from the sea.

The party of which we speak comprised two men not quite reached the middle age, and a fine, noble-looking boy of perhaps eight years old or a little more; but all the conversation was between the two elder, who bore a slight family likeness to each other. The one had a cloak thrown over his arm, and a blue handkerchief bound round his left hand. His dress in other respects was that of a military man of the period; a long-waisted, broad-tailed coat, with a good deal of gold lace and many large buttons upon it, enormous riding boots, and a heavy sword. He had no defensive armour on, indeed, though those were days when the soldierly cuirass was not yet done away with; and on his head he only wore an ordinary hat trimmed round with feathers.

He seemed, however, to be a personage perfectly well able to defend his own, being not much short of six feet in height; and though somewhat thin, extremely muscular, with long, bony arms, and a wide deep chest. His forehead was high and open, and his eye frank and clear, having withal some shrewdness in its quick twinkle. The countenance was a good one; the features handsome, though a little coarse; and if it was not altogether prepossessing, the abatement was made on account of a certain indescribable look of dissipation--not absolutely to say debauchery, but approaching it--which mingled with the expression of finer things, like nightshade filling up the broken masses of some ruined temple. His hair was somewhat prematurely grizzled; for he yet lacked several years of forty, and strong lines, not of thought, were marked upon his brow.

He was, upon the whole, a man whom many people would have called a handsome, fine-looking man; and there was certainly in his countenance that indescribable something, which can only be designated by the term engaging.

While conversing with his companion, which he did frankly and even gaily, laughing, as we have said, from time to time, there was still a peculiarity which might be supposed to show that for some reason he was not perfectly at his ease, or perfectly sure of the man to whom he spoke. In general, he did not look at him, though he gazed straight forward; but, as is very frequently the case with us all, when we are talking to a person whom we doubt or dislike, he looked beyond him, from time to time, however, turning his eyes full upon the countenance of his comrade, and keeping them fixed upon him for several moments.

The second personage of the party was a man somewhat less in height than the other, but still tall. He was two or three years younger; handsome in features; graceful in person; and withal possessing an air of distinction which the other might have possessed also, had it not been considerably diminished by the certain gay and swaggering look which we have already noticed. His dress was not so completely military as that of the first, though there was scarf and sword-knot, and gold-fringed belt and leathern gloves, with wide cuffs, which swallowed up the arms almost to the elbows.

He laughed not at all, and his tone was grave, but smooth and courtly, except when, ever and anon, there mingled with what he was saying in sweet and placid words, some bitter and sarcastic tirade, which made his companion smile, though it moved not a muscle of his own countenance.

We have said that there was a third in the group, and that third was a boy of about eight years of age. It is scarcely possible to conceive anything more beautiful than his countenance, or to fancy a form more replete with living grace than his. His hair swept round his clear and open countenance in dark wavy curls; and while he held the taller of the two gentlemen by the hand, he gazed forward over the wide melancholy sea, which came rolling up towards their feet, with a look full of thought, and perhaps of anxiety. There was certainly grief in that gaze; for the black eyelashes which surrounded those large blue eyes became, after a moment or two, moistened with something bright like a tear; and apparently utterly inattentive to the conversation between his two companions, he still turned away, fully occupied with the matter of his own thoughts.

It is time, however, for us to take notice of that to which he did not attend.

"Not a whit, Harry, not a whit," said the taller of the two: "there are certain portions of good and evil scattered through the world, and every man must take his share of both. I have taken care, as you well know, to secure a certain portion of the pleasures of this life. It was not natural that the thing should last for ever, so I have quite made up my mind to drinking the bitters since I have sipped the sweets. On this last business I have staked my all, and lost my all; and if my poor brother had not done the same, and lost his life into the bargain, I should not much care for my part. On my honour and soul, it does seem to me a strange thing, that here poor Morton, who would have done service to everybody on earth, who was as good as he was brave, and as clever as he was good, should fall at the very first shot, and I go through the whole business with nothing but this scratch of the hand. I did my best to get myself killed, too; for I will swear that I was the last man upon our part that left the bank of the Boyne. But just as half a dozen of the fellows had got me down, and were going to cut my throat because I would not surrender, there came by the fellow they call Bentinck, I think, who called to them not to kill me now that the battle was over. I started up, saying, 'There is one honest Dutchman at least,' and made a dart through them. They would have caught me, I dare say, but he laughed aloud; and I heard him call to them not to follow me, saying, 'That one on either side made no great difference.' I may chance to do that fellow a good turn yet in my day."

"That may well be," replied the other; "for since your brother's death, if you are sure he is killed, you are the direct heir to an earldom, and to estates that would buy a score of German princes."

While he thus spoke, the person he addressed suddenly turned his eyes full upon his face, and looked at him intently for a minute. He then answered, "Sure he is dead, Harry? Did I not tell you that he died in my arms? Would it not have been a nice thing now, if I had been killed too? There would have been none between you and the earldom then. Upon my life, I think you ought to have it: it would just suit you; you would make such a smooth-tongued, easy courtier to this Dutch vagabond, whom you are going over to, I can see, notwithstanding all your asseverations;" and he laughed aloud as he spoke.

"Nonsense, Lennard, nonsense!" replied his companion: "I neither wish you killed, my good cousin, nor care for the earldom, nor am going over to the usurper, though, Heaven knows, you'll do no good to any one, the earldom will do no good to you, and the usurper, perhaps, may do much good to the country. But had either of the three been true, I should certainly have given you up to the Prince of Orange, instead of sharing my last fifty guineas with you, to help you off to France."

His companion gazed down upon the ground with a grim smile, and remained for a moment without answering; he then looked up, gave a short laugh, and replied, "I must not be ungrateful, cousin mine; I thank you for the money with all my heart and soul; but I cannot think that you have run yourself so hard as that either; you must have made mighty great preparations which have not appeared, to spend your snug little patrimony upon a king who did not deserve it, and for whom you did not fight, after all."

"I should have fought if I could have come up in time," replied the other, with his brows darkening. "I suppose you do not suspect me of being unwilling to fight, Lennard?"

"Oh, no, man! no!" replied his cousin: "it does not run in our blood; we have all fighting drops in our veins; and I know you can fight well enough when it suits your purpose. As for that matter, I might think myself a fool for fighting in behalf of a man who won't fight in his own behalf; but it is his cause, not himself, Harry, I fought for."

"Bubbles, bubbles, Lennard," replied the other, "'tis but a mere name!"

"And what do we all fight for, from the cradle to the grave?" demanded his cousin--"bubbles, bubbles, Harry. Through England and Ireland, not to say Scotland, there will be tomorrow morning, which I take it is Sunday, full five thousand priests busily engaged in telling their hearers, that love, glory, avarice, and ambition are nothing but--bubbles! So I am but playing the same game as the rest. I wish to Heaven the boat would come round though, for I am beginning to think it is as great a bubble as the rest.--Run down, Wilton, my boy," he said, speaking to the youth that held him by the hand--"run down to that point, and see if you can discover the boat creeping round under the cliffs."

The boy instantly darted off without speaking, and the two gentlemen watched him in silence. After a moment, however, the shorter of the two spoke, with his eyes still fixed on the child, and the slight sneer curling his lip--"A fine boy that, Lennard!" he said. "A child of love, of course!"

"Doubtless," answered the other; "but you will understand he is not mine.--It is a friend's child that I have promised to do the best for."

"He is wondrous like your brother Morton," rejoined his companion: "it needs no marriage certificate to tell us whose son he is."

"No; God speed the poor boy!" replied the other gentleman, "he is like his father enough. I must do what I can for him, though Heaven knows what I am to do either for him or myself. It is long ere he can be a soldier, and I am not much accustomed to taking heed of children."

"Where is his mother?" demanded the cousin: "whatever be her rank, she is most likely as rich as you are, and certainly better able to take care of him."

"Pshaw!" replied the other--"I might look long enough before I found her. The boy has never known anything about her either, so that would not do. But here he comes, here he comes, so say no more about it."

As he spoke, the boy bounded up, exclaiming, "I see the boat, I see the boat coming round the rock!" and the moment after, a tolerable-sized fishing boat was seen rounding the little point that we have mentioned; and the two cousins, with the boy, descended to the water's edge. During the few minutes that elapsed before the boat came up to the little landing-place where they stood, the cousins shook hands together, and bade each other adieu.

"Well, God speed you, Harry!" said the one; "you have not failed me at this pinch, though you have at many another."

"Where shall I write to you, Lennard," demanded the other, "in case that anything should happen to turn up to your advantage?"

"Oh! to the Crown, to the Crown, at St. Germains," replied the elder; "and if it be for anything to my advantage, write as quickly as possible, good cousin.--Come, Wilton, my boy; come, here's the boat! Thank God we have not much baggage to embark.--Now, my man," he continued, speaking to one of the fishermen who had leaped out into the water, "lift the boy in, and the portmanteau, and then off to yonder brig, with all the sail you can put on."

Thus saying, he sprang into the boat, received the boy in his arms, and waved his hand to his cousin, while the fishermen pushed off from the shore.

The one who was left behind folded his arms upon his chest, and gazed after the boat as she bounded over the water. His brow was slightly clouded, and a peculiar sort of smile hung upon his lip; but after thus pausing for a minute or two, he turned upon his heel, walked up a narrow path to the top of the cliff, and mounting a horse which was held for him by a servant, at a distance of about a hundred yards from the edge, he rode away, whistling as he went, not like Cimon, for want of thought, but from the very intensity of thought.

CHAPTER II

The horseman of whom we have spoken in the last chapter rode slowly on about two hundred yards farther, and there the servant advanced and opened a gate, by means of which the path they were then upon communicated with a small road between two high banks leading down to the sea-side. The moment that the gentleman rode forward through the gate, his eyes fell upon a figure coming up apparently from the sea-shore. It was that of a woman, seemingly well advanced in life, and dressed in the garb of the lower orders: there was nothing particular in her appearance, except that in her gait and figure she was more decrepit than from her countenance might have been expected. The tears were streaming rapidly down her face, however; and though she suddenly paused on perceiving the stranger, she could not command those tears from flowing on, though she turned away her head to conceal them.

The stranger slightly pulled in his horse's rein, looked at her again, and then gazed thoughtfully down the road towards the sea, as if calculating what the woman could have been doing there, and whether she could have seen the departure of his two late companions.

The servant who was behind him seemed to read his master's thoughts; for being close to him shutting the gate, he said in a low tone, "That's the old woman with whom the young gentleman lodged; for I saw her when the Colonel went there this morning to fetch him away."

The moment the man had spoken, his master pushed forward his horse again, and riding up to the woman, accosted her at once.

"Ah, my good woman," he said, "you are grieving after your poor little boy; but do not be cast down, he will be taken good care of."

"God bless your honour," replied the woman, "and thank you, too, for comforting me: he's a dear good boy, that's true; but the Colonel has taken him to France, so I shall never see him more."

"Oh yes, you may, my good lady," replied the stranger: "you know I am his cousin--his father's first cousin; so if you want to hear of him from time to time, perhaps I could put you in the way of it. If I knew where you lived, I would come and call upon you to-night, and talk to you about it before I go on to Dublin."

"Your honour's going to Dublin, are you?" said the woman, suddenly and sharply, while the blood mounted into the cheek of her companion, as if from some feeling of embarrassment. She continued, however, before he could reply, saying, "With a thousand thanks to your honour, I shall be glad to see you; and if I could but hear that the poor boy got well to France, and was comfortable, I think I should be happy all my life."

"But where do you live, my good woman?" demanded the horseman: "we have not much time to lose, for the sun is going down, and the night is coming on."

"And a stormy night it will be," said the woman, who, though she had very little of the Irish accent, seemed to have not a little of that peculiar obliquity of mind, which so often leads the Irishman to follow the last idea started, however loosely it may be connected with the main subject of discourse. "As to where I live," she continued, "it's at the small neat cottage at the end of the lane; the best house in the place to my mind, except the priest's and the tavern; and for that matter, it's my own property, too."

"Well, I will come there in about an hour," said her companion, "and we will talk it all over, my good lady, for I must leave this place early to-morrow."

Away went the stranger as he spoke, at a rapid pace, towards an Irish village or small town of that day, which lay at the distance of about a mile and a half from the sea-shore. It was altogether a very different place, and bore a very different aspect, from any other collection of houses, of the same number and extent, within the shores of the Sister Island. It was situated upon the rise of a steep hill, at the foot of which ran a clear shallow stream, from whose margin, up to the top of the acclivity, ran two irregular rows of houses, wide apart, and scattered at unequal distances, on the two sides of the high road. They were principally hovels, of a single story in height; a great proportion of them formed of nothing but turf, with no other window but a hole covered with a board, and sometimes not that. Others, few and far between, again, were equally of one story, but were neatly plastered with clay, and ornamented with a wash of lime; and besides these, were three or four houses which really deserved the name--the parish priest's, the tavern, and what was called the shop.

These rows of dwellings were raised on two high but sloping banks, which were covered with green turf, and extended perhaps fifty yards in width between the houses and the road: this long strip of turf affording the inhabitants plenty of space for dunghills and dust-heaps, with occasional stacks of turf, and a detached sort of summer-house now and then for a pig, in those cases where his company was not preferred in the parlour.

Here, too, the chickens used to meet in daily convocation; and here the priest's bull would occasionally take a morning walk, to the detriment of the dunghills and the frailer edifices, to the danger of the children, and the indignation of the other animals, who might seem to think that they had a right prescriptive to exclusive possession.

Between these two tracts of debatable land was interposed a paved high road, twice as broad as it needed to have been, and furnished with a stone gutter down the centre, into which flowed, from every side, streams not Castalian; while five or six ducks, belonging to the master of the shop, acted as the only town scavengers; and a large black sow, with a sturdy farrow of eleven young pigs, rolled about in the full enjoyment of the filth and dirt, seeming to represent the mayor and town council of this rural municipality.

At the top of the hill two or three lanes turned off, and in one of these was situated the cottage which the old lady had indicated as her dwelling. The stranger, however, rode not thither at once, but, in the first place, stopped at the tavern, as it was called (being neither more nor less than a small public-house), and throwing his rein to the servant, he dismounted, and paused to order some refreshment. When this was done, he took his way at once to the house of the priest, which was a neat white building, showing considerable taste in all its external arrangements. The stranger was immediately admitted, and remained for about half an hour; at the end of which time he came out, accompanied as far as the little wicket gate by a very benign and thoughtful-looking man, past the middle age, whose last words, as he took leave of the stranger, were, "Alas, my son! she was so beautiful, and so charitable, that it is much to be lamented that she was in all respects a cast-away."

The stranger then returned to the tavern, and sat down to a somewhat black and angular roasted fowl, which, however, proved better to the palate than the eye; and to this he added somewhat more than a pint of claret, which--however strange it may seem to find such a thing in an Irish pot-house--might, for taste and fragrance, have competed with the best that ever was found at the table of prince or peer: nor was such a thing uncommon in that day. This done, and when five or six minutes of meditation--that kind of pleasant meditation which ensues when the inner man is made quite comfortable--had been added to his moderate food and moderate potation, the stranger rose, and with a slow and thoughtful step walked forth from the inn, and took his way towards the cottage to which the old woman had directed him.

The sun was by this time sinking below the horizon, and a bright red glow from his declining rays spread through the atmosphere, tinging the edges of the long, liny, lurid clouds which were gathering thickly over the sky. The wind, too, had risen considerably, and was blowing with sharp quick gusts increasing towards a gale, so that the stranger was obliged to put his hand to his large feathered hat to keep it firm upon his head.

In the meantime, the old woman had returned home, and her first occupation was to indulge her grief; for, sitting down at the little table in her parlour, she covered her eyes with her hands, and wept till the tears ran through her fingers. After a time, however, she calmed herself, and rising, looked for a moment into a small looking-glass, which showed her face entirely disfigured with tears. She then went into a little adjacent room, which, as well as the parlour, was the image of neatness and cleanness. She there took a towel, dipped it in cold water, and seemed about to bathe away the traces from her cheeks. The next moment, however, she threw the towel down, saying, "No, no! why should I?" She then returned to the parlour, and called down the passage, "Betty, Betty!"

An Irishwoman, of about fifty years of age, clothed much in the same style, and not much worse than her mistress, appeared in answer to her summons; and, according to the directions she now received, lighted a single candle, put up a large heavy shutter against the parlour window, and retired. The mistress of the house remained for some time sitting at the table, and apparently listening for every step without; though from time to time, when a heavier and heavier blast of wind shook the cottage where she sat, she gazed up towards the sky, and her lips moved as if offering a prayer.

At length, some one knocked loudly at the door, and starting up, she hurried to open it and give entrance to the stranger whom we have mentioned before. She put a chair for him, and stood till he asked her to sit down.

"So, my good lady," he said, "you lived a long time with Colonel and Mrs. Sherbrooke."

"Oh! bless you, yes, sir," replied the woman, "ever since the Colonel and the young lady came here, till she died, poor thing, and then I remained to take care of the boy, dear, beautiful fellow."

"You seem very sorry to lose him," rejoined the stranger, "and, doubtless, were sadly grieved when Mrs. Sherbrooke died."

"You may well say that," replied the woman; "had I not known her quite a little girl? and to see her die, in the prime of her youth and beauty, not four-and-twenty years of age. You may well say I was sorry. If her poor father could have seen it, it would have broke his heart; but he died long before that, or many another thing would have broken his heart as well as that."

"Was her father living," demanded the stranger, "when she married Colonel Sherbrooke?"

The woman, without replying, gazed inquiringly and steadfastly on the stranger's countenance for a moment or two; who continued, after a short pause--"Poo, poo, I know all about it; I mean, when she came away with him."

"No, sir," replied the woman; "he had been dead then more than a year."

"Doubtless," replied the stranger, "it was, as you implied, a happy thing for him that he did not live to see his daughter's fate; but how was it, I wonder, as she was so sweet a creature, and the Colonel so fond of her, that he never married her?"

The woman looked down for a moment; but then gazed up in his face with a somewhat rueful expression of countenance, and a shake of the head, answering, "She was a Protestant, you know."

The stranger looked surprised, and asked, "Did she always continue a Protestant, my good woman? I should have thought love could have worked more wonderful conversions than that."

"Ah! she died as she lived, poor thing," replied the woman, "and with nobody with her either, but I and one other; for the Colonel was away, poor man, levying troops for the king--that is, for King James, sir; for your honour looks as if you were on the other side."

The stranger was silent and looked abstracted; but at length he answered, somewhat listlessly, "Really, my good woman, one does not know what side to be of. It is raining very hard to-night, unless those are the boughs of the trees tapping against your window."

"Those are the large drops of rain," replied the woman, "dashed against the glass by the south-west wind. It will be an awful night; and I think of the ship."

"I will let you hear of the boy," rejoined the stranger in an indifferent tone, "as soon as I hear of him myself;" and taking up his hat from the table, he seemed about to depart, when a peculiar expression upon the woman's countenance made him pause, and, at the same time, brought to his mind that he had not even asked her name.

"I thought your honour had forgotten," she replied, when he asked her the question at length. "They call me Betty Harper; but Mrs. Harper will find me in this place, if you put that upon your letter: and now that we are asking such sort of questions, your honour wouldn't be offended, surely, if I were to ask you your name too?"

"Certainly not, my good lady," he replied; "I am called Harry Sherbrooke, Esquire, very much at your service.--Heavens, how it blows and rains!"

"Perhaps it is nothing but a wind-shower" replied the woman; "if your honour would like to wait until it has ridden by."

"Why, I shall get drenched most assuredly if I go," he answered, "and that before I reach the inn; but I will look out and see, my good lady."

He accordingly proceeded into the little passage, and opened the door, followed by his companion. They were instantly saluted, however, by a blast of wind that almost knocked the strong man himself down, and made the woman reel against the wall of the passage.

Everything beyond--though the cottage, situated upon a height, looked down the slope of the hill, over the cliffs, to the open sea--was as dark as the cloud which fell upon Egypt: a darkness that could be felt! and not the slightest vestige of star or moon, or lingering ray of sunshine, marked to the eye the distinction between heaven, earth, and sea.

Sherbrooke drew back, as the wind cut him, and the rain dashed in his face; but at that very moment something like a faint flash was seen, apparently at a great distance, and gleaming through the heavy rain. The woman instantly caught her companion's wrist tight in her grasp, exclaiming, "Hark!"--and in a few seconds after, in a momentary lull of the wind, was heard the low booming roar of a distant cannon.

"It is a signal of distress!" cried the woman. "Oh! the ship, the ship! The wind is dead upon the shore, and the long reef, out by the Battery Point, has seen many a vessel wrecked between night and morning."

While she spoke, the signal of distress was seen and heard again.

"I will go down and send people out to see what can be done," said the stranger, and walked away without waiting for reply. He turned his steps towards the inn, muttering as he went, "There's one, at least, on board the ship that won't be drowned, if there's truth in an old proverb! so if the vessel be wrecked to-night, I had better order breakfast for my cousin to-morrow morning--for he is sure to swim ashore." It was a night, however, on which no hope of reaching land could cheer the wrecked seamen. The tide was approaching the full; the wind was blowing a perfect hurricane; the surf upon a high rocky beach, no boat could have lived in for a minute; and the strongest swimmer--even if it had been within the scope of human power and skill to struggle on for any time with those tremendous waves--must infallibly have been dashed to pieces on the rocks that lined the shore. The minute guns were distinctly heard from that town, and several other villages in the neighbourhood. Many people went to the tops of the cliffs, and some down to the sea-shore, where the waves did not reach the bases of the rocks. One gentleman, living in the neighbourhood, sent out servants and tenantry with links and torches, but no one ever could clearly distinguish the ship; and could only perceive that she must be in the direction of a dangerous rocky shoal called the Long Reef, at about two miles' distance from the shore.

The next morning, however, her fate was more clearly ascertained; not that a vestige of her was to be seen out at sea, but the whole shore for two or three miles was covered with pieces of wreck. The stern-post of a small, French-built vessel, and also a boat considerably damaged in the bow, and turned keel upwards, came on shore as Harry Sherbrooke and his servant were themselves examining the scene. The boat bore, painted in white letters, "La Coureuse de Dunkerque."

"That is enough for our purpose, I should suppose," said the master, pointing to the letters with a cane he had in his hand, and addressing his servant--"I must be gone, Harrison, but you remain behind, and do as I bade you."

"Wait a moment, yet, sir," replied the man: "you see they are bringing up a body from between those two rocks,--it seems about his size and make, too;" and approaching the spot to which he pointed, they found some of the country people carrying up the body of a French officer, which afterwards proved to be that of the commander of the brig, which had been seen during the preceding day. After examining the papers which were taken from the pockets of the dead man, one of which seemed to be a list of all the persons on board his vessel, Sherbrooke turned away, merely saying to his servant, "Take care and secure that paper, and bring it after me to Dublin as fast as possible."

The man bowed his head, and his master walked slowly and quietly away.

CHAPTER III

Now whatever might be the effect of all that passed, as recorded in the last chapter, upon the mind of Harry Sherbrooke, it is not in the slightest degree our intention to induce the reader to believe that the two personages, the officer and the little boy, whom we saw embark for the brig which was wrecked, were amongst the persons who perished upon that occasion. True it is that every person the ship contained found a watery grave, between sunset and sunrise on the night in question. But to explain how the whole took place, we must follow the track of the voyagers in the boat.

As soon as they were seated, Lennard Sherbrooke threw his arms affectionately round the boy, drew him a little closer to his bosom, and kissed his broad fair forehead; while the boy, on his part, with his hand leaning on the officer's knee, and his shoulder resting confiding on his bosom, looked up in his face with eyes of earnest and deep affection. In such mute conference they remained for some five or ten minutes; while the hardy sailors pulled away at the oars, their course towards the vessel lying right in the wind's eye. After a minute or two more, Lennard Sherbrooke turned round, and gazed back towards the shore, where he could now plainly perceive his cousin beginning to climb the little path up the cliff. After watching him for a moment with a look of calculating thought, he turned towards the boy again, and saw that there were tears in his eyes, which sight caused him to bend down, saying, in a low voice, "You are not frightened, my dear boy?"

"Oh no, no!" replied the boy--"I am only sorry to go away to a strange place."

Lennard Sherbrooke turned his eyes once more towards the shore, but the form of his cousin had now totally disappeared. He then remained musing for a minute or two, while the fishermen laboured away, making no very great progress against the wind. At the distance of about a mile or a mile and a half from the shore,

Lennard Sherbrooke turned round towards the man who was steering, and made some remarks upon the excellence of the boat. The man, proud of his little vessel, boasted her capabilities, and declared that she was as sea-worthy as any frigate in the navy.

"I should like to see her tried," said Sherbrooke. "I should not wonder if she were well tried to-night," replied the man.

For a moment or two the officer made no rejoinder; but then approaching the steersman nearer still, he said, in a low voice, "Come, my man, I have something to tell you. We must alter our course very soon; I am not going to yon Frenchman at all."

"Why, then, where the devil are you going to?" demanded the fisherman; and he proceeded, in tones and in language which none but an Irishman must presume to deal with, to express his astonishment, that after having been hired by the other gentleman to carry the person who spoke to him and the boy to the French brig of war, where berths had been secured for them, he should be told that they were not going there at all.

The stranger suffered him to expend all his astonishment without moving a muscle, and then replied, with perfect calmness, "My good friend, you are a Catholic, I have been told, and a good subject to King James--"

"God bless him!" interrupted the man, heartily; but Sherbrooke proceeded, saying, "In these days one may well be doubtful of one's own relations; and I have a fancy, my man, that unless I prevent any one from knowing my course, and where I am, I may be betrayed where I go, and betrayed if I stay. Now what I want you to do is this, to take me over to the coast of England, instead of to yonder French brig."

The man's astonishment was very great; but he seemed to enter into the motives of his companion with all the quick perception of an Irishman. There were innumerable difficulties, however, which he did not fail to start; and he asserted manfully, that it was utterly impossible for them to proceed upon such a voyage at once. In the first place, they had no provisions; in the next place, there was the wife and children, who would not know what was become of them; in the third place, it was coming on to blow hard right upon the coast. So that he proved there was, in fact, not only danger and difficulty, but absolute impossibility, opposed to the plan which the gentleman wished to follow.

In the meanwhile, the four seamen, who were at the oars, laboured away incessantly, but with very slow and difficult efforts. Every moment the wind rose higher and higher, and the sun's lower limb touched the waters, while they were yet two miles from the French brig.

A part of the large red disk of the descending orb was seen between the sea and the edge of the clouds that hung upon the verge of the sky, pouring forth from the horizon to the very shore a long line of blood-red light, which, resting upon the boiling waters of the ocean, seemed as if the setting star could indeed "the multitudinous sea incarnadine, making the green one red."

That red light, however, showed far more clearly than before how the waters were already agitated; for the waves might be seen distinctly, even to the spot in the horizon where they seemed to struggle with the sun, heaving up their gigantic heads till they appeared to overwhelm him before he naturally set.

The arguments of the fisherman apparently effected that thing which is so seldom effected in this world; namely, to convince the person to whom they were addressed. I say SELDOM, for there have been instances known, in remote times, of people being convinced. They puzzled him, however, and embarrassed him very much, and he remained for full five minutes in deep and anxious thought.

His reverie, however, was brought to an end suddenly, by a few words which the fisherman whispered to him. His countenance brightened; a rapid and brief conversation followed in a low tone, which ended in his abruptly holding out his hand to the good man at the helm, saying, "I trust to your honour."

"Upon my soul and honour," replied the fisherman, grasping his proffered hand.

The matter now seemed settled,--no farther words passed between the master of the boat and his passenger; but the seaman gave a rapid glance to the sky, to the long spit of land called the Battery Point, and to the southward, whence the wind was blowing so sharply.

"We can do it," he muttered to himself, "we can do it;" and he then gave immediate orders for changing the boat's course, and putting out all sail. His companions seemed as much surprised by his change of purpose, as he had been with the alteration of his passenger's determination. His orders were nevertheless obeyed promptly, the head of the boat was turned away from the wind, the canvas caught the gale, and away she went like lightning, heeling till the little yard almost touched the water. Her course, however, was not bent back exactly to the same spot from which she started, and it now became evident that it was the fisherman's intention to round the Battery Point.

Lennard Sherbrooke was not at all aware of the dangerous reef that lay so near their course; but it soon became evident to him that there was some great peril, which required much skill and care to avoid; and, as night fell, the anxiety of the seamen evidently became greater. The wind by this time was blowing quite a hurricane, and the rushing roaring sound of the gale and the ocean was quite deafening. But about half an hour after sunset that peculiar angry roar, which is only heard in the neighbourhood of breakers, was distinguished to leeward; and looking in that direction, Sherbrooke perceived one long white line of foam and surf, rising like an island in the midst of dark and struggling waters.

Not a word was said: it seemed as if scarcely a breath was drawn. In a few minutes the sound of the breakers became less distinct; a slight motion was perceivable in the arm of the man who held the tiller, and in about ten minutes the effect of the neighbouring headlands was found in smoother water and a lighter gale, as the boat glided calmly and steadily on, into a small bay, not many hundred miles from Baltimore. The rest of their voyage, till they reached the shore again, was safe and easy: the master of the boat and his men seemed to know every creek, cove, and inlet, as well as their own dwelling places; and, directing their coarse to a little but deep stream, they ran in between two other boats, and were soon safely moored.

The boy, by Sherbrooke's direction, had lain himself down in the bottom of the boat, wrapped up in a large cloak; and there, with the happy privilege of childhood, he had fallen sound asleep, nor woke till danger and anxiety were passed, and the little vessel safe at the shore. Accommodation was easily found in a neighbouring village, and, on the following day, one, and only one, of the boat's crew went over to the spot from which they had set out on the preceding evening. He returned with another man, both loaded with provisions. There was much coming and going between the village and the boat during the day. By eventide the storm had sobbed itself away; the sea was calm again, the sky soft and clear; and beneath the bright eyes of the watchful stars, the boat once more took its way across the broad bosom of the ocean, with its course laid directly towards the English shore.

CHAPTER IV.

Those were days of pack-saddles and pillions--days certainly not without their state and display; but yet days in which persons were not valued according to the precise mode of their dress or equipage, when hearts were not appraised by the hat or gloves, nor the mind estimated by the carriages or horses.

Man was considered far more abstractedly then than at present; and although illustrious ancestors, great possessions, and hereditary claims upon consideration, were allowed more weight than they now possess, yet the minor circumstances of each individual,--the things that filled his pocket, the dishes upon his table, the name of his tailor, or the club that he belonged to,--were seldom, if ever, allowed to affect the appreciation of his general character.

However that might be, it was an age, as we have said, of pack-saddles and pillions; and no one, at any distance from the capital itself, would have been the least ashamed to be seen with a lady or child mounted behind him on the same horse, while he jogged easily onward on his destined way.

It was thus that, about a quarter of an hour before nightfall, a, tall powerful man was seen riding along through one of the north-western counties of England, with a boy of about eight years of age mounted on a pillion behind him, and steadying himself on the horse by an affectionate embrace cast round the waist of his elder companion.

Lennard Sherbrooke--for the reader has already divined that this was no other than the personage introduced to him in our first chapter--Lennard Sherbrooke, then, was still heavily armed, but in other respects had undergone a considerable change. The richly laced coat had given place to a plain dark one of greenish brown; the large riding boots remained; and the hat, though it kept its border of feathers, was divested of every other ornament. There were pistols at the saddle-bow, which indeed were very necessary in those days to every one who performed the perilous and laborious duty of wandering along the King's Highway; and in every other respect the appearance of Lennard Sherbrooke was well calculated neither to attract cupidity nor invite attack.

About ten minutes after the period at which we have again introduced him to our readers, the traveller and his young companion stopped at the door of an old-fashioned inn, or rather at the porch thereof; for the door itself, with a retiring modesty, stood at some distance back, while an impudent little portico with carved oak pillars, of quaint but not inelegant design, stood forth into the road, with steps leading down from it to the sill of the sunk doorway. An ostler ran out to take the horse, and helped the boy down tenderly and carefully. Sherbrooke himself then dismounted, looked at his beast from head to foot, and then ordering the ostler to give him some hay and water, he took the boy by the hand and entered the house.

The ostler looked at the beast, which was tired, and then at the sky, over which the first shades of evening were beginning to creep, thinking as he did so that the stranger might quite as well put up his beast for the night. In the meantime, however, Sherbrooke had given the boy into the charge of the hostess, had bidden her prepare some supper for him, and had intimated that he himself was going a little farther, but would soon return to sleep at her hospitable dwelling. He ordered to be brought in and given into her charge also a small portmanteau,--smaller than that which he had taken with him into the boat,--and when all this was done, he kissed the boy's forehead tenderly, and left him, mounting once more his weary beast, and plodding slowly along upon his way.

It was a very sweet evening: the sun, half way down behind one of the distant hills, seemed, like man's curiosity, to overlook unheeded all the bright and beautiful things close to him, and to gaze with his eyes of light full upon the objects further from him, through which the wayfarer was bending his way. The line of undulating hills, the masses of a long line of woodland, some deep valleys and dells, a small village with its church and tower on an eminence, were all in deep blue shadow; while, in the foreground, every bank and slope was glittering in yellow sunshine, and a small river, that wound along through the flatter part of the ground, seemed turned into gold by the great and glorious alchymist, as he sunk to his rest.

The heart of the traveller who wandered there alone was ill, very ill at ease. Happily for himself, as he was now circumstanced, the character of Sherbrooke was a gay and buoyant one, not easily depressed, bearing the load lightly; but still he could not but feel the difficulties, the dangers, and the distresses of a situation, which, though shared in by very many at that moment, was rather aggravated by such being the case, and had but small alleviation even from hope.

In the first place, he had seen the cause to which he had attached himself utterly ruined by the base irresolution of a weak monarch, who had lost his crown by his tyranny, and who had failed to regain it by his courage. In the next place, for his devotion to that cause, he was a banished and an outlawed man, with his life at the mercy of any one who chose to take it. In the next he was well nigh penniless, with the life of another, dear, most dear to his heart, depending entirely upon his exertions.

The heart of the traveller, then, was ill, very ill at ease, but yet the calm of that evening's sunshine had a sweet and tranquillizing effect. There is a mirror--there is certainly a moral mirror in our hearts, which reflects the images of the things around us; and every change that comes over nature's face is mingled sweetly, though too often unnoticed, with the thoughts and feelings called forth by other things. The effect of that calm evening upon Lennard Sherbrooke was not to produce the wild, bright, visionary dreams and expectations which seem the peculiar offspring of the glowing morning, or of the bright and risen day; but it was the counterpart, the image, the reflection of that evening scene itself to which it gave rise in his heart. He felt tranquillized, he felt more resolute, more capable of enduring. Grief and anxiety subsided into melancholy and resolution, and the sweet influence of the hour had also an effect beyond: it made him pause upon the memories of his past life, upon many a scene of idle profligacy, revel, and riot,--of talents cast away and opportunity neglected,--of fortune spent and bright hopes blasted,--and of all the great advantages which he had once possessed utterly lost and gone, with the exception of a kind and generous heart: a jewel, indeed, but one which in this world, alas! can but too seldom be turned to the advantage of the possessor.

On these things he pondered, and a sweet and ennobling regret came upon him that it should be so--a regret which might have gone on to sincere repentance, to firm amendment, to the retrieval of fortunes, to an utter change of destiny, had the circumstances of the times, or any friendly voice and helping hand, led his mind on upon that path wherein it had already taken the first step, and had opened out before him a way of retrieval, instead of forcing him onward down the hill of destruction. But, alas! those were not times when the opportunity of doing better was likely to be allowed to him; nor were circumstances destined to change his course. His destiny, like that of many Jacobites of the day, was but to be from ruin to ruin; and let it be remembered, that the character and history of Lennard Sherbrooke are not ideal, but are copied faithfully from a true but sad history of a life in those times.

All natural affections sweeten and purify the human heart. Like everything else given us immediately from God, their natural tendency is to wage war against all that is evil within us; and every single thought of amendment and improvement, every regret for the past, every better hope for the future, was connected with the thought of the beautiful boy he had left behind at the inn; and elevated by his love for a being in the bright purity of youth, he thought of him and his situation again and again; and often as he did so, the intensity of his own feelings made him murmur forth half audible words all relating to the boy, or to the person he was then about to seek, for the purpose of interesting him in the poor youth's fate.

"I will tell him all and everything," he said, thus murmuring to himself as he went on: "he may drive me forth if he will; but surely, surely, he will protect and do something for the boy. What, though there have been faults committed and wrong done, he cannot be so hard-hearted as to let the poor child starve, or be brought up as I can alone bring him up."

Such was still the conclusion to which he seemed to come; and at length when the sun had completely gone down, and at the distance of about three miles from the inn, he paused before a large pair of wooden gates, consisting of two rows of square bars of painted wood placed close together, with a thick heavy rail at the top and bottom, while two wooden obelisks, with their steeple-shaped summits, formed the gate posts. Opening the gates, as one well familiar with the lock, he now entered the smaller road which led from them through the fields towards a wood upon the top of the hill. At first the way was uninteresting enough, and the faint remains of twilight only served to show some square fields within their hedge-rows cut in the most prim and undeviating lines around. The wayfarer rode on, through that part of the scene, with his eyes bent down in deep thought; but when he came to the wood; and, following the path--which, now kept with high neatness and propriety, wound in and out amongst the trees, and then sweeping gently round the shoulder of the hill, exposed a beautiful deer park--he had before his eyes a fine Elizabethan house, rising grey upon a little eminence at the distance of some four or five hundred yards,--it seemed that some old remembrance, some agitating vision of the days gone by, came over the horseman's mind. He pulled in his rein, clasped his hands together, and gazed around with a look of sad and painful recognition. At the end of a minute or two, however, he recovered himself, rode on to the front of the house we have mentioned, and dismounting from his horse, pulled the bell-rope which action was instantly followed by a long peal heard from within.

"It sounds cold and empty," said the wayfarer to himself, "like my reception, and perhaps my hopes."

No answer was made for some time; and though the sounds had been loud enough, as the traveller's ears bore witness, yet they required to be repeated before any one came to ask his pleasure.

"This is very strange!" he said, as he applied his hand to the bell-rope again. "He must have grown miserly, as they say, indeed. Why I remember a dozen servants crowding into this porch at the first sound of a horse's feet."

A short time after, some steps were heard within; bolts and bars were carefully withdrawn, and an old man in a white jacket, with a lantern in his hand, opened the heavy oaken door, and gazed upon the stranger.

"Where is the Earl of Byerdale?" demanded the horseman, in apparent surprise. "Is he not at home?"

The old man gazed at him for a moment from head to foot, without replying, and then answered slowly and somewhat bitterly, "Yes, he is at home--at his long home, from which he'll never move again! Why, he has been dead and buried this fortnight."

"Indeed!" cried the traveller, putting his hand to his head, with an air of surprise, and what we may call dismay; "indeed! and who has discharged the servants and shut up the house?"

"Those who have a right to do it," replied the old man, sharply; "for my lord was not such a fool as to leave his property to be spent, and his place mismanaged, by two scape-graces whom he knew well enough."

As he spoke, without farther ceremony he shut the door in the stranger's face, and then returned to his own abode in the back part of the house, chuckling as he went, and murmuring to himself, "I think I have paid him now for throwing me into the horsepond, for just telling a little bit of a lie about Ellen, the laundry maid. He thought I had forgotten him! Ha! ha! ha!"

The traveller stood confounded; but he made no observation, he uttered no word, he seemed too much accustomed to meet the announcement of fresh misfortune to suffer it to drive him from the strong-hold of silence. Sweeter or gentler feelings might have done it: he might have been tempted to speak aloud in calm meditation and thought, either gloomy or joyful; but his heart, when wrung and broken by the last hard grasp of fate, like the wolf at his death, was dumb.

He remained for full two minutes, however, beneath the porch, motionless and silent; then springing on his horse's back, he urged him somewhat rapidly up the slope. Ere he had reached the top, either from remembering that the beast was weary, or from some change in his own feelings, he slackened his pace, and gave himself up to meditation again. The first agony of the blow that he had received was now over, and once again he not only reasoned with himself calmly, but expressed some of his conclusions in a murmur.

"What!" he said, "a peer without a penny! the name attainted, too, and all lands and property declared forfeit! No, no! it will never do! Years may bring better times!--Who knows? the attainder may be reversed; new fortunes may be gained or made! The right dies not, though it may slumber; exists, though it be not enforced. A peer without a penny! no, no!--far better a beggar with half a crown!"

Thus saying he rode on, passed through the wood we have mentioned,--the dull meadows, and the wooden gates; and entering the high road, was proceeding towards the inn, when an event occurred which effected a considerable change in his plans and purposes.

It was by this time one of those dark nights, the most propitious that can be imagined for such little adventures as rendered at one time the place called Gad's Hill famous alike in story and in song. It wasn't that the night was cloudy, for, to say sooth, it was a fine night, and manifold small stars were twinkling in the sky; but the moon, the sweet moon, was at that time in her infancy, a babe of not two days old, so that the light she afforded to her wandering companions through the fields of space was of course not likely to be much. The stars twinkled, as we have said, but they gave no light to the road; and on either side there were sundry brakes, and lanes, and hedges, and groups of trees which were sufficiently shady and latitant in the mid-day, and which certainly were impervious to any ray of light then above the horizon.

The mind of Lennard Sherbrooke, however, was far too busy about other things to think of dangers on the King's Highway. His purse was certainly well armoured against robbery; and the defence was on the inside and not on the out; so that--had he thought on the matter at all, which he did not do--he might very probably have thought, in his light recklessness, he wished he might meet with a highwayman, in order to try whether he could not rob better than be robbed.

However, as I have said, he thought not of the subject at all. His own situation, and that of the boy Wilton, occupied him entirely; and it was not till the noise of a horse's feet coming rapidly behind him sounded close at his shoulder, that he turned to see by whom he had been overtaken.

All that Sherbrooke could perceive was, that it was a man mounted on a re-markably fine horse, riding with ease and grace, and bearing altogether the appear-ance of a gentleman.

"Pray, sir," said the stranger, "can you tell me how far I am from the inn called the Buck's Horns, and whether this is the direct road thither?"

"The inn is about two miles on," replied Sherbrooke, "on the left-hand side of the way, and you cannot miss it, for there is no other house for five miles."

"Only two miles!" said the stranger; "then there is no use of my riding so fast, risking to break my neck, and my horse's knees."

Sherbrooke said nothing, but rode on quietly, while the stranger, still reining in his horse, pursued the high road by the traveller's side.

"It is a very dark night," said the stranger, after a minute or two's silence.

"A very dark night, indeed!" replied Sherbrooke, and the conversation again ended there.

"Well," said the stranger, after two or three minutes more had passed, "as my conversation seems disagreeable to you, sir, I shall ride on."

"Goodnight, sir," replied Sherbrooke, and the other appeared to put spurs to his horse. At the first step, however, he seized the traveller's rein, uttering a whistle: two more horsemen instantly darted out from one side of the road, and in an instant the well-known words, "Stand and deliver!" were audibly pronounced in the ears of the traveller.

Now it is a very different thing, and a much more difficult thing, to deal in such a sort with three gentlemen of the road, than with one; but nevertheless, as we have before shown, Lennard Sherbrooke was a stout man, nor was he at all a faint-hearted one. A pistol was instantly out of one of the holsters, pointed, and fired, and one of his assailants rolled over upon the ground, horse and man together. His heavy sword was free from the sheath the moment after; and exclaiming, "Now there's but two of you, I can manage you," he pushed on his horse against the man who had seized his bridle, aiming a very unpleasant sort of oblique cut at the worthy personage's head, which, had it taken effect, would probably have left him with a considerable portion less of skull than that with which he entered into the conflict.

Three things, however, happened almost simultaneously, which gave a new aspect altogether to affairs. The man upon Sherbrooke's left hand fired a pistol at his head, but missed him in the darkness of night. At the same moment the other man at whom he was aiming the blow, and who being nearer to him of course saw better, parried it successfully, but abstained from returning it, exclaiming, "By Heavens! I believe it is Leonard Sherbrooke!"

"If you had asked me," replied Sherbrooke, "I would have told you that long ago: pray who are you?"

"I am Frank Bryerly," replied the man: "hold your hands, hold your hands every one, and let us see what mischief's done! Dick Harrison, I believe, is down. Devilish unfortunate, Sherbrooke, that you did not speak."

"Speak!" returned Sherbrooke, "what should I speak for? these are not times for speaking over much."

"I am not hurt, I am not hurt!" cried the man called Harrison; "but hang him, I believe he has killed my horse, and the horse had well nigh killed me, for he reared and went over with me at the shot:--get up, brute, get up!" and he kicked the horse in the side to make him rise. Up started the beast upon his feet in a moment, trembling in every limb, but still apparently not much hurt; and upon examination it proved that the ball had struck him in the fleshy part of the shoulder, producing a long, but not a deep wound, and probably causing the animal to rear by the pain it had occasioned.

As soon as this was explained satisfactorily, a somewhat curious scene was presented, by Leonard Sherbrooke standing in the midst of his assailants, and shaking hands with two of them as old friends, while the third was presented to him with all the form and ceremony of a new introduction. But such things, alas! were not uncommon in those days; and gentlemen of high birth and education have been known to take to the King's Highway--not like Prince Hal, for sport, but for a mouthful of bread.

"Why, Frank," said Sherbrooke, addressing the one who had seized his horse's rein, "how is this, my good fellow?"

"Why, just like everything else in the world," replied the other in a gay tone. "I'm at the down end of the great see-saw, Sherbrooke, that's all. When last you knew me, I was a gay Templer, in not bad practice, bamboozling the juries, deafening the judges, making love to every woman I met, ruining the tavern-keepers, and astounding the watch and the chairman. In short, Sherbrooke, very much like yourself."

"Exactly, Frank," replied Sherbrooke, "my own history within a letter or so: we were always called the counterparts, you know; but what became of you after I left you, a year and a half ago, when this Dutch skipper first came over to usurp his father-in-law's throne?"

"Why, I did not take it quite so hotly as you did," replied the other; "but I remained for some time after the King was gone, till I heard he had come back to Ireland; then, of course, I went to join him, fared with the rest, lost everything, and here I am--after having been a Templer, and then a captain in the king's guards-- doing the honours of the King's Highway."

"Stupidly enough," replied Lennard Sherbrooke; "for here the first thing that you do is to attack a man who is just as likely to take as to give, and ask for a man's money who has but a guinea and a shilling in all the world."

"I am but raw at the trade, I confess," replied the other, "and we are none of us much more learned. The truth is, we were only practising upon you, Sherbrooke, we expect a much better prize to-morrow; but what say you, if your condition be such, why not come and take a turn upon the road with us? It is the most honourable trade going now-a-days. Treason and treachery, indeed, carry off the honours at court; but there are so many traitors of one gang or another, that betraying one's friend is become a vulgar calling. Take a turn with us on the road, man! take a turn with us on the road!"

"Upon my soul," replied Sherbrooke, "I think the plan not a bad one; I believe if I had met you alone, Frank, I should have tried to rob you."

"Don't call it rob," replied Frank Bryerly, "call it soliciting from, or relieving. But it is a bargain, Sherbrooke, isn't it?"

Lennard Sherbrooke paused and thought for a moment, with the scattered remains of better feelings, like some gallant party of a defeated army trying still to rally and resist against the overpowering force of adverse circumstances. He thought, in that short moment, of what other course he could follow; he turned his eyes to the east and the west, to the north and the south, for the chance of one gleam of hope, for the prospect of any opening to escape. It was in vain, his last hope had been trampled out that night. He had not even money to fly, and seek, on some other shore, the means of support and existence. He had but sufficient to support himself and his horse, and the poor boy, for three or four more days. Imagination pictured that poor boy's bright countenance, looking up to him for food and help, and finding none, and grasping Bryerly's hand, he said, in a low voice, "It is a bargain. Where and how shall I join you?"

"Oh!" replied the other, "we three are up at Mudicot's inn, about four miles there: you had better turn your horse and go back with us."

"No," replied Sherbrooke, "I have some matters to settle at the little inn down there: all that I have in the world is there, and that, Heaven knows, is little enough; I will join you to-morrow."

"Sherbrooke," said Bryerly, drawing him a little on one side and speaking low, "I am a rich man, you know: I have got ten guineas in my pocket: you must share them with me."

Pride had already said "No!" but Bryerly insisted, saying, "You can pay me in a day or two."

Sherbrooke thought of the boy again, and accepted the money; and then bidding his companions adieu for the time, he left them and returned to the inn.

The poor boy, wearied out, had once more fallen asleep where he sat, and

Sherbrooke, causing him to be put to bed, remained busily writing till a late hour at night. He then folded up and sealed carefully that which he had written, together with a number of little articles which he drew forth from the portmanteau; he then wrote some long directions on the back of the packet, and placing the whole once more in the portmanteau, in a place where it was sure to be seen, if any inquisitive eye examined the contents of the receptacle, he turned the key and retired to rest. The whole of the following day he passed in playing with and amusing little Wilton; and so much childish gaiety was there in his demeanour, that the man seemed as young as the child. Towards evening, however, he again ordered his horse to be brought out; and, having paid the landlady for their accommodation up to that time, he again left the boy in her charge and put his foot in the stirrup. He had kissed him several times before he did so; but a sort of yearning of the heart seemed to come over him, and turning back again to the door of the inn, he once more pressed him to his heart, ere he departed.

CHAPTER V.

Journeys were in those days at least treble the length they are at present. It may be said that the distance from London to York, or from Carlisle to Berwick, could never be above a certain length. Measured by a string probably such would have been the case; but if the reader considers how much more sand, gravel, mud, and clay, the wheels of a carriage had to go through in those days, he will easily see how it was the distances were so protracted.

At all events, fifty or sixty miles was a long, laborious journey; and at whatever hour the traveller might set out upon his way, he was not likely to reach the end of it, without becoming a "borrower from the night of a dark hour or two."

Such was the case with the tenant of a large cumbrous carriage, which, drawn heavily on by four stout horses wended slowly on the King's Highway, not very far from the spot where the wooden gates that we have described raised their white faces by the side of the road.

The panels of that carriage, as well as the ornaments of the top thereof, bore the arms of a British earl; and there was a heavy and dignified swagger about the vehicle itself, which seemed to imply a consciousness even in the wood and leather of the dignity of the person within. He, for his own part, though a graceful and very courtly personage, full of high talent, policy, and wit, had nothing about him at all of the pomposity of his vehicle; and at the moment which we refer to, namely, about two hours after nightfall, tired with his long journey, and seated with solitary thought, he had drawn a fur-cap lightly over his head, and, leaning back in the carriage, enjoyed not unpleasant repose.

To be woke out of one's slumbers suddenly at any time, or by any means, is a very unpleasant sensation; but there are few occasions that we can conceive, on which such an event is more disagreeable than when we are thus woke, to find a pistol at our breast, and some one demanding our money.

The Earl of Sunbury was sleeping quietly in his carriage with the most perfect feeling of security, though those indeed were not very secure times; when suddenly the carriage stopped, and he started up. Scarcely, however, was he awake to what was passing round, than the door of the carriage was opened, and a man of gentlemanly appearance, with a pistol in his right hand, and his horse's bridle over the left arm, presented himself to the eyes of the peer. At the same time, through the opposite window of the carriage, was seen another man on horseback; while the Earl judged, and judged rightly, that there must be others of the same fraternity at the heads of the horses, and the ears of the postilions.

The Earl was usually cool and calm in his demeanour under most of the circumstances of life; and he therefore asked the pistol-bearing gentleman, much in the same tone that one would ask one's way across the country, or receive a visitor whom we do not know, "Pray, sir, what may be your pleasure with me?"

"I am very sorry to delay your lordship even for a moment," replied the stranger, very much in the same tone as that with which the Earl had spoken; "but I do it for the purpose of requesting, that you would disburden yourself of a part of your baggage, which you can very well spare, and which we cannot. I mean, my lord, shortly and civilly, to say, that we must have your money, and also any little articles of gold and jewellery that may be about your person."

"Sir," replied the Earl, "you ask so courteously, that I should be almost ashamed to refuse you, even were your request not backed by the soft solicitation of a pistol. There, sir, is my purse, which probably is not quite so full as you might desire, but is still worth something. Then as to jewellery, my watch, seals, and these trinkets are at your disposal. Farther than these I have but this ring, for which I have a very great regard; and I wish that some way could be pointed out by which I might be able to redeem it at a future time it may be worth some half dozen guineas, but certainly not more, to any other than myself. In my eyes, however, it only appears as a precious gage of old affection, given to me in my youth by one I loved, and which has remained still upon my finger, till age has wintered my hair."

"I beg that you will keep the ring," replied the highwayman; "you have given enough already, my lord, and we thank you."

He was now retiring with a bow, and closing the door, but the Earl stopped him, saying, in a tone of some feeling, "I beg your pardon; but your manner, language, and behaviour, are so different from all that might be expected under such circumstances, that I cannot but think necessity more than inclination has driven you to a dangerous pursuit."

"Your lordship thinks right," replied the highwayman "I am a poor gentleman, of a house as noble as your own, but have felt the hardships of these times more severely than most."

He was again about to retire; but the Earl once more spoke, saying, "Your behaviour to me, sir, especially about this ring, has been such that, without asking impertinent questions, I would fain serve you.--Can I do it ?"

"I fear not, my lord; I fear not," replied the stranger. Then seeming to recollect himself, with a sudden start, he approached nearer to the carriage, saying, "I had forgot--you can, my lord!--you can."

"In what manner?" demanded the peer.

"That I cannot tell your lordship here and now," replied the highwayman: "time is wanting, and, doubtless, my companions' patience is worn away already."

"Well," replied the Earl, "if you will venture to call upon me at my own house, some ten miles hence, which, as you know me, you probably know also, I will hear all you have to say, serve you if I can, and will take care that you come and go with safety."

"I offer you a thousand thanks, my lord," replied the other, "and will venture as fearlessly as I would to my own chamber."[1]

Thus saying, he drew back and closed the door; and then making a signal to his companions to withdraw from the heads of the horses, he bade the postilions drive on, and sprang upon his own beast.

"What have you got, Lennard? what have you got?" demanded the man who was at the other door of the carriage: "what have you got--you have had a long talk about it?"

"A heavy purse," replied Sherbrooke; "what the contents are, I know not--a watch, a chain, and three gold seals.--I'm almost sorry that I did this thing."

---

1 It may be interesting to the reader to know that the whole of this scene, even to a great part of the dialogue, actually took place in the beginning of the reign of William III.

"Sorry!" cried the other; "why you insisted upon doing it yourself, and would let no other take the first adventure out of your hands."

"I did not mean that," replied Sherbrooke "I did not mean that at all! If the thing were to be done, and I standing by, I might as well do it as see you do it. What I mean is, that I am sorry for having taken the man's money at all!"

"Pshaw!" replied the other: "You forget that he is one of the enemy, or rather, I should say, a traitor to his king, to his native-born prince, and therefore is fair game for every true subject of King James."

"He stood by him a long time," replied Sherbrooke, "for all that--as long, and longer than the King stood by himself."

"Never mind, never mind, Colonel," said one of the others, who had come up by this time; "you won't need absolution for what's been done to-night; and I would bet a guinea to a shilling, that if you ask any priest in all the land, he will tell you, that you have done a good deed instead of a bad; but let us get back to the inn as quick as we can, and see what the purse contains."

The road which the Earl of Sunbury was pursuing passed the very inn to which the men who had lightened him of his gold were going; but there was a back bridle-path through some thick woods to the right of the road, which cut off a full mile of the way, and along this the four keepers of the King's Highway urged their horses at full speed, endeavouring, as was natural under such circumstances, to gallop away reflection, which, in spite of all that they assumed, was not a pleasant companion to any of the four. It very often happens that the exhilaration of success occupies so entirely the portion of time during which remorse for doing a bad action is most ready to strike us, that we are ready to commit the same error again, before the last murmurs of conscience have time to make themselves heard. Those who wish to drown her first loud remonstrances give full way and eager encouragement to that exhilaration; and now, each of the men whom we have mentioned, except Sherbrooke, went on encouraging their wild gaiety, leaping the gates that here and there obstructed their passage, instead of opening them; and in the end arriving at the inn a full quarter of an hour before the carriage of the Earl passed the house on its onward way.

The vehicle stopped there for a minute or two, to give the horses hay and water; and much was the clamour amongst the servants, the postilions, and the ostlers, concerning the daring robbery that had been committed; but the postilions of those days, and eke the keepers of inns, were wise people in their generation, and discreet withal. They talked loudly of the horror, the infamy, and the shamefulness, of making the King's Highway a place of general toll and contribution; but still they abstained most scrupulously from taking any notice of gentlemen who were out late upon the road, especially if they went on horseback.

CHAPTER VI.

It was about two days after the period of which we have spoken, when the Earl of Sunbury, caring very little for the loss he had met with on the road, and thinking of it merely as one of those unpleasant circumstances which occur to every man now and then, sat in his library with every sort of comfort and splendour about him, enjoying in dignified ease the society of mighty spirits from the past, in those works which have given and received an earthly immortality. His hand was upon Sallust; and having just been reading the awful lines which present in Catiline the type of almost every great conspirator, he raised his eyes and gazed on vacancy, calling up with little labour, as it were, a substantial image to his mind's eye of him whom the great historian had displayed.

The hour was about nine o'clock at night, and the windows were closed, when suddenly a loud ringing of the bell made itself heard, even in the Earl's library. As the person who came, by applying at the front entrance, evidently considered himself a visitor of the Earl, that nobleman placed his hand upon the open page of the book and waited for a farther announcement with a look of vexation, muttering to himself, "This is very tiresome: I thought, at all events, I should have had a few days of tranquillity and repose."

"A gentleman, my lord," said one of the servants, entering, "is at the gate, and wishes to speak with your lordship."

"Have you asked what is his business?" demanded the Earl.

"He will not mention it, my lord," replied the servant, "nor give his name either; but he says your lordship told him to call upon you."

"Oh! admit him, admit him," said the peer; "put a chair there, and bring some chocolate."

After putting the chair, the man retired, and a moment after returned, saying,

"The gentleman, my lord."

The door opened wide, and the tall fine form of Lennard Sherbrooke entered, leading by the hand the beautiful boy whom we have before described, who now gazed about him with a look of awe and surprise.

Little less astonishment was visible on the countenance of the Earl himself; and until the door was closed by the servant, he continued to gaze alternately upon Sherbrooke and the boy, seeming to find in the appearance of each much matter for wonder.

"Do me the favour of sitting down," he said at length "I think I have had the advantage of seeing you before."

"Once, my lord," replied Sherbrooke, "and then it must have been but dimly."

"Not more than once?" demanded the Earl: "your face is somewhat familiar to me, and I think I could connect it with a name."

"Connect it with none, my lord," said Sherbrooke: "that name is at an end, at least for a time: the person for whom you take me is no more. I should have thought that you knew such to be the case."

"I did, indeed, hear," said the Earl, "that he was killed at the Boyne; but still the likeness is so great, and my acquaintance with him was so slight, that--"

"He died at the Boyne, my lord," said Sherbrooke, looking down, "in a cause which was just, though the head and object of that cause was unworthy of connexion with it." The Earl's cheek grew a little red; but Sherbrooke continued, with a slight laugh, "I did not, however, come here, my lord, to offend you with my view of politics. We have only once met, my lord, that I know of in life, but I have heard you kindly spoken of by those I loved and honoured. You, yourself, told me, that if you could serve me you would; and I come to claim fulfilment of that offer, though what I request may seem both extraordinary and extravagant to demand."

The Earl bent down his eyes upon the table, and drew his lips in somewhat close, for he in no degree divined what request was coming; and he was much too old a politician to encourage applications, the very proposers of which announced them as extravagant. "May I ask," he said, at length, "what it is you have to propose? I am quite ready to do any reasonable thing for your service, as I promised upon an occasion to which I need not farther refer."

Three servants at that moment entered the room, with chocolate, long cut slices of toast, and cold water; and the conversation being thus interrupted, the Earl invited his two guests to partake; and calling the boy to him, fondled him for some moments at his knee, playing with the clustering curls of his bright hair, and asking him many little kindly questions about his sports and pastimes.

The boy looked up in his face well pleased, and answered with so much intelligence, and such winning grace, that the Earl, employing exactly the same caress that Sherbrooke had often done before, parted the fair hair on his forehead, and kissed his lofty brow.

When the servants were gone, Sherbrooke instantly resumed the conversation. "My request, my lord," he said, "is to be a very strange one; a request that will put you to some expense, though not a very great one; and will give you some trouble, though, would to God both the trouble and expense could be undertaken by myself."

"Perhaps," said the Earl, turning his eyes to the boy, "it may be better, sir, that we speak alone for a minute or two. I am now sure that I cannot be mistaken in the person to whom I speak, although I took you at first for one that is no more. We will leave your son here, and he can amuse himself with this book of pictures."

Thus saying he rose, patted the boy's head, and pointed out the book he referred to. He then threw open a door between that room and the next, which was a large saloon, well lighted, and having led the way thither with Sherbrooke, he held with him a low, but earnest conversation for some minutes.

"Well, sir," he said at length, "well, sir, I will not, and must not refuse, though it places me in a strange and somewhat difficult situation; but indeed, indeed, I wish you would listen to my remonstrances. Abandon a hopeless, and what, depend upon it, is an unjust cause,--a cause which the only person who could gain by it has abandoned and betrayed. Yield to the universal voice of the people; or if you cannot co-operate with the government that the popular voice has called to power, at all events submit; and, I doubt not in the least, that if, coupled with promises and engagements to be a peaceful subject, you claim the titles and estates--"

"My lord, it cannot be," replied Sherbrooke, interrupting him: "you forget that I belong to the Catholic church. However, you will remember our agreement respecting the papers, and other things which I shall deposit with you this night: they are not to be given to him till he is of age, under any circumstances, except that of the King's restoration, when you may immediately make them public."

As he spoke, he was turning away to return to the library; but the Earl stopped him, saying, "Stay yet one moment: would it not be better to give me some farther explanations? and have you nothing to say with regard to the boy's education? for you must remember how I, too, am situated."

"I have no farther explanations to give, my lord," replied Sherbrooke; "and as to the boy's education, I must leave it entirely with yourself. Neither on his religious nor his political education will I say a word. In regard to the latter, indeed, I may beg you to let him hear the truth, and, reading what is written on both sides, to judge for himself. Farther I have nothing to say."

"But you will understand," replied the other, with marked emphasis, "that I cannot and do not undertake to educate him as I would a son of my own. He shall have as good an education as possible; he shall be fitted, as far as my judgment can go, for any station in the state, to enter any gentlemanly profession, and to win his way for himself by his own exertions. But you cannot and must not expect that I should accustom him to indulgence or expense in any way that the unfortunate circumstances in which he is placed may render beyond his power to attain, when you and I are no longer in being to support or aid him."

"You judge wisely, my lord," replied Sherbrooke, "and in those respects I trust him entirely to you, feeling too deeply grateful for the relief you have given me from this overpowering anxiety, to cavil at any condition that you may propose."

"I have only one word more to say," replied the Earl, "which is, if you please, I would prefer putting down on paper the conditions and circumstances under which I take the boy: we will both sign the paper, which may be for the security of us both."

Sherbrooke agreed without hesitation; and on their return to the library, the Earl wrote for some time, while his companion talked with and caressed the boy. When the Earl had done, he handed one of the papers he had written to Sherbrooke, who read it attentively, and then signing it returned it to the Earl. That nobleman in the mean time, had signed a counterpart of the paper which he now gave to Sherbrooke; and the latter, taking from his pocket the small packet of various articles which we have seen him make up at the inn before he went out on the very expedition which produced his present visit to the Earl, gave it into the peer's hands, who put his seal upon it also.

This done, a momentary pause ensued, and Lennard Sherbrooke gazed wistfully at the boy. A feeling of tenderness, which he could not repress, gained upon his heart as he gazed, and seemed to overpower him; for tears came up, and dimmed his sight. At length, he dashed them away; and taking the boy up in his arms, he pressed him fondly to his bosom; kissed him twice; set him down again; and then, turning to the Earl, with a brow on which strong resolution was seen struggling with deep emotion, he said, "Thank you, my lord, thank you!"

It was all he could say, and turning away hastily he quitted the room. The Earl rang the bell, and ordered the servant to see that the gentleman's horse was brought round. He then turned and gazed upon the boy with a look of interest; but little Wilton seemed perfectly happy, and was still looking over the book of paintings which the Earl had given to him to examine.

"What can this be?" thought the Earl, as he looked at him; "can there be perfect insensibility under that fair exterior?" And taking the boy by the hand he drew him nearer.

"Are you not sorry he is gone?" the nobleman asked.

"Oh! he will not be long away," replied the boy: "he will come back in an hour or two as he always does, and will look at me as I lie in bed, and kiss me, and tell me to sleep soundly."

"Poor boy!" said the Earl, in a tone that made the large expressive eyes rise towards his face with a look of inquiry: "You must not expect him to be back to-night, my boy. Now tell me what is your name?"

"Wilton," replied the boy; but remembering that that was not sufficient to satisfy a stranger, he added, "Wilton Brown. But how long will it be before he comes back?"

"I do not know," replied the Earl, evading his question. "How old are you, Wilton?"

"I am past eight," replied the boy.

"Happily, an age of quick forgetfulness!" said the Earl, in a low tone to himself; and then applying his thoughts to make the boy comfortable for the night, he rang for his housekeeper, and gave her such explanations and directions as he thought fit.

CHAPTER VII.

There is a strange and terrible difference in this world between the look forward and the look back. Like the cloud that went before the hosts of the children of Israel, when they fled from the land of Egypt, an inscrutable fate lies before us, hiding with a dark and shadowy veil the course of every future day: while behind us the wide-spread past is open to the view; and as we mark the steps that we have taken, we can assign to each its due portion of pain, anxiety, regret, remorse, repose, or joy. Yet how short seems the past to the recollection of each mortal man! how long, and wide, and interminable, is the cloudy future to the gaze of imagination!

Many years had passed since the eventful night recorded in our last chapter; and to the boy, Wilton Brown, all that memory comprised seemed but one brief short hour out of life's long day.

The Earl of Sunbury had fulfilled what he had undertaken towards him, exactly and conscientiously. He was a man, as we have shown, of kindly feelings, and of a generous heart: although he was a politician, a courtier, and a man of the world. He might, too--had not some severe checks and disappointments crushed many of the gentler feelings of his heart--he might, too, have been a man of warm and enthusiastic affections. As it was, however, he guarded himself in general very carefully against such feelings; acted liberally and kindly; but never promised more, or did more, than prudence consented to, were the temptation ever so strong.

He had promised Lennard Sherbrooke that he would take the boy, and give him a good education, would befriend him in life, and do all that he could to serve him. He kept his word, as we have said, to the letter. During the first six weeks, after he had engaged in this task, he saw the boy often in the course of every day; grew extremely fond of him; took him to London, when his own days of repose in the country were past; and solaced many an hour, when he returned home fatigued with business, by listening to the boy's prattle, and by playing with, as it were, the fresh and intelligent mind of the young being now dependent upon him for all things.

It is a false and a mistaken notion altogether, that men of great mind and intense thought are easily wearied or annoyed by the presence of children. The man who is wearied with children must always be childish himself in mind; but, alas! not young in heart. He must be light, superficial, though perhaps inquiring and intelligent; but neither gentle in spirit nor fresh in feeling. Such men must always soon become wearied with children; for very great similarity of thought and of mind--the paradox is but seeming--is naturally wearisome in another; while, on the contrary, similarity of feeling and of heart is that bond which binds our affections together. Where both similarities are combined, we may be most happy in the society of our counterpart; but where the link between the hearts is wanting there will always be great tediousness in great similarity.

Thus the Earl of Sunbury, though, Heaven knows, no man on earth could be less childish in his keen and calculating thoughts, or in all his ordinary habits and occupations, yet found a relief, and an enjoyment, in talking with the boy, in eliciting all his fresh and picturesque ideas, and in marking the train and course which thought naturally takes before it is tutored to follow the direction of art. His own heart--for a man of the world--was very fresh; but still the worldly mind ruled it when it would; and the moment that he began to find that the boy might become too much endeared, and too necessary to him, he determined to deprive himself of the present pleasure, rather than risk the future inconvenience.

He accordingly determined to send the boy to school, and little Wilton heard the announcement with pleasure; for though by this time he had become greatly attached to the Earl, he longed for the society of beings of the same age and habits as himself. When he was with the Earl he saw that nobleman was interested with him, but he saw that he was amused with him too; and in this respect children are very like that noblest of animals, the dog. Any one who has remarked a dog when people jest with him, and speak to him mockingly, must have seen that the creature is not wholly pleased, that he seems as if made to feel a degree of inferiority. Such also is the case with children; and little Wilton felt that the Earl was making a sort of playful investigation of his mind, even while he was jesting with him. I have said felt, because it was feeling, not thought, that discovered it; and, therefore, though he loved the Earl notwithstanding all this, he was glad to go where he heard there were many such young beings as himself.

The Earl did not think him ungrateful on account of the open expression of his delight. He saw it all, and understood it all; for he had very few of the smaller selfishnesses, which so frequently blind our eyes to the most obvious facts which impinge against our own vanities. His was a high and noble mind, chained and thralled by manifold circumstances and accidents to the dull pursuits of worldly ambitions. One trait, however, may display his character: he had practised in regard to the boy a piece of that high delicacy of feeling of which none but great men are capable. He had learned and divined, from the short conversation which had taken place between himself and Lennard Sherbrooke, sufficient in regard to the boy's unfortunate situation to guide his conduct in respect to him; and now, even when alone with him in his own drawing-room or library, he asked no farther questions; he pryed not at all into what had gone before; and though the youth occasionally prattled of the wild Irish shores, and the cottage where he had been brought up, the Earl merely smiled, but gave him no encouragement to say more.

At length, Wilton Brown went to school; and as the Earl gradually lost a part of that interest in him which had given prudence the alarm, time had its effect on Wilton also, drawing one thin airy film after another over the events of the past, not obliterating them; but, like the effect of distance upon substantial objects, gathering them together in less distinct masses, and diminishing them both in size and clearness. When the time approached for his holidays, which were few and far between, he was called to the Earl's house, and treated with every degree of kindness; though with mere boyhood went by boyhood's graces, and the lad could not be fondled and played with as the child. The Earl never did anything to make him feel that he was a dependant--no, not for a single moment; but as the boy's mind expanded, and as a certain degree of the knowledge of the world was gained from the habits of a public school, he explained to him, clearly and straight-forwardly, that upon his own exertions he must rely for wealth, fame, and honour. He told him, that in the country where he lived, the road to fortune, dignity, and power, was open to every man; but that road was filled with eager and unscrupulous competitors, and obstructed in many parts by obstacles difficult to be surmounted.

"They can be surmounted, Wilton, however," he added; "and with energy, activity, and determination, that road can be trod, from one end to the other, within the space of a single life, and leave room for repose at the end.--You have often seen," he continued, "a gentleman who visits me here, who rose from a station certainly not higher, or more fortunate than your own,--who is called, even now, the Great Lord Somers, and doubtless the same name will remain with him hereafter. He is an example for all men to follow; and his life offers an encouragement for every sort of exertion. He rose even from a very humble station of life, outstripped all competitors, and is now, as you see, in the post of Lord Keeper, owing no man anything, but all to his own talents and perseverance. The same may be the case with you, Wilton. All that I can do, to place you in the way of winning fortune and station for yourself, I will do most willingly; but in every other respect you must keep in mind, that you are to be the artisan of your own fortune, and shape your course accordingly."

Such was the language held towards Wilton Brown by the Earl, upon more than one occasion; and the boy took what he said to heart, remembered, pondered it, and after much thought and reflection formed the great and glorious resolution of winning honour and renown, by every exertion of his mind and body. It is a resolution that may, perhaps, have often been taken by those who ultimately have never succeeded in the attempt. It is a resolution from which some may have been wiled away by pleasure, or driven by accident. But it is a resolution which no man who afterwards proved great ever failed to take, ay, and to take early. On the head of mediocrity: on the petty statesmen who figure throughout two thirds of the world's history; on the tolerable generals who conduct the ordinary wars of the world; on the small poets and the small philosophers who fill up the ages that intervene between great men, fortune and accident may shower down the highest honours, the greatest power, the most abundant wealth; but the man who in any pursuit has reached the height of real greatness, has set out on his career with the resolution of winning fame in despite of circumstances.

Such was the resolution which was taken, as we have said, by Wilton Brown, and the effect of that very resolution upon him, as a mere lad, was to make him thoughtful, studious, and different from any of the other youths of the school, in habits and manners.

The change was beneficial in many respects, even then. It made him strive to acquire knowledge of every sort and kind that came within his reach, and he always succeeded in some degree. It made him cultivate every talent which he felt that he possessed, and an accurate eye and a musical ear were not neglected as far as he could obtain instruction. He not only acquired much knowledge, but also much facility in acquiring; and his eager and anxious zeal did not pass unnoticed by those who taught him, so that others contributed to his first success, as well as his own efforts.

That first success was, perhaps, unexpected by any one else. The period came, at which he was barely qualified by age to strive in competition with his schoolfellows, for one of those many excellent opportunities afforded by the kindness and wisdom of past ages, for obtaining a high education at one of the universities. He had never himself proposed to be one of the competitors on this occasion, as there was a year open before him to pursue his studies, and there were many boys at the school far older than himself.

The Earl had not an idea that such a thing would take place, as Wilton himself had always expressed the utmost anxiety to pursue a military career. He had never, indeed, even pressed him to adopt another pursuit, although he had pointed out to his protege, that his own influence lay almost entirely in the political world; and his surprise, therefore, was very great, when he heard that Wilton, at the suggestion of the head master, had presented himself for examination on this very first occasion, and had carried off the highest place from all his competitors.

On his arrival in London he received him with delight, showered upon him praises, and fitted him out liberally for his first appearance at the University.

Here, however, Wilton's first fortune seemed to abandon him. About six months after his matriculation, he had the grief to hear that the Earl had been thrown from his horse in hunting, and received various severe injuries. He hastened to one of his country seats, where that nobleman had been sojourning for the time, but found him a very different man from that which he had appeared before. He was not ill enough to need or to desire nursing and tendance, but he was quite ill enough to be irritable, impatient, and selfish; for it is a strange fact, that the very condition which renders us the most dependent on our fellow-creatures too often renders us likewise indifferent to their comfort, in our absorbing consideration of our own. Although he could sit up and walk about, and go forth into his gardens, yet he suffered great pain, which did not seem to diminish; and a frequent spitting of blood rendered him impatient and querulous, whenever his lowest words were not instantly heard and comprehended.

It was a painful lesson to the youth he had brought up; and when the time for Wilton's return to Oxford arrived, and the Earl, with seeming satisfaction, put him in mind that it was time to go, the young gentleman, in truth, felt it a relief from a situation in which he neither well knew how to satisfy himself, or to satisfy the invalid, towards whom he was so anxious to show his gratitude.

He returned, then, to the university, where the allowance made him by the Earl, of two hundred per annum, together with the little income which a successful competition at school had placed at his disposal, enabled him to maintain the society of that class with which he had always associated in life, and to do so with ease to himself; though not without economy.[2] The Earl had asked him twice, if he had found the sum enough, and seemed much pleased when Wilton had replied that it was perfectly so. But from that expression he easily divined, that had it been otherwise, the Earl might have said nothing reproachful, but would not have been well satisfied.

Wilton did not mistake the motives of the Earl: he knew him to be anything but a penurious man; and he had long seen and been aware of the motives on which that nobleman acted towards him. He knew that it was with a wish to give him everything that was necessary and appropriate to the situation in which he was placed, but by no means to encourage expensive habits, or desires which might unfit him for the first laborious steps which he was destined to tread in the path of life. He felt, indeed, that there was an ambitious spirit in his own heart, and it cost him many a struggle in thought, to regulate its action: to guide it in the course of all that was good and right, but resolutely to restrain it from following any other path. "Ambition," he thought, "is like a falcon, and must be trained to fly only at what game I will. Its proud spirit must be broken, to bend to this, and to submit to that; to yield even to imaginary indignities, provided they imply no sacrifice of real honour, and to strive for no false show, while I am striving for a greater object."

---

2   I think that the same was the college allowance of the well-known Evelyn.

Thus passed a year, but during that time the Earl's health had been in no degree improved; and a number of painful events had taken place in his political course which had left his mind more irritable than before, while continual suffering had brought upon him a sort of desponding recklessness, which made him cast behind him altogether those things which he had previously considered the great objects of existence, and desire nothing but to quit for ever the scene of political strife, and pass the rest of his days in peace, if not in comfort.

Such had been the state of his mind when Wilton had last seen him in London, towards the beginning of the year 1695; but the young gentleman was somewhat surprised, about a month afterwards, to receive a sudden summons to visit the Earl in town, coupled with information, that it was his friend's design immediately to proceed to Italy, on account of his health. The summons was very unexpected, as we have implied; but the Earl informed him in his letter that he was going without loss of time; and as the shortest way of reaching him, Wilton determined to mount his horse at once, and ride part of the way to London that night. Of his journey, however, and its results, we will speak in another chapter.

CHAPTER VIII.

That there are epochs in the life of every man, when all the concurrent circumstances of fortune seem to form, as it were, a dam against the current of his fate, and turn it completely into another direction, when the trifling accident and the great event work together to produce an entirely new combination around him, no one who examines his own history, or marks attentively the history of others, can doubt for a moment. It is very natural, too, to believe that there are at those moments indications in our own hearts--from the deep latent sympathies which exist between every part of nature and the rest--that the changes which reason and observation do not point out are about to take place in our destiny: for is it to be supposed, that when the fiat has gone forth which alters a being's whole course of existence--when the electric touch has been communicated to one end of the long chain of cause and effect which forms the fate of every individual being--is it to be supposed that it will not tremble to its most remote link, especially towards that point where the greatest action is to take place?

There come upon us, it seems to me, in those times, fits of musing far deeper and more intense, excitability of feeling--perhaps of imagination too--more acute than at any other time. Perhaps, also, a determination, an energy of will is added, necessary to carry us through, with power and firmness, the struggle, or the change, or the temptation that awaits us.

When Nelson stood upon the quarter-deck of his ship, but a few minutes before the last great victory that closed a career of glory, he felt and expressed a sense that his last hour was come, that the great and final change of fate was near, and that but a few moments remained for the accomplishment of his destiny. But the indication was given to a mind that could employ it nobly; and he to whom the foreshadowing of his fate had been afforded, even as a boy--when he determined that he would, and felt that he could, be a hero--in that last moment, when he knew that the hero's life was done, determined to die as he had lived, and used the prescience of his coming death but to promote the objects for which he had existed.

There may be some men who would say these things are not natural; but if we could see all the fine relationships of one being to another, if the mortal eye refined could view the unsubstantial as well as the substantial world, could mark the keen sympathies and near associations, and all the essences which fill up the apparent gaps between being and being, we should see, undoubtedly, that these things are most natural, and wonder at the blindness with which we have walked in darkling ignorance through the thronged and multitudinous universe.

It was somewhat late in the afternoon when Wilton Brown put his foot in the stirrup, and set off to ride towards London. He did not hope to reach the metropolis that night, but he intended to go as far as he could, so as to insure his arrival before the hour of the Earl's breakfast on the following morning. He had ridden his horse somewhat hard during the morning before he had received the summons to town, and he consequently now set out at a slow pace. Not to weary the noble beast was, in truth, and in reality, his motive; but there was, at the same time, in his mind, a temporary inclination to deep and intense thought, which he could by no means shake off, and which naturally disposed him to a slow and equable pace.

The sudden announcement of the Earl's determination to go abroad, without any intimation that the young man whom he had fostered from youth to manhood was to accompany him, or to follow him to the continent, might very well set Wilton musing on his circumstances and his prospects; but that was not the cause of his meditative mood on the present occasion, though it was the immediate cause of his giving way to it. In truth, the inclination which he felt to low, desponding, though deep and clear thought, had pursued him for the last four-and-twenty hours, and it was to cast it off that he had in fact ridden so hard that very morning. Now, however, he found it necessary to yield to it; and as he rode along, he gave up his mind entirely to the consideration of the past, of the present, and the future.

The Earl had announced to him at once in his letter, that he was about to leave England, but he had made no reference whatsoever to the future fate of him whom he had hitherto protected and supported. Was that protection and support still to continue? Wilton asked himself. His friend had told him that he was to win his way in the world, and was the struggle now to begin? The next question that came was, naturally, Who and what am I, then? and his thoughts plunged at once into a gulf where they had often lost themselves before.

His boyhood had passed away unheeding, and he had attached no importance to his previous fate, nor made any effort to impress upon his own recollection the circumstances which preceded the period of his reception into the Earl's house. Indeed, he had never thought much upon the matter, till at length, when he had reached the age of fifteen, the Earl had kindly and judiciously spoken with him upon his future prospects; and in order to stimulate him to exertion, had pointed out to him that his fortunes depended on himself. He had then, for the first time, asked himself, "Who and what am I?" and had striven to recollect as much as possible of the past, in order to gather thence some knowledge of the present. His efforts had not been very successful.

Time, the great destroyer, envies even memory the power of preserving images of the things that he has done away or altered; and he is sure, if possible, to deface the pictures altogether, or to leave the lines less clear. With Wilton he had done much to blot out and to confuse. At first, memory seemed all a blank beyond the period of his schoolboy days; but gradually one image after another rose out of the void, and one called up another as they came. Still they were clouded and indistinct, like the vague phantoms of a dream. It was with great difficulty that he recollected any names, and could not at all tell in what land it was, that some of the brightest of his memories lay. It was all unconnected, too, with the present, and from it Wilton could derive no clue in regard to the great change that was coming. Between him and the future there appeared to hang a dark pall, which his eye could not penetrate, but behind which was Fate. He tried to combat such feelings: he tried long, as he rode, to conquer them; to put them down by the power of a vigorous mind; to overthrow sensation by thought.

When, however, he found that he could not succeed, when, after many efforts, the oppression--for I will not call it despondency--remained still as powerful as ever, he mentally turned, as if to face an enemy that pursued him, and to gaze full upon the inevitable power itself; all the more awful as it was, in the misty grandeur which shrouded the frowning features from his view. He nerved his heart, too, and resolved, whatever it might be that was in store for him, whatever might be the change, the loss, the adversity, which all his sensations seemed to prophesy, that he would bear it with unshrinking courage, with resolute determination; nay, with what was still more with one of his disposition, with unmurmuring patience.

In the meanwhile, however, he strove, as he went along, to persuade himself that the presentiment was but the work of fancy; that there was nothing real in it; that he had excited himself to fears and apprehensions that were groundless; that the expedition of the Earl to Italy was but a temporary undertaking, and that it would most probably make no change in his situation, no alteration in his fortunes.

Thus thought he, as he rode slowly onward, when, at the distance of about a quarter of a mile, he perceived another horseman, proceeding at a pace perhaps still slower than his own. The aspect of the country between Oxford and London was as different in that day from that which it is at present as it is possible to conceive. There is nothing in all England--with all the changes which have taken place, in manners, morals, feelings, arts, sciences, produce, manufactures, and government--which has undergone so great a change, as the high roads of the empire during the last hundred and fifty years. No one can now tell, where the roads which lay between this place and that then ran. They have been dug into, ploughed up, turned hither and thither, changed into canals, or swallowed up in railroads. The face of the country, too, has been altered, by many a village built, and many an old mansion pulled down, long tracts of country brought into cultivation, and deep plantations of old trees shadowing that ground which in those days was unwholesome marsh, or barren moor. Even Hounslow Heath, beloved by many of the frequenters of the King's Highway, has disappeared under the spirit of cultivation, and left no trace of places where many a daring deed was clone.

However that may be, the road which the young traveller was following, lay not at all in the direction taken by either of the present roads to Oxford; but at a short distance from High Wycombe turned off to the right--that is, supposing the traveller to be going towards London--and approached the banks of the Thames not far from Marlow. In so doing, it passed over a long range of high hills, and a wide extent of flat, common ground upon the top, which was precisely the point whereat Wilton Brown had arrived, at the very moment we began this digression upon the state of the King's Highways in those times.

This common ground of which we speak was as bleak as well might be, for the winds of heaven had certainly room to visit it as roughly as they chose; it was also uncultivated, and yet it cannot be said to have been unproductive; for, probably, there never was a space of ground of equal size, unless it were Maidenhead Thicket, which could show so rich and luxuriant a crop of gorse, heath, and fern. For a shelter to the latter, appeared scattered at unequal distances over the ground a few stunted trees--hawthorns, beeches, and oaks. The beech, however, predominated, in honour of the county in which the common was situated; for though, probably, if we knew the origin of the name bestowed on each county in England, we should find them all significant, yet none, I believe, would be found more picturesque or appropriate than that given by our good Saxon ancestors to the county in question--being Buchen-heim, or Buckingham: the home or land of the beeches.

The gorse, fern, and heath, besides a small quantity of not very rich grass, and a few wild flowers, were the only produce of the ground, except the trees that I have mentioned; and the only tenants of the place were a few sheep, by far too lean to need any one to look after them. On the edges of the common, indeed, might be found an occasional goose or two, but they were like the white settlers on the coast of Africa: venturing rarely and timidly into the interior. A high road went across this track, as I have shown; but it being necessary, from time to time, that farmers' carts, and other conveyances, horses, waggons, tinkers' asses, and flocks of sheep, should cross it in different directions, and as each of these travelling bodies, in common with the world in general, liked to have a way of its own, the furze and fern had been cut down in many long straight lines; and paths for horse and foot, as well as long tracks of wheels, and deep ruts, crossed and recrossed each other all over the common. To have seen it--nay, to see it now, for it exists very nearly in its primeval state--one would suppose, from all the various tracks, that it was a place of great thoroughfare, when, to say truth, though I have crossed it some twenty times or more, I never saw any travelling thing upon it but a solitary tax-cart and a gipsy's van.

It was just about the middle of this common, then, that Wilton Brown, as I have said, perceived another horseman riding along at the same slow pace as himself. Their faces were both turned one way, with a few hundred yards between them; and it appeared to the young gentleman, that the other personage whom we have mentioned was coming in an oblique line towards the high road to which he himself was journeying. This supposition proved to be correct, as the stranger, riding along the path that he was following, came abreast of Wilton Brown upon the high road, just at the spot where a comfortable direction-post pointed with the forefinger of a rude hand carved in the wood, along a path to the left, bearing inscribed, in large letters, "To Woburn."

The young traveller examined the other with a hasty but marking glance, and perceived thereby, that he was a stout man of the middle age, between the unpleasant ages of forty and fifty, but without any loss of power or activity. He was mounted on a strong black horse, had a quick and eager eye, and altogether possessed a fine countenance, but there was some degree of shy suspicion in his look, which did not seem to indicate any very great energy or force of determination.

It now wanted not more than a quarter of an hour to sunset, and there was a bright rich yellow light in the western sky, which gave each traveller a fair excuse for staring into the face of the other, as if their eyes were dazzled by the beams of the declining sun.

When he had satisfied himself, Wilton Brown turned away his eyes, and rode on, gazing quietly over the wide extent of bleak common, which, to say sooth, offered a picturesque scene enough, with its scrubby trees, and its large masses of tall gorse, lying in the calm evening air; while deep blue shadows, and clear lights resting here and there in the hollows and upon the swells, marked them out distinctly to the view.

In a moment after, however, Wilton's ears were saluted by the stranger's voice, saying, "Give you good evening, young gentleman--it has been a fine afternoon."

Now this might appear somewhat singular in the present day--when human beings have adopted a particular sort of mysterious ordinance, by which alone they can become thoroughly known and acquainted with each other--and when no man, upon any pretence or consideration whatsoever, dare speak to a fellow-creature, until some one known to both of them has whispered some cabalistic words between them, which, in general, neither of them hear distinctly. At the time I speak of, however, acquaintance was much more easily made, so far, at least, as common civility and the ordinary charities of life went. A man might speak to another at that time, if any accidental circumstances threw them close together, without any risk of being taken for a fool, a swindler, or a brute; and there was, in short, a good-humoured frankness and simplicity in those days, which formed, to say the truth, the best part about them; for the good old times, as they are called, were certainly desperately coarse, and a trifle more vicious than the present.

Such being the case then, Wilton Brown was not in the least surprised at the address of the stranger, but turned, and replied civilly; and being, indeed, somewhat dissatisfied with the companionship of his own thoughts, he suffered his horse to jog on side by side with the beast of the stranger, and entered into conversation with him willingly enough. He found him an intelligent and clever man, with a tone and manner superior, in many points, to his dress and equipage. He seemed to speak with authority, and was conversant with the great world of London, with the court, and the camp. He knew something also of France, and its self-called great monarch. He spoke with a shrug of the shoulder and an Alas! of the court of Saint Germain, and the exiled royal family of England; but he said nothing that could commit him to either one party or the other; and though he certainly left room for Wilton to express his own sentiments, if he chose to do so, he did not absolutely strive to lead him to any political subject, which formed in those days a more dangerous ground than at present.

Wilton, however, had not the slightest inclination to discuss politics with a stranger. Brought up by a Whig minister, educated in the Protestant religion, and fond of liberty upon principle, it may easily be imagined, that he not only looked upon those who now swayed, and were destined to sway, the British sceptre as the lawful and rightful possessors of power in the country, but he regarded the actual sovereign himself--though he might not love him in his private character, or admire him in those acts, where the man and the monarch were too inseparably blended to be considered apart--as a great deliverer of this country, from a tyranny which had been twice tried and twice repudiated. At the same time, however, he felt for the exiled monarch. But he felt still more for his noble wife, and for his unhappy son. His own heart told him that those two had been unjustly dealt with, the one calumniated, the other punished without a fault. Nor did he blame the true and faithful servants whom adversity could not shake, and who were only loyal to a crime, who still adhered to their old allegiance, loved still the sovereign, who had never ill-treated them, and were ready again to shed their blood for the house in whose service so much noble blood had already flowed. He did not--he did not in his own heart--blame them, and he loved not to consider what necessity there might be for putting down with the strong and unsparing hand of law the frequent renewal of those claims which had been decided upon by the awful sentence of a mighty nation.

But upon none of these subjects spoke he with the stranger. He refrained from all such topics, though they were with some skill thrown in his way; and thus the journey passed pleasantly enough for about half an hour. By that time the sun had gone down; but it was a clear, bright evening with a long twilight; and the evening rays, like gay children unwilling to go to sleep, lingered long in rosy sport with the light clouds before they would sink to rest beneath the western sky. The twilight was becoming grey, however, and the light falling short, when, at about the distance of half a mile before they reached the spot where the common terminated, the two travellers approached a rise and fall in the ground, beyond which ran a little stream with a small old bridge of one arch, not in the best repair, carrying the highway over the water with a sharp and sudden turn. Scattered about in the neighbourhood of the bridge, and on the slope that led down to it, perched upon sundry knolls and banks, and pieces of broken ground, were a number of old beeches, mostly hollowed out by time, but still flourishing green in their decay. These trees, together with the twilight, prevented the bridge itself from being seen by the travellers; but as they came near, they heard a sudden cry, as if called forth by either terror or surprise, and Wilton instantly checked his horse to listen.

"Did you not hear a scream?" he said, addressing his companion in a low voice.

"Yes," answered the other, "I thought I did: let us ride on and see."

Wilton's spurs instantly touched his horse's side, and he rode quickly down the slope towards the bridge, which he well remembered, when a scene was suddenly presented to his view, which for a moment puzzled and confounded him.

Just at the turn of the bridge lay overturned upon the road one of the large, heavy, wide-topped vehicles, called a coach in those days, while round about it appeared a group of persons whose situation, for a moment, seemed to him dubious, but which soon became more plain. A gentleman, somewhat advanced in life--perhaps about fifty-eight or fifty-nine, if not more--stood by the door of the carriage, from which he had recently emerged, and with him two women, one of whom was a young lady, apparently of about seventeen years of age, and the other her maid. Three men--servants stood about their master; but they had not the slightest appearance of any intention of giving aid to any one; for, though sundry were the situations and attitudes in which they stood, each of those attitudes betokened, in a greater or a less degree, the uncomfortable sensation of fear. One of them, indeed, had a brace of pistols in his two hands, but those hands dropped, as it were, power-less by his side, and his knees were bent into a crooked line, which certainly indi-cated no great firmness of heart.

To account for the trepidation displayed by several of the persons present, it may be necessary to state that round the overthrown vehicle stood five personages, each of whom held a cocked pistol in his hand, and, in two instances, the hands that held those pistols were raised in an attitude of menace not to be mistaken. In one instance, the weapon of offence was pointed towards the gentleman who appeared to be the owner of the carriage; in the other, it was directed towards the head of the poor girl, his daughter, who seemed to have not the slightest intention of resisting.

This formidable gesture was accompanied by words, which were spoken loud enough for Wilton to hear, as he pushed his horse down the hill; and those words were, "Come, madam! your ear-rings, quick: do not keep us all night with your hands shaking. By the Lord, I will get them out in a quicker fashion, if you do not mind."

Before we can proceed to describe what occurred next, it may be necessary to state one feature in the case, which was very peculiar--this was, that at about forty yards from the spot where the robbery was taking place, upon the top of a small bank, with his horse grazing near, and his arms crossed upon his chest, stood a man of gentlemanly appearance and powerful frame, taking no part whatsoever in the affray; not opposing the proceedings of the plunderers, indeed, but gnawing his nether lip, as if anything rather than well contented. He fixed a keen, even a fierce eye upon Wilton as he rode down; but neither the young gentleman himself, nor the other traveller, who followed him at full speed, took any notice of him, but coming on with their pistols drawn from their holsters, they were soon in the midst of the group round the carriage.

Wilton, unaccustomed to such encounters, was not very willing to shed blood, and therefore--the chivalrous spirit in his heart leading him at once towards one particular spot in the circle--he struck the man who was brutally pointing his pistol at the girl, a blow of his clenched fist, which hitting him just under the ear, as he turned at the sound of the horse's feet, laid him in a moment motionless and stunned upon the ground.

The young gentleman, by the same impulse, and almost at the same instant, sprang from his horse, and cast himself between the lady and the assailants; but at that moment the voice of his travelling companion met his ear, exclaiming, in a thundering tone, "That is right! that is right! Now stand upon the defensive till my men come up!"

Wilton did not at all understand what this might mean; but turning to the servants already on the spot, he exclaimed, in a sharp tone, "Stand forward like men, you scoundrels!" and they, seeing some help at hand, advanced a little with a show of courage.

The gentlemen of the King's Highway, however, had heard the words which Wilton's companion had shouted to him; and seeing themselves somewhat overmatched in point of numbers already, they did not appear to approve of more men coming up on the other side, before they had taken their departure. There was, consequently, much hurrying to horse. The man who had been knocked down by Wilton was dragged away by the heels, from the spot where he lay somewhat too near to the other party; and the sharp application of the gravel to his face, as one of his companions pulled him along by the legs, proved sufficiently reviving to make him start up, and nearly knock his rescuer down.

Wilton--not moved by the spirit of an ancient Greek--felt no inclination to fight for the dead or the living body of his foe; and the whole party of plunderers were speedily in the saddle and on the retreat, with the exception of the more sedate personage on the bank. He, indeed, was more slow to mount, calling the man who had been knocked down "The Knight of the Bloody Nose" as he passed him; and then with a light laugh springing into the saddle, he followed the rest at an easy canter.

"Ha! ha! ha!" exclaimed Wilton's companion of the road, laughing, "let me be called the master of stratagems for the rest of my life! Those five fools have suffered themselves to be terrified from their booty, simply by three words from my mouth and their own imaginations."

"Then you have no men coming up?" said Wilton.

"Not a man," replied the other: "all my men are busy in my own house at this minute; most likely saying grace over roast pork and humming ale."

CHAPTER IX.

The events that happen to us in life gather themselves together in particular groups, each group separated in some degree from that which follows and that which goes before, but yet each united, in its own several parts, by some strong bond of connexion, and each by a finer and less apparent ligament attached to the other groups that surround it. In short, if, as the great poet moralist has said, "All the world is a stage, and all the men and women in it only players," the life of each man is a drama, with the events thereof divided into separate scenes, the scenes gathered into grand acts, and the acts all tending to the great tragic conclusion of the whole. Happy were it for man if he, like a great dramatist, would keep the ultimate conclusion still in view.

In the life of Wilton Brown, the scene of the robbers ended with the words which we have just said were spoken by his travelling companion, and a new scene was about to begin.

The elderly gentleman to whom the carriage apparently belonged, took a step forward as the stranger spoke the last sentence, exclaiming, "Surely I am not mistaken--Sir John Fenwick, I believe." The stranger pulled off his hat and bowed low. "The same, your grace," he replied: "it is long since we have met, and I am happy that our meeting now has proved, in some degree, serviceable to you."

"Most serviceable, indeed, Sir John," replied the Duke, shaking him warmly by the hand; "and how is your fair wife, my Lady Mary? and my good Lord of Carlisle, and all the Howards?"

"Well, thank your grace," replied Sir John Fenwick, "all well. This, I presume, is your fair daughter, my Lady."

"She is, sir, she is," interrupted the Duke: "you have seen her as a child, Sir John. But pray, Sir John, introduce us to your gallant young friend, to whom we are also indebted for so much."

"He must do that for himself," replied Sir John Fenwick: "we are but the companions of the last half hour, and comrades in this little adventure."

Although accustomed to mingle with the best society; and, in all ordinary cases, free and unrestrained in his own manners, Wilton Brown felt some slight awkwardness in introducing himself upon the present occasion. He accordingly merely gave his name, expressing how much happiness he felt at the opportunity he had had of serving the Duke; but referred not at all to his own station or connexion with the Earl of Sunbury.

"Wilton Brown!" said the Duke, with a meaning smile, and gazing at him from head to foot, while he mentally contrasted his fine and lofty appearance, handsome dress, and distinguished manners, with the somewhat ordinary name which he had given. "Wilton Brown! a NOM DE GUERRE, I rather suspect, my young friend?"

"No, indeed, my lord," replied Wilton: "were it worth anybody's while to search, it would be found so written in the books of Christchurch."

"Oh! an Oxonian," cried the Duke, "and doubtless now upon your way to London. But how is this, my young friend, you are in midst of term time!"

Wilton smiled at the somewhat authoritative and parental tone assumed by the old gentleman. "The fact is, my Lord Duke," he said, "that I am obliged to absent myself, but not without permission. The illness of my best friend, the Earl of Sunbury, and his approaching departure for Italy, oblige me to go to London now to see him before he departs."

"Oh, the Earl of Sunbury, the Earl of Sunbury," replied the Duke: "a most excellent man, and a great statesman, one on whom all parties rely.* That alters the case, my young friend; and indeed, whatever might be the cause of your absence from Alma Mater, we have much to thank that cause for your gallant assistance--especially my poor girl here. Let me shake hands with you--and now we must think of what is to be clone next, for it is well nigh dark: the carriage is broken by those large stones which they must have put in the way, doubtless, to stop us; and it is hopeless to think of getting on farther to-night."[3]

"Hopeless, indeed, my lord," replied Sir John Fenwick; "but your grace must

---

3 Let it be remarked that this was not the Earl of Sunderland, of whom the exact reverse might have been said.

have passed on the way hither a little inn, about half a mile distant, or somewhat more. There I intended to sleep to-night, and most probably my young friend, too, for his horse seems as tired as mine. If your grace will follow my advice, you would walk back to the inn, make your servants take everything out of the carriage, and send some people down afterwards to drag it to the inn-yard till to-morrow morning."

"It is most unfortunate!" said the Duke, who was fond of retrospects. "We sent forward the other carriage about three hours before us, in order that the house in London might be prepared when we came."

The proposal of Sir John Fenwick, however, was adopted; and after giving careful and manifold orders to his servants, the Duke took his way back on foot towards the inn, conversing as he went with the Knight. His daughter followed with Wilton Brown by her side; and for a moment or two they went on in silence; but at length seeing her steps not very steady over the rough road upon which they were, Wilton offered his left arm to support her, having the bridle of his horse over the right.

She took it at once, and he felt her hand tremble as it rested on his arm, which was explained almost at the same moment. "It is very foolish, I believe," she said, in a low, sweet voice, "and you will think me a terrible coward, I am afraid; but I know not how it is, I feel more terrified and agitated, now that this is all over, than I did at the time."

The communication being thus begun, Wilton soon found means to soothe and quiet her. His conversation had all that ease and grace which, combined with carefulness of proprieties, is only to be gained by long and early association with persons of high minds and manners. There was no restraint, no stiffness--for to avoid all that could give pain or offence to any one was habitual to him--and yet, at the same time, there was joined to the high tone of demeanour a sort of freshness of ideas, a picturesqueness of language and of thought, which were very captivating, even when employed upon ordinary subjects. It is an art--perhaps I might almost call it a faculty--of minds like his, insensibly and naturally to lead others from the most common topics, to matters of deeper interest, and thoughts of a less every-day character. It is as if two persons were riding along the high road together, and one of them, without his companion remarking it, were to guide their horses into some bridle-path displaying in its course new views and beautiful points in the scenery around.

Thus ere they reached the inn, the fair girl, who leaned upon the arm of an acquaintance of half an hour, seemed to her own feelings as well acquainted with him as if she had known him for years, and was talking with him on a thousand subjects on which she had never conversed with any one before.

The Duke, who, although good-humoured and kindly, was somewhat stately, and perhaps a very little ostentatious withal, on the arrival of the party at the inn, insisted upon the two gentlemen doing him the honour of supping with him that night, "as well," he said, "as the poorness of the place would permit;" and a room apart having been assigned to him, he retired thither, with the humbly bowing host, to issue his own orders regarding their provision. The larder of the inn, however, proved to be miraculously well stocked; the landlord declared that no town in Burgundy, no, nor Bordeaux itself, could excel the wine that he would produce; and while the servants with messengers from the inn brought in packages, which seemed innumerable, from the carriage, the cook toiled in her vocation, the host and hostess bustled about to put all the rooms in order, Sir John Fenwick and Wilton Brown talked at the door of the inn, and Lady Laura retired to alter her dress, which had been somewhat deranged by the overthrow of the carriage.

At length, however, it was announced that supper was ready, and Wilton with his companion entered the room, where the Duke and his daughter awaited them. On going in, Wilton was struck and surprised; and, indeed, he almost paused in his advance, at the sight of the young lady, as she stood by her father. In the grey of the twilight, he had only remarked that she was a very pretty girl; and as they had walked along to the inn, she had shown so little of the manner and consciousness of a professed beauty, that he had not even suspected she might be more than he had first imagined. When he saw her now, however, in the full light, he was, as we have said, struck with surprise by the vision of radiant loveliness which her face and form presented. Wilton was too wise, however, and knew his own situation too well, even to dream of falling in love with a duke's daughter; and though he might, when her eyes were turned a different way, gaze upon her and admire, it was but as a man who looks at a jewel in a king's crown, which he knows he can never possess.

Well pleased to please, and having nothing in his thoughts to embarrass or trouble him on that particular occasion, he gave way to his natural feelings, and won no small favour and approbation in the eyes of the Duke and his fair daughter. The evening, which had begun with two of the party so inauspiciously, passed over lightly and gaily; and after supper, Wilton rose to retire to rest, with a sigh, perhaps, from some ill-defined emotions, but with a recollection of two or three happy hours to be added to the treasury of such sweet things which memory stores for us in our way through life.

As the inn was very full, the young gentleman had to pass through the kitchen to reach the staircase of his appointed room. Standing before the kitchen fire, and talking over his shoulder to the landlord, who stood a step behind him, was a tall, broad-shouldered, powerful man, dressed in a good suit of green broad cloth, laced with gold. His face was to the fire, and his back to Wilton, and he did not turn or look round while the young gentleman was there. The landlord hastened to give his guest a light, and show him his room; and Wilton passed a night, which, if not dreamless, was visited by no other visions but sweet ones.

On the following morning he was up early, and approached the window of his room to throw it open, and to let in the sweet early air to visit him, while he dressed himself; but the moment he went near the window, he saw that it looked into a pretty garden laid out in the old English style. That garden, however, was already tenanted by two persons apparently deep in earnest conversation. One of those two persons was evidently Sir John Fenwick, and the other was the stranger in green and gold, whom Wilton had remarked the night before at the kitchen fire.

Seeing how earnestly they were speaking, he refrained from opening his window, and proceeded to dress himself; but he could not avoid having, every now and then, a full view of the faces of the two, as they turned backwards and forwards at the end of the garden. Something that he there saw puzzled and surprised him: the appearance of the stranger in green seemed more familiar to him than it could have become by the casual glance he had obtained of it in the inn kitchen; and he became more and more convinced, at every turn they took before him, that this personage was no other than the man he had beheld standing on the bank, taking no part with the gentlemen of the road, indeed, but evidently belonging to their company.

This puzzled him, as we have said, not a little. Sir John Fenwick was a gentleman of good repute, whom he had heard of before now. He had married the Lady

Mary Howard, daughter of the Earl of Carlisle, and, though a stanch Jacobite, it was supposed, he was nevertheless looked upon as a man of undoubted probity and honour. What could have been his business, then, with thieves, or at best with the companions of thieves? This was a question which Wilton could no ways solve; and after having teased himself for some time therewith, he at length descended to the little parlour of the inn, and ordered his horse to be brought round as speedily as possible. He felt in his own bosom, indeed, some inclination to wait for an hour or two, in order to take leave of the Duke and his fair daughter; but remembering his own situation with the Earl, as well as feeling some of his gloomy sensations of the day before returning upon him, he determined to set out without loss of time. He mounted accordingly, and took his way towards London at a quick pace, in order to arrive before the Earl's breakfast hour.

There are, however, in that part of the country, manifold hills, over which none but a very inhumane man, unless he were pursued by enemies, or pursuing a fox, would urge his horse at a rapid rate; and as Wilton Brown was slowly climbing one of the first of these, he was overtaken by another horseman, who turned out to be none other than the worthy gentleman in the green coat.

"Good morrow to you, Master Wilton Brown," said the stranger, pulling up his horse as soon as he had reached him: "we are riding along the same road, I find, and may as well keep companionship as we go. These are sad times, and the roads are dangerous."

"They are, indeed, my good sir," replied Wilton, who was, in general, not without that capability of putting down intrusion at a word, which, strangely enough, is sometimes a talent of the lowest and meanest order of frivolous intellects, but is almost always found in the firm and decided--"they are, indeed, if I may judge by what you and I saw last night."

The stranger did not move a muscle, but answered, quite coolly, "Ay, sad doings though, sad doings: you knocked that fellow down smartly--a neat blow, as I should wish to see: I thought you would have shot one of them, for my part."

"It is a pity you had not been beforehand with me," answered Wilton: "you seemed to have been some time enjoying the sport when we came up."

The stranger now laughed aloud. "No, no," he said, "that would not do; I could not interfere; I am not conservator of the King's Highway; and, for my part, it should always be open for gentlemen to act as they liked, though I would not take any share in the matter for the world."

"There is such a thing," replied Wilton, not liking his companion at all--"there is such a thing as taking no share in the risk, and a share in the profit."

A quick flush passed over the horseman's cheek, but remained not a moment. "That is not my case," he replied, in a graver tone than he had hitherto used; "not a stiver would I have taken that came out of the good Duke's pocket, had it been to save me from starving. I take no money from any but an enemy; and when we cannot carry on the war with them in the open field, I do not see why we should not carry it on with them in any way we can. But to attack a friend, or an indifferent person, is not at all in my way."

"Oh! I begin to understand you somewhat more clearly," replied Wilton; "but allow me to say, my good sir, that it were much better not to talk to me any more upon such subjects. By so doing, you run a needless risk yourself, and can do neither of us any good. Of course," he added, willing to change the conversation, "it was Sir John Fenwick who told you my name."

"Yes," replied the other; "but it was needless, for I knew it before."

"And yet," said Wilton, "I do not remember that we ever met."

"There you are mistaken," answered the traveller; "we met no longer ago than last Monday week. You were going down the High-street in your cap and gown, and you saw some boys looking into a tart shop, and gave them some pence to buy what they longed for."

The ingenuous colour came up into Wilton Brown's cheek, as he remembered the little circumstance to which the man alluded. "I did not see you," he said.

"But I saw you," answered the man, "and was pleased with what I saw; for I am one of those whom the hard lessons of life have taught to judge more by the small acts done in private, than by the great acts that all mankind must see. Man's closet acts are for his own heart and God's eye; man's public deeds are paintings for the world. However, I was pleased, as I have said, and I have seen more things of you also that have pleased me well. You saw me, passed me by, and would not know me again in the same shape to-morrow; but I take many forms, when it may suit my purposes; and having been well pleased with you once or twice, I take heed of what you are about when I do see you."

Wilton Brown mused over what he said for a moment or two, and then replied, "I should much like to know what it was first induced you to take any notice of my actions at all--there must have been some motive, of course."

"Oh, no," replied the other--"there is no MUST! It might have been common curiosity. Every likely youth, with a pair of broad shoulders and a soldier-like air, is worth looking after in these times of war and trouble. But the truth is, I know those who know something of you, and, if I liked, I could introduce you to one whom you have not seen for many a year."

"What is his name?" demanded Wilton Brown, turning sharply upon the stranger, and gazing full in his face.

"Oh! I name no names," replied the stranger; "I know not whether it would be liked or not. However, some day I will do what I have said, if I can get leave; and now I think I will wish you good morning, for here lies my road, and there lies yours."

"But stay, stay, yet a moment," said Wilton, checking his horse; "how am I to hear of you, or to see you again?"

"Oh!" replied the stranger, in a gay tone, "I will contrive that, fear not!--Nevertheless, in case you should need it, you can ask for me at the tavern at the back of Beaufort House: the Green Dragon, it is called."

"And your name, your name?" said Wilton, seeing the other about to ride away.

"My name! ay, I had forgot--why, your name is Brown--call me Green, if you like. One colour's just as good as another, and I may as well keep the complexion of my good friend, the Dragon, in countenance. So you wont forget, it is Mister Green, at the Green Dragon, in the Green Lane at the back of Beaufort House; and now, Mister Brown, I leave you a brown study, to carry you on your way."

So saying, he turned his horse's head, and cantered easily over the upland which skirted the road to the left. After he had gone about a couple of hundred yards, Wilton saw him stop and pause, as if thoughtfully, for a minute. But without turning back to the road, he again put spurs to his horse, and was out of sight in a few moments.

Wilton then rode on to London, without farther pause or adventure of any kind; but it were vain to say that, in this instance, "care did not sit behind the horseman;" for many an anxious thought, and unresolved question, and intense meditation, were his companions on his onward way. Fortunately, however, his horse was not troubled in the same manner; and about five minutes before the hour he had proposed to himself, Wilton was standing before the house of the Earl in St. James's-square. The servants were all rejoiced to see him, for, unlike persons in his situation in general, he was very popular amongst them; but the Earl, he was informed, had not yet risen, and the account the young gentleman received of his health made him sad and apprehensive.

CHAPTER X.

I N about an hour's time, the Earl of Sunbury descended to breakfast; and he expressed no small pleasure at the unexpected appearance of his young protege.

"You were always a kind and an affectionate boy, Wilton," he said; "and you have kept your good feelings unchanged, I am happy to find. Depend upon it, when one can do so, amongst all the troubles, and cares, and corrupting things of this world, we find in the feelings of the heart that consolation, when sorrows and disappointments assail us, which no gift or favour of man can impart. I believe, indeed, that within the last six months, with all the bodily pains and mental anxieties I have had to suffer, I should either have died or gone mad, had not my mind obtained relief, from time to time, in the enjoyment of the beauties of nature, the works of art, and the productions of genius. Nor have my thoughts been altogether unoccupied with you," he added, after a moment's pause, "and that occupation would have been most pleasant to my mind, Wilton, inasmuch as through your whole course you have given me undivided satisfaction. But, alas! I cannot do for you all that I should wish to do. You know that my own estates are all entailed upon distant relatives, whom I do not even know. I am not a man, as you are well aware, to accumulate wealth; and all I can possibly assure to you is the enjoyment of the same income I have hitherto allowed you, and which, in case of my death, I will take care shall be yours."

Wilton listened, as may be supposed, with affection and gratitude; but he tried, after expressing all he felt, and assuring the Earl that he possessed as much as he desired, to put an end to a conversation which was rendered the more painful to him by the marked alteration which he perceived in the person of his friend since he had last seen him.

The Earl, however, would not suffer the subject to drop, replying, "I know well that you are no way extravagant, Wilton, and maintain the appearance of a gentle-man upon smaller means than many could or would; but yet, my good youth, you are naturally ambitious; and there are a thousand wants, necessities, and desires still to be gratified, which at present you neither perceive nor provide for. You are not destined, Wilton, to go on all your life, content in the seclusion of a college, with less than three hundred a year. Every man should strive to fulfil to the utmost his destiny--I mean, should endeavour to reach the highest point in any way which God has given him the capability of attaining. You must become more than you are, greater, higher, richer, by your own exertions. Had my health suffered me to re-main here, I could have easily facilitated your progress in political life. Now I must trust your advancement to another; and you will perhaps think it strange, that the person I do trust it to should not be any of my old and intimate political friends. But I have my reasons for what I do, which you will some day know; and before I go, I must exact one promise of you, which is to put yourself under the guidance of the person whom I have mentioned, and to accept whatever post he may think the best calculated to promote your future views. As he now holds one of the highest stations in the ministry, I could have wished him to name you his private secretary, but that office is at present filled, and he has promised me most solemnly to find you some occupation within the next half-year. Your allowance shall be regularly transmitted to you till my return; and, until you receive some appointment, you had better remain at Oxford, which may give you perhaps the means of taking your first degree. And now, my dear boy, that I have explained all this, what were you about to say regarding the adventures you met with in your journey?"

"First let me ask, sir," replied Wilton, "who is the gentleman you have so kindly interested for me?"

"Oh! I thought you had divined: it is the Earl of Byerdale, now all potent in the counsels of the King--at least, so men suppose and say. However, I look upon it that you have given me the promise that I ask."

"Undoubtedly, my lord," replied Wilton: "in such a case, I must ever look upon your wishes as a command."

The conversation then turned to other and lighter matters, and Wilton amused his friend with the detail of the adventures of the preceding night.

"Sir John Fenwick!" exclaimed the Earl, as soon as Wilton came to the events that succeeded the robbery--"he is a dangerous companion, Sir John Fenwick! We know him to be disaffected, a nonjuror, and a plotter of a dark and intriguing character. Who was the Duke he met with? Duke of what?"

"On my word, I cannot tell you, sir," replied Wilton; "I did not hear his name: they called his daughter Lady Laura."

"You are a strange young man, Wilton," replied the Earl; "there are probably not two men in Europe who would have failed to inquire, if it were no more than the name of this pretty girl you mention."

"If there had been the slightest probability of my ever meeting her again," replied Wilton, "I most likely should have inquired. But my story is not ended yet;" and he went on to detail what had occurred during his ride that morning.

This seemed to strike and interest the Earl more than the rest; and he immediately asked his young companion a vast number of questions, all relating to the personal appearance of the gentleman in green, who had been the comrade of his early ride.

After all these interrogatories had been answered, he mused for a minute or two, and then observed, "No, no, it could not be. This personage in green, Wilton, depend upon it, is some agent of Sir John Fenwick, and the Jacobite party. He has got some intimation of your name and situation, and has most likely seen you once or twice in Oxford, where, I am sorry to say, there are too many such as himself. They have fixed their eyes upon you, and, depend upon it, there will be many attempts to gain your adherence to an unsuccessful and a desperate party. Be wise, my dear Wilton, and shun all communication with such people. No one who has not filled such a station as I have, can be aware of their manifold arts."

Wilton promised to be upon his guard, and the conversation dropped there. It had suggested, however, a new train of ideas to the mind of the young gentleman--new, I mean, solely in point of combination, for the ideas themselves referred to subjects long known and often thought of. It appeared evident to him, that the question which the Earl had put to himself in secret, when he heard of his conversation with the man in green, was, "Can this be any one, who really knows the early history of Wilton Brown?" and the question which Wilton in turn asked himself was, "How is the Earl connected with that early history?"

Many painful doubts had often suggested themselves to the mind of Wilton

Brown in regard to that very subject; and those doubts themselves had prevented him from pressing on the Earl questions which might have brought forth the facts, but which, at the same time, he thought, might pain that nobleman most bitterly, if his suspicions should prove accurate.

The Earl himself had always carefully avoided the subject, and when any accidental words led towards it, had taken evident pains to change the conversation. What had occurred that morning, however, weighed upon Wilton's mind, and he more than once asked himself the question--"Who and what am I?"

There was a painful solution always ready at hand; but then again he replied to his own suspicions--"The Earl certainly treats me like a noble and generous friend, but not like a father." The conclusion of all these thoughts was,--

"Even though I may give the Earl a moment's pain, I must ask him the question before he goes to Italy;" and he watched his opportunity for several days, without finding any means of introducing such a topic.

At length, one morning, when the Earl happened to be saying something farther regarding the young man's future fate, Wilton seized the opportunity, and replied, "With me, my dear lord, the future and the past are alike equally dark and doubtful. I wish, indeed, that I might be permitted to know a little of the latter, at least." "Do not let us talk upon that subject at present, Wilton," said the Earl, somewhat impatiently; "you will know it all soon enough. At one-and-twenty you shall have all the information that can be given to you."

But few words more passed on that matter, and they only conveyed a reiteration of the Earl's promise more distinctly. On the afternoon of that day another person was added to the dinner table of the Earl of Sunbury. Wilton knew not that anybody was coming, till he perceived that the Earl waited for some guest; but at length the Earl of Byerdale was announced, and a tall good-looking man, of some fifty years of age, or perhaps less, entered the room, with that calm, slow, noiseless sort of footstep, which generally accompanies a disposition either naturally or habitually cautious. It is somewhat like the footstep of a cat over a dewy lawn.

Between the statesman's brows was a deep-set wrinkle, which gave his countenance a sullen and determined character, and the left-hand corner of his mouth, as well as the marking line between the lips and the cheek, were drawn sharply down, as if he were constantly in the presence of somebody he disliked and rather scorned.

Yet he strove frequently to smile, made gay and very courteous speeches too, and said small pleasant things with a peculiar grace. He was, indeed, a very gentlemanly and courtly personage, and those who liked him were wont to declare, that it was not his fault if his countenance was somewhat forbidding. By some persons, indeed--as is frequently the case with people of weak and subservient characters--the very sneer upon his lip, and the authoritative frown upon his brow, were received as marks of dignity, and signs of a high and powerful mind.

Such things, however, did not at all impose upon a man so thoroughly acquainted with courts and cabinets as the Earl of Sunbury, and the consequence was, that Lord Byerdale, with all his coolness, self-confidence, and talent, felt himself second in the company of the greater mind, and though he liked not the feeling, yet stretched his courtesy and politeness farther than usual.

When he entered, he advanced towards the Earl with one of his most bright and placid smiles, apologized for being a little later than his time, was delighted to see the Earl looking rather better, and then turned to see who was the other person in the room, in order to apportion his civility accordingly. When he beheld Wilton Brown, the young gentleman's fine person, his high and lofty look, and a certain air of distinction and self-possession about him, though so young, appeared to strike and puzzle him; but the Earl instantly introduced his protege to the statesman, saying, "The young friend, my lord, of whom I spoke to you, Mr. Wilton Brown."

Lord Byerdale was now as polite as he could be, assured the young gentleman that all his small interest could command should be at his service; and while he did so, he looked from his countenance to that of the Earl, and from the Earl's to his, as if he were comparing them with one another. Then, again, he glanced his eyes to a beautiful picture by Kneller, of a lady dressed in a fanciful costume, which hung on one side of the drawing-room.

Wilton remarked the expression of his face as he did so; and his own thoughts, connecting that expression with foregone suspicions, rendered it painful. Quitting the room for a moment before dinner was announced, he retired to his own chamber, and looked for an instant in the glass. He was instantly struck by an extraordinary resemblance, between himself and the picture, which had never occurred to him before.

In the meanwhile, as soon as he had quitted the room, the Earl said, in a calm, grave tone to his companion, pointing at the same time to the picture which the other had been remarking, "The likeness is indeed very striking, and might, perhaps, lead one to a suspicion which is not correct."

"Oh, my dear lord," replied the courtier, "you must not think I meant anything of the kind. I did remark a slight likeness, perhaps; but I was admiring the beauty of the portrait. That is a Kneller, of course; none could paint that but Kneller."

The Earl bowed his head and turned to the window. "It is the portrait," he said, "of one of my mother's family, a third or fourth cousin of my own. Her father, Sir Harry Oswald, was obliged to fly, you know, for one of those sad affairs in the reign of Charles the Second, and his estates and effects were sold. I bought that picture at the time, with several other things, as memorials of them, poor people."

"She must have been very handsome," said Lord Byerdale.

"The painter did her less than justice," replied the Earl, in the same quiet tone: "she and her father died in France, within a short time of each other; and there is certainly a strong likeness between that portrait and Wilton.--There is no relationship, however."

Notwithstanding the quiet tone in which the Earl spoke, Lord Byerdale kept his own opinion upon the subject, but dropped it as a matter of conversation. The evening passed over as pleasantly as the illness of the Earl would permit; and certainly, if Wilton Brown was not well pleased with the Earl of Byerdale, it was not from any lack of politeness on the part of that gentleman. That he felt no particular inclination towards him is not to be denied; but nevertheless he was grateful for his kindness, even of demeanour, and doubted not--such was his inexperience of the world--that the Earl of Byerdale would always treat him in the same manner.

After this day, which proved, in reality, an eventful one in the life of Wilton Brown, about a week elapsed before the Earl set out for the Continent. Wilton saw him on board, and dropped down the river with him; and after his noble friend had quitted the shores of England, he turned his steps again towards Oxford, without lingering at all in the capital. It must be confessed, that he felt a much greater degree of loneliness, than he had expected to experience on the departure of the Earl. He knew now, for the first time, how much he had depended upon, and loved and trusted, the only real friend that he ever remembered to have had. It is true, that while the Earl was resident in London, and he principally in Oxford, they saw but little of each other; but still it made a great change, when several countries, some at peace and some at war with England, lay between them, and when the cold melancholy sea stretched its wide barrier to keep them asunder. He felt that he had none to appeal to for advice or aid, when advice or aid should be wanting; that the director of his youth was gone, and that he was left to win for himself that dark experience of the world's ways, which never can be learned, without paying the sad price of sorrow and disappointment.

Such were naturally his first feelings; and though the acuteness of them wore away, the impression still remained whenever thought was turned in that direction. He was soon cheered, however, by a letter from the Earl, informing him of his having arrived safely in Piedmont; and shortly after, the first quarter of his usual allowance was transmitted to him, with a brief polite note from the Earl of Byerdale, in whose hands Lord Sunbury seemed entirely to have placed him. Wilton acknowledged the note immediately, and then applied himself to his studies again; but shortly after, he was shocked by a rumour reaching him, that his kind friend had been taken prisoner by the French. While he was making inquiries, as diligently as was possible in that place, and was hesitating, as to whether, in order to learn more, he should go to London or not, he received a second epistle froth the Earl of Byerdale, couched in much colder terms than his former communication, putting the question of the Earl's capture beyond doubt, and at the same time stating, that as he understood this circumstance was likely to stop the allowance which had usually been made to Mr. Brown, he, the Earl of Byerdale, was anxious to give him some employment as speedily as possible, although that employment might not be such as he could wish to bestow. He begged him, therefore, to come to London with all speed, to speak with him on the subject, and ended, by assuring him that he was-- what Wilton knew him not to be--his very humble and most obedient servant.

On first reading the note, Wilton had almost formed a rash resolution--had almost determined neither to go to London at all, nor to repose upon the friendship and assistance of the Earl of Byerdale. But recollecting his promise to his noble friend before his departure, he resolved to endure anything rather than violate such an engagement; and consequently wrote to say he would wait upon the Earl as soon as the term was over, to the close of which there wanted but a week or two at that time.

In that week or two, however, Wilton was destined to feel some of the first inconveniences attending a sudden change in his finances. Remembering, that, for the time at least, more than two-thirds of his income was gone, he instantly began to contract all his expenses, and suffered, before the end of the term, not a few of the painful followers of comparative poverty.

He now felt, and felt bitterly, that the small sum which he received from his college would not be sufficient to maintain him at the University, even with the greatest economy; so that, besides his promise to the Earl, to accept whatever Lord Byerdale should offer him, absolute necessity seemed to force him as a dependent upon that nobleman, at least till he could hear some news of his more generous friend.

It is an undoubted fact, that small annoyances are often more difficult to bear than evils of greater magnitude; and Wilton felt all those attendant upon his present situation most acutely. To appear differently amongst his noble comrades at the University; to have no longer a horse, to join them in their rides; to be obliged to sell the fine books he had collected, and one or two small pictures by great masters which he had bought; to be questioned and commiserated by the acquaintances who cared the least for him;--all these were separate sources of great and acute pain to a feeling and sensitive heart, not yet accustomed to adversity. Wilton, however, had not been schooling his own mind in vain for the last two years; and though he felt as much as any one, every privation, yet he succeeded in bearing them all with calmness and fortitude, and perhaps even curtailed every indulgence more sternly than was absolutely necessary at the time, from a fear that the reluctance which he felt might in any degree blind his eyes to that which was just and right.

A few instruments of music, a few books not absolutely required in his studies, his implements for drawing, and all the little trinkets or gifts of any kind which he had received from the Earl of Sunbury, were the only things that he still preserved, which merited in any degree the name of superfluities. With the sum obtained from the sale of the rest, he discharged to the uttermost farthing all the expenses of the preceding term, took his first degree with honour, and then set out upon his journey to London.

No adventure attended him upon the way; and on the morning after his arrival, he presented himself at an early hour at the house of the Earl of Byerdale. After waiting for some time, he was received by that nobleman with a cold and stately air; and having given him a hint, that it would have been more respectful if he had come up immediately to London, instead of waiting at Oxford till the end of the term, the Earl proceeded to inform him of his views.

"Our noble and excellent friend, the Earl of Sunbury," said the statesman, "was very anxious, Mr. Brown, that I should receive you as my private secretary. Now, as I informed him, the gentleman whom I have always employed cannot of course be removed from that situation without cause; but, at the same time, what between my public and my private business, I have need of greater assistance than he can render me. I have need, in fact, of two private secretaries, and one will naturally succeed the other, when, as will probably be the case, in about six months the first is removed by appointment to a higher office. I will give you till to-morrow to consider, whether the post I now offer you is worth your acceptance. The salary we must make the same as the allowance which has lately unfortunately ceased; and I am only sorry that I can give you no further time for reflection, as I have already delayed three weeks without deciding between various applicants, in order to give you time to arrive in London."

Wilton replied not at the moment; for there was certainly not one word said by the Earl which could give him any assignable cause of offence, and yet he was grieved and offended. It was the tone, the manner, the cold haughtiness of every look and gesture that pained him. He was not moved by any boyish conceit; he was always willing, even in his own mind, to offer deep respect to high rank, or high station, or high talents. He would have been ready to own at once, that the Earl was far superior to himself in all these particulars; but that which did annoy him, as it might annoy any one, was to be made to feel the superiority, at every word, by the language and demeanour of the Earl himself.

He retired, then, to the inn, where, for the first time during all his many visits to London, he had taken up his residence; and there, pacing up and down the room, he thought bitterly over Lord Byerdale's proposal. The situation offered to him was far inferior to what he had been led to expect; and he evidently saw, that the demeanour of the Earl himself would render every circumstance connected with it painful, or at least unpleasant. Yet, what was he to do? There were, indeed, a thousand other ways of gaining his livelihood, at least till the Earl of Sunbury were set free; but then, his promise that he would not refuse anything which was offered by Lord Byerdale again came into his mind, and he determined, with that resolute firmness which characterized him even at an early age, to bear all, and to endure all; to keep his word with the Earl to the letter, and to accept an office in the execution of which he anticipated nothing but pain, mortification, and discomfort.

Such being the case, he thought it much better to write his resolutions to the Earl, than to expose himself to more humiliation by speaking with him on the subject again. He had suffered sufficiently in their last conversation on that matter, and he felt that he should have enough to endure in the execution of his duties. He wrote, indeed, as coldly as the Earl had spoken; but he made no allusion to his disappointment, or to any hopes of more elevated employment.

He expressed himself ready to commence his labours as soon as the Earl thought right; and in the course of three days was fully established as the second private secretary of the Earl.

The next three or four months of his life we shall pass over as briefly as possible, for they were chequered by no incident of very great interest. The Earl employed him daily, but how did he employ him?--As a mere clerk. No public paper, no document of any importance, passed through his hands. Letters on private business, the details of some estates in Shropshire, copies of long and to him meaningless accounts, and notes and memorandums, referring to affairs of very little interest, were the occupations given to a man of active, energetic, and cultivated mind, of eager aspirations, and a glowing fancy. It may be asked, how did the Earl treat him, too?--As a clerk! and not as most men of gentlemanly feeling would treat a clerk. Seldom any salutation marked his entrance into the room, and cold, formal orders were all that he received.

Wilton bore it all with admirable patience; he murmured not, otherwise than in secret; but often when he returned to his own solitary room, in the small lodging he had taken for himself in London, the heart within his bosom felt like a newly-imprisoned bird, as if it would beat itself to death against the bars that confined it.

Amidst all this, there was some consolation came. A letter arrived one morning, after this had continued about two months, bearing one postmark from Oxford, and another from Italy. It was from the Earl of Sunbury, who was better, and wrote in high spirits. He had been arrested by the French, and having been taken for a general officer of distinction, bad been detained for several weeks. But he had been well treated, and set at liberty, as soon as his real name and character were ascertained. Only one of Wilton's letters, and that of an early date, had reached him, so that he knew none of the occurrences which placed his young friend in so painful a situation, but conceived him to be still at Oxford, and still possessing the allowance which he had made him.

The moment he received these tidings, Wilton replied to it with a feeling of joy and a hope of deliverance, which showed itself in every line of the details he gave. This letter was more fortunate than the others, and the Earl's answer was received within a month. That answer, however, in some degree disappointed his young friend. Lord Sunbury praised his conduct much for accepting the situation which had been offered; but he tried to soothe him under the conduct of the Earl of Byerdale, while he both blamed that conduct and censured the Earl in severe terms, for having suffered the allowance which he had authorized him to pay to drop in so sudden and unexpected a manner. To guard against the recurrence of such a thing for the future, the Earl enclosed an order on his steward for the sum, with directions that it should be paid in preference to anything else whatsoever. At the same time, however, he urged Wilton earnestly not to quit the Earl of Byerdale, but to remain in the employment which he had accepted, at least till the return of a more sincere friend from the Continent should afford the prospect of some better and more agreeable occupation.

Wilton resolved to submit; and as he saw that the Earl was anxious upon the subject, wrote to him immediately, to announce that such was the case. Hope gave him patience; and the increased means at his command afforded him the opportunity of resuming the habits of that station in which he had always hitherto moved. In these respects, he was now perfectly at his ease, for his habits were not expensive; and he could indulge in all, to which his wishes led him, without those careful thoughts which had been forced upon him by the sudden straitening of his means. Such, then, was his situation when, towards the end of about three months, a new change came over his fate, a new era began in the history of his life.

CHAPTER XI.

How often is it that a new acquaintance, begun under accidental circumstances, forms an epoch in life? How often does it change in every respect the current of our days on earth--ay! and affect eternity itself? The point of time at which we form such an acquaintance is, in fact, the spot at which two streams meet. There, the waters of both are insensibly blended together--the clear and the turbid, the rough and the smooth, the rapid and the slow. Each not only modifies the manner, and the direction, and the progress of the other with which it mingles, but even if any material object separates the united stream again into two, the individuality of both those that originally formed it is lost, and each is affected for ever by the progress they have had together.

Wilton Brown was now once more moving at ease. He had his horses and his servant, and his small convenient apartments at no great distance from the Earl of Byerdale's. He could enjoy the various objects which the metropolis presented from time to time to satisfy the taste or the curiosity of the public, and he could mingle in his leisure hours with the few amongst the acquaintances he had made in passing through a public school, or residing at the University, whom he had learned to love or to esteem. He sought them not, indeed, and he courted no great society; for there was not, perhaps, one amongst those he knew whose taste, and thoughts, and feelings, were altogether congenial with his own. Indeed, when any one has found such, in one or two instances, throughout the course of life, he may sit himself down, saying, "Oh! happy that I am, in the wide universe of matter and of spirit I am not alone! There are beings of kindred sympathies linked to myself by ties of love which it never can be the will of Almighty Beneficence that death itself should break!"

If Wilton felt thus towards any one, it was towards the Earl of Sunbury; but yet there was a difference between his sensations towards that kind friend and those of which we have spoken, on which we need not pause in this place. Except in his society, however, Wilton's thoughts were nearly alone. There were one or two young noblemen and others, for whom he felt a great regard, a high esteem, a certain degree of habitual affection, but that was all, and thus his time in general passed solitarily enough.

With the Earl of Byerdale he did not perhaps interchange ten words in three months, although when he was writing in the same room with him he had more than once remarked the eyes of the Earl fixed stern and intent upon him from beneath their overhanging brows, as if he would have asked him some dark and important question, or proposed to him some dangerous and terrible act which he dared hardly name.

"Were he some Italian minister," thought Wilton, sometimes, "and I, as at present, his poor secretary, I should expect him every moment to commend the assassination of some enemy to my convenient skill in such affairs."

At length one morning when he arrived at the house of the Earl to pursue his daily task, he saw a travelling carriage at the door with two servants, English and foreign, disencumbering it from the trunks which were thereunto attached in somewhat less convenient guise than in the present day. He took no note, however, and entered as usual, proceeding at once to the cabinet, where he usually found the Earl at that hour. He was there and alone, nor did the entrance of Wilton create any farther change in his proceedings than merely to point to another table, saying, "Three letters to answer there, Mr. Brown--the corners are turned down, with directions."

Wilton sat down and proceeded as usual; but he had scarcely ended the first letter and begun a second, when the door of the apartment was thrown unceremoniously open, and a young gentleman entered the room, slightly, but very gracefully made, extremely handsome in features, but pale in complexion, and with a quick, wandering, and yet marking eye, which seemed to bespeak much of intelligence, but no great steadiness of character. He was dressed strangely enough, in a silk dressing-gown of the richest-flowered embroidery, slippers of crimson velvet embroidered with gold upon his feet, and a crimson velvet nightcap with gold tassels on his head.

"Why, my dear sir, this is really cruel," cried he, advancing towards the Earl, and speaking in a tone of light reproach, "to go away and leave me, when I come back from twelve or fourteen hundred miles' distance, without even waiting to see my most beautiful dressing-gown. Really you fathers are becoming excessively un-dutiful towards your children! You have wanted some one so long to keep you in order, my lord, that I see evidently, I shall be obliged to hold a tight hand over you. But tell me, in pity tell me, did you ever see anything so exquisite as this dressing-gown? Its beauty would be nothing without its superbness, and its splendour nothing without its delicacy. The richness of the silk would be lost without the radiant colours of the flowers, and the miraculous taste of the embroidery would be entirely thrown away upon any other stuff than that. In short, one might write a catechism upon it, my lord. There is nothing on all the earth equal to it. No man has, or has had, or will have, anything that can compete with it. Gold could not buy it. I was obliged to seduce the girl that worked it; and then, like Ulysses with Circe, I bound her to perform what task I liked. 'Produce me,' I exclaimed, 'a dressing-gown!' and, lo! it stands before you."

Wilton Brown turned his eyes for an instant to the countenance of the Earl of Byerdale, when, to his surprise, he beheld there, for the first time, something that might be called a good-humoured smile. The change of Wilton's position, slight as it was, seemed to call the attention of the young gentleman, who instantly approached the table where he sat, exclaiming, "Who is this? I don't know him. What do you mean, sir," he continued, in the same light tone--"what do you mean, by suffering my father to run riot in this way, while I am gone? Why, sir, I find he has addicted himself to courtierism, and to cringing, and to sitting in cabinets, and to making long speeches in the House of Lords; and to all sorts of vices of the same kind, so as nearly to have fallen into prime ministerism. All this is very bad--very bad, indeed--"

"My dear boy," said the Earl, "you will gain the character of a madman without deserving it."

"Pray, papa, let me alone," replied the young man, affecting a boyish tone; "you only interrupt me: may I ask, sir, what is your name?" he continued, still addressing Wilton.

"My name, sir," replied the other, slightly colouring at such an abrupt demand, "is Wilton Brown."

"Then, Wilton, I am very glad to see you," replied the other, holding out his hand--"you are the very person I wanted to see; for it so happens, that my wise, prudent, and statesmanlike friend, the Earl of Sunbury, having far greater confidence in the security of my noddle than has my worthy parent here, has entrusted to me for your behoof one long letter, and innumerable long messages, together with a strong recommendation to you, to take me to your bosom, and cherish me as any old man would do his grandson; namely, with the most doting, short-sighted, and depraving affection, which can be shown towards a wayward, whimsical, tiresome, capricious boy; and now, if you don't like my own account of myself, or the specimen you have had this morning, you had better lay down your pen, and come and take a walk with me, in order to shake off your dislike; for it must be shaken off, and the sooner it is done the better."

The Earl's brow had by this time gathered into a very ominous sort of frown, and he informed his son in a stern tone, that his clerk, Mr. Brown, was engaged in business of importance, and would not be free from it, he feared, till three o'clock.

"Well, my lord, I will even go and sleep till three," replied the young man. "At that hour, Mr. Brown, I will come and seek you. I have an immensity to say to you, all about nothing in the world, and therefore it is absolutely necessary that I should disgorge myself as soon as possible."

Thus saying, he turned gaily on his heel, and left the Earl's cabinet.

"You must excuse him, Mr. Brown," said the Earl, as soon as he was gone; "he is wild with spirits and youth, but he will soon, I trust, demean himself more properly." Wilton made no reply, but thought that if the demeanour of the son was not altogether pleasant, the demeanour of the father was ten times worse. When the three letters were written, Lord Byerdale immediately informed Wilton that he should have no farther occupation for him that day, although the clock had not much passed the first hour after noon; and as it was evident that he had no inclination to encourage any intimacy between him and his son, the young gentleman retired to his own lodgings, and ordering his horse to be brought round quickly, prepared to take a lengthened ride into the country.

Before the horse could be saddled, however, a servant announced Lord Sherbrooke, and the next moment the son of the Earl of Byerdale entered the room.

There was something in the name that sounded familiar in the ears of Wilton Brown, he could not tell why. Ile almost expected to see a familiar face present itself at the open door; for so little had been the communication between himself and the Earl of Byerdale, that he had never known till that morning that the Earl had a son, nor ever heard the second title of the family before. He received his visitor, however, with pleasure, not exactly for the young nobleman's own sake, but rather on account of the letters and messages which he had promised from the Earl of Sunbury.

Lord Sherbrooke was now dressed as might well become a man of rank in his day; with a certain spice of foppery in his apparel, indeed, and with a slight difference in the fashion and materials of his clothes from those ordinarily worn in England, which might just mark, to an observing eye, that they had been made in a foreign country.

His demeanour was much more calm and sedate than it had been in the morning; and sitting down, he began by a reproach to Wilton, for having gone away without waiting to see him again.

"The fact is, my lord," replied Wilton, "that the Earl, though he did not absolutely send me away, gave me such an intimation to depart, that I could not well avoid it."

"It strikes me, Wilton," said Lord Sherbrooke, familiarly, "that my father is treating you extremely ill; Lord Sunbury gave me a hint of the kind, when I saw him in Rome; and I see that he said even less than the truth."

"I have no right to complain, my lord," answered Wilton, after pausing for a moment to master some very painful emotions--"I have no reason to complain, my lord, of conduct that I voluntarily endure."

"Very well answered, Wilton!" replied the young lord, "but not logically, my good friend. Every gentleman has a right to expect gentlemanly treatment. He has a right to complain if he does not meet with that which he has a right to expect; and he does not bar himself of that right of complaint, because any circumstances render it expedient or right for him not to resist the ill-treatment at which he murmurs. However, it is more to your honour that you do not complain; but I know my father well, and, of course, amongst a great many high qualities, there are some not quite so pleasant. We must mend this matter for you, however, and what I wish to say to you now, is, that you must not spoil all I do, by any pride of that kind which will make you hold back when I pull forward."

"Indeed, my lord," replied Wilton, "you would particularly oblige me by making no effort to change the position in which I am placed. All the communication which takes place between your lordship's father and myself is quite sufficient for the transaction of business, and we can never stand in any other relation towards each other than that of minister and private secretary."

"Or CLERK, as he called you to me to-day," said Lord Sherbrooke, drily.

"The name matters very little, my lord," replied Wilton; "he calls me SECRETARY to myself, and such he stated me to be in the little memorandum of my appointment, which he gave me, but if it please him better to call me clerk, why, let him do it."

"Oh! I shall not remonstrate," replied Lord Sherbrooke; "I never argue with my father. In the first place, it would be undutiful and disrespectful, and I am the most dutiful of all sons; and in the next place, he generally somehow gets the better of me in argument--the more completely the more wrong he is. But, nevertheless, I can find means to drive him, if not to persuade him; to lead him, if not to convince him; and having had my own way from childhood up to the present hour--alas! that I should say it, after having taken the way that I have taken--I do not intend to give it up just now, so I will soon drive him to a different way with you, while you have no share in the matter, but that of merely suffering me to assume, at once, the character of an old friend, and not an insincere one. On the latter point, indeed, you must believe me to be just as sincere as my father is insincere, for you very well know, Wilton, that, in this world of ours, it is much more by avoiding the faults than by following the virtues of our parents, that we get on in life. Every fool can see where his father is a fool, and can take care not to be foolish in the same way; but it is a much more difficult thing to appreciate a father's wisdom, and learn to be wise like him."

"The latter, my lord, I should think, would be the nobler endeavour," replied Wilton; "though I cannot say what would have been my own case, if I had ever had the happiness of knowing a father's care."

Lord Sherbrooke for a moment or two made no reply, but looked down upon the ground, apparently struck by the tone in which Wilton spoke. He answered at length, however, raising his eyes with one of his gay looks, "After all, we are but mortals, my dear Wilton, and we must have our little follies and vices. I would not be an angel for the world, for my part; and besides--for so staid and sober a young man as you are--you forget that I have a duty to perform towards my father, to check him when I see him going wrong, and to put him in the right way; to afford him, now and then, a little filial correction, and take care of his morals and his education. Why, if he had not me to look after him, I do not know what would become of him. However, I see," he added in a graver tone, "that I must not jest with you, until you know me and understand me better. What I mean is, that we are to be friends, remember. It is all arranged between the Earl of Sunbury and myself. We are to be friends, then; and such being the case, I will take care that my lord of Byerdale does not call my friend his clerk, nor treat him in any other manner than as my friend. And now, Wilton, set about the matter as fast as ever you can. There is my letter of recommendation from the Earl of Sunbury, which I hope will break down some barriers, the rest I must do for myself. You will find me full of faults, full of follies, and full of vices; for though it may be a difficult thing to be full of three things at once, yet the faults, follies, and vices within me seem to fill me altogether, each in turn, and yet altogether. In fact, they put me in mind of two liquids with which I once saw an Italian conjurer perform a curious trick. He filled a glass with a certain liquid, which looked like water, up to the very brim, and then poured in a considerable quantity of another liquid without increasing the liquid in the glass by a drop. Now sometimes my folly seems to fill me so completely, that I should think there was no room for vices, but those vices find some means to slip in, without incommoding me in the least. However, I will leave you now to read your letters, and to wonder at your sage and prudent friend, the Earl of Sunbury, having introduced to your acquaintance, and recommended to your friendship, one who has made half the capitals of Europe ring with his pranks. The secret is, Wilton, that the Earl knows both me and you. He pays you the high compliment of thinking you can be the companion of a very faulty man, without acquiring his faults; and he knows that, though I cannot cure myself of my own errors, I hate them too much to wish any one to imitate them. When you have done reading," he added, "come and join me at Monsieur Faubert's Riding School, in the lane going up to the Oxford Road: I see your horse at the door--I will get one there, and we will have a ride in the country. By heavens, what a beautiful picture! It is quite a little gem. That child's head must be a Correggio."

"I believe it is," replied Wilton: "I saw it accidentally at an auction, and bought it for a mere trifle."

"You have the eye of a judge," replied his companion.

"Do not be long ere you join me;" and looking at every little object of ornament or luxury that the room contained, standing a minute or two before another picture, taking up, and examining all over, a small bronze urn, that stood on one of the tables, and criticising the hilts of two or three of Wilton's swords, that stood in the corner of the room, he made his way out, like Hamlet, "without his eyes," and left his new acquaintance to read his letter in peace.

In that letter, which was in every respect most kind, Wilton found that the Earl gave a detailed account of the character of the young nobleman who had just left him. He represented him, very much as he had represented himself, full of follies, and, unfortunately, but too much addicted to let those follies run into vices. "Though he neither gambled nor drank for pleasure," the Earl said, "yet, as if for variety, he would sometimes do both to excess. In other respects, he had lived a life of great profligacy, seeming utterly careless of the reproaches of any one, and rather taking means to make any fresh act of licence generally known, than to conceal it. Nor is this," continued the Earl, "from that worst of all vanities, which attaches fame to what is infamous, and confounds notoriety with renown, but rather from a sort of daringness of disposition, which prompts him to avow openly any act to which there may be risk attached. With all these bad qualities," the Earl proceeded, "there are many good ones. To be bold as a lion is but a corporeal endowment, but he adds to that the most perfect sincerity and frankness.

"He would neither falsify his word nor deny an act that he has committed for the world. His mind is sufficiently acute, and his heart sufficiently good, to see distinctly the evils of unbridled licence, and to condemn it in his own case; and he is the last man in the world who would lead or encourage any one in that course which he has pursued himself. In short, his own passions are as the bonds cast around the Hebrew giant when he slept, to give him over into the hands of any one who chooses to lead him into wrong. The consecrated locks of the Nazarite--I mean, purity and innocence of heart--have been shorn away completely in the lap of one Delilah or another; and though he hates those who hold him captive, he is constrained to follow where they lead. I think you may do him good, Wilton; I am certain he can do you no harm: I believe that he is capable, and I am certain that he is willing, to make your abode in London more pleasant to you, and to open that path for your advancement, which his father would have put you in, if he had fulfilled the promises that he made to me."

CHAPTER XII.

A few weeks made a considerable change in the progress of the life of Wilton Brown. He found the young Lord Sherbrooke all that he had been represented to be in every good point of character, and less in every evil point. He did not, it is true, studiously veil from his new friend his libertine habits, or his light and reckless character; but it so happened, that when in society with Wilton, his mind seemed to find food and occupation of a higher sort, and, on almost all occasions, when conversing with him, he showed himself, as he might always have appeared, a high-bred and well-informed gentleman, who, though somewhat wild and rash, possessed a cultivated mind, a rich and playful fancy, and a kind and honourable heart.

Wilton soon discovered that he could become attached to him, and ere long he found a new point of interest in the character of his young companion, which was a sort of dark and solemn gloom that fell upon him from time to time, and would seize him in the midst of his gayest moments, leaving him, for the time, plunged in deep and sombre meditations. This strange fit was very often succeeded by bursts of gaiety and merriment, to the full as wild and joyous as those that went before; and Wilton's curiosity and sympathy were both excited by a state of mind which he marked attentively, and which, though he did not comprehend it entirely, showed him that there was some grief hidden but not vanquished in the heart.

Lord Sherbrooke did not see the inquiring eyes of his friend fixed upon him without notice; and one day he said,

"Do not look at me in these fits, Wilton; and ask me no questions. It is the evil spirit upon me, and he must have his hour."

As the time passed on, Wilton and the young lord became daily companions, and the Earl could not avoid showing, at all events, some civility to the constant associate of his son. He gradually began to converse with him more frequently. He even ventured, every now and then, upon a smile. He talked for an instant, sometimes, upon the passing events of the day; and, once or twice, asked him to dine, when he and his son would otherwise have been tete-a-tete. All this was pleasant to Wilton; for Lord Sherbrooke managed it so well, by merely marking a particular preference for his society, that there was no restraint or force in the matter, and the change worked itself gradually without any words or remonstrance. In the midst of all this, however, one little event occurred, which, though twenty other things might have been of much more importance and much more disagreeable in their consequences, pained Wilton in a greater degree than anything he had endured.

One day, when the Earl was confined to his drawing-room by a slight fit of gout, Wilton had visited him for a moment, to obtain more particular directions in regard to something which he had been directed to write. Just as he had received those directions, and was about to retire, the Duke of Gaveston was announced; and in passing through a second room beyond, into which the Earl could see, Wilton came suddenly upon the Duke, and in him at once recognised the nobleman whom he had aided in delivering from the clutches of some gentlemen practitioners on the King's Highway. Their meeting was so sudden, that the Duke, though he evidently recollected instantly the face of Wilton Brown, could not connect it with the circumstances in which he had seen it. Wilton, on his part, merely bowed and passed on; and the Duke, advancing to Lord Byerdale, asked at once, "Who is that young gentleman?--his face is quite familiar to me."

"It is only my clerk," replied the Earl, in a careless tone. "I hope your grace received my letter."

Wilton had not yet quitted the room, and heard it all; but he went out without pause. When the door was closed behind him, however, he stood for a moment gazing sternly upon the ground, and summoning every good and firm feeling to his aid. Nor was he unsuccessful: he once more conquered the strong temptation to throw up his employment instantly; and, asking himself, "What have I to do with pride?" he proceeded with his daily task as if nothing had occurred.

No consequences followed at the moment; but before we proceed to the more active business of our story, we must pause upon one other incident, of no great apparent importance, but which the reader will connect aright with the other events of the tale.

Two mornings after that of which we have spoken, the Earl came suddenly into the room where Wilton was writing, and interrupted him in what he was abort, by saying, "I wish, Mr. Brown, you would have the goodness to write, under my dictation, a letter, which is of some importance."

Brown bowed his head, and taking fresh paper, proceeded to write down the Earl's words, as follows:--

"Sir,--Immediately upon the receipt of this, you will be   pleased to proceed to the village of ------, in the county   of ------, and make immediate inquiries, once more, in   regard to the personages concerning whom you instituted an   investigation some ten or twelve years ago. Any additional   documents you may procure, concerning Colonel Sherbrooke,   Colonel Lennard Sherbrooke, or any of the other parties   concerned in the transactions which you know of as taking   place at that time, you will be pleased to send to me forthwith."

Wilton perceiving that the Earl did not proceed, looked up, as if to see whether he had concluded or not. The Earl's eyes were fixed upon him with a stern, intense gaze, as if he would have read his very soul. Wilton's looks, on the contrary, were so perfectly unconscious, so innocent of all knowledge that he was doing anything more than writing an ordinary letter of business, that--if the Earl's gaze was intended to interpret his feelings by any of those external marks, which betray the secrets of the heart, by slight and transitory characters written on nature's record book, the face--he was convinced at once that there was nothing concealed below. His brow relaxed, and he went on dictating, while the young gentleman proceeded calmly to write.

"You will be particular," the letter went on, "to inquire what became of the boy, as his name was not down in the list found upon the captain's person; and you will endeavour to discover what became of the boat that carried Lennard Sherbrooke and the boy to the ship, and whether all on board it perished in the storm, or not."

The Earl still watched Wilton's countenance with some degree of earnestness; and, to say the truth, if his young companion had not been put upon his guard, by detecting the first stern, dark glance the minister had given him, some emotion might have been visible in his countenance, some degree of thoughtful inquiry in his manner, as he asked, "To whom am I to address it, my lord?"

The words of the Earl, in directing an inquiry about the fisherman, the boy, the boat, and the wreck, seemed to connect themselves with strange figures in the past- -figures which appeared before his mind's eye vague and misty, such as we are told the shadows always appear at first which are conjured up by the cabalistic words of a necromancer. He felt that there was some connecting link between himself and the subject of the Earl's investigation; what, he could not tell: but whatever it was, his curiosity was stimulated to tax his memory to the utmost, and to try by any means to lead her to a right conclusion, through the intricate ways of the past.

That first gaze of the Earl, however, had excited in his bosom not exactly suspicion, but that inclination to conceal his feelings, which we all experience when we see that some one whom we neither love nor trust is endeavouring to unveil them. He therefore would not suffer his mind to rest upon any inquiry in regard to the past, till the emotions which it might produce could be indulged unwatched; and, applying to the mechanical business of the pen, he wrote on to the conclusion, and then demanded, simply, "To whom am I to address it?"

"To Mr. Shea," replied the Earl, "my agent in Waterford, to whom you have written before;" and there the conversation dropped.

The Earl took the letter to sign it; but now that it was done, he seemed indifferent about its going, and put it into a portfolio, where it remained several days before it was sent.

As soon as he could escape, Wilton Brown retired to his own dwelling, and there gave himself up to thought; but the facts, which seemed floating about in the dark gulf of the past, still eluded the grasp of memory, as she strove to catch them. There was something, indeed, which he recollected of a boat, and a storm at sea, and a fisherman's cabin, and still the name of Sherbrooke rang in his ears, as something known in other days. But it came not upon him with the same freshness which it had done when first he heard the title of the Earl of Byerdale's soil; and he could recall no more than the particulars we have mentioned, though the name of Lennard seemed familiar to him also.

While he was in this meditative mood, pondering thoughtfully over the past, and extracting little to satisfy him from a record which time, unfortunately, had effaced, he was interrupted by the coming of the young Lord Sherbrooke, who now was accustomed to enter familiarly without any announcement. On the present occasion his step was more rapid than usual, his manner more than commonly excited, and the moment he had cast himself into a chair he burst into a long loud peal of laughter. "In the name of Heaven," he exclaimed, "what piece of foolery do you think my worthy father has concocted now? On my honour, I believe that he is mad, and only fear that he has transmitted a part of his madness to me. Think of everything that is ridiculous, Wilton, that you can conceive; let your mind run free over every absurd combination that it is possible to fancy; think of all that is stupid or mad-like in times present or past, and then tell me what it is that my father intends to do."

"I really do not know, Sherbrooke," replied his friend "but nothing, I dare say, half so bad as you would have me believe. Your father is much too prudent and careful a man to do anything that is absurd."

"You don't know him--Wilton, you don't know him," replied Lord Sherbrooke; "for the sake of power or of wealth he has the courage to do anything on earth that is absurd, and for revenge he has the courage to do a great deal more. In regard to revenge, indeed, I don't mind: he is quite right there; for surely if we are bound to be grateful to a man that does good to us, we are bound to revenge ourselves upon him who does us wrong. Besides, revenge is a gentlemanlike passion; but avarice and ambition are certainly the two most ungentlemanlike propensities in human nature."

"Not ambition, surely," exclaimed Wilton.

"The worst of all!" cried his friend--"the worst of all! Avarice is a gentleman to ambition! Avarice is merely a tinker, a dealer in old metal; but ambition is a chimney-sweep of a passion: a mere climbing-boy, who will go through any dirty hole in all Christendom only to get out at the top of the chimney. But you have not guessed, Wilton--you have not guessed. To it; and tell me, what is the absurd thing my father proposes to do?"

Wilton shook his head, and said that he could in no way divine.

"To marry me, Wilton--to marry me to a lady rich and fair," replied the young lord: "what think you of that, Wilton?--you who know me, what think you of that?"

"Why, if I must really say the truth," replied Wilton, "I think the Earl has very naturally considered your happiness before that of the lady."

"As well gilded a sarcasm that," replied Lord Sherbrooke, "as if it had come from my father's own lips. However, what you say is very true: the poor unfortunate girl little knows what the slave merchants are devising for her. My father has dealt with hers, and her father has dealt with mine, and settled all affairs between them, it seems, without our knowledge or participation in any shape. I was the first of the two parties concerned who received the word of command to march and be married, and as yet the unfortunate victim is unacquainted with the designs against her peace and happiness for life."

"Nay, nay," replied Wilton, almost sorrowfully, "speak not so lightly of it. What have you done, Sherbrooke? for Heaven's sake, what have you done? If you have consented to marry, let me hope and trust that you have determined firmly to change your conduct, and not indeed, as you say, to ruin the poor girl's peace and happiness for life."

"Oh! I have consented," replied Lord Sherbrooke, in the same gay laughing tone; "you do not suppose that I would refuse beauty, and sweetness, and twenty thousand a year. I am not as mad as my father. Oh! I consented directly. I understand, she is the great beauty of the day. She will see very little of me, and I shall see very little of her, so we shall not weary of one another. Oh! I am a very wise man, indeed. I only wanted what our friend Launcelot calls 'a trifle of wives' to be King Solomon himself. Why you know that for the other cattle which distinguished that great monarch I am pretty well provided."

Wilton looked down upon the ground with a look of very great pain, while imagination pictured what the future life of some young and innocent girl might be, bound to one so wild, so heedless, and dissolute as Lord Sherbrooke. He remained silent, however, for he did not dare to trust himself with any farther observations; and when he looked up again, he found his friend gazing at him with an expression on his countenance in some degree sorrowful, in some degree reproachful, but with a look of playful meaning flickering through the whole.

"Now does your solemnity, and your gravity," said Lord Sherbrooke, "and your not yet understanding me, almost tempt me, Wilton, to play some wild and inconceivable trick, just for the purpose of opening your eyes, and letting you see, that your friend is not such an unfeeling rascal as the world gives out."

"I know you are not, my dear Sherbrooke--I am sure you are not," replied

Wilton, grasping warmly the hand which Lord Sherbrooke held out to him; "I was wrong for not seeing that you were in jest, and for not discovering at once that you had not consented. But how does the Earl bear your refusal?"

"You are as wrong as ever, my dear Wilton," replied his friend, in a more serious tone--"I have consented; for if I had not, it must have made an irreparable breach between my father and myself, which you well know I should not consider desirable--I must obey him sometimes, you know, Wilton--He had pledged himself, too, that I should consent. However, to set your mind at rest, I will tell you the loophole at which I creep out. Her father, it seems, is not near so sanguine as my father, in regard to his child's obedience, and he is, moreover, an odd old gentleman, who has got into his head a strange antiquated notion, that the inclinations of the people to be married have something to do with such transactions. He therefore bargained, that his consent should be dependent upon the young lady's approbation of me when she sees me. In fact, I am bound to court, and she to be courted. My father is bound that I shall marry her if she likes me, her father is bound to give her to me if she likes to be given. Now what I intend, Wilton, is, that she should not like me. So this very evening you must come with me to the theatre, and there we shall see her together, for I know where she is to be. To-morrow, I shall be presented to her in form, and if she likes to have me, after all I have to say to her, why it is her fault, for I will take care she shall not have ignorance to plead in regard to my worshipful character."

Wilton would fain have declined going to the theatre that night, for, to say the truth, his heart was somewhat heavy; but Lord Sherbrooke would take no denial, jokingly saying that he required some support under the emotions and agitating circumstances which he was about to endure. As soon as this was settled, Lord Sherbrooke left him, agreeing to call for him in his carriage at the early hour of a quarter before five o'clock; for such, however, were the more rational times and seasons of our ancestors, that one could enjoy the high intellectual treat of seeing a good play performed from beginning to end, without either changing one's dinner hour, or going with the certainty of indigestion and headache.

CHAPTER XIII.

Far more punctual than was usual with him. Lord Sherbrooke was at the door of Wilton Brown exactly at the hour he had appointed; and, getting into his carriage, they speedily rolled on from the neighbourhood of St. James's-street, then one of the most fashionable parts of the metropolis, to Russell-street, C however, though evidently anxious to be early at the theatre, could not resist his inclination to take a look into the Rose, and, finding several persons whom he knew there, he lingered for a considerable time, introducing Wilton to a number of the wits and celebrated men of the day.

The play had thus begun before they entered the theatre, and the house was filled so completely that it was scarcely possible to obtain a seat.

As if with a knowledge that his young companion was anxious to see the ill-fated lady destined by her friends to be the bride of a wild and reckless libertine, Lord Sherbrooke affected to pay no attention whatsoever to anything but what was passing on the stage. During the first act Wilton was indeed as much occupied as himself with the magic of the scene: but when the brief pause between the acts took place, his eyes wandered round those boxes in which the high nobility of the land usually were found, to see if he could discover the victim of the Earl of Byerdale's ambition.

There were two boxes on the opposite side of the house, towards one or the other of which almost all eyes were turned, and to the occupants of which all the distinguished young men in the house seemed anxious to pay their homage. In one of those boxes was a very lovely woman of about seven or eight and twenty, sitting with a queenly air to receive the humble adoration of the gay and fluttering admirers who crowded round her. Her brow was high and broad, but slightly contracted, so that a certain haughtiness of air in her whole figure and person was fully kept in tone by the expression of her face. For a moment or two, Wilton looked at her with a slight smile, as he said in his own heart, "if that be the lady destined for Sherbrooke, I pity her less than I expected, for she seems the very person either to rule him or care little about him."

The next moment, however, a more perfect recollection of all that Lord Sherbrooke had said, led him to conclude that she could not be the person to whom he alluded. He had spoken of her as a girl, as of one younger than himself; whereas the lady who was reigning in the stage-box was evidently older, and had more the appearance of a married than a single woman.

Wilton then turned his eyes to the other box of which we have spoken; and in it there was also to be seen a female figure seated near the front with another lady; while somewhat further back, appeared the form of an elderly gentleman with a star upon the left breast. Towards that box, as we have before said, many eyes were turned; and from the space* below, as well as from other parts of the house, the beaux of the day were gazing in evident expectation of a bow, or a smile, or a mark of recognition. Nevertheless, in neither of the ladies which that box contained was there, as far as Wilton could see, any of those little arts but too often used for the purpose of attracting attention, and which, to say the truth, were displayed in a remarkable manner by the lady in the other box we have mentioned. There was no fair hand stretched out over the cushions; no fringed glove cast negligently down; no fan waved gracefully to give emphasis to that was said; but, on the contrary, the whole figure of the lady in front remained tranquil and calm, with much grace and beauty in the attitude, but none even of that flutter of consciousness which often betrays the secrets of vanity. The expression of the face, indeed, Wilton could not see, for the head was turned towards the stage; and though the lady looked round more than once during the interval between the acts to speak to those behind her in the box, the effect was only to turn her face still farther from his gaze.[4]

At length, the play went on, and at the end of the second act a slight movement enabled Lord Sherbrooke and Wilton to advance further towards the stage, so that the latter was now nearly opposite to the box in which one of the beauties of the day was seated. He immediately turned in that direction, as did Lord Sherbrooke at

---

4 I have not said "the pit," because the intruders of fashion had not then been driven from the STAGE itself, especially between the acts.

the same moment; and Wilton, with a feeling of pain that can scarcely be described, beheld in the fair girl who seemed to be the unwilling object of so much admiration, no other than the young lady whom he had aided in rescuing when attacked, as we have before described, by the gentry who in those days frequented so commonly the King's Highway.

Though now dressed with splendour, as became her rank and station, there was in her whole countenance the same simple unaffected look of tranquil modesty which Wilton had remarked there before, and in which he had fancied he read the story of a noble mind and a fine heart, rather undervaluing than otherwise the external advantages of beauty and station, but dignified and raised by the consciousness of purity, cultivation, and high thoughts. The same look was there, modest yet dignified, diffident yet self-possessed; and while he became convinced that there sat the bride selected by the Earl of Byerdale for his son, he was equally convinced that she was the person of all others whose fate would be the most miserable in such an union.

At the same moment, too, his heart was moved by sensations that may be very difficult accurately to describe. To talk of his being in love with the fair girl before him would, in those days as in the present, have been absurd; to say that he had remembered her with anything like hope, would not be true, for he had not hoped in the slightest degree, nor even dreamed of hope. But what he had done was this-- he had thought of her often and long; he had recollected the few hours spent in her society with greater pleasure than any he had known in life; he had remembered her as the most beautiful person he had ever seen--and indeed to him she was so; for not only were her features, and her form, and her complexion, all beautiful according to the rules of art, but they were beautiful also according to that modification of beauty which best suited his own taste. The expression, too, of her countenance--and she had much expression of countenance when conversing with any one she liked--was beautiful and varying; and the grace of her movements and the calm quietness of her carriage were of the kind which is always most pleasing to a high and cultivated mind.

He had recollected her, then, as the most beautiful creature he had ever seen; but there was also a good deal of imaginative interest attached to the circumstances in which they had first met; and he often thought over them with pleasure, as forming a little bright spot in the midst of a somewhat dull and monotonous existence. In short, all these memories made it impossible for him to feel towards her as he did towards other women. There was admiration, and interest, and high esteem.--It wanted, surely, but a little of being love. One thing is very certain: Wilton would have heard that she was about to be married to any one with no inconsiderable degree of pain. It would have cost him a sigh; it would have made him feel a deep regret. He would not have been in the slightest degree disappointed, for hope being out of the question he expected nothing; but still he might regret.

Now, however, when he thought that she was about to be importuned to marry one for whom he might himself feel very deep and sincere regard, on account of some high and noble qualities of the heart, but whose wild and reckless libertinism could but make her miserable for ever, the pain that he experienced caused him to turn very pale. The next moment the blood rushed up again into his cheek, seeing Lord Sherbrooke glance his eyes rapidly from the box in which she sat to his countenance, and then to the box again.

At that very same moment, the Duke, who was the gentleman sitting on the opposite side of the box, bent forward and whispered a few words to his daughter: the blood suddenly rushed up into her cheek; and with a look rather of anxiety and apprehension than anything else, she turned her eyes instantly towards the spot where Wilton stood. Her look was changed in a moment; for though she became quite pale, a bright smile beamed forth from her lip; and though she put her hand to her heart, she bowed markedly and graciously towards her young acquaintance, directing instantly towards that spot the looks of all the admirers who surrounded the box.

The words which the Duke spoke to her were very simple, but led to an extraordinary mistake. He had in the morning communicated to her the proposal which had been made for her marriage with Lord Sherbrooke, and she, who had heard something of his character, had shrunk with alarm from the very idea. When her father, however, now said to her, "There is Lord Sherbrooke just opposite," and directed her attention to the precise spot, her eyes instantly fell upon Wilton.

She recollected her father's observation in regard to the name he had given at the inn being an assumed one: his fine commanding person, his noble countenance, his lordly look, and the taste and fashion of his dress, all made her for the moment believe that in him she beheld the person proposed for her future husband. At the same time she could not forget that he had rendered her an essential service. He had displayed before her several of those qualities which peculiarly draw forth the admiration of women--courage, promptitude, daring, and skill; his conversation had delighted and surprised her; and to say truth, he had created in her bosom during the short interview, such prepossessions in his favour, that to her he was the person who now solicited her hand, instead of the creature which her imagination had portrayed as Lord Sherbrooke, was no small relief to her heart. It seemed as if a load was taken off her bosom; and such was the cause of those emotions, the expression of which upon her countenance we have already told.

It was not, indeed, that she believed herself the least in love with Wilton Brown, but she felt that she COULD love him, and that feeling was quite enough. It was enough, while she fancied that he was Lord Sherbrooke, to agitate her with joy and hope; and, though the mistake lasted but a short time, the feelings that it produced were sufficient to effect a change in all her sensations towards him through life. During the brief space that the mistake lasted, she looked upon him, she thought of him, as the man who was to be her husband. Had it not been for that misunderstanding, the idea of such an union between herself and him would most likely never have entered her mind; but once having looked upon him in that light, even for five minutes, she never could see him or speak to him without a recollection of the fact, without a reference, however vague, ill-defined, and repressed in her own mind, to the feelings and thoughts which she had then entertained.

Lord Sherbrooke remarked the changing colour, the look of recognition on both parts, the glad smile, and the inclination of the head.

"Why, Wilton," he said in a low voice--"Wilton! it seems you are already a great deal better acquainted with my future wife than I am myself; and glad to see you does she seem! and most gracious is her notice of you! Why, there are half of those gilded fools on the other side of the house ready to cut your throat at this moment, when it is mine they would seek to cut if they knew all; but pray come and introduce me to my lovely bride, I had no idea she was so pretty. I'm sure I am delighted to have some other introduction than that of my father, and so unexpected a one."

All this was said in a bantering tone, but not without a shrewd examination of

Wilton's countenance while it was spoken. What were the feelings of the young nobleman it was impossible for Wilton to divine; but he answered quite calmly, the first emotion being by this time passed--"My acquaintance with her is so slight, that I certainly could not venture to introduce any one, far less one who has so much better an introduction ready prepared."

"By heavens, Wilton," replied his friend, "by the look she gave you and the look you returned, one would not have judged the acquaintance to be slight; but as you will not introduce me, I will introduce you; for, I suppose, in common civility, I must go and speak to her father, as the old gentleman's eye is upon me. There! He secures his point by a bow. Dearly beloved, I come, I come!"

Thus saying, he turned to proceed to the box, making a sign to Wilton to follow, which he did, though at the time he did it, he censured his own weakness for yielding to the temptation.

"I am but going," he thought, "to augment feelings of regret at a destiny I cannot change--I only go to increase my own pain, and in no degree to avert from that sweet girl a fate but too dark and sorrowful."

As he thus thought, he felt disposed, even then, to make some excuse for not going to the Duke's box; but by the time they were half way thither, they were met by several persons coming the other way, amongst whom was a gentleman richly but not gaudily dressed, who immediately addressed Lord Sherbrooke, saying, that the Duke of Gaveston requested the honour of his company in his box, and Wilton immediately recognised his old companion of the road, Sir John Fenwick. Sir John bowed to him but distantly; and Wilton was more than ever hesitating whether he should go on or not, when some one touched him on the arm, and turning round he beheld his somewhat doubtful acquaintance, who had given himself the name of Green.

Sir John Fenwick and the stranger looked in each other's faces without the slightest sign of recognition: but to Wilton himself Green smiled pleasantly, saying, "I very much wish to speak a word with you, Mr. Wilton Brown. Will you just step aside with me to the lobby for a moment?"

The recollection of what had passed when last they met, together with the wish of avoiding an interview with the Duke and his daughter, from which he augured nought but pain, overcame Wilton's repugnance to hold any private communication with one whom he had certainly seen in a situation at the least very equivocal; and merely saying to Lord Sherbrooke, "I must speak with this gentleman for a moment, and therefore cannot come with you," he left the young lord to follow Sir John Fenwick, and turned with the stranger into the lobby. There was no one there at the moment, for at that time the licensed abomination, of which it has since been the scene, would not have been tolerated in any country calling itself Christian. Wilton was indeed rather glad that it was vacant, for he was not anxious to be observed by many people in conversation with his present companion. Not that anything in his appearance or manner was calculated to call up the blush of idle pride. The stranger's dress was as rich and tasteful as any in the house, his manner was easy and free, his look, though not particularly striking, distinguished and gentlemanly.

The stranger was the first to speak. "Do not alarm yourself, Mr. Brown," he said: "Mr. Green is a safe companion here, whatever he might be in Maidenhead Thicket. But I wanted to speak a word to you yourself, and to give you a hint that may be beneficial to others. As to yourself, I told you when last we met that I could bring you into company with some of your old friends. I thought your curiosity would have carried you to the Green Dragon long ago. As, however, you do not seem to wish to see your old friends, I have now to tell you that they wish to see you, and therefore I have to beg you to meet me there to-morrow at six o'clock."

"You are mistaken entirely," replied Wilton, "in regard to my not wishing to see my old friends. I very much wish it. I wish to hear more of my early history, about which there seems to me to be some mystery."

"Is there?" said the stranger, in a careless tone. "Whether anything will be explained to you or not, I cannot say. At all events, you must meet me there; and, in the meantime tell me, have you seen Sir John Fenwick since last we met?"

"No, I have not," replied Wilton. "Why do you ask?"

"Because," replied the other, "Sir John Fenwick is a dangerous companion, and it were better that you did not consort with him."

"That I certainly shall not do," replied Wilton, "knowing his character sufficiently already."

"Indeed!" replied the other. "You have grown learned in people's characters of late, Master Brown: perhaps you know mine also; and if you do, of course you will give me the meeting to-morrow at the Green Dragon."

He spoke with a smile; and Wilton replied, "I am by no means sure that I shall do so, unless I have a better cause assigned, and a clearer knowledge of what I am going there for."

"Prudent! Prudent!" said the stranger. "Quite right to be prudent, Master Wilton. Nevertheless, you must come, for the matter is now one of some moment. Therefore, without asking you to answer at present, I shall expect you. At six of the clock, remember--precisely."

"I by no means promise to come," replied Wilton, "though I do not say that I will not. But you said that you wished to tell me something which might be useful to others. Pray what may that be?"

"Why," answered the stranger, "I wish you to give a little warning to your acquaintance, the Duke of Gaveston, regarding this very Sir John Fenwick and his character."

"Nay," said Wilton, "nay--that I can hardly do. My acquaintance with the Duke himself is extremely small. The Duke is a man of the world sufficiently old to judge for himself, and with sufficient experience to know the character of Sir John Fenwick without my explaining it to him."

"The Duke," replied the other, "is a grown baby, with right wishes and good intentions, as well as kind feelings; but a coral and bells would lure him almost anywhere, and he has got into the hands of one who will not fail to lead him into mischief. I thought you knew him well; but nevertheless, well or ill, you must give him the warning."

"I beg your pardon," replied Wilton, drawing himself up coldly: "but in one or two points you have been mistaken. My knowledge of the Duke is confined to one interview. I shall most probably never exchange another word with him in my life; and even if I were to do so, I should not think of assailing, to a mere common acquaintance, the character of a gentleman whom I may not like or trust myself, but who seems to be the intimate friend of the very person in whose good opinion you wish me to ruin him."

"Pshaw!" replied the stranger--"you will see the Duke again this very night, or I am much mistaken. As to Sir John Fenwick, I am a great deal more intimately his friend than the Duke is, and I may wish to keep him from rash acts, which he has neither courage nor skill to carry through, and will not dare to undertake, if he be not supported by others. I am, in fact, doing Sir John himself a friendly act, for I know his purposes, which are both rash and wrong; and if I cannot. stop them by fair means, I must stop them by others."

"In that," replied Wilton, "you must act as you think fit. I know nothing of Sir John Fenwick from my own personal observation; and therefore will not be made a tool of, to injure his reputation with others."

"Well, well," replied his companion--"in those circumstances you are right; and, as they say in that beggarly assemblage of pettifogging rogues and traitors called the House of Commons, I must shape my motion in another way. The manner in which I will beg you to deal with the Duke, is this. Find an opportunity, before this night be over, of entreating him earnestly not to go to-morrow to the meeting at the Old King's Head, in Leadenhall-street. This is clear and specific, and at the same time you assail the character of no one."

Wilton thought for a moment or two, and then replied, "I cannot even promise you absolutely to do this; but, if I can, I will. If I see the Duke, and have the means of giving him the message, I will tell him that I received it from a stranger, who seemed anxious for his welfare."

"That will do," answered the other--"that will do. But you must tell him without Sir John Fenwick's hearing you. As to your seeing him again, you will, I suppose, take care of that; for surely the bow, and the smile, and the blush, that came across the house to you, were too marked an invitation to the box, for such a gallant and a courteous youth not to take advantage of at once."

Wilton felt himself inclined to be a little angry at the familiarity with which his companion treated him, and which was certainly more than their acquaintance warranted. Curiosity, however, is powerful to repress all feelings, that contend with it; and if ever curiosity was fully justifiable, it surely was that of Wilton to know his own early history. Thus, although he might have felt inclined to quarrel with any other person who treated him so lightly, on the present occasion he smothered his anger, and merely replied that the stranger was mistaken in supposing that there was any such acquaintance between him and Lady Laura as to justify him in visiting her box.

Even while he was in the act of speaking, however, Lord Sherbrooke entered the lobby in haste, and advanced immediately towards him, saying, "Why, Wilton, I have been seeking you all over the house. Where, in Fortune's name, have you been? The Duke and Lady Laura have both been inquiring after you most tenderly, and wondering that you have not been to see them in their box."

The stranger, whom we shall in future call Green, turned away with a smile, saying merely, "Good evening, Mr. Brown; I won't detain you longer."

"Why, who the devil have you got there, Wilton?" exclaimed Lord Sherbrooke: "I think I have seen his face before."

"His name is Green," replied Wilton, not choosing to enter into particulars; "but I am ready now to go with you at once, and make my apologies for not accompanying you before."

"Come then, come," replied Lord Sherbrooke; and, leading the way towards the Duke's box, he added, laughingly, "If there had been any doubt before, my good Wilton, as to my future fate, this night has been enough to settle it."

"In what way?" said Wilton; but ere the young nobleman could answer, otherwise than by a smile, they had reached the box, and the door was thrown open.

Wilton's heart beat, it must be confessed; but he had sufficient command over himself to guard against the slightest emotion being perceptible upon his countenance; and he bowed to the Duke and to Lady Laura, with that ceremonious politeness which he judged that his situation required. Lady Laura at once, however, held out her hand to him, and expressed briefly, how glad she was of another opportunity to thank him for the great service which he had rendered her some time before. The Duke also spoke of it kindly and politely; and the other persons in the box, who were several in number, began to inquire into the circumstances thus publicly mentioned, so that the conversation took a more general turn, till the curtain again arose.

A certain degree of restraint, which had at first affected both Wilton and the lady, soon wore off, and the evening went by most pleasantly. It was not strange--it was not surely at all strange--that a young heart should forget itself in such circumstances. Wilton gave himself up, not indeed to visions of joy, but to actual enjoyment. Perhaps Lady Laura did the same. At all events, she looked far happier than she had done before; and when at length the curtain fell, and the time for parting came, they both woke as from a dream, and the waking was certainly followed by a sigh on either part. It was then that Wilton first recollected the warning that he had promised to give, and he was considering how he should find the means of speaking with the Duke alone, when that nobleman paused for a moment, as the rest of the party went out of the box, and drawing Wilton aside, said in a hasty but kindly wanner, "Lord Sherbrooke informs me that you are his most intimate friend, Mr. Brown; and as it is very likely that we shall see him frequently, I hope you will sometimes do us the favour of accompanying him."

Wilton replied by one of those unmeaning speeches which commit a man to nothing; for though his own heart told him that he would really be but too happy, as he said to take advantage of the invitation, yet it told him, at the same time, that to do so would be dangerous to his peace. The Duke was then about to follow his party; but Wilton now in turn detained him, saying, "I have a message to deliver to you, my lord duke, from a stranger who stopped me as I was coming to your box."

"Ha!" said the Duke, with a somewhat important air, "this is strange; but still I have so many communications of different kinds--what may it be, Mr. Brown?"

"It was, my lord," replied Wilton, in a low voice, "a warning which I think it best to deliver, as, not knowing the gentleman's name who gave it to me, I cannot tell whether it may be a mere piece of impertinence from somebody who is perhaps a stranger to your grace, or an intimation from a sincere friend--"

"But the warning, the warning!" said the Duke, "pray, what was this warning?"

"It was," replied Wilton, "a warning not to go to a meeting which you proposed to attend in the course of tomorrow."

"Ha!" said the Duke, with a look of some surprise--"did he say what meeting?"

"Yes, my lord," replied Wilton--"he said it was a meeting at the old King's Head in Leadenhall Street, and he added that it would be dangerous for you to do so."

"I will never shrink from personal danger, Mr. Brown," said the Duke, holding up his head, and putting on a courageous look. But the moment after, something seemed to strike him, and he added with a certain degree of hesitation, "But let me ask you, Mr. Brown, does my lord of Byerdale know this?--You have not told Lord Sherbrooke?"

"Neither the one nor the other, my lord," replied Wilton--"I have mentioned the fact to nobody but yourself."

"Pray, then, do not," replied the Duke; "you will oblige me very much, Mr. Brown, by keeping this business secret. I must certainly attend the meeting at four to-morrow, because I have pledged my word to it; but I shall enter into nothing that is dangerous or criminal, depend upon it--"

The nobleman was going on; and it is impossible to say how much he might have told in regard to the meeting in question, if Wilton had not stopped him.

"I beg your pardon, my lord," he said; "but allow me to remind you that I have no knowledge whatsoever of the views and intentions with which this meeting is to be held. I shall certainly not mention the message I have brought your grace to any one, and having delivered it, must leave the rest to yourself, whose judgment in such matters must be far superior to mine."

The Duke looked gratified, but moved on without reply, as the rest of his party were waiting at a little distance. Wilton followed; and seeing the Duke and Lady Laura with Sir John and Lady Mary Fenwick into their carriages, he proceeded homeward with Lord Sherbrooke, neither of them interchanging a word till they had well nigh reached Wilton's lodgings. There, however, Lord Sherbrooke burst into a loud laugh, exclaiming--

"Lack-a-day, Wilton, lack-a-day! Here are you and I as silent and as meditative as two owls in a belfry: you looking as wise as if you were a minister of state, and I as sorrowful as an unhappy lover, when, to say the truth, I am thinking of some deep stroke of policy, and you are meditating upon a fair maid's bright eyes. Get you gone, Wilton; get you gone, for a sentimental, lack-a-daisical shepherd! Now could we but get poor old King James to come back, the way to a dukedom would be open before you in a fortnight."

"How so?" demanded Wilton, "how so? You do not suppose, Sherbrooke, that I would ever join in overturning the religion, and the laws, and the liberties of my country--how so, then?"

"As thus," replied Lord Sherbrooke--"I will answer you as if I had been born the grave-digger in Hamlet. King James comes over--well, marry go to, now--a certain duke that you wot of, who is a rank Jacobite, by the by, instantly joins the invader; then comes King William, drives me his fellow-king and father-in-law out of the kingdom in five days, takes me the duke prisoner, and chops me his head off in no time. This headless father leaves a sorrowful daughter, who at the time of his death is deeply and desperately in love, without daring to say it, her father's head being the only obstacle in the way of the daughter's heart. Then comes the lover to console the lady, and finding her without protection, offers to undertake that very needful duty. Now see you, Wilton? Now see you?--But there's the door of your dwelling. Get you in, man, get you in, and try if in your dreams you can get some means of bringing it about. By my faith, Wilton, you are in a perilous situation; but there's one thing for your comfort,--if I can get out of all the scrapes that at this moment surround me on every side, like the lines of a besieging enemy, you can surely make your escape out of your difficulties, when you have love, and youth, and hope, to befriend you."

"Hope?" said Wilton, in bitter sadness; but at the moment he spoke, the door of the house was opened, and, bidding Lord Sherbrooke "Good night," he went in.

CHAPTER XIV.

During the greater part of the next day Wilton did not set eyes upon Lord Sherbrooke. The Earl of Byerdale, however, was peculiarly courteous and polite to his young secretary. There was much business, Earl was obliged to be very rapid in all his movements; but the terms in which he gave his directions were gentle and placable, and some letters received in the course of the day from Ireland seemed to please him well. He hinted even in a mysterious tone to Wilton that he had something of importance to say to him, but that he had not time to say it at the moment, and he ended by asking his secretary to dine at his house on the following day, when he said the Duke of Gaveston and Lady Laura were to be present, with a large party.

He went out about three o'clock: and Wilton had not long returned to his lodgings when Lord Sherbrooke joined him, and insisted on his accompanying him on horseback for a ride into the country.

Wilton was at that moment hesitating as to whether he should or should not go to the rendezvous given him by his strange acquaintance, Green. He had certainly left the theatre on the preceding night determined so to do; for the various feelings which at this time agitated his heart had changed the anxiety which he had always felt to know the circumstances of his birth and family into a burning thirst, which would have led him almost anywhere for satisfaction.

A night's thought, however--for we cannot say that he slept--had again revived all the doubts which had before prevented him from seeking the stranger, and had once more displayed before his eyes all the many reasons which in those days existed for holding no communication with persons whose characters were not known; or were in the least degree suspicious. Thus before Lord Sherbrooke joined him, he had fully convinced himself that the thing which he had so great an inclination to do was foolish, imprudent, and wrong. He had seen the man in a situation which left scarcely a doubt of his pursuits; he had seen him in close communication with a gentleman principally known as a virulent and unscrupulous enemy of the reigning dynasty; and he had not one cause for thinking well of him, except a certain off-hand frankness of manner which might easily be assumed.

All this he had repeated to himself twenty times, but yet he felt a strong inclination to go, when Lord Sherbrooke's sudden appearance, and invitation to ride out with him, cast an additional weight into the opposite scale, and determined his conduct at once. It is wonderful, indeed, how often those important acts, in regard to which we have hesitated and weighed every point with anxious deliberation, are ultimately determined by the most minute and trifling circumstance, totally unconnected with the thing itself. The truth is, under such circumstances we are like a man weighing fine gold dust, who does it to such a nicety that a hair falling into the scale turns it one way or the other.

In the present instance, our friend Wilton was not unwilling that something should come in aid of his better judgment; and ordering his horse t was soon beyond the precincts of London, and riding through the beautiful fields which at that time extended over ground where courtiers and ministers have now established their town dwellings.

From the whole demeanour of his companion, from the wild and excited spirits which he displayed, from the bursts of merriment to which he gave way, apparently without a sufficient cause, Wilton evidently saw that there was either some wild scheme working in Lord Sherbrooke's brain, or the knowledge of some happy event gladdening his heart. What it was, however, he could not divine, and the young nobleman was evidently determined on no account to explain. He laughed and jested with Wilton in regard to the gravity which he could not conquer, declared that he was the dullest companion that ever had been seen, and vowed that there could be no more stupid and tiresome companion for a long ride than a man in love, unless, indeed, it were a lame horse.

"Indeed, my dear Sherbrooke," replied Wilton, "you should prove, in the first place, that I am in love, which I can assure you is not the case, before you attempt to attribute my being grave to that reason. My very situation in life, and a thousand things connected therewith, are surely enough to make me sad at times."

"Why, what is there sad in your situation, my dear Wilton?" demanded Lord Sherbrooke, in the same tone of raillery: "here are you a wealthy young man--ay, wealthy, Wilton. Have you not yourself told me that your income exceeds your expenses; while I, on the other hand, have no income at all, and expenses in abundance? Well, I say you are here a wealthy young man, with the best prospects in the world, destined some day to be prime minister for aught I know."

"And who, at this present moment," interrupted Wilton, "has not a relation upon earth that he knows of; who has never enjoyed a father's care or a mother's tenderness; who can only guess that his birth was disgraceful to her whom man's heart is naturally bound to reverence, without knowing who or what was his father, or who even was the mother by whose shame he was brought into being."

Lord Sherbrooke was immediately grave, for he saw that Wilton was hurt; and he replied frankly and kindly, "I beg your pardon, my dear Wilton--I did not intend to pain you, and had not the slightest idea of how you were circumstanced. To tell the truth, I took it for granted that you were the son of good Lord Sunbury; and thought that you were, of course, well aware of all the particulars."

"Of none, Sherbrooke, of none," replied Wilton. "Suspicions may have crossed my mind that it is as you supposed, but then many other things tend to make me believe that such is not the case. At all events, one thing is clear--I have no family, no kindred; or if I have relations, they are ashamed of the tie that binds me to them, and voluntarily disown it."

"Pshaw! Wilton," exclaimed Lord Sherbrooke--"family! What matters a family? Make yourself one, Wilton. The best of us can but trace his lineage back to some black-bearded Northman, or yellow-haired Saxon, no better than a savage of some cannibal island of the South Sea--a fellow who tore his roast meat with unwashed fingers, and never knew the luxury of a clean shirt. Make a family for yourself, I say; and let the hundredth generation down, if the world last so long, boast that the head of the house was a gentleman, and wore gold lace on his coat."

Wilton smiled, saying, "I fear the prospect of progeny, Sherbrooke, will never be held as an equivalent for the retrospect of ancestors."

"An axiom worthy of Aristotle!" exclaimed Lord Sherbrooke; "but here we are, my dear Wilton," he continued, pulling up his horse at the gates of a house enclosed within walls, situated about a quarter of a mile beyond Chelsea, and somewhat more from the house and grounds belonging at that time to the celebrated Earl of Peterborough.

"But what do you intend to do here?" exclaimed Wilton, at this pause.

"Oh! nothing but make a call," replied his companion.

"Shall I ride on, or wait till you come back?" demanded Wilton.

"Oh, no!--come in, come in," said Lord Sherbrooke--"I shall not be long, and I'll introduce you, if you are not acquainted."

While he was speaking he had rung the bell, and his own two servants with Wilton's rode up to take the horses. Almost at the same moment a porter threw open the gates, and to his companion's surprise, Lord Sherbrooke asked for the Duke of Gaveston. The servant answered that the Duke was out, but that his young lady was at home; and thus the hero of our tale found himself suddenly, and even most unwillingly, brought to the dwelling of one whose society he certainly liked better than that of any one else on earth.

Lord Sherbrooke looked in his face with a glance of malicious pleasure; and then, as nothing on earth ever stopped him in anything that he chose to do or say, he burst forth into a gay peal of laughter at the surprise which he saw depicted on the countenance of his friend.

"Take the horses," he continued, turning to his own servants--"take the horses round to the Green Dragon, in the lane behind the house, wet their noses, and give them a book to read till we come to them. Come, Wilton, come! It is quite fitting," he said, in a lower tone, "that in execution of my plan I should establish a character for insanity in the house. Now that fat porter with the mulberry nose will go and report to the kitchen-maid that I order my horses a book to read, and they will decide that I am mad in a minute. The news will fly from kitchen-maid to cook, and from cook to housekeeper, and from housekeeper to lady's maid, and from lady's maid to lady. There will be nothing else talked of in the house but my madness; and when they come to add madness to badness they will surely give me up, if they haven't a mind to add sadness to madness likewise."

While he spoke, they were following a sort of groom of the chambers, who, after looking into one of the rooms on the ground-floor, turned to Lord Sherbrooke, saying, in a sweet tone,

"Lady Laura is walking in the gardens I see, my lord. I will show your lordship the way."

"So you have the honour of knowing who my lordship is, Mr. Montgomery Styles?" said Lord Sherbrooke, looking him full in the face.

"I beg your lordship's pardon," said the man, in the same mincing manner--"my name is not Montgomery Styles--my name is Josiah Perkins."

"Well, Jos. Perkins," said the young nobleman, "I PRAE SEQUOR, which means, get on as fast as you can, Mr. Perkins, and I'll come after; though you may tell me as you go, how it was you discovered my lordliness."

"Oh! by your look, my lord: I should have discovered it at once," replied the groom of the chambers; "but his grace told me that your lordship was likely to call."

"Oh, ho!" cried Lord Sherbrooke, with a laughing look to Wilton. But the next moment the servant threw open a glass door, and they issued forth into the gardens, which were very beautiful, and extended down to the river, filled with fine old trees, and spread out in soft green terraces and gravel walks. Lord Sherbrooke gazed round at first, with a look of criticising inquiry, upon the gardens; but the eyes of Wilton had fixed immediately upon the figure of a lady who was walking slowly along on the terrace, some way beneath them, at the very edge of the river. She did not remark the opening of the glass door in the centre of the house, which was at the distance of about two hundred yards from the spot where she was at the time; but continued her walk with her eyes bent upon the ground, and one hand playing negligently with the bracelet which encircled the wrist of the other arm. Her thoughts were evidently deeply busied with matters of importance, at least to herself. She was walking slowly, as we have said--a thing that none but a high-bred woman can do with grace--and though the great beauty of her figure was, in some degree, hidden by the costume of the day, yet nothing could render its easy, gliding motion aught but exquisitely graceful, and (if I may use a far-fetched term, but, perhaps, the only one that will express my meaning clearly,) musical to the eye. It must not be understood that, though she was walking slowly, the grace with which she did so had anything of the cold and stately air which those who assume it call dignity. Oh no! it was all easy: quiet, but full of youth, and health, and life it was the mere movement of a form, perfect in the symmetry of every limb, under the will of a spirit harmonizing entirely with the fair frame that contained it. She walked slowly because she was full of deep thought; but no one who beheld her could doubt that bounding joy might in its turn call forth as much grace in that young form as the calmer mood now displayed.

Wilton turned his eyes from the lady to his young companion, and he saw that he was now gazing at her too, and that not a little admiration was painted in his countenance. Wilton was painfully situated, and felt all the awkwardness of the position in which Lord Sherbrooke had placed him fully. Yet how could he act? he asked himself--what means of escape did there exist? What was the motive, too? what the intentions of Lord Sherbrooke? for what purposes had he brought him there? in what situation might he place him next?

All these, and many another question, he asked his own heart as they advanced across the green slopes and little terraces towards that in which the young lady "walked in beauty." There was no means for him to escape, however; and though he never knew from one moment to another what would be the conduct of Lord Sherbrooke, he was obliged to go on, and take his chance of what that conduct might be.

When they were about fifty yards from Lady Laura, she turned at the end of the walk, and then, for the first time, saw them as they approached; but if the expression of her countenance might be believed, she saw them with no great pleasure. An expression of anxiety, nay, of pain, came into her beautiful eyes; and as they were turned both upon Lord Sherbrooke and Wilton, the latter came in for his share also of that vexed look.

"You see, Wilton," said Lord Sherbrooke in a low voice, "how angry she is to behold you here. It was for that I brought you. I want to tease her in all possible ways," and without waiting for any reply, he hurried his pace, and advanced towards the lady.

She received him with marked coldness and distance of manner; but now the difference in her demeanour towards him and towards Wilton was strongly marked--not that the smile with which she greeted the latter when he came up was anything but very faint, yet her lip did relax into a smile.

The colour, too, came up a little into her cheek; and her manner was a little agitated. In short--though without openly expressing any very great pleasure at seeing him--it was evident that she was not displeased; and the secret of the slight degree of embarrassment which she displayed was, that for the first moment or so after she saw him, she thought of her mistake of the night before, and of her feelings while she had imagined that the Duke had pointed him out to her as one who, if she thought fit, might be her future husband.

The lady soon conquered the momentary agitation, however; and the conversation went on, principally maintained, of course, between herself and Lord Sherbrooke. Wilton would have given worlds indeed to have escaped, but there was no possibility of so doing, Lady Laura signified no intention of returning to the house; and they continued walking up and down the broad gravelled terrace, which of all things on earth affords the least opportunity for lingering behind, or escaping the embarrassment of being the one too many.

Wilton had too much good taste to suffer his annoyance to appear; and though he strove to avoid taking any greater part in the conversation than he could help, still when he joined in, what he did say was said with ease and grace. Lord Sherbrooke forced him, indeed, to speak more than he was inclined, and, to Lady Laura, there seemed a strange contrast between the thoughts and language of the two. The young nobleman's conversation was light, witty, poignant, and irregular. It was like the flowing of a shallow stream amongst bright pebbles which it causes to sparkle, and from which it receives in return a thousand various shades and tints, but without depth or vigour; while that of Wilton was stronger, more profound, more vigorous both in thought and expression, and was like a deeper river flowing on without so much sunshine and light, but clear, deep, and powerful, and not unmusical either, between its banks.

It was towards the latter that Lady Laura turned and listened, though she could not but smile at many of the gay sallies of him who walked on the other side: but it seemed as if the conversation of Lord Sherbrooke rested in the ear, while that of Wilton sunk into the heart.

It would not be very interesting, even if we had times to detail all that took place upon that occasion; but it must be confessed that, though once or twice Lord Sherbrooke felt inclined to put forth all his powers of pleasing, out of pique at the marked preference which Lady Laura showed for Wilton, he in no degree concealed the worst points of his character. He said nothing, indeed, which could offend in mere expression: but every now and then he suffered some few words to escape him, which clearly announced that the ties of morality and religion were in no degree recognised by him amongst the principles by which he intended to guide his actions. He even forced the conversation into channels which afforded an opportunity of expressing opinions of worse than a dangerous character. Constancy, he said, was all very well for a turtledove, or an old man of seventy with a young wife; and as for religion, there were certain people paid for having it, and he should not trouble himself to have any unless he were paid likewise. This was not, indeed, all said at once, nor in such distinct terms as we have here used, but still the meaning was the same; and whether expressed in a jesting or more serious manner, that meaning could not be misunderstood.

Wilton looked grave and sad when he heard such things said to a pure and high-minded girl; and Lady Laura herself turned a little pale, and cast her eyes down upon the ground without reply.

At length, after this had gone on for some time, Lord Sherbrooke inquired for Lady Mary Fenwick, saying that he had hoped to see her there, and to inquire after her health.

"Oh, she is here still," replied Lady Laura; "but she complained of headache this morning, and is sitting in the little library. I do not know whether she would be inclined to see any one or not."

"Oh, she will see me, beyond all doubt," exclaimed Lord Sherbrooke--"no lady ever refuses to see me. Besides, her great-grandmother, on old Lady Carlisle's side, was my great- grandfather's forty-fifth cousin; so that we are relations. I will go and find her out. Stay you, Wilton, and console Lady Laura, till I come back again. I shall not be five minutes."

Thus saying, away he darted, leaving Lady Laura and Wilton alone in the middle of the walk. The lady seemed to hesitate for a moment what she should do, whether she should follow to the house or not, and she paused for an instant in the walk; but inclination, if the truth must be said, got the better of what she might consider strictly decorous, and after that momentary pause, she walked on with Wilton by her side. In saying that it was inclination determined her conduct, I did not mean to say that it was solely the inclination to walk and converse with Wilton Brown, though that had some share in the business, but there was besides, an inclination to be freed from the presence of Lord Sherbrooke, who had succeeded to a miracle in making her thoroughly disgusted with him.

As they walked on, there was a certain degree of embarrassment hung over both Wilton and Laura; both felt, perhaps, that they could be very happy in each other's society, but both felt afraid of being too happy. With Wilton, there were a thousand causes to produce that slight embarrassment, and with Lady Laura several also. But one, and a very principal cause was, that there was something which she longed exceedingly to say, and yet doubted whether she ought to say it.

It does not unfrequently happen that a person of the highest rank and station, possessing every quality to secure friendship, with wealth and every gift of fortune at command, surrounded by numerous acquaintances, and mingling with a wide society, is nevertheless totally alone--alone in spirit and in heart--alone in thought and mind. Such was the case with Lady Laura. It is true she had yet but very little experience of the world, and her search for a congenial spirit had not been carried far or prosecuted long; but she was one of those who had learned to think and to feel early. Her mother, who had died three years before, had taught her to do so, not alone for her own sake, but also for that of her father; for the Duchess had early felt the conviction that her own life would be brief, and knew that the mind and character of her daughter must have a great effect upon the Duke, whom she loved much, though she could not venerate very highly.

With a heart, then, full of deep and pure feelings, with a mind not only originally bright and strong, not only highly cultivated and stored with fine tastes, but highly directed and fortified with strong principles, with an enthusiastic love of everything that was beautiful and graceful, generous, noble, and dignified--it is not to be wondered at that, in the wide society of the capital, or amongst all the acquaintances who thronged her father's house, Lady Laura had seen no spirit congenial to her own, no heart with the same feelings, no mind with the same objects. In every one she had met with, there had still been some apparent weakness, some worldliness, some selfishness; there had been coldness, or apathy, or want of principle, or want of feeling; and the bright enthusiasms of her young nature had been confined to the tabernacle of her own heart.

She had seen Wilton Brown but seldom, it is true, but nevertheless she felt differently towards him and other people. There were several causes which had produced this; and perhaps, as Lady Laura was not absolutely an angel, his personal appearance might have something to do with it, though less than might be supposed. His fine person, his noble carriage, his bright and intelligent countenance, the rapid variety of its expressions, the dignified character of the predominant one to which it always returned, after those more transient had passed away--all gave the idea of there being a high heart and mind beneath. In the next place, Wilton had, as we have told, commenced his acquaintance with her by an act of personal service, performed with gallantry, skill, and decision, at the risk of his own life. In the third place, in all his conversation, as far as she had ever known or remarked, there were those small casual traits of good feelings, fine tastes, and strong principles, expressed sometimes by a single word, sometimes by a look or gesture, which are a thousand-fold more convincing, in regard to the real character of the person, than the most laboured harangue, or essay, or declaration.

Thus it was that Laura hoped, and fancied, and believed, she had now seen one person upon earth whose feelings, thoughts, and character might assimilate with her own. Pray let the reader understand, that I do not mean to say Laura was in love with Wilton; but she did believe that he was one of those for whose eyes she might draw away a part of that customary veil with which all people hide the shrine of their deeper feelings from the sight of the coarse multitude.

There was something, then, as we have seen, that she wished to say--there was something that she believed she might say, without risk or wrong. But yet she hesitated; and she and Wilton went on nearly to the end of the walk in perfect silence. At length she cast a timid glance, first towards the house where Lord Sherbrooke was seen just entering one of the rooms from the upper terrace, and then to the face of Wilton Brown, whose eye chanced at that moment to be upon her with a look of inquiry. The look gave her courage, and she said--

"I am going to say a very odd thing, Mr. Brown, I believe; but your great intimacy with Lord Sherbrooke puzzles me. He told my father last night that you were his dearest and most intimate friend. I always thought that friendship must proceed from a similarity of feelings and pursuits, and I am sure, from what I have heard you say, at least I think I may be sure, that you entertain ideas the most opposite to those with which he has just pained us."

Wilton smiled somewhat sadly; but he did not dare deny that such opinions were Lord Sherbrooke's real ones; for his well-known conduct was too much in accordance with them.

"Would to Heaven, dear lady," he said, "that Sherbrooke would permit me to be as much his friend as I might be! I must not deny that he has many faults--faults, I am sure, of education and habit alone, for his heart is noble, honourable, and high"

"Nay," cried Lady Laura--"could a noble or an honourable heart entertain such sentiments as he has just expressed?"

"You do not know him, nor understand him yet, Lady Laura," replied Wilton. "Most men strive to make themselves appear better than they really are: Sherbrooke labours to make himself appear worse--not alone, Lady Laura, in his language--not alone in his account of himself, but even by his very actions. I am confident that he has committed more than one folly, for the sole purpose, if his motives were thoroughly sifted and investigated, of establishing a bad reputation."

"What a sad vanity!" exclaimed Lady Laura. "On such a man no reliance can be placed. But his plain declaration, a few minutes ago, is quite sufficient to mark his character, I mean his declaration, that he considers no vows taken to a woman at all binding on a man. Is that the principle of an honourable heart, Mr. Brown?"

Wilton was silent for a moment, but Lady Laura evidently looked for a reply; and he answered at length, "No, it is not, Lady Laura; but I fully believe, ere taking any such vows, Sherbrooke would openly acknowledge his view of them, and, having done so, would look upon them as mere empty air."

Lady Laura laughed, evidently applying her companion's words to her own situation with Lord Sherbrooke; and Wilton, unwilling that one word from his lips should have a tendency to thwart the purposes of the Earl of Byerdale, in a matter where he had no right to interfere, hastened to add, "Let me assure you, Lady Laura, however, at the same time that I make this acknowledgment with regard to Sherbrooke, that I am fully convinced, if he were to pledge his word of honour to keep those voles, he would die rather than violate that pledge."

"That is to say," replied Lady Laura, somewhat bitterly, "that he has erected an idol whose oracles he can interpret as he will, and calls it honour, denying that there is any other God. But let us speak of it no more, Mr. Brown; these things make one sad."

Wilton was glad to speak of something else; for he felt himself bound by every tie to say all that he could in favour of Lord Sherbrooke; and yet he could not find in his heart to aid, in the slightest degree, in forwarding a scheme which could end in nothing but misery to the sweet and innocent girl beside him. He changed the topic at once, then, and exerted himself to draw her mind away from the matter on which they had just been speaking.

Nevertheless, that subject, while they went on, remained in the mind of each; and Lady Laura might have discovered--if she had been at all apprehensive of her own feelings--that it is a dangerous thing to do as she had done, and raise, for any eye, even a corner of that veil which bides the heart, unless we are inclined to raise it altogether. Her subsequent conversation with Wilton took its tone throughout, entirely from what had gone before. Without knowing it, or rather, we should say, without perceiving it, they suffered it to be mingled with deep feelings; shadowed forth, perhaps, more than actually expressed. A softness, too, came over it--we insist not, though, perhaps, we might, call it a tenderness the ceremonious terms were soon dropped; and because the speakers would have been obliged to use those ceremonious terms, if they had spoken each other's names, they seemed by mutual consent to forget each other's names, and never spoke them at all. Lady Laura did not address him as Mr. Brown, and Wilton uttered not the words, "Lady Laura." From time to time, too, she gazed up in his face, to see if he understood what she meant but could not fully express; and he, while he poured forth any of the deep thoughts long treasured in his own bosom, looked often earnestly into her countenance, to discover by the expression the effect produced on her mind.

Lord Sherbrooke was absent for more than half an hour; and, during that half hour, Wilton and the lady had gone farther on the journey they were taking than ever they had gone yet.--What journey?

Cannot you divine, reader? When Wilton entered those gardens, we might boldly say, as we did say, that he was not in love. When he left them, we should have hesitated. He would have hesitated himself! Was not that going far upon a journey?

However, Lord Sherbrooke at length joined them; and after a moment more of cold and ceremonious leave-taking with Lady Laura, he turned, and, accompanied by Wilton, left the house.

Lady Laura remained upon the terrace, walking more rapidly than before, and with her eyes bent upon the ground. Two minutes brought Wilton to the gates of the court-yard; but oh, in those two minutes, how his heart smote him, and how his brain reeled!

"Shall I run for the horses, my lord?" cried the groom of the chambers--"Shall I go for the horses, my lord?" exclaimed one of the running footmen who was loitering in the hall.

"No," said Lord Sherbrooke--"we will walk and fetch them," and taking Wilton's arm, he sauntered quietly on from the house.

"Sherbrooke, Sherbrooke, this is all very wrong," said Wilton, the moment they were out of hearing.

"Very wrong, Solon!" exclaimed Lord Sherbrooke--"what do you mean? Heavens and earth, what a perverse generation it is! When I expected to be thanked over and over again for the kindest possible act, to be told that it is all very wrong! You ungrateful villain! I declare I have a great mind to turn round and draw my sword upon you, and cut your throat out of pure friendship. Very wrong, say you?"

"Ay, very wrong, Sherbrooke," replied Wilton. "You have placed me in an unpleasant and dangerous situation, and without giving me notice or a choice, have made me co-operate in doing what I do not think right."

"Pshaw!" cried Lord Sherbrooke--"Pshaw! At your heart, my dear Wilton, you are very much obliged to me; and if you are not the most ungrateful and the most foolish of all men upon earth, you will take the goods the gods provide you, and make the best use of time and opportunity."

"All I can say, Sherbrooke," replied Wilton, "is, that I shall never return to that house again, except for a formal visit to the Duke."

"Fine resolutions speedily broken!" exclaimed Lord Sherbrooke: and he was right.

CHAPTER XV.

Had Wilton Brown wanted an immediate illustration of the fragile nature of man's purposes, of how completely and thoroughly our firmest resolutions are the sport of fate and accident, it could have been furnished to him within five minutes after he left the gates of the house where he had paid an unintended visit.

Lord Sherbrooke seemed perfectly well acquainted with the house and its neighbourhood, and led the way round through a green lane at the back, which presently, in one of its most sequestered spots, offered to the eyes a somewhat large old-fashioned public-house, standing back in a small paved court: while planted before it, on the edge of the road, was a sign-post, bearing on its top the effigy of a huge green dragon.

Now, whether it be from some unperceived association in the minds of the English people between the chimerical gentleman we have lately mentioned and the patron saint of this island, who, it seems, if all tales were told, was not a bit better than the dragon that he slew; or for what other reason I know not, yet there is no doubt of the fact, that in all ages English vintners have had a particular predilection for green dragons; and that name was so commonly attached to a public-house, in those days, that it had not at all struck Wilton Brown that the Green Dragon to which Lord Sherbrooke ordered the horses to be led, was that very identical Green Dragon where his acquaintance Mr. Green had given him the rendezvous.

He might not, indeed, have heard Lord Sherbrooke's order at all; but it is still more probable, that he only did not attend to it, as all his thoughts were taken up at the moment by the discovery of what place Lord Sherbrooke had brought him to. It now, however, struck him--when he saw the Green Dragon standing in the Green Lane, precisely as it had been described by Green--that it might very likely be the identical house to which he had been directed; and on asking Lord Sherbrooke what was the name of the mansion they had just visited, the matter was placed beyond doubt by his replying, "Beaufort House. The Duke only hires it for a time."

Brown hesitated now for an instant, as to how he should act. His watch told him that it was close upon the hour to the appointment: curiosity raised her voice: the natural longing after kindred had also its influence; and if the society of Lord Sherbrooke was any impediment, that was instantly removed by the young noble-man saying, "Come, Wilton, as you are an unsociable devil, and seem out of temper, I shall leave you to ride home by yourself--The truth is," he added, after a moment's pause, "I am going upon an expedition, that the character I have given myself to my fair Lady Laura may be fully and completely established on the day that it is given.".

"Nay, Sherbrooke, nay!" cried Wilton--"I hope and trust such is not the case."

The other only laughed, and called loudly for his servants and horses.

Well disciplined to his prompt and fiery disposition, his grooms led the horses out in a moment, and the young nobleman sprang into the saddle. Before his right foot was in the stirrup, he had touched the horse with the spur, and away he went like lightning, waving his hand to Wilton with a light laugh.

Wilton's horses and groom had appeared also, but he paused before the door without mounting; and the next moment, a fat, well-looking host, as round, as well fed, and as rosy, as beef, beer, and good spirits, ever made the old English innkeeper, appeared at the door in his white night-cap and apron, and approaching the young gentleman, invited him in with what seemed a meaning look.

"Perhaps I may come in," replied Wilton, "and taste your good ale, landlord."

"Sir, the ale is both honoured and honourable," replied the host. "I can assure you many a high gentleman tastes it at the Green Dragon."

Bidding his servant lead the horse up and down before the door, Wilton slowly entered the well-sanded passage, and passed through the doorway of a room to which the landlord pointed. The moment he entered, he heard voices speaking very loud, there being nothing apparently between that and the adjoining chamber but a very thin partition of wood-work. The landlord hemmed and coughed aloud, and Wilton made his footfalls sound as heavily as possible, but all in vain: the person who was speaking went on in the same tone; and before the landlord could get out of the room again and down the passage to the door of the next chamber, which was some way farther on, Wilton distinctly heard the words, "Nonsense, Sir George! don't attempt to cajole me! I tell you, I will have nothing to do with it. To bring in foreigners is bad enough, when we are quite strong enough to do it without: but I will take no man's blood but in fair fight."

"Well!" exclaimed the other, in the same loud and vehement manner--"you know, sir, I could hang you if I liked!"

At that moment the door was evidently opened, and the landlord's voice, exclaiming, "Hush! hush!" was heard; but he could not stop the reply, which was,--

"I know that! But I could hang you, too; so that we are each pretty safe. This is that villain Charnock's doing. Tell him I will blow his brains out the first time I meet him, for spoiling, by his bloody-minded villany, one of the most hopeful plans--"

But the landlord's "Hush! hush!" was again repeated, and the voices were thenceforth moderated, though the discussion seemed still to endure some time.

Wilton's curiosity was now more excited than ever; and when the landlord brought him a foaming jug of ale, together with a long Venice glass having a wavy pearl-coloured line up the stalk, he asked the simple question, "Is Mr. Green here?"

On this the landlord put down his head, saying, in a low voice, "The Colonel will be with you directly: he expects you, sir."

"The Colonel!" thought Brown--"this is a new dignity. However, with his state and station I have little to do, if I could but discover my own."

At the end of about five minutes the conversation in the other room ceased, and in a moment or two more the door was opened, and Green made his appearance. We have so accurately described him before that we should not pause upon his appearance now, had there not been a great change in his dress, which had such an effect as to render it scarcely possible to recognise him.

Now, instead of a military-looking suit of green, he had on a long-waisted broad-cut coat of black, with jet buttons; a light-coloured periwig filled full of powder; black breeches and silk stockings, and a light black-hilted sword. In fact, he bore much more the appearance of a French lawyer of that day than anything else. The features, indeed, were there; but it was wonderful what the highly-powdered wig had done to soften the strong-marked lines of his face, and to blanch the weather-beaten appearance of his complexion.

The suit of black, too, made him look thinner and even taller than he really was; and on his first entrance into the room, Wilton certainly did not know him.

"You have come before your time," he said, "though perhaps it is as well, for I must go out as soon as it is dusk;" and as he spoke he cast himself into a chair, fixed his eyes upon some scanty embers which were smouldering in the grate, and fell into a deep and apparently painful fit of thought. His broad but heavy brow was knitted with a wrinkled frown; the muscles of his face worked from time to time; and Wilton could see the sinews of his large powerful hand, as it lay upon his knee, standing out like cords, though he uttered not a word.

After pausing for a moment or two, his companion thought it time to recall this strange acquaintance to the subject of his coming, and said, "You told me I might see some of my old friends here, Mr. Green. Let me remind you it grows late."

"Don't be impatient, my good boy," replied the other, abstractedly, at the same time rising and drinking a deep draught of the ale--"you SHALL see some of your old friends! Don't you see me?"

"Yes," replied Wilton, "you are an acquaintance, certainly, of some months, but nothing more that I know of."

"Well, well, do not be impatient, I say," answered Green "you shall see some one else, if I don't satisfy you. But you are before your time, as I said."

He had scarcely spoken, when the door of the little room opened once more, and a woman apparently of no very high class, and considerably advanced in years, so as to be somewhat decrepit, came in. She was dressed in a large grey cloak of common serge, with a stick in her hand, and mittens on her hands, while over her head was a large black wimple or hood, which covered a great part of her face.

The moment Green saw her, he crossed over, and said in a low but not inaudible voice, "Not a word, till all this business is over! They will ruin the cause and themselves, and all that are engaged with them, by committing all sorts of crimes. It will plunge him into the greatest dangers, if you say a word."

Much of what he said was heard by Brown; and in the meantime Green aided the woman to disembarrass herself of her hood and cloak, taking the staff out of her hand, and at the same time turning the key of the door. The moment that he did so, his female companion drew herself up; the appearance of bowed decrepitude vanished; and she stood before Brown a tall graceful woman, apparently scarcely forty years of age, with a countenance still beautiful, and a demeanour which left no doubt of the society with which at one time she must have mingled.

Of Wilton himself the lady had as yet had but once glance, as she first entered the room; for, ever since, Green had stood between them so that she could not see. When she did behold him fully, however, she gazed upon him earnestly, clasping her hands, and exclaiming, "Is it--is it possible?"

The next moment her feelings seemed to overpower her--"Oh yes, yes," she cried, advancing "it is he himself--the same dear, blessed likeness of the dead!" and casting her arms round the young gentleman's neck, she wept long and profusely on his bosom.

Wilton was surprised and agitated, as may well be conceived. He was not sufficiently ignorant of the world not to know that there are a thousand tricks and artifices daily practised, which assume such appearances as the scene now performing before him displayed. He might, indeed, have entertained suspicions of all sorts of transformations and disguises; but there was an earnestness, a truth, in the lady's manner that was in itself convincing, and there was something more, also--there was a most extraordinary resemblance in her whole face and person to the picture which we have before mentioned in the house of the Earl of Sunbury. The features were the same, the height, the figure: the eyes were the same colour, there was the same peculiar expression about the mouth, and the only difference seemed to be the difference of age. The picture represented a girl of eighteen or nineteen: the person who stood beside him must have seen well nigh forty summers.

Though the likeness was complete, there was a certain difference. Have we not all beheld a beautiful scene spread out in the morning light, full of radiance, and sparkling, and glorious sunshine? and have we not seen a grey cloud creep over the sky, leaving the landscape the sauce, but taking from it the resplendent beams in which it shone at first? So did it seem with her. All appeared the same as in the bright being whom the painter had depicted in her gay day of youth; but that Time had since brought, as it were, a grey shadow over the loveliness which it could not take away.

All these things took from Wilton every doubt; and after he had suffered the lady for a moment to give way to her feelings without a word: even throwing his arm slightly round her, and pressing her towards him, he said, "Are you--are you my mother?"

"Alas! no, my dear boy," she replied, raising her head and wiping away the tears, while the colour rose slightly in her cheek. "I am not your mother, but one who has loved you scarcely less than ever mother loved her son; one who nursed and fondled you in infancy; one who has now come from another land but for the sake of seeing you, and of holding once more to her heart the nursling of other years, even more sad and terrible than these."

"From another land!" said Wilton, thoughtfully, while through the dim and misty vista of the past, strange figures seemed to move before his eyes, as if suddenly called up out of the darkness of oblivion by some enchanter's voice. "Another land!" he said, thoughtfully--"Your face and your voice seem to wake strange memories. I think, I remember having been with you in another land, and I recollect--surely I recollect, a pretty cottage with a rose-tree at the door--a rose-tree in full bloom; and tying the knot of an officer's scarf, and his holding me long to his heart, and blessing me again and again--"

"Before he went to battle!" said the lady, "before he went to death!" Her voice became choked in suffocating sobs, and she wept again long and bitterly.

"Nay, but tell me more," said Wilton--"in pity, tell me more. Do I not surely recollect his face, too?" and he pointed to Green, "and the sparkling sea-shore? and sailing long upon the ocean? Tell me more, oh, tell me more!"

"I must not yet, Wilton," she replied--"I must not yet. They tell me it is dangerous, and I believe it is. Struggles must soon take place, changes must inevitably ensue, and I would not--no, not for all the world, I would not that your young life should be plunged into those terrible contentions, which have swallowed up, as a dark whirlpool, the existence of so many of your race. If our hopes be true, the way to fortune and rank will be open to you at once: or there is no such a thing as gratitude in the world. If not, you will have the means of living in quiet and tranquillity, and if you will, of struggling for higher things; for within six months the whole shall be told to you. Ask me not! ask me not!" she added, seeing him about to speak--"I have promised in this matter to be guided by others, and I must say no more."

"But who is he?" continued Wilton, pointing to Green. The lady looked first at him, and then at their companion, with a faint, even a melancholy, smile.

"He is one," she replied, "whom you must trust, for he has ever guided others better and more successfully than he has guided himself. He is one who has every title to direct you."

"This is all very strange," said Wilton, "and it is painful, too. You do not know--you cannot tell, how painful it is to live, as it were, in a dark cloud, knowing nothing either of the future or the past."

The lady looked down sadly upon the ground.

"There are, sometimes," she said, "certainties which are far more terrible than doubts. Be contented, Wilton, till you hear more: when you do hear more, you will hear much painful matter; you will have much to undergo, and you will need courage, determination, and strength of mind. In the meanwhile, as from your earliest years, careful, anxious, zealous, eyes have watched over you, marked your every movement, traced your every step, even while you thought yourself abandoned, forgotten, and neglected: so shall it be till the whole is explained to you. Thenceforth you will rule your own conduct, judge, determine, and act for yourself. We know, we are sure, that you will act nobly, uprightly, and well in the meanwhile, and that you will do no deed which at a future period may not befit any station and any race to acknowledge."

Wilton mused deeply for several moments, and then raising his eyes to the lady's face, he demanded, in a low tone--

"Answer me only one question more. Am I the son of Lord Sunbury?"

The blood rushed violently up into the lady's countenance.

"Lord Sunbury was never married," she exclaimed--"was he?"

"I know not," replied Wilton--"all I ask is, am I his son? I ask it, because he has shown me generous kindness, care, and consideration; and at times I have seen him gazing in my face, when he thought I did not remark it, as if there were some deeper feelings in his bosom than mere friendship. Yet I cannot say that he has ever taught me to look upon myself as his son."

"Your imagination is only leading you into a labyrinth, Wilton," replied the personage calling himself Green, "from which you will find it difficult to extricate yourself. Be contented with what you know, and ask no more."

"I much wish, and I do entreat," replied Wilton, "that you would give me an answer to the question I have asked. There might be circumstances--indeed, I may say, that circumstances are very likely to occur, in which it would be absolutely necessary for me to know what claim I have upon the Earl of Sunbury. I have never yet asked him for anything of importance; but I foresee that the time may soon come when I may have to demand of him what I would not venture to demand, did I consider myself but the claimless child of his bounty."

The lady looked at Green, and Green at her, and they paused for several minutes. At length she answered, "I will give you a claim upon Lord Sunbury;" and she took from her finger a large ring, such as were commonly worn in those days, presenting on one side a shield of black enamel surrounded with brilliants, and in the centre a cipher, formed also of small diamonds. "Keep this," said the lady, "till all is explained to you, Wilton, and then return it to me. Should the Earl's assistance be required in anything of vital importance, show him that ring, if he be in England, or if he be abroad, tell him that you possess it, and beseech him by all the thoughts which that may call up in his mind, to aid you to the utmost of his power.--I think he will not fail you."

Wilton was about to answer; and though it was now growing dusk, he might have lingered on much longer, striving to gain more information, but at that moment there came a sound of many feet at the passage, and the voice of some one speaking apparently to the landlord, and demanding,--"Who the devil's horses are those walking up and down there?"

Almost at the same time, a hand was laid upon the latch of the door, and it would have been thrown open, had not Green previously taken the precaution of locking it. He now partially opened it, however, and spoke a few words to those without.

"Go into the next room," he said; "go into the next room--I will be with you directly." He then closed the door again, and turning to Wilton, took him by the arm, saying, "Now mount your horse, and be gone instantly: your time for staying here is over; make the best of your way home, without delay; and only remember, that whenever we meet in future, you do not appear to know me, unless I speak to you. Should you want advice, direction, and assistance--and remember, that though poor and powerless as I seem, I may know more, and be able to do far more, than you imagine--ask for me here; or the first time you see me, lay your finger upon that ring which she has given you, and I will find means to learn your wishes, and to promote them instantly--Now you must go at once."

Wilton saw that the attempt to learn more, at that moment, would be vain: but before he departed, he took the lady by the hand, bidding her adieu, and saying, "At all events, I have one consolation. Since I came here, I feel less lonely in the world; I feel that there are some to whom I am dear; and yet I would fain ask you one thing more. It is, how, when I think of you, I shall name you in my thoughts. Your image will be frequently before me; the affection which you have shown me, the words you have spoken, will never be forgotten. But there is a pleasure in connecting all those remembrances with a name. It seems to render them definite; to give them a habitation in the heart for ever."

"Call me Helen," replied the lady, quickly. "Where I now dwell they call me the Lady Helen. I must not add any more; and now adieu, for it is time that both you and I should leave this place."

Green once more urged him to depart; and Brown, with his curiosity not satisfied, but even more excited than ever, quitted the house, mounted his horse, and rode away slowly towards his own dwelling, meditating as he went.

CHAPTER XVI.

Onward! onward!" cries the voice of youth; whether it may be that the days are bright, passing in joy and tranquillity, and we can say with the greatest French poet of the present day--ay, the greatest, however it may seem--Beranger,

"Sur une onde tranquille,
Voguant soir et matin,
Ma nacelle est docile
Au souffle du destin.
La voile s'enfie-t-elle,
J'abandonne le bord.
(O doux zephir, sois-moi fidele!)
Eh! vogue, ma nacelle;
Nous trouverons un port"--

or whether the morning is overcast with clouds and storms, still "Onward! onward!" is the cry, either in the hope of gaining new joys, or to escape the sorrows that surround us. It is for age to stretch back the longing arms towards the Past: the fate of youth is to bound forward to meet the Future.

Wilton reached his home, and bending down his head upon his hands, passed more than an hour in troublous meditation. All was confused and turbid. The stream of thought was like a mountain torrent, suddenly swelled by rains, overflowing its banks, knowing no restraint, no longer clear and bright, but dark and foaming and whirling in rapid and uncertain eddies round every object that it touched upon. The scene at Beaufort House, the thought of Laura, and all that had been said there, mingled strangely and wildly with everything that had taken place afterwards, and nothing seemed certain, but all confused, and indistinct, and vague. But still there came a cry from the bottom of his heart: the cry of "Onward! onward! onward! towards the fated future!"

Nor was that cry the less vehement or less importunate because lie had no power whatsoever to advance or retard the coming events by a single hour: nor had it less influence because--unlike most men, who generally have some lamp, however dim, to give them light into the dark caverns of the future--he had not even one faint ray of probability to show him what was before his footsteps.

On the contrary, the yearning to reach that future, to pass on through that darkness to some brighter place beyond, was all the more strong and urgent. In short, excited imagination had produced some hope, without the slightest probability to foster it. He had even been told that he was to expect information of a painful kind. Not one word had been said to give him the expectation of a bright destiny: and yet there was something so sweet, so happy, in having found any one whose tenderness had been bestowed upon his infant years, and whose affection had remained unchanged by time and absence, that hope--as hope always is--was born of happiness; and though that hope was wild, uncertain, and unfounded, it made the natural eagerness of youth all the more eager.

When he lay down to rest he slept not, but still many a vision floated before his waking eyes, and thought made the night seem short. On the following morning he was early up and dressed; but by seven o'clock a note was put into his hand, in a writing which he did not know. On opening it, however, he found it to contain a request, couched in the most courteous terms, from the Duke of Gaveston, that he would call upon him immediately, and before he went to the house of Lord Byerdale. There was scarcely time to do so; but he instantly ordered his horse, and galloped to Beaufort House as fast as possible. He was ushered immediately into a small saloon, and thence into the dressing-room of the Duke, whom he found in a state of considerable agitation, and evidently embarrassed even in explaining to him what he wanted.

"I have sent for you, Mr. Brown," he said,--"I have sent for you to speak on a matter that may be of great consequence:--not that I know that it will be--not that I have heard anything--for I would not hear, after I found out what was the great object; but--but--"

Wilton was inclined to imagine that some unexpected obstacles had occurred in regard to the proposed alliance between the families of the Duke and of the Earl of Byerdale, and he certainly felt no inclination to aid in removing those obstacles. He replied, therefore, coldly enough, "If there is anything in which I can serve your grace, I am sure it will give me much pleasure to do so."

His coldness, however, only seemed to increase the Duke's eagerness and also his agitation.

"You can, indeed, Mr. Brown," he said, "render me the very greatest service, and I'm sure you are an honourable and an upright man, and will not refuse me. If you had explained yourself more clearly the night before last, I am sure I would have taken your advice at once, and would not have gone at all; but, as it is, I stayed not a moment longer than I could help, and have now broken with Fenwick and Barklay for ever. They vow that I am pledged to their cause, and must take a part, but they will find themselves mistaken."

Wilton now found that the good nobleman's fancy had misled him, and that his agitation arose from something that had taken place at the meeting at the Old King's Head, in regard to which he certainly knew nothing, nor indeed wished to know anything. He replied, however, somewhat more warmly,--

"In regard to these transactions, my lord duke, I know nothing, as I before informed you: but if you will tell me how I can serve you, I will do it with pleasure."

"I was sure you would, Mr. Brown, I was sure you would," said the Duke. "You can do me the greatest service, my dear young friend, by promising me positively upon your word of honour never to mention to any one that I went to this meeting at the Old King's Head, or, in fact, that I knew anything about it. I especially could wish that it be not mentioned to the Earl of Byerdale; for I know that he is a very fierce and vindictive man, and I do not wish to put myself in his power, just at present, above all times. Nobody on earth knows it but you and the people engaged in the affair, whose mouths are stopped, of course. We left the carriage on this side of Paul's, and I sent the two running footmen different ways, so that, if you give me your honour, I am quite safe."

"I give you my honour, most assuredly, my lord duke," replied Wilton, "that I will never, under any circumstances, or at any time, mention one word of that which has taken place between us on the subject. Rest perfectly sure of that. Indeed, I know nothing; I therefore have nothing to tell. But, at all events, I will utter not one word."

"Thank you, thank you!" cried the Duke, grasping his hand with joy and enthusiasm--"thank you, thank you a thousand times, my dear young friend!" and in the excitement of the moment, in his dressing-gown and slippers as he was, he led Wilton out to the room where his daughter was seated, and without any explanation informed her that he, Wilton, was one of his best and dearest friends. He then rushed back again to conclude the little that wanted to the labours of his toilet, leaving Wilton alone with her at the breakfast-table.

"Oh, Mr. Brown," exclaimed Laura, with her face glowing with eagerness, "I hope and trust that you have settled this business, for I have been most anxious ever since last night. Sir John Fenwick behaved so ill, and quitted the house in such fury, and that dark-looking man who accompanied him back, used such threatening language towards my father, that indeed--indeed, I feared for the consequences this morning."

Wilton evidently saw that her fears pointed in any direction but the right one, and that she apprehended some hostile rencontre between her father and the two rash Jacobites with whom he had suffered himself to be entangled. Knowing, however, that it could be anything but the desire of such men to call public attention to their proceedings, he did not scruple to give her every assurance that no duel, or angry collision of any kind, was likely, to take place: at which news her face glowed with pleasure, and her lips flowed with many an expression of gratitude, although he assured hex again and again that he had done nothing on earth to merit her thanks.

The smiles were very beautiful, however, and very grateful to his heart; but he found that every moment was adding to feelings which it was madness to indulge; and, therefore, as soon as the Duke had returned, he took his leave, and turned his steps homeward. He knew, indeed, that he should have to encounter the same pleasant danger again that very afternoon; that he should have to see her, to be in the same room, to sit at the same table with her, to speak to her, even though it were but for a moment; but then it would be all under restraint; the eyes of the many would be upon them; there would be no open communication, no speaking the real feelings of the heart, no freedom from the dull routine of society.

He was perhaps five minutes behind his time, but the Earl was all complaisance: the arrangements that he had made for his son; the unexpected facility with which Lord Sherbrooke had apparently entered into those arrangements; the political importance of the alliance with the Duke; the immense accession of wealth to his family; the aspect of public affairs, were all sufficient to mellow down a demeanour which, to his inferiors at least, was generally harsh and proud. But yet Wilton could not help believing that there was a peculiar expression in the Earl's countenance when that nobleman's eyes turned upon him; that there was a smile which was not a smile of benignity, that there was a courtesy which was not of the heart. Why or wherefore Wilton could hardly tell, but he fancied that the Earl's conduct was what it might be towards a person who had suddenly fallen completely into his power, and whom he intended to use as a tool in any way that he might think fit. He pictured to his own imagination the Earl bidding his victim perform some action the most revolting to his feelings in the sweetest tone possible; the victim beginning to resist; the cold blooded politician calmly showing his power, and exercising it with bitter civility.

However, the courtesy lasted all day: there was nothing said to confirm Wilton in this fancy; and when he took leave, the Earl reminded him of the dinner hour, adding, "Be punctual, be punctual, Mr. Brown. We shall dine exactly at the hour; and my cook is a virago, you know."

Wilton did not fail to be to the moment, and he, the Earl, and Lord Sherbrooke, were some time in the great saloon before the guests began to arrive. At length the large heavy coaches of those days began to roll into the court-yard, and one after another many a distinguished man and many a celebrated beauty of the age appeared. Still, however, the Earl evidently looked upon the Duke and his daughter as the principal guests, and waited in anxious expectation for their coming.

They arrived later than any one, Laura herself looking grave, if not sad, the Duke evidently embarrassed and not at ease. Nor did the particular attentions paid by the Earl to both remove in any degree the sadness of the one or the embarrassment of the other. This was so marked that the Earl soon felt it; and though the sort of determined calmness of his manner, and habitual self-command, prevented him from showing the least uneasiness, yet, from a particular glance of his eye and momentary quiver of his lip, Wilton divined that he was angry and irritable.

It must be admitted, also, that Lord Sherbrooke did not take the means to put his father more at ease. To Lady Laura he paid no attention whatsoever, devoted himself during the greater part of the evening to a beautiful woman of not the most pure and unsullied character in the world, and showed himself disposed to flirt with everybody, except the very person to whom his father wished him to pay court. The dinner party was followed by an entertainment in the evening; and still the same scene went on; till at length the Earl came round to Wilton, and said, in a low voice, "I wish, my dear young gentleman, you would try your influence upon Sherbrooke."

The Earl was going on, but Wilton rose immediately, saying, "I understand you, my lord," and approaching the place where Lord Sherbrooke was seated, he waited till the laughter which was going on around him was over, and then said in a low voice, "For pity's sake, Sherbrooke, and for decency's sake, do pay some attention to the Duke and his daughter; remember, they are new guests of your father's, and merit, at all events, some respect."

The young Lord looked up in his friend's countenance with a malicious smile, replying, "They do, my dear Wilton, they do! and you see I keep at a respectful distance. But I will do anything to please."

He accordingly rose from his seat, and Wilton saw him first approach the Duke, speak a few words to him, and then take a seat beside Lady Laura. Her air was evidently cold and reserved, but what passed more, Wilton, of course, did not know. The young lord, however, seemed suddenly struck by something that she said, turned quickly towards her, and made a rejoinder; she answered, apparently, with perfect calmness. But the instant after, Lord Sherbrooke rose from his chair, made her a low bow, and was crossing the room. His father, however, met him half-way, and they spoke for a moment or two. The Earl's cheek became very red, and his brow contracted; but Lord Sherbrooke passed quietly on, and came up to where Wilton stood.

"She has just told me what she thinks of my character, Wilton," said the young nobleman, "and I have transmitted the same to my father, who must settle the matter with the Duke as he likes."

"The Earl's plans are certainly in a prosperous condition," thought Wilton; and though he could not, of course, approve of the unceremonious means which Lord Sherbrooke took to defeat his father's intentions, and to cast the burden of refusal on Lady Laura, yet he could not grieve, it must be admitted, that she should determining for herself.

During the whole evening her conduct towards Wilton Brown had been exactly what he had expected--kind, gentle, and courteous. She evidently treated him more as a friend than any one else in the room; and though he purposely spoke to her but seldom, and then merely with the terms of formal respect, yet whenever he did approach her, she greeted him with a smile, which showed that his society was not at all unpleasant to her.

To the eyes of Wilton it was very evident that Lord Byerdale was extremely irritated by what he had heard. No one else perceived it, however, for, as was usual with him, the irritation of the moment, though likely to produce very serious effects at an after period, clothed itself for the time in additional smiles and stately courtesies, only appearing now and then in an additional drop of sarcastic bitterness mingling with all the civil things that he said. As usual, also, he was peculiarly soft and reverential in his manner towards those with whom he was most angry, and the Duke and Lady Laura were more the objects of his particular attention than ever. He sat beside her; he talked to her; he paid her that marked attention which his son had neglected to offer; and at length, when the Duke proposed to retire, he himself handed her to the carriage, paying her some well turned compliment at every step, and relieving his heart of its bitterness by some stinging sneer at the rest of womankind.

Thus passed over the evening; and Wilton, it must be acknowledged with a mind more at ease on account of the decided part that Lady Laura seemed to have taken, slept soundly and dreamt happily, though he still resolved, sooner or later, to crush feelings which could only end in misery.

On the following morning he went to the house of Lord Byerdale at the usual hour, and proceeded at once to the cabinet of the Earl. It was already occupied by that nobleman and his son, however; and though there were no loud words spoken, no angry tones audible, yet there were sufficient indications of angry feeling, at least on the part of the Earl, to make Wilton immediately pause and draw back a step.

"Come in, come in," said the Earl--"you know all this affair, and I believe have done what you could to make this young man reasonable."

Wilton accordingly entered the room, and Lord Byerdale again turned to his son, laying his finger upon the letter before him. "I repeat, Sherbrooke," he said, "that you yourself have done all this. I did not ask you, sir, to be virtuous, I did not ask you to be temperate, I did not bid you cast away the dice or abandon drunkenness and revelling, or turn off three or four of your mistresses, or to give over going to the resort of every sort of vice in the metropolis. I asked you none of these things, because it would be hard and ungenerous to require a man to do what his nature and habits render perfectly impossible. I turn to his vomit again, or the sow to refrain from wallowing in the mire."

"Savoury similes, my lord," said Lord Sherbrooke--"most worthy of Solomon and your lordship. May I ask what it is you did demand then?"

"That you should assume a virtue if you had it not," replied Lord Byerdale; "that you should put a certain cloak of decency over your vices, and that you should at least be commonly courteous to the person selected for your future wife: especially when I pointed out to you the immense, the inconceivable advantages of such an alliance not only to you but to me."

"Well, but, my dear father," said Lord Sherbrooke, "I will grant all that you say. It is altogether my fault; I have behaved very stupidly, very wildly, very rudely, very viciously. But there is no reason that you should be so angry with the young lady, or with my good lord duke."

"Ay, sir! think you so?" said the Earl--"you are mighty wise in your own conceit. You have had your share, certainly; but I do not avenge myself on my own son. They have had their share, however, too. Their pride, their would-be importance, their insufferable arrogance, which makes them think that kings or princes are not too good for her--these have all had no light share; and if I live for six months I will bring that pride down to the very lowest pitch. I will degrade her till she thinks herself a servant wench."

Wilton certainly did feel his blood boil, but he knew that he had neither any right nor any power to interfere; and he turned to some papers that were upon the tables, and hid the expression which his thoughts might communicate to his countenance, by apparent attention to something else.

Some more words passed between the father and son, but they were few. Lord Sherbrooke, upon the whole, behaved better than Wilton could have expected. He neither treated the subject lightly and jocularly as he was accustomed to do in most cases, nor bitterly and sarcastically, which his father's evident want of principle in the whole business gave him but too fair an opportunity of doing. He acknowledged fairly and straight-forwardly his errors and his vices; and all that he said in regard to the offence he had given his father was, that he imagined he could not in honour suffer Lady Laura to decide without letting her know the character at least of the man who was proposed for her husband.

"Well, sir," replied his father, sharply, "you have convinced her of your character very soon. Mine, she may be longer in finding out; but she shall not fail to be made equally well aware of it in the end."

Thus saying, he turned and quitted the room, giving some casual directions to Wilton as he passed.

"Well, that business is so far done and over," exclaimed Lord Sherbrooke, as soon as his father was gone; "and, as it is pleasant, my dear Wilton, to do a good action now and then, by way of a change, you and I must enter into a conspiracy together, to prevent my worthy, subtle, and revengeful father from executing a this poor girl, who has only done her duty to herself, and to me, and to her father."

"I trust," replied Wilton, "that the Earl's threat was but one of those bursts of disappointment which will pass away with time. I cannot imagine that, after a little consideration, he will have any inclination really to injure either the Duke or his daughter; nor, indeed, do I see that he could have the means either."

Lord Sherbrooke shook his head with a gloomy air, and answered, "He will make them, Wilton--he will make the means; and as to inclination, you do not know him as well as I do. He will not forget what has occurred this day, as long as he remembers how to write his own name. This same goodly desire of revenge is henceforth a part of his nature, and nothing will ever remove it, unless self-interest or ambition be brought into action against it."

"But what sort of revenge think you he will seek?" demanded Wilton--"situated as the Duke is, I see no opportunity that your father can have of injuring him."

"Heaven only knows," replied Lord Sherbrooke. "The fire will go on smouldering for months, perhaps for years, but it will not go out. He said, just before you came in, that because she had refused to marry me, he would make her marry a footman; and, as I really believe his lordship is occasionally endowed with superhuman powers of executing what he thinks fit, it would not surprise me at all to see my Lady Laura led to the altar by John Noakes, our porter's son, dressed up for the occasion as a foreign prince."

"I do not fear that," replied Wilton with a smile; "I should rather apprehend that he may entangle the good Duke, who does not seem overburdened with sense, in some of these sad plots which are daily taking place. Should we find out that such is the case, we may indeed aid in preventing it."

Lord Sherbrooke shook his head. "It is the poor girl he will aim at first, depend upon it," the young nobleman answered. "I wish to Heaven she had told me her intention of refusing me in such a formal manner; I would have shown her how to manage the matter without calling down this storm. But, instead of that, she sits down and deliberately writes him a letter, which, just in the proportion that it is honest, true, and straightforward, is the thing best calculated to excite his wrath. Yet, as if she had some idea of his character, and wished to shield her father, she takes the whole responsibility of the thing upon herself, telling him that the Duke had pressed her much upon the subject, but that she felt it would be utterly impossible to give her hand to your very humble servant. All this has, of course, brought the storm more directly upon herself, though her father will be screened thereby in no degree. I doubt not he has gone there now."

"Do you think there is any chance of an actual and open quarrel between them?" demanded Wilton.

"Not in the least," answered Lord Sherbrooke with a scoff: "my dear Wilton, you must be as blind as a mole, if you do not see that my father, though as brave as a lion, is not a man to quarrel with any one. He is a great deal too good a politician for that; he knows that in quarrelling with any one he hates, he must suffer something himself, and may suffer a good deal. No, no, he takes a better plan, and contrives to make his enemies suffer while he suffers not at all. In general, if you see him particularly civil to anybody, you may suppose that he looks upon them as an enemy, and is busy in getting them quietly into his power. Quarrel with the Duke? Oh no, a thousand to one, ere half an hour be over, he will be shaking him cordially by the hand, putting him quite at his ease, begging him to let the matter be forgotten altogether, saying that it was natural he should seek so illustrious an alliance, which, indeed, he had scarcely a right to hope for. Then he will see the lady herself, and say that he perfectly enters into her feelings, that a person so richly gifted as herself, and having already all that wealth and rank can give, has a right to consult, before all other things, the feelings of her own heart. It would not surprise me at all if he were to offer to send me abroad again, lest my presence in London, after the pretensions which have been formed, should prove, in any degree, annoying to her."

The conversation continued for some time longer in the same strain: and Wilton could not but feel that Lord Sherbrooke gave an accurate though a terrible picture of his father's character.

At length, the young nobleman rose as if to depart; but standing ere he did so before the table at which his young friend was seated, he gazed upon his face earnestly and silently for a minute or two, and then said,--

"I don't know why, Wilton, but I have a great and a strong regard for you, and I have been dreaming dreams for you, that I see you are unwilling to dream for yourself: However, you must have the same regard for me; and--even if you are not inclined, in any degree, to take advantage of what I must say is evident regard on the part of this young lady towards you--yet, for my sake, you must let me know, aid me, and assist me, if you should see any scheme forming against her happiness or peace. I am not so bad, Wilton, even as I seem to you. I am sorry for this girl--really sorry for her. I ought to have taken the burden upon my own shoulders, instead of casting it upon hers; for I could have removed all these difficulties by speaking one single word. But that word would have cost me much to speak, and I shrunk from saying it. If, however, I find that through my fault she is likely to suffer, I will speak that word, Wilton, at all risks, so you must give me help and support, at least in doing what is right."

"That I will, Sherbrooke," replied Wilton, grasping his hand, "that I will most zealously. But in regard to what you say of Lady Laura's kind feeling towards me, depend upon it you are wholly mistaken. The only reason, be you sure, why she makes any difference in her manner towards me, and towards men of higher rank than myself; is, that she knows the difference of our station and fortunes must ever prevent my entertaining any of those hopes which others might justly feel."

Before Wilton concluded, Lord Sherbrooke had cast himself into a chair; his eyes were fixed on the ground, his brow had become contracted. It was one of those moments when, as he said, his evil spirit was upon him; and seeing that such was the case, Wilton left him to his own meditations and proceeded to write the letters which the Earl had directed him to despatch.

In about half an hour, the young nobleman roused himself from his reverie, with a light laugh, apparently causeless; and without speaking another word to Wilton, quitted the room.

Wilton only saw the Earl for a few minutes during the rest of the day, and with him the statesman was so captious, irritable, and sneering, that, reading his feelings by the key his son had given, Wilton had every reason to believe himself to be in high favour. Various matters of business, however, occurred to keep him late at the Earl's house, and night had fallen when he returned to his own lodgings.

In about an hour after, however, one of the Earl's servants brought him a note in Lord Sherbrooke's handwriting, and marked "In haste." Wilton tore it open immediately, and read,--

"MY DEAR WILTON,

"My father directs me to request your immediate return.
The Duke is now here. Lady Laura has been carried off,
or, at all events, has disappeared; and we want your wise
head to counsel, perhaps your strong hand to execute. Come
directly, for we are all in agitation.

"Yours, SHERBROOKE."

Written below, in smaller characters, and marked "Private," two lines to the following effect:--

"This business is not my father's doing. It is too coarse for his
handiwork. He may, perhaps, take advantage of it, however, if he
finds an opportunity. Burn this instantly."

CHAPTER XVII.

Having now run on for some time, following almost entirely the course and history of one individual, painting none but the characters with whom he was brought into immediate contact, and making him, as it were, a lantern in the midst of our dark story, all the characters appearing in bright light as long as they were near him, and sinking back into darkness as soon as they were removed from him, we must follow our old wayward and wandering habits; and just at the moment when we have contrived to create the first little gleam of interest in the reader's breast, must leave our hero entirely to his fate, open out new scenes, introduce new personages, and devote a considerable space to matters which have APPARENTLY not the slightest connexion whatsoever with that which went before.

About thirty miles from London, towards the sea-coast, there then stood a small ancient house, built strongly of brick. It was not exactly castellated in its appearance, but yet in the days of Cromwell it had endured a short siege by a small body of the parliamentary troops, and had afforded time, by the resistance which it offered, for a small body of noblemen and gentlemen attached to the cause of King Charles to make their escape from a superior party of pursuers. It was built upon the edge of a very steep slope, so that on one side it was very much taller than the other. It was surrounded by thick trees also; and though by no means large, it had contrived to get into a small space as many odd corners as a Chinese puzzle. The walls were very thick, the windows few and small, the chimneys numerous, and the angles innumerable.

Into one of the small rooms of this house, at about eleven o'clock at night, I must now introduce the reader.

In that chamber, with her head resting on her hand, her eyes fixed upon a wood-fire that was burning before her, one small and beautiful foot stretched out towards it, while the other was concealed by the drapery of her long robe; and with the whole graceful line of her figure thrown back in the large arm-chair which she occupied--except, indeed, the head, which was bent slightly forward--sat a very lovely young woman, perhaps of two or three and twenty years of age, in meditations evidently of a somewhat melancholy cast. The hand on which her head leaned, and which was very soft, round, and fair, was covered with rings, while the other was quite free from such ornaments, with the exception of one small ring of gold upon the slender third finger. In that hand she had been holding an open letter; but, buried in meditation, she had suffered the paper to drop from her hold, and it had fallen upon the ground beside her.

We had said that she was very beautiful, but her beauty was of a different sort and character altogether from that of the lady whom we have described under the name of Lady Laura Gaveston. Her hair was of the richest, brightest, glossy black, as fine as silk, yet bending, wherever it escaped, into rich and massy curls. There was one of these which fell upon the back of her fair neck, and another upon either temple. Upon the forehead, as was then customary, the hair was divided into smaller curls, and cut much shorter, which fashion was a great disfigurement to beauty, and certainly left her less handsome than she otherwise would have appeared. Still, however, she was very, very lovely; and the fine lines of her features, the clear rich brown of her complexion, the glorious light of her large dark eyes, softened by the long thick lashes that overshadowed them, the full and rounded beauty of every limb, left it impossible even for human heart to do away what nature's cunning hand had done.

There are certainly moments in which, as every one must have remarked, a beautiful human countenance is more beautiful than at any other period, when it acquires, from some accidental circumstance, a temporary and extraordinary degree of loveliness. Sometimes it is the mere disposition of light and shade that produces this effect--the background behind it, the objects that surround it. Sometimes it is that the tone of the mind at the moment gives the peculiar expression which harmonizes best with the lines of the features and the colouring of the complexion, and which is in perfect accord with all those expectations which fine, indistinct, but sweet associations produce in our mind from every particular style of beauty that we see. Associations are, in fact, the bees of the imagination, and, wandering through all nature, may be said to distil honey from every fair object on which they light. Why does a rich and warm complexion, and a glowing cheek, call up instantly in our mind the idea of joyous health and pleasant-heartedness? Less because we have been accustomed to see that complexion attended by such qualities than because it connects itself with the idea of summer, gay summer and all its fruits and flowers, and merry sports and light amusements, and a thousand memories of happy days, and thousands upon thousands still of other things of which we have no consciousness, but which are present to sensation though not to thought, all the while that we are gazing upon a ruddy cheek, and thinking that the pleasure is derived from the white and red alone.

When the expression is perfectly suited to the style of beauty, it is natural to suppose that it will add to the charm; but there is a case where the cause of the increase is not so easily discovered--I mean when the mind gives to the countenance a temporary-expression totally opposed to the style of beauty itself. Yet this is sometimes the case: for how often do we see high and majestic features soften into playful smiles, and seem to gain another grace. In the lady we have mentioned, the whole style of the countenance and of the form gave the idea of joyous gaiety, of happy, nay, exuberant life and cheerfulness; but the expression was now all sad; and from the contrast--which produced deeper associations than perfect harmony would have called forth--her beauty itself was heightened. It was like some gay and splendid scene by moonlight.

She had remained in this meditating attitude for some time, when the door quietly opened, and a personage entered the room, of whom we must say a few words, though he is not destined to play any very prominent part in our tale. Monsieur Plessis was a Frenchman, a soi-disant Protestant. One thing, at all events, is certain, that his father had been so, and had been expelled from France many years before by persecution. The gentleman before us exercised many trades, by which, perhaps, he had not acquired so much wealth as his father had by one. His father's calling had been that of cook and major domo to a fat, rich, gluttonous, careless English peer; and as he employed his leisure time in distilling various simples, he had classed his noble patron under that head, and distilled from him what he himself would jocosely have called "Golden Water."

Amongst the various trades which, as we have said, were carried on by the son, was smuggling, under which were included the conveyance of contraband men, women, and children, as well as other sorts of merchandise; swindling a little, when occasion presented itself; clipping the golden coin of the kingdom, which at that time was a great resource to unfortunate gentlemen; not exactly forging exchequer tallies, and other securities of the same kind, but aiding by a certain dexterity of engraving in the forging, which he did not choose actually to commit; and over and above all these several occupations, callings, and employments, he was one of the best reputed spies which the French court had in England, as well as the most industrious agent which England had in obtaining intelligence from France. In fact, he sold each country to the other with the greatest possible complaisance. The great staple of the intelligence that he gave to both was false; but he took care to mingle a sufficient portion of truth with what he told, to acquire a considerable degree of reputation. He was, indeed, much too well versed in the practices of coiners, not to know that a bad piece of money is best passed off between two good ones; and though he was a sort of bonding warehouse, where an immense quantity of manufactured intelligence lay till it was wanted, yet he had means of obtaining better information, which he did not fail to make use of when he judged it needful.

Strange, however, are the perversities of human character: this practical betrayer of trust was not without certain good points in his character. The cheating a king or a statesman had a touch of grandeur in it, which suited his magnificent ideas; a little robbery on the King's Highway seemed to him somewhat chivalrous; and he could admire those who did it, though he did not meddle with the business himself: but there was a certain class of persons whom he would as soon have cheated, betrayed, or deceived, even to keep himself in practice, which he considered one of the most legitimate excuses for anything he liked to do, as he would have cut his hand off. These were the poor French emigrants in England, and the unfortunate adherents of the House of Stuart in France.

As is now well known, though it was only suspected at the time, thousands of these men were daily coming and going between France and Britain, in the very midst of the war; and they were always sure to find at the house of Plessis kind and civil treatment, perfect security, and the most accurate intelligence which could be procured of all that was taking place.

In cases of danger he had a thousand ways of secreting them or favouring their escape. If ever, as was frequently the case, they wished to communicate with some kind friend, who was willing to relieve them, or to frighten some timid enemy upon whom they had some hold, Plessis could generally find them the means; and in cases where some one in danger required to be brought off speedily and secretly, Plessis had often been known to spend very large sums, and risk even life itself, rather than suffer an enterprise to fail in which he had taken a part.

The Duke of Shrewsbury and Trumbull, while they were secretaries of state, employed Plessis actively, and overlooked not a few little peccadilloes for the sake of the intelligence they obtained; and Torcy, though he had been known to vow more than once that he would hang him if he set his foot in France, held two or three long conferences with him at Versailles, and dismissed him with a present of several thousand livres.

His apparel was very peculiar, as he generally wore above his ordinary dress a large long waisted red coat, hooked round his neck at the collar, somewhat in the manner of a cloak, without his arms being thrust into the sleeves; his shoes were very high in the instep, and buckled with a small buckle over the front; but as he was a little man, and of a somewhat aspiring disposition, the heels of those shoes were enormously high, sufficient to raise him nearly two inches from the ground, and make his foot in external appearance very like that of a calf or a Chinese lady. Indeed, in body and in mind likewise, he was upon tiptoes the whole day long.

His entrance into the room where the lady was, roused her at once from the reverie into which she had fallen; and taking up the letter from the ground, she turned to see who it was that came in.

"Madam," he said, speaking in French, which, be it remarked, was the language used between them during the whole conversation, "were it not better for you to retire to rest? You spoil your complexion, you impair your beauty, by these long vigils."

"Beauty!" she said, with something of a scoff. "But why should I retire, as you call it, to rest, Plessis? You mean to say, retire to think more deeply still, in darkness as well as in solitude."

"Madam," replied Plessis, "you take these things too heavily. But the truth is, I have a fair company coming here, by whom you might not well like to be seen.

Far be it from me, if you think otherwise, to disturb you in possession of the apartments. But they come here at midnight to consult, it would seem, upon business of importance; whereof I know nothing, indeed, but which I know requires secrecy and care."

"Business of importance!" said the lady, somewhat scornfully--"to seat a bigoted dotard on the throne of England! That is what they come to consult about. Are they not some of those whom I saw yesterday morning from the window? that dark Sir George Barkley, who used to walk through the halls of St. Germain's, in gloomy silence, till the profane courtiers called him the shadow of the cloud? and that sanguinary Charnock, whom I once heard conferring with the banished queen, and vowing that there was no way but one of dealing with usurpers, and that was by the dagger? If these are your guests, Plessis, I know the business that they come for full well."

"I neither know, beautiful lady," replied Plessis, "nor do I seek to know. So pray tell me nothing thereof. Many a grown man in his day has been hanged for knowing too much, and nobody but a schoolboy was ever punished for knowing too little. These gentlemen come about their own business. I meddle not with it; and I must not shame my hospitality so much as to say, 'Good gentlemen, you shall not meet at my house!'"

"You are a wise and prudent man, Plessis," replied the lady: "bid the girl take a light to my chamber; I will go there and muse--not that I fear their seeing me; but the Lady Helen, perhaps, might wish it otherwise."

With a bow down to the very ground, Plessis retired, and the lady paused for a minute or two longer, leaning upon a small table in the middle of the room, and apparently thinking over what had passed.

"It is a strange thing," she said to herself, after a moment, "a most strange thing, that the customs of the world, and what we call honour, so often requires us to do those things that every principle of right and justice, truth and religion, commands us not to do. God's word tells us not to murder, yet men daily do it, and women think them all the nobler for trading in blood. If we violate the law, and do what is really wicked, we risk punishment on earth, and incur punishment hereafter; yet if we do strictly what honesty and justice tells us, in all cases, how many instances would be found, where men would shun us, and where our own hearts would condemn us also. Here I have it in my power to stop the effusion of much blood, to prevent the commission of many crimes, to strangle, perhaps, a civil war in its birth, merely by discovering the presence of these men in a land from which they are exiled--I have it in my power thereby to spare even themselves from evil acts and certain punishment: and yet my lips must be sealed, lest men should say I dealt treacherously with them. 'Tis a hard-dealing world, and I have suffered too much already by despising it, to despise it any more."

As she thus came to the conclusion, which every woman, perhaps, will come to sooner or later, she turned and left the room; and while her foot was still upon the staircase, there came a sound of many horses' feet from the small paved esplanade in front of the house.

"Ay, there they are," murmured the lady in a low voice--"the men who would use any treacherous art whatever to accomplish their own purpose, and who would yet call any one traitor who divulged their schemes. Would to God that Helen would come back! I am weary of all this, and sick at heart, as well I may be."

A sound in the hall below made her quicken her footsteps; and in two or three minutes more the room she had just quitted was occupied by five or six tenants of a very different character and appearance from herself.

CHAPTER XVIII.

The first person that entered the room after the lady quitted it was Monsieur Plessis himself, who, with a light in his hand, came quickly on before the rest, and gave a rapid glance round, as if to insure that no little articles belonging to its last tenant remained scattered about, to betray the fact of her dwelling in his house.

He was followed soon after by a tall, thin, gloomy-looking personage, dressed in dark clothing, and somewhat heavily armed, for a period of internal peace. His complexion was saturnine, his features sharp and angular, his eyes keen and sunk deep under the overhanging brows; and across one cheek, not far below the eye, was a deep gash, which drew down the inner corners of the eyelid, and gave a still more sinister expression to the countenance than it originally possessed. He was followed by two others, both of whom were much younger men than himself. One was gaily dressed, and had a fat and somewhat heavy countenance, which indeed seemed unmeaning, till suddenly a quick fierce glance of the eye and a movement of the large massy lower jaw, like that which is seen in the jaws of a dog eager to bite, showed that under that dull exterior there were passions strong and quick, and a spirit not so slow and heavy as a casual observer might imagine.

Besides these, there were one or two other persons whose dress denoted them of some rank and station in society, though those who had seen them in other circumstances might now have remarked that various devices had been employed to disguise their persons in some degree.

One of these, however, has been before introduced to the reader, being no other than that Sir John Fenwick whom we have more than once had occasion to mention. He was now no longer dressed with the somewhat affected neatness and coxcombry which had marked his appearance in London, but, on the contrary, was clad in garments comparatively coarse, and bore the aspect of a military man no longer in active service, and enduring some reverses. He also was heavily armed, though many of the others there present bore apparently nothing but the ordinary sword which was carried by every gentleman in that day.

The first of the personages we have mentioned approached with a slow step towards the fire, saying to Plessis as he advanced, "So the Colonel has not come, I see?"

"No, Sir George," replied Plessis with a lowly inclination of the head, "he has not arrived yet; but I had a messenger from him at noon to-day, saying that he would be here to-night."

"Ha!" exclaimed Sir George Barkley, "that is more than I expected--But he will not come, he will not come! Make us a bowl of punch, good Plessis--make us a bowl of punch--the night is very cold.--But he will not come, I feel very sure he will not come."

"I think I hear his horse's feet even now," replied Plessis--"at all events, there is some one arrived."

"Keep him some minutes down below, good Plessis," exclaimed Sir George Barkley hastily. "Run down and meet him. Make up some story, and delay him as long as possible; for I have got something to consult with these gentlemen upon before we see him."

Plessis hastened away; and as soon as the door was closed, Barkley turned to the gaily dressed man we have mentioned, saying, "Charnock, tell Sir John Friend and Captain Rookwood what we were saying as we came along; and all that has happened in London."

The dull countenance of Charnock was lighted up in a moment by one of those quick looks we have mentioned. "Listen, Parkyns, too," he said, "for you have not heard the whole."

"Be quick, be quick, Charnock," said Sir George Barkley.

"Well, thus it is then, gentlemen," said Charnock--"matters do not go so favourably as we could have wished. Sir John Fenwick, here, the most active of us all, had got the Duke of Gaveston to join us heartily, to concur in the rising, or, at all events, to hear all that we propose, with a promise of perfect secrecy; but most unfortunately, at the meeting at the Old King's Head, some one unwisely suffered it to slip out that we were to have thirty thousand French troops, forgetting that what is good to tell the lower classes and those who are timid and fearful of not having means enough, does not do to be told to the bold and high-minded, who are apt to be foolishly confident. The Duke cried out at that, and vowed that if his opinion were to have any weight, or if his co-operation was of any import, not a foreign soldier should come into the land. This was bad enough; but we might have smoothed that down, had not Lowick chanced to hint the plan for getting rid of this Prince of Orange as the first step. Thereupon both the Duke and the Earl of Aylesbury, who were present, flew out like fire; and the Duke, vowing he would hear no more, took up his hat and sword and walked away, in spite of all that could be said. The Earl, for his part, stayed the business out, saying, that he would have nothing to do with the affair, but that he remained to show us that he would not betray anything."

"That is to say," exclaimed one of the others, "that the Duke will betray all."

"Not exactly," said Sir John Fenwick, with a grim smile. "We have taken care of that, and perhaps may compel the Duke to join us whether he likes it or not, when once the matter's done. However, Sir George and I have determined that it is absolutely necessary and needful for us all to understand, that we, who take the deeper part in the matter, must keep our own counsel better for the future. Of course, we must still endeavour to enrol as many names as possible; but to all ordinary supporters we must tell nothing more, than that the general rising is to take place, and that we have the most perfect certainty of success by means which we cannot divulge."

"You will remark, gentlemen," said Sir George Barkley, "that the assistance of the French troops is to be mentioned to no one at all, without the general consent of the persons here present."

"And the execution, or putting to death, or call it what you will, of the Prince of Orange," added Charnock, "is to be told to nobody on any account whatever. We have quite sufficient hands to do it ourselves without any more help; and if you and your men will take care of the guards, I will undertake the pistoling work with my own hand."

"But the Colonel," said one of the others, "you forgot to mention about the Colonel, Charnock."

"Why, that is the worst spot in the whole business," said Sir George Barkley.

"No one expected his stomach to be queasy; but by heavens he's worse than either the Duke or the Earl. He did not so much seem to dislike the idea of foreign troops--though that did not please him--but one would have thought him a madman to hear how he talked about that very necessary first step, the getting rid of the usurper. He said, not only that he would have nothing to do with it, but that it should not be done; and he used very high and threatening language even towards me--at present his Majesty's representative. He used words most injurious to us all, and which I would have resented to the death if it had not been for consideration of the high cause in which we are all here engaged."

"What did he say? What did he say?" demanded two or three voices.

"In the first instance," answered Sir George Barkley, "he would not come to the last meeting at the King's Head; and his first question, when I went to seek him, was, whether the King knew of what we were about to do? I said, certainly not; that I had a general commission, which was quite enough, and that we had not told the King of an act which was very necessary, but might not be pleasant for him to hear. With that he tossed up his head and laughed, in his way, saying that he thought so; and that the King did not know what bloody-minded villains he had got in his service.--Bloody minded villains was the word.--It is rather impudent, too, and somewhat strange, that he, of all men, should talk thus--he who, for many a year now, has lived by taking toll upon the King's Highway."

"Ay; but I insist say, Sir George," replied one of the others, "he has always been very particular. I, who have been with him now these many years, can answer for it, that in all that time he has never taken a gold piece from any one but the King's enemies, nor I either; and he vows that the King's commission which he still has, justifies him in stripping them."

"Ay, so it does," replied Sir George Barkley, "and the King's commission, too, justifies us in killing them. This gentleman only makes nice distinctions when it suits him. However, we are taking means to get all his people away from him. Byerly won't be such a stickler, no doubt, and five or six of the others we can bribe."

"Ay, but will he not betray us," said Sir William Parkyns.

"I think not," said Sir George Barkley; and unwittingly he paid the person he spoke of the highest compliment in his power, saying, "I rather fancy the same sort of humour that prevents him from going on in the business with us will keep him from betraying what he knows. But we shall soon see that; and now having said all we have to say, you had better go down, Fenwick, and see if he be come or not."

During the time that this conversation had been going on, there had been various sounds of different descriptions in the house; and when Sir John Fenwick rose and opened the door to seek the person last spoken of, he was met face to face by Monsieur Plessis, and a maid-servant, carrying an immense bowl of punch, at that time the favourite beverage of a great part of the English nation.

"Was that the Colonel?" demanded Fenwick, as soon as he beheld Plessis.

"Yes," replied the Frenchman; "but he is busy about his horses and things, and said he would be up immediately."

"Has he got anybody with him?" demanded Sir John Fenwick in a low voice, for Plessis had left the door partly open behind him.

"Only two," rejoined the other.

"Put down the punch, Plessis," said Sir George Barkley--"run down and see if you cannot stop the others from coming up with him."

Before Plessis could do as he was bid, however, the door was flung farther open, and our old acquaintance Green entered the room alone. He was dressed as upon the first occasion of his meeting with Wilton Brown, except that he had a sort of cloak cast over his other garments, and a much heavier sword by his side. Plessis, who did not seem very much to like the aspect of affairs, made his exit with all speed, and closed the door; and Green, with a firm step and a somewhat frowning brow, advanced to the table, saying, "I give you good evening, gentlemen."

Sir John Fenwick, who was nearest to him, held out his hand as to an old friend; but Green thrust his hands behind his back, and made him a low bow, saying, "I must do nothing, Sir John, that may make you believe me your comrade when I am not."

"Nay, nay, Colonel," said Sir John Fenwick, still holding out his hand to him, "at least as your friend of twenty years' standing."

"That as you please, sir," replied Green, giving him his hand coldly.

"We have requested your presence here, Colonel," said Charnock, "to speak over various matters--"

"Mr. Charnock," interrupted Green, "I have nothing to do with you. It is with this gentleman I wish to have a word or two more than we could have the other afternoon," and he walked directly up to Sir George Barkley.

"Well, sir, what is it that you want with me?" said Sir George. "I hope you have thought better of what you said that night."

"Thought, sir," answered Green, "has only served to confirm everything that I then felt. In the first place, Sir George Barkley, you have dealt with me in this business uncandidly; and if I had not had better information than that which you gave me, pretending to be a friend, I should have been smuggled into a transaction which I abhor and detest."

"How mean you, sir? How mean you? I was perfectly candid with you," said Sir George Barkley.

"Ha, ha, ha!" exclaimed Green, laughing scornfully. "Perfectly candid! Yes, when you could not be otherwise. You told me, sir, that you wanted my assistance with ten men well armed for a service of great honour and danger; but until I put the question straightforward to you--having already obtained a knowledge of your proceedings--you did not tell me that the service you required was the cold-blooded murder of William, wrongly called King of England."

"That, sir, was to be explained to you afterwards," said Sir George Barkley.

"Afterwards!" exclaimed Green: "ay, sir, how soon afterwards? After the deed was done, ha? or after I was so far committed that I could not retract? And let me ask you, why it was that I was not to be informed till afterwards, when every other person here present knew it long before--I, who remained by the bloody waters of the Boyne when you acted as the King's running footman, and heralded him back to France? Nay, nay, you shall hear me out, sir, now. I believe not that you would ever have told me, had it not been that this intercepted letter fell into my hands, and informed me of all your proceedings, when you thought I knew them not."

And as he spoke he held the letter out before him, and struck his hand fiercely upon the paper.

The others looked round, each in his neighbour's face, with a doubtful, and disconcerted look, and Green went on before any one could answer.

"Why was all this, Sir George Barkley?" he said. "Why was this concealment? I will tell you why: because you dared not for your life propose such a thing to me, till you thought I was so far committed that I could not escape you; and if I had not asked you myself the question, I should never have heard the truth till this day."

Dark and darker shades of passion had come over the countenance of Sir George Barkley while Green had been speaking; and he, Charnock, and one of the others, during the latter part of their new companion's somewhat vituperative address, had been exchanging looks very significant and menacing. At length, however, Sir George Barkley exclaimed, "Come, come, Colonel--this language is too much. You have been asking questions and answering them yourself. We have now one or two to ask you, and we hope you will answer them as much to our satisfaction as you have answered the others to your own."

"What are your questions, sir?" demanded Green, fixing his eye upon him sternly. "Let me hear them, and if it suits me I will reply; if not, you must do without an answer."

"To one question, at least," replied Sir George Barkley, "to one question, at least, we must compel an answer!"

"Compel!" exclaimed Green, "compel!" and he took a step back towards the door.

"Look to the door, Fenwick!" exclaimed Sir George Barkley. "Parkyns, help Sir John! I should be sorry to take severe measures with you, Colonel; but before you stir a step from this room you must pledge yourself by all you hold sacred that you will not betray us."

Green heard him to an end without any further movement than the step back which he had taken, and which placed him in such a position that he could front either Barkley and the rest on the one side, or those who were at the door upon the other, without the possibility of any one coming upon him from behind without being seen. The moment the other had done, however, he shook back the cloak from his shoulders, and took from the broad horseman's girdle which girt him round the middle, a pistol, the barrel of which was fully eighteen inches long, while its counterpart appeared on the other side of the belt, in which also were two more weapons of the same kind, but of less dimensions. He leaned the muzzle calmly upon his hand for a moment, and looking tranquilly in the face of Sir John Fenwick he said, in a quiet tone, "Sir John Fenwick, you are in my way. You will do wisely to retire from the door, and take your friend with you."

"Rush upon him!" cried a man named Cranburne; and as he spoke he sprang forward himself, while Sir George Barkley and the rest came somewhat more slowly after. The pistol was in a moment transferred to Green's left hand, and with a back-handed blow of the right, which seemed in fact but a mere touch, Cranburne was laid prostrate on the ground, with his whole face and neck swimming in blood from his mouth and nose. In his fall he nearly knocked down Sir George Barkley, who took it as a signal for retreat towards the fire-place, and at the same moment Green, who had not moved a step from the spot where he stood, repeated in a louder voice, "You are in my way, Sir John Fenwick! Move from the door!" and at the same instant, in the silence which had followed the overthrow of Cranburne, the ringing sound occasioned by a pistol being suddenly cocked made itself distinctly heard.

"Move, move, Sir John Fenwick!" cried one of the others, a Captain Porter--"this is all very silly: we risk a great deal more by making a fracas here, than in trusting to the honour of a gentleman, such as the Colonel."

Sir John Fenwick did not require two recommendations to follow this suggestion, but he and Parkyns drew back simultaneously, leaving the way free for Green to go out. He advanced, in consequence, as if to take advantage of this movement; but before he quitted the room, he turned and fronted the party assembled.

"Sir George Barkley," he said, looking at him with a scornful smile, "you are, all of you, afraid of my telling what I know; but now that the way is clear, I will so far relieve you as to say, that nothing which any of you have told me shall ever pass my lips again. The knowledge that I have gained or may gain by other means is my own property, with which I shall do as I like; but there are one or two pieces of information which I carry under my doublet, and which you may not be sorry to hear. As for you. Sir George Barkley, the secret I have to reveal to you is, that you are a white-livered coward. This I shall tell to nobody but yourself--Ha, ha, ha!--because your friends know it already, and to your enemies you will never do any harm. Fenwick, you are just sufficient of a fool to get yourself into a scrape, and sufficient of a knave to drag your friends in too, in the hopes of getting out yourself. Sir William Parkyns and Sir John Friend, knights and gentlemen of good repute, with full purses and with empty heads, you are paving a golden road to the gallows. Charnock, you are a butcher; but depend upon it, you were not made to slaughter any better beast than a bullock. The rest of you, gentlemen, good night. As for you, Porter, I wish you were out of this business. You are too honest a man to be in it; but take care that you do not make a knave of yourself in trying to shake yourself free from a cloak that you should never have put on."

It may easily be conceived that this speech was not particularly palatable to any of the parties present. But Sir George Barkley was the only one who answered, and he only did it by a sneer.

"Oh! we know very well," he said, "my good Colonel, that you can turn your coat as well as any man. We have heard of certain visits to Kensington, and interviews with the usurper; and, doubtless, we shall soon see a long list of our names furnished by you, and stuck up against Whitehall."

"He who insinuates a falsehood, sir," replied Green, turning sharply upon him, "is worse than he who tells a lie, for a lie is a bolder sort of cowardice than a covered falsehood. I have never been but once to Kensington in my life, and that was to see Bentinck, Lord Portland--whom I did not see. William of Nassau I have never spoken to in my life, and never seen, that I know of, except once through a pocket-glass, upon the banks of the Boyne. All that you have said, sir, you know to be false; and as to my giving a list of your names, that you know to be false also. What I may do to prevent evil actions I do not know, and shall hold it over your heads. But of one thing you may be quite sure, that no man's name would ever be compromised by me, however much he may deserve it."

Thus saying, he turned upon his heel and quitted the room, still holding the pistol in his hand. After closing the door, he paused for an instant and meditated, then thrust the pistol back into his belt, and walked along one of the many passages of the house, with the intricacies of which he seemed perfectly well acquainted.

The scene of dismay and confusion, however, which he left behind is almost indescribable. Every person talked at once, some addressing the general number, not one of whom was attending; some speaking vehemently to another individual, who in turn was speaking as vehemently to some one else. The great majority of those present, however, seemed perfectly convinced that their late companion would betray them, or, at all events, take such measures for frustrating their schemes, as to render it perilous in the extreme to proceed in them. Sir John Friend was for giving it all up at once, and Parkyns seemed much of the same opinion. Rookwood, Fenwick, and others hesitated, but evidently leaned to the safer course.

Sir George Barkley and Charnock were the only persons who, on the contrary, maintained the necessity and the propriety of abandoning none of their intentions.

To this, indeed, after great efforts, they brought back the judgment of the rest; but it required all their skill and art to accomplish that object. In regard to the general question of proceeding, they urged, at first, that they might as well go on, though cautiously, inasmuch as they were all committed to such a degree, that they could not be more so, let them do what they would. They were already amenable to the law of high treason, which was sure not to be mitigated towards them, and therefore they had nothing farther to fear but discovery. This having been conceded, and fear beginning to wear away, after a little consideration, it was easily shown to some of those present who proposed to abandon the idea of calling in foreign troops, in the hope of bringing back the Duke and the Earl of Aylesbury, with others, to their party, that their great hope of security lay in the actual presence of those foreign troops, who would, at all events, enable them to effect their escape, even if they did not insure them success in their design. The assassination was the next thing touched upon: but here Sir George Barkley argued, that what had occurred should only be considered as a motive for urging on their proceedings with the utmost rapidity.

"Let us leave it to be understood," he said, "by the great multitude of King James's loyal subjects, that the matter of aid from France is a thing yet to be considered of. In regard to the death of the usurper, whatever it may be necessary to say to others, none of us here present can doubt that it is absolutely necessary to our success. The whole of the information possessed by the man who has just left us is evidently gained from a letter which I wrote to Sir John Hubbard in the north, which has somehow unfortunately fallen into his hands. In that letter, however, I stated that the usurper's life would come to an end in April next, as we at first proposed. If the man have any design of betraying us--"

"No, no, he will not betray us," said several voices; "he has pledged himself not to disclose our names; and when his word is once given, it is sure."

"But," said Sir John Fenwick, "he straight-forwardly said that he would frustrate our scheme, and in so doing, it is a thousand chances to one that he causes the whole to be discovered."

"Then the way," exclaimed Sir George Barkley, "the only way is to proceed in the business at once. This letter to Hubbard is what he goes upon; he has no suspicion of our being ready to accomplish the thing at once. Let us then take him by surprise; and while he is waiting to see what April will produce, let us, I say, within this very week, execute boldly that which we have boldly undertaken. We can easily have sharp spies kept constantly watching this good friend of ours in the green doublet, who seems to fancy himself a second-hand sort of Robin Hood. Half of his people are mine already, and the other half will be so soon. Let the thing be done before the year be a week older; and let us to-morrow night meet at Mrs. Mountjoy's in St. James's-street, and send over to hurry the preparations in France. Gentlemen, it is time for action. Here several months have slipped by, and nothing is done. It is high time to do something, lest men should say we promised much and performed little."

Gradually all those who were present came round to the opinion of Sir George Barkley, and everything was arranged as he had proposed it. Some farther time was then spent in desultory conversation; and it seemed as if every one lingered, under the idea that they were all to go away together. Sir George Barkley, however, and Fenwick, seemed somewhat uneasy, and whispered together for a moment or two; and at length the latter said, "It may be better, gentlemen, for us to go away by two or three at a time. You, Parkyns, with Sir John Friend, had better take along the upper road; three others can take the low road by the waterside; and Sir George with Charnock and myself will wait here till you are safely on your way."

This proposal was instantly agreed to; but still some of the gentlemen lingered, evidently to the discomposure of Sir George Barkley, who at length gave them another hint that it was time to depart.

"By Heaven!" he exclaimed, as soon as they were all gone, "I thought they would have hung drivelling on here till the boat came down. The tide served at ten o'clock, and before one they must be off the end of the garden. How far is it from Erith?"

"Oh, certainly not four hours' sail," answered Charnock. "But had I not better now write the letter we talked of to the Duke? I can conceal my own hand well enough, and then if Fenwick is asked anything about it, he can swear most positively that it is not his writing."

"Oh! I care nothing about it," replied Fenwick. "The foolish old man cannot betray me without betraying himself; and you will see he will soon come round. In the meantime, however, I will go down and talk to old Plessis about the ship. I should think it could be got ready two days sooner easily; and as this that we have in view is a great object, we must not mind paying a few pounds for speed."

Thus saying, he left the room; and Charnock, taking paper out of a drawer, proceeded to write a letter according to the suggestions of Sir George Barkley. Presently after, there was a sound of several voices speaking, which apparently proceeded from some persons approaching the front of the house. Both Sir George Barkley and Charnock started up, the first exclaiming, "Hark! there they are!"

"Yes," exclaimed Charnock, "there's a woman's voice, sure enough! Why the devil don't they stop her talking so loud?"

"You write out the letter, Charnock," said Sir George. "I must go down and see that all is right."

Charnock nodded his head, and the other left the room.

CHAPTER XIX.

When Wilton Brown reached the house of the Earl of Byerdale, he found that nobleman, the Duke of Gaveston, and Lord Sherbrooke, sitting together in the most amicable manner that it is possible to conceive. The countenance of the Duke was certainly very much distressed and agitated; but making allowance for the different characters of the two men, Lord Byerdale himself did not seem to be less distressed. Lord Sherbrooke, too, was looking very grave, and was thoughtfully scribbling unmeaning lines with a pen and ink on some quires of paper before him.

"Oh, Mr. Brown, I am very glad to see you," exclaimed the Duke.

"My dear Wilton," said the Earl, addressing him by a title which he had never given him in his life before, "we are particularly in need of your advice and assistance. I know not whether Sherbrooke, in his note, told you the event that has occurred."

"He did so, to my great grief and surprise, my lord," replied Wilton. "How I can be of any assistance I do not know; but I need not say that I will do anything on earth that I can to aid my lord duke and your lordship."

"The truth is," replied Lord Byerdale, "that I am as greatly concerned as his grace: it having happened most unfortunately, this very morning--I am sorry, through Sherbrooke's own fault--that Lady Laura found herself compelled to break off the proposed alliance between our two families, which was one of my brightest day-dreams. The Duke knows well, indeed, that however high I may consider the honour which I had at one time in prospect, I am perfectly incapable of taking any unjustifiable means, especially of such a rash and desperate nature, to secure even an alliance such as his. But other people--the slanderous world at large--may insinuate that I have had some share in this business; and therefore it is absolutely necessary for me to use every exertion for the purpose of discovering whither the young lady has been carried. At the same time, the circumstances in which we are placed must, in a great degree, prevent Sherbrooke from taking that active part in the business which I know he could wish to do, and I therefore must cast the burden upon you, of aiding the Duke, on my part, with every exertion to trace out the whole of this mysterious business, and, if possible, to restore the young lady to her father."

The Earl spoke rapidly and eagerly, as if he feared to be interrupted, and wished, in the first instance, to give the matter that turn which seemed best to him.

"I am very anxious, too, Mr. Brown," said the Duke, "to have your assistance in this matter, for I am sure, you well know I place great confidence in you."

Wilton bowed his head, not exactly perceiving the cause of this great confidence at the moment, but still well pleased that it should be so.

"May I ask," he said, in as calm a voice as he could command, for his own heart was too much interested in the subject to suffer him to speak altogether tranquilly--"may I ask what are the particulars of this terrible affair, for Lord Sherbrooke's note was very brief? He merely told me the Lady Laura had disappeared; but he told me not where she had last been seen."

"She was last seen walking on the terrace in the garden," said the Duke, "just as it was becoming dusk. The afternoon was cold, and I thought of sending for her; but she had been a good deal agitated and anxious during the day, and I did not much like to disturb her thoughts."

"On which terrace?" demanded Wilton, eagerly.

"On the low terrace near the water," replied the Duke.

"Good God!" exclaimed Wilton, clasping his hands, "can she have fallen into the river?" and the horrible image presented to his mind made his cheek turn as pale as ashes. In a moment after, however, it became red again, for he marked the eye of the Earl upon him, while the slightest possible smile crept round the corners of that nobleman's mouth.

"My apprehensions, at first, were the same as yours, my young friend," replied the Duke. "I was busy with other things, when one of the servants came to tell me that they thought they had heard a scream, and that their young lady was not upon the terrace, though she had not returned to the house. We went down instantly with lights, for it was now dark; and my apprehensions of one terrible kind were instantly changed into others, by finding the large footmarks of men in the gravel, part of which was beaten up, as if there had been a struggle. The footsteps, also, could be traced down the stone steps of the landing-place, where my own barge lies, and there was evidently the mark of a foot, loaded with gravel, on the gunwale of the boat itself, showing that somebody had stepped upon it to get into another boat."

This intelligence greatly relieved the mind of Wilton; and at the same time, Lord Sherbrooke, who had not yet spoken a word, looked up, saying, "The Duke thinks, Wilton, that it will be better for you to go home with him, and endeavour to trace this business out from the spot itself. One of the messengers will be sent to you immediately with a warrant, under my father's hand,[5] to assist you in apprehending any of the participators in this business. Do you think anything can be done to-night?"

Wilton was accustomed to read his friend's countenance with some attention, and, from his whole tone and manner, he gathered that Lord Sherbrooke was somewhat anxious to bring the conference to an end.

"Perhaps something may be done to-night," he replied, "especially if no inquiry has yet been made amongst the watermen upon the river."

"None," replied the Duke, "none! To say the truth, I was so confounded and confused, that I came away here instantly--for advice and assistance," he added; but there was a pause between the words, which left his real views somewhat doubtful. The rest of the business was speedily arranged. The Duke's coach was at the door, and Wilton proceeded into the Earl's library to write a note to his own servant, containing various directions. He was followed in a minute or two by Lord Sherbrooke, who seemed looking for something in haste.

"Where are the blank warrants, Wilton?" he said: "my father will sign one at once."

As he spoke, however, he bent down his head over Wilton's shoulder, and then added, "Get away as fast as you can, or you will betray yourself to the keen eyes

---

5   It may be as well to remark here, that much of the business which is now entirely entrusted to police magistrates was then carried on by the secretaries of state and high official persons; and a "secretary's warrant" was an instrument of very dangerous and extensive power.

that are upon you. Go with the Duke, rescue the girl, and the game is before you. I, too, will exert myself to find her, but with different views, and you shall have the benefit of it."

"Sherbrooke, Sherbrooke," said Wilton, "what madness is it that you would put into my head?"

"It is in your heart already, Wilton," replied Lord Sherbrooke. "But after all, it is no madness, Wilton; for I have this very night heard my father acknowledge to the Duke that he knows who you really are; that the blood in your veins is as good as that of any one in the kingdom; and that your family is more ancient than that of the Duke himself, only that on account of some of the late troubles and changes it has been judged necessary to keep you, for a time, in the shade. Thus, you see, it is no madness--Nay, nay, collect your thoughts, Wilton.--Where are these cursed warrants? I say the game is before you.--There is my father's voice calling. He has an intuitive perception that I am spoiling his plans. Look to Sir John Fenwick, Wilton--look to Sir John Fenwick. I suspect him strongly. Hark how that patient and dignified father of mine is making the bell of the saloon knock its head against the wall! By heavens, there's his step! Fold up your note quickly! Where can these cursed warrants be?--My lord," he continued, turning to his father, who entered at that moment, "before you sent me for the warrants, you should have given me a warrant to discover and take them up, for I can neither do one nor the other."

The warrants were soon found, however; the Earl signed one and filled up the blanks; one of the ordinary Messengers of State was sent for, in order to follow Wilton and the Duke as soon as possible; and the young gentleman, taking his place in the carriage, was soon upon the way to Beaufort House, conversing over the events that had occurred.

What between agitation, grief, and apprehension, the Duke was all kindness and condescension towards his young companion. He seemed, indeed, to cast himself entirely upon Wilton for support and assistance; and it speedily became apparent that his suspicions also pointed in the direction of Sir John Fenwick, and the rash and violent men with whom he was engaged.

"I could explain myself on this subject," said the Duke, "to no one but you, my dear young friend, as you are the only person acquainted with the fact of my having been at that unfortunate meeting, except, indeed, the people themselves. Of course

I could not say a word upon the subject to Lord Byerdale or Lord Sherbrooke; but in you I can confide, and on your judgment and activity I rely entirely for the recovery of my poor girl."

"I will do my best, my lord," replied Wilton, "and trust I shall be successful. Perhaps I may have more cause for anticipating a fortunate result than even your grace, as I have means of instantly ascertaining whether the persons to whom you have alluded have any share in this matter or not; means which I must beg leave to keep secret, but which I shall not fail to employ at once."

"Oh, I was sure," replied the Duke, "that if there was a man in England could do it, you would be the person. I know your activity and your courage too well, not to have every confidence in you."

The coachman had received orders to drive quick; and the hour of nine was just striking on the bell of an old clock at Chelsea when the carriage drove into the court-yard. Wilton sprang out after the Duke; but he did not enter the house.

"I will but go to make some inquiries," he said, "and join your grace in half an hour. I may learn something tonight, and under these circumstances it is right to lose no time. I should be well pleased, however, to have a cloak, if one of your grace's servants could bring me either a common riding cloak or a roquelaure."

One was immediately procured; and, somewhat to the surprise and admiration of the Duke, who was, as the reader may have perceived, one of those people that are expressively denominated SLOW MEN, he set off instantly to pursue his search, animated by feelings which had now acquired even a deeper interest than ever, and by hopes of the extraordinary circumstances in which he was placed proving the means of attaining an object well worth the exertion of every energy and every thought.

It was a fine frosty night, with the stars twinkling over head, but no moon, so that his way amongst the narrow lanes which surrounded Beaufort House at that time, was not very easily found. As he walked on, he heard a sharp whistle before him, but it produced nothing, though he proposed to himself to stand upon the defensive, judging from one or two little signs and symptoms which he had seen, that the Green Dragon might protect under the shadow of its wings many persons of a far more fierce and dangerous description than it had itself proved, either as an adversary of St. George, or as an inhabitant of the marshes near Wantley.

He walked on fast, and a glimmering light in the direction from which he had heard the sound proceed at length led him to the hospitable door of the Green Dragon. One sign of hospitality, indeed, it wanted. It stood not open for the entrance of every one who sought admission; and a precautionary minute or two was suffered to pass before Wilton obtained one glance of the interior.

At length, however, a small iron bolt, which prevented any impertinent intrusion into the penetralia of the Green Dragon, was drawn back, and the lusty form of the landlord made its appearance in the passage. He instantly recognised Wilton, whose person, indeed, was not very easily forgotten; and laying his finger on the side of his nose, with a look of much sagacity, he led Wilton into a little room which seemed to be his own peculiar abode.

"The Colonel is out, sir," he said, as soon as the door was closed; "and there are things going on I do not much like."

Wilton's mind, full of the thought of Lady Laura, instantly connected the landlord's words with the fact of her disappearance, but refrained from asking any direct question regarding the lady. "Indeed, landlord," he said, "I am sorry to hear that. What has happened?"

"Why, sir," answered the landlord, "nothing particular; but only I wish the Colonel was here--that is all. I do not like to see tampering with a gentleman's friends. You understand, sir--I wish the Colonel was here."

"But, landlord," said Wilton, "can he not be found? I wish he were here, too, and if you know where he is, I might seek him. I have something important to say to him."

"Bless you, sir," replied the landlord, "he's half-way to Rochester by this time. He went well nigh two hours ago, and he is not a man to lose time by the way. You'll not see him before to-morrow night, and then, may be, it will be too late. I'd tell you, sir, upon my life," he continued, "if you could find him, for he bade me always do so; but you will not meet with him on this side of Gravesend till to-morrow night, when he will most likely be at the Nag's Head in St. James's Street about the present blessed hour. I've known him a long time now, sir, and I will say I never saw such another gentleman ON THE WAY, though there is Mr. Byerly and many others that are all very gentlemanlike--but bless you, sir, they do it nothing like the Colonel, so I do not wish him to be wronged."

"Of course not," answered Wilton; "but tell me, landlord, had he heard of this unfortunate business of the lady being carried off, before he went?"

"Lord bless you, no, sir," replied the man--"I only heard of it myself an hour ago. But one of our people was talking with a waterman just above there, and he said that there was a covered barge--like a gentleman's barge--came down at a great rate, about six o'clock; and he vowed that he heard somebody moaning and crying in it; but likely that is not true, for he never said a word till after he heard of the Duke's young lady having been whipped up."

Wilton obtained easily the name and address of the waterman, and finding that there was no chance whatever of gaining any further intelligence of Green, or any means of communicating with him at an earlier period than the following night, he took his leave of the good host, and rose to depart. The landlord, however, stopped him for a moment.

"Stay a bit, Master Brown," he said. "You see, I rather think there are one or two gentlemen in the lane waiting just to talk a word with my good Lord Peterborough, who is likely to pass by; and as the Colonel told me that you were not just in that way of business yourself, you had better take the boy with you."

"No, indeed," replied Wilton, somewhat bitterly, "I am not exactly, as you say, in that way of business myself. I am being taught to rob on a larger scale."

"Oh, sir!" exclaimed the landlord, not at all understanding Wilton's allusion to his political pursuits, "all these gentlemen keep the highway a horseback too. This foot-padding is only done just for a bit of amusement, and because the Colonel is out of the way. He would be very angry if he knew it.--But I did not know you were upon the road at all, sir."

"No, no," replied Wilton, smiling, "I was only joking, my good friend. The sort of robbery I meant was aiding kings and ministers to rob and cheat each other."

"Ay, ay, sir!" said the landlord, now entering into his meaning, and taking as a good joke what Wilton had really spoken in sadness--"you should have called it miching, sir--miching on a great scale. Well, that's worse than t'other. Give me the King's Highway, I say! only I'm too fat and pursy now."

This said, he went and called a little boy well trained in bearing foaming pots from place to place, who soon conducted Wilton back in safety to the house of the Duke, and then undertook to send up the waterman with all speed. By this time the

Messenger from the Earl of Byerdale had arrived; but although the good gentlemen called Messengers, in those days, exercised many of the functions of a Bow-street officer, and possessed all the keen and cunning sagacity of that two-legged race of ferrets, neither he nor Wilton could elicit any farther information from the waterman than that which had been already obtained.

"I think, sir, I think, your grace," said the Messenger, bowing low to the statesman's secretary, and still lower to the Duke, "I think that we must give the business up for tonight, for we shall make no more of it. Tomorrow morning, as early as you please, Mr. Brown, I shall be ready to go down the river with you, and I think we had better have this young man's boat, as he saw the barge which he thinks took the young lady away. Hark ye, my man," he continued, addressing the waterman, "you've seen fifty guineas, haven't you?"

"Why, never in my own hand, your honour," replied the man, with a grin.

"Well, then, you'll see them in your hand, and your own money too, if by your information we find out this young lady; so go away now, and try to discover any one of your comrades who knows something of the matter, and come with a wherry to the Duke's stairs tomorrow morning as soon as it is daylight."

"Ay, ay, we'll find her, sir, I'll bet something," said the man; and with this speech, the only consolatory one which had yet been made by any of the party, he left them. The Messenger having now done all that he thought sufficient, retired comfortably to repose, shaking from his mind at once all recollection of a business in which his heart took no part. Nothing on earth marks more distinctly that the Spirit or the Soul, with all its fine sensibilities and qualities, both of suffering and acting, is of distinct being from the mere Intellect, which is, in fact, but the soul's prime minister, than the manner in which two people of equal powers of mind will act in circumstances where the welfare of a third person, dear to the one, and not dear to the other, is concerned. A sense of what is right, some accidental duty, or mere common philanthropy, may often cause the one to exert all his powers with the utmost activity to obtain the object in view; but the moment that he has done all that seems possible, the soul tells the mind to throw off the burden for the time; and, casting away all thought of the matter, he lays himself down comfortably to sleep and forgetfulness. The other, however, in whose bosom some more deep interest exists, pursues the object also by every means that can be suggested; but when all is done, and the mind is wearied, the soul does not suffer the intellect to repose, but, still engaged in the pursuit, calls the mind to labour with anxious thought, even though that thought may be employed in vain.

For some hours after the Messenger was sound asleep, and had forgotten the whole transaction in the arms of slumber, Wilton sat conversing with the Duke, and endeavouring to draw from him even the smallest particulars of all that had taken place during the last few days, with the hope of discovering some probable cause for the event. The Duke, however, though disposed to be communicative towards Wilton on most subjects, showed a shyness of approaching anything connected with the meeting in Leadenhall-street.

It was evident, indeed, that all his suspicions turned upon Sir John Fenwick, and he admitted that a violent quarrel had occurred after the meeting; but he showed so evident an inclination to avoid entering into the subject farther, that Wilton in common delicacy could not press him. Finding it in vain to seek any more information in that quarter, Wilton at length retired to rest, but sleep came not near his eyelids. He now lay revolving all that had occurred, endeavouring to extract from the little that was really known some light, however faint, to lead to farther discovery. In the darkness of the night, imagination, too, came in, and pictured a thousand vague but horrible probabilities regarding the fate of the beautiful girl with whom he had so lately walked in sweet companionship on the very terrace from which it appeared that she had been violently taken away. Fancy had wide range to roam, both in regard to the objects of those who had carried her off, to the place whither they had borne her, and to the probability of ever recovering her or not. But Fancy stopped not there--she suggested doubts to Wilton's mind as to the fact of her having been carried off at all. The terrible apprehension that she might, by some accident, have fallen into the river returned upon him. The feet-marks upon the gravel, he thought, might very naturally have been produced by the servants in their first search; and it was not at all improbable that some one of them, thinking that his young mistress had fallen into the water, might have placed his foot upon the gunwale of the barge to lean forward for a clearer view of the river under the terrace.

As he thought of all these things, and tortured his heart with apprehensions, the conviction came upon the mind of Wilton, that, notwithstanding every difference of station, and the utter hopelessness of love in his case, Laura had become far,

far dearer to him than any other being upon earth; had produced in his bosom sensations such as he had never known before; sensations which were first discovered fully in that hour of pain and anxiety, and which, alas! promised but anguish and disappointment for the years to come.

There was, nevertheless, something fascinating in the conviction, which, once admitted, he would not willingly have parted with; and it gradually led his thoughts to what Lord Sherbrooke had told him concerning his own fate and family. That information, indeed, brought him but little hope in the present case, though we should speak falsely were we to assert that it brought him no hope. The gleam was faint, and doubting that it would last, he tried voluntarily to extinguish it in his own heart. He called to mind how many there were, whose families, engaged in the late troubles during the reigns of Charles and James, had never been able to raise themselves again, but had sunk into obscurity, and died in poverty and exile. He recollected how many of them and of their children had been driven to betake themselves to the lowest, and even the most criminal courses; and he bethought him, that if he were the child of any of these, he might think himself but too fortunate in having obtained an inferior station which gave him competence at least. The cloud might never be cleared away from his fate; and he recollected, that even if it were so, there was but little if any chance of his obtaining, with every advantage, that which he had learned to desire even without hope. He knew that the Duke was a proud man, proud of his family, proud of his wealth, proud of his daughter, proud of his rank, and that he had judged it even a very great condescension to consent to a marriage between his daughter and the son of the Earl of Byerdale, a nobleman of immense wealth, vast influence, most ancient family, and one who, from his power in the counsels of his sovereign, might, in fact, be considered the prime minister of the day. He knew, I say, that the Duke had considered his consent as a very great condescension; and he had remarked that very night, that Laura's father, even in the midst of his grief and anxiety, had made the Earl feel, by his whole tone and manner, that in the opinion of the Duke of Gaveston there was a vast distinction between himself and the Earl of Byerdale. What chance was there, then, he asked himself, for one without any advantages, even were the happiest explanation to be given to the mystery of his own early history?

Thus passed the night, but before daylight on the following morning he was up and dressed; and, accompanied by the Messenger, he went down the river with two watermen; both of whom declared that they had seen the covered barge pass down at the very hour of Lady Laura's disappearance, and had heard sounds as if from the voice of a person in distress.

We shall not follow Wilton minutely on his search, as not a little of our tale remains to be told. Suffice it to say, that from Chelsea to Woolwich he made inquiries at every wharf and stairs, examined every boat in the least like that which had been seen, and spoke with every waterman whom he judged likely to give information; but all in vain. At that time almost every nobleman and gentleman in London, as well as all merchants, who possessed any ready means of access to the Thames, had each a private stairs down to the river, with his barge, which was neither more nor less than a large covered boat, somewhat resembling a Venetian gondola, but much more roomy and comfortable.

Thus the inquiries of Wilton and the Messenger occupied a considerable space of time, and the day was far spent when they turned again at Woolwich, and began to row up the stream. Wilton, on his part, felt inclined to land, and, hiring a horse, to proceed to the Duke's house with greater rapidity--but the Messenger shook his head, saying, "No, no, sir: that wont do. We must go through the same work all over again up the river. There's quite a different set of people at the water-side in the morning and in the evening. We are much more likely to hear tidings this afternoon than we were in the early part of the day."

Wilton saw the justice of the man's remark, and acquiesced readily. But he did so only to procure for himself, as it turned out, a bitter and painful addition to the apprehensions which already tormented him. In passing London bridge, one of the heavy barges used in the conveyance of merchandise was seen moored at a little distance below the bridge, and in the neighbourhood of the fall. A great number of men were in her, rolling up various ropes and grappling irons, while a personage dressed as one of the city officers appeared at their head. Ile was directing them at the moment to unmoor the barge, and bring her to one of the wharfs again; but the boatmen of Wilton's boat, without any orders, immediately rowed up to the barge, and the Messenger inquired what the officer and his comrades were about.

The officer, who seemed to know him, replied at once, "Why, Mr. Arden, we are dragging here to see if we can get hold of the boat or any of the bodies that went down last night."

"Ay, Smith," replied the Messenger, "what boat was that? I haven't heard of it."

"Why, some stupid fools," replied the officer, "dropping down the river in a barge about half-past eight last night, tried to shoot the arch at half tide, struck the pier, got broadside on at the fall, and of course capsized and went down. If it had been a wherry, the boat would have floated, but being a covered barge, and all the windows shut, she went down in a minute, and there she sticks; but we can't well tell where, though I saw the whole thing happen with my own eyes."

"Did you see who was in the barge?" demanded the Messenger.

"I saw there were three men in her," the officer replied, "but I couldn't see their faces or the colour of their clothes, for it was very dark; and if it had not been for the two great lamps at the jeweller's on the bridge, I should not have seen so much as I did. We are going home now, for we have not light to see; but we got up one of the bodies, drifted down nearly half a mile on the Southwark side there."

"Was it a man or a woman?" demanded Wilton, eagerly.

"A man, sir," replied the officer. "It turns out to be Jones, the waterman by Fulham."

Wilton did not speak for a moment, and the Messenger was struck, and silent likewise. When they recovered a little, however, they explained to the officer briefly the object of their search upon the river, and he was easily induced to continue dragging at the spot where he thought the boat had disappeared. He was unsuccessful, however; and, after labouring for about half an hour, the total failure of light compelled them to desist without any farther discovery. Wilton then landed with the Messenger; and with his brain feeling as if on fire, and a heart wrung with grief, he rode back, as soon as horses could be procured, to carry the sad tidings which he had obtained to Laura's father.

CHAPTER XX.

A spirit--though rather of a better kind than that which drags too many of our unfortunate countrymen into the abodes of wickedness and corruption, now called Gin Pal--es, so liberally provided for them in the metropolis--abodes licensed and patronised by the government for the temptation of the lower orders of the populace to commit and harden themselves in the great besetting vice of this country--a spirit, I say, of a better kind than this, drags me into a house of public entertainment, called the Nag's Head, in St. James's Street.

The Nag's Head, in St. James's Street!!!

Now, though nobody would be in the least surprised to have read or heard of the Nag's Head in the Borough, yet there is probably not a single reader who will see this collocation of the "Nag's Head" with "St. James's Street" without an exclamation, or at least a feeling of surprise, at it being possible there should ever have been such a thing in St. James's Street at all--that is to say, not a nag's head, either horsically or hobbyhorsically speaking, but tavernistically; for be it known to all men, that the Nag's Head here mentioned was an inn or tavern actually in the very middle of the royal and fashionable street called St. James's. One might write a whole chapter upon the variations and mutations of the names of inns, and inquire curiously whether their modification in various places and at various times depends merely upon fashion, or whether it is produced by some really existing but latent sympathy between peculiar names, as applied to inns, and particular circumstances, affecting localities, times, seasons, and national character.

Having already touched upon this subject, however, though with but a slight and allusive sentence or two, in reference to our friend the Green Dragon, and being at this moment pressed for time and room, we shall say no more upon the subject here, but enter at once into the Nag's Head, and lead the reader by the hand to the door of a certain large apartment, which, at about half-past nine o'clock, on the night we have just been speaking of, was well nigh as full as it could hold.

The people whom it contained were of various descriptions, but most of them were gentlemanly men enough in their appearance, and these were ranged round little tables in parties of five or six, or sometimes more. It cannot, indeed, be said that their occupations were particularly edifying. Dice, backgammon-boards, and cards were spread on many of the tables; punch smoked around with a very fragrant odour; and whatever might have been the nature of the conversation in general, the oaths and expletives, with which it was interlarded from time to time, spoke not very well for either the morality or the eloquence of our ancestors: for such, indeed, I must call these gentlemen, forming as they did part of the great ancestral body of a hundred and fifty years ago; though I devoutly hope and pray that none of my own immediate progenitors happened to be amongst the number there assembled. The smell of punch and other strong drink was, to the atmosphere of the place, exactly what the dissolute and swaggering air of a great number of the persons assembled there was to the natural expression of the human countenance. The noise, too, was very great; so that the ear of a new comer required to become accustomed to it before he could hear anything that was taking place.

Gradually, however, as habit reconciled the visitor to the din, the oaths and objurgations, together with the words "cheat, liar, knave," &c. &c., separated themselves from the rest of the conversation, and swam like a sort of scum upon the top of the buzz. Though all were met there for enjoyment, too, it is worthy of remark, that many of the countenances around bore strong marks of fierce and angry passions, disappointment, hatred, revenge; and many a flushed cheek and flashing eye told the often-told tale, that in the amusements which man devises for himself he is almost always sure to mingle a sufficient quantity of vice to bring forth a plentiful return of sorrow.

While all this was proceeding in full current, the door, which opened with a weight and pulley, rattled and squeaked as it was cast back, and our often-mentioned friend Green--or the Colonel, as he was called--entered the room. Giving a casual glance around him, he proceeded to the other end of the saloon, where there was a small table vacant, and called in a loud but slow voice for a pint of claret.

Whether this was his habit, or whether it was merely an accidental compliance with the tavern etiquette of taking something in the house which we visit, the claret was brought to him instantly, as if it had been ready prepared, together with a large glass of the kind now called a tumbler, and a single biscuit.

Green took no notice of any one in the room, for some minutes, but ate the biscuit and drank the claret in two drafts of half a pint at a time. When this was done, he gazed round him gravely and thoughtfully; after which he walked up to one of the tables where some people were playing at hazard, and spoke a word or two across it to the man who was holding the dice-box. The man looked up with a frank smile, and for his only reply nodded his head, saying, "In five minutes, Colonel."

Green then went on to the next table, and spoke in the same low voice to a person on the left-hand side, but the man looked down doggedly, shrugged his shoulders, and said, "I can't leave my game now, Colonel. If you had told me half an hour ago, it might have been different."

"Oh! you are very busy in your game, are you?" said Green. "And so I suppose are you," he added, turning to another who was sitting at the same table.

That man answered also in the same tone; and Green, muttering to himself "Very well!" went on to two more tables at little distances from each other, from one of which only, he received a nod in answer to what he said, with the words, "Directly, Colonel--directly."

He was just going on to another, when the door again opened, and a tall, graceful young man, APPARENTLY of one or two and twenty years of age, entered the room, and advanced towards the table which Green had left vacant. His whole manner and appearance was totally different from that of the persons by whom the room had been previously tenanted, and a number of inquiring eyes were naturally turned towards him. Green looked him full in the face without taking the slightest notice; nor did the stranger show any sign of remarking him, except by brushing against him as he passed, and then turning round and begging his pardon, while at the same time he laid the finger of his right hand upon a diamond ring which he wore upon the little finger of the left. He then advanced straight to the vacant table, as we have said, and sat down, looking towards a drawer who stood at the other end of the room, and saying--

"Bring me some claret."

At the same moment, Green advanced to the table, and bowing his head with the air and grace of a distinguished gentleman, said--

"I beg your pardon, sir, for saying that this is my table; but there is perfectly room at it for us both, and if you will permit me the honour, I will join you in your wine. Shall we say a bottle of good Burgundy, which will be better than cold claret on this chilly night?"

"With all my heart," replied Wilton Brown, for we need hardly tell the reader that it was he who had last entered the room at the Nag's Head; and Green, turning to the drawer, said, "This gentleman and I will take a bottle of Burgundy. Let it be that which the landlord knows of."

"I understand, sir--I understand," replied the drawer, "last Monday night's;" and Wilton and his companion were soon busily discussing their wine, and talking together, upon various indifferent things, in a voice which could be heard at the neighbouring tables. Green spoke with ease and grace, and had altogether so much the tone of a well-bred man of the world, that he might have passed for such in the highest society in the realm. Wilton found the task a more difficult one, for his mind was eagerly bent upon other subjects. He laboured to play his part to the best, however; and Green, laughing, showed him how to drink his wine out of goblets, as he called it; so that the matter was brought to a conclusion sooner than he had ventured to hope.

As the bottle drew to its close, Green took an opportunity of saying, in a low voice, "Come with me when I go out."

Wilton answered in the same tone, "Must you not make some excuse?"

"Oh, I will show you one--I will show you one!" exclaimed Green, aloud--"if you have never seen one, I will show you one within five minutes from this time. I have but to speak a word to some of my friends at these different tables, and then you shall come with me."

This was heard all through the room; and Wilton seeing that the excuse was already made, said no more, but, "Very well, I am ready when you like."

Green then rose, and went round those to whom he had before spoken, addressing each of them again in the same order.

"I will meet you, Harry," he said to the first, who had so readily made an affirmative answer, "in three quarters of an hour. Don't be longer, my good fellow, if you can help it. Master Williamson," he added, when he came up to the other, speaking in as low a tone as possible, "I think you would have given up your game at cards, if you had known what I had to tell you and Davis there, opposite."

There was something dark and meaning in Green's look as he spoke, a knitting of the brows, a drawing together of the eyelids, and a tight shutting of the mouth between every three or four words, which made the man turn a little white.

"Why, what is the matter, Colonel?" he said, in a much civiler tone than before. "Cannot you tell me now?"

"Oh, yes," replied Green, in the same low tone, "I can tell you now, if you like. It is no great matter: only that there are warrants out against you and Davis; and against Ingram there at the other table, for robbing the Earl of Peterborough last night in the Green Lane, behind Beaufort House. They have got hold of Jimmy Law, poor fellow, already, and he will be hanged to a certainty. It was discovered who you all were by Harry Brown, who was one of your party when you went, without my knowledge, to do business between Gravesend and Rochester. He's one of my Lord Peterborough's led captains now, and was in the carriage with him, though you didn't see him to know him. He gave all your names, and they have sent down to the Green Dragon after you, and have also people on the Rochester road. Tell Davis, and I will tell Ingram; for it is better you should all get out of the way for awhile."

This was said in so low a tone, that none of those around could hear distinctly; but the worthy gentleman to whom the words were addressed did not seem near so cautious as the Colonel; for, after having suffered his eyes and his mouth to expand gradually with a look of increasing horror at every word, he started up from the table as Green concluded, exclaiming, "By--!" and dashed the cards down upon the board before him, scattering one half of them over the floor. Green gave him one momentary look of sovereign contempt, and then proceeded to the opposite table, where he told the same story to the personage named Ingram, whose attention had been called by the vehement excitement of his comrade. The effect now produced seemed fully as deep, though not quite so demonstrative; for Master Ingram sat in profound silence at the table for at least five minutes, with his face assuming various hues of purple and green, as he revolved the matter in his own mind.

It is probable, that very seldom any three men, except three sailors, have ever thought so much of a rope at the same moment; and before Green could finish his tour round the room and rejoin Wilton, those to whom he had spoken were all hastening up St. James's Street as fast as they could go. Green returned to the table where he had been seated, called the drawer to receive the money for the Burgundy, and then bowing his head to Wilton, with somewhat of a stiff air, he said, "Now, sir, if you please, I am ready to show you the way; and as I have not much time-"

"I am quite ready," replied Wilton; and turning to the door, he and Green left the house together, while those who remained behind, immediately they were gone, gathered into two or three little knots, discussing the scene which had just taken place.

In the meantime, Green led Wilton into St. James's Square, the centre of which was not at that time enclosed, as now, by iron railings; and walking to and fro there, he demanded eagerly what was the matter, and heard with surprise all that his young companion had to tell him of the sudden disappearance of the Duke's daughter, of which he had previously received no intelligence.

We need not recapitulate the whole of Wilton's account to the reader; but will only add, to that which is already known, one fact of some importance with which the young gentleman concluded the detail of his inquiries during that very day.

"When I arrived at Beaufort House," he said, "fully and painfully impressed with the notion that this poor young lady was drowned, I was met by the Duke at the very door of his library with a letter in his hand. His eyes were full of tears of joy, for the news of a boat having been lost had, by this time, reached him; and the letter, which was dated from a distant part of the country, informed him of his daughter's safety, in these words:-'Lady Laura Gaveston will be restored to Beaufort House as soon as her father can make up his mind to behave with spirit and patriotism, and follow out the only plans which can save his country. This must be done by actions, not by words; but a positive engagement under his hand will be considered sufficient. In the meantime, she remains a hostage for his good faith.' At the bottom was written, in a hand which he says is that of Lady Laura herself--'My dear father, I am well; but this is all they will let me write.'"

"Whence was it dated?" demanded Green sharply.

"Newbury," replied Wilton; "and the letter was brought by a person who spoke with a foreign accent."

"This is strange," said Green: "I should think it was some of that troop of--I know not well whether to call them villains or madmen. I should think some of them had done this, were it not that I had seen them all--I may say all the principal ones--last night, and they certainly had not a woman with them then."

"The Duke's suspicions turn principally upon Sir John Fenwick," said Wilton.

"It could not well be him," replied Green: "he was there, and none but men with him. It is very strange! I wish I could see that letter. Perhaps I might recognise the hand."

"That is evidently feigned," answered Wilton; "but I should think the date of Newbury must be false, too."

"To be sure, to be sure," replied Green--"the exact reverse most likely. They must have taken her towards the sea, not inland--Newbury!--More likely towards Rochester or Sheerness; yet I can't think there was any woman there. Yet stay a minute, Wilton," he continued, "stay a minute. I expect tidings to-night, from the very house at which I met them last night. There is a chance, a bare chance, of there being something on this matter in the letters; it is worth while to see, however. Where can I find you in ten minutes from this time ?-I saw the boy waiting near the palace when we came out."

"I will go into the Earl of Sunbury's, on that side of the square," replied Wilton, "where you see the two lights. There is nobody in it but the old housekeeper, but she knows me and will admit me."

"She knows me, too," replied Green, drily; "and I will join you there in ten minutes with any intelligence I may gain."

Green left him at once, with that peculiar sharpness and rapidity of movement which Wilton had always remarked in him from their first meeting. The young gentleman, on his part, went over to the house of the Earl of Sunbury, and telling the old housekeeper, and the girl who opened the door to him, that a gentleman would soon be there to speak with him on business, he went up to the saloon, and as soon as he was alone, raised the light that was left with him, to gaze upon the picture which we have mentioned more than once, and to compare it by the aid of memory with the lady whom he had seen but a few days before. The likeness was very strong, the height was the same, the features, examined strictly one by one, presented exactly the same lines. The complexion, indeed, in the picture, was more brilliant; and it was that, perhaps, as well as a certain roundness, which marked a difference of age; but then the expression was precisely the same--a depth, a tenderness even approaching to melancholy--in the picture, as in her whom he had seen; and though he gazed, and wondered, and wearied imagination for probabilities, he found none, but could only end by believing that, in the facts connected with that picture, lay the mystery of his fate, and of the link between him and the Earl of Sunbury.

He was still gazing, when Green was ushered into the room, and setting down the light, Wilton turned to meet him. There was a dark and heavy frown upon the countenance of him whom we have so often heard called the Colonel, as he entered: an expression of bitterness mingled with sadness; but, nevertheless, he took up the light, and walking up to the picture, gazed upon it for a minute or two, as Wilton had done.

"It is wonderfully like," he said, after pausing for a moment or two--"how beautiful she was! However, I have no time to think of such things now. I have here tidings for you, Wilton. I know not yet rightly what they are, for I caught but a glance of them; and had other things to think of bitter enough, and requiring instant attention. Here, let us look what this epistle says."

Setting down the lamp upon the table, he opened the letter and held it to the light, reading it attentively, while Wilton, who stood beside him did the same. It was written in fine small hand, and in French; but the page at which Green had opened the sheet, after a few words connected with a sentence that had gone before, went on as follows:--"I should not have sent this till we were safe across, but that circumstances have induced us to delay our departure; and you would scarcely think that it is I who have urged Caroline to remain for yet a little while: I, who some days ago was so fearful of remaining, so anxious to depart. Nor is it solely an inclination to linger near that dear boy, although I own the sight of him has been to me like the foretaste of a new existence. Bless him for me, my friend--bless him for me! But I found that the dear wild girl who is with me had neither ceased to love, nor ceased entirely to hope. In the last letter she received, mingled with reproaches for coming hither, there was every now and then a burst of tenderness and affection which made her trust, and me almost believe, that all good and honourable feeling is not extinct. She thinks that if she could see him, the better angel might gain the dominion, and I have not only counselled her to remain yet a little while, but also even to go to London should it be required. While we were talking over all these things," the letter proceeded, "just after you were gone, we heard a fresh arrival at this house, and, as I thought, a woman's voice speaking in tones of remonstrance and complaint. I have this morning learned who it is, and now write in great haste to ask you if these things are right in any cause, or if you can have anything to do with it. I will not believe it, Lennard--I will not believe it. Rash as you have been in choosing your own fate--hasty as you have been in all things connected with yourself--you would not, I am sure, countenance a thing that is cruel as well as criminal."

Green laughed bitterly. "I am forced," he said, "to bear much that I would not countenance. But look here--she goes on to say that it is the daughter of the Duke. 'Young, and beautiful, and gentle,' she says--that matches well, does it not, Wilton, ha?--I Who has been torn from her father, the Duke of Gaveston, in this daring and shameful manner, and brought hither by water with the intention, as I believe, of sending her over to France in the ship that we have hired. I have seen her twice, and spoken with her for some time, and I beseech you, if it be possible, find means of setting her free.'--Ay, but how may that be?" continued Green. "If they have got her, and risk their necks to have her, they will take care to keep her sure. They have men enough for that purpose, and they have taken care to render me nearly powerless."

"I should have thought," replied Wilton, whose joy at the discovery of where Laura really was had instantly blown up the flame of hope so brightly, that objects distant and difficult to be reached seemed by that light to be close at hand--"I should have thought, from what I have seen and what I suspect, that you could have commanded a sufficient force at any moment to set all opposition at defiance, especially when you were engaged in a lawful and generous cause."

"I should have thought so, too," replied Green, "two days ago. But times have changed, Wilton, times have changed, and, like the wind of a tropical climate, turned round in a single moment. On my soul," he continued, vehemently, "one would think that men were absolutely insane. Here a set of people, whose lives are all in my own hand, dare to tamper with my friends and comrades, to bribe them, to hire them away from me, ay, and to do it so openly that I cannot fail to see it, and that too, at the very moment when they know that I hate and abhor their proceedings, and when they have just reason to suppose that I will take means to frustrate their base and cowardly designs, and only waver between the propriety of doing so, and the wish not to give them over to the death they well deserve."

"If they have so acted," replied Wilton--"if they have shown such base ingratitude towards you, as well as designs dangerous to the country--for I will not affect to doubt or misunderstand you--why not boldly, and at once, give them up to justice? Understand me, I wish to hear nothing more of these men. I wish to be perfectly ignorant of their whole proceedings. I wish to have no information whatsoever, except my own suspicions, for if I had, I should feel myself bound immediately to cause their arrest. But from what you have said in regard to Sir John Fenwick; from what the Duke has said on various occasions; and from what I myself have remarked, I am strongly inclined to believe that there are matters going on which can but end in ruin to those engaged in them, if not in all the horrors of a civil war."

"That I should not mind--that I should not mind!" cried Green--"let us have a civil war; let every man lay his hand upon his sword and betake him to his standard. That is the true, the right, the only right way to get rid of an usurper. It has been with the very view of that civil war you talk of that I have banished myself from the station in which I was born, that I have walked by night instead of by day, and that I have kept in constant preparation, throughout the whole of the south of England, the seeds, as it were, of a future army. And now what have they done? Not only trusted the command of all things to others, but given that command to men who would do, by the basest and most dastardly means, that which I would do by open force and bold exertion: men who have mixed up crimes of the blackest die with the noblest aspirations that ever led on men of honour to the greatest deeds; who have soiled and sullied, disgraced and degraded, the cause for which I have shed my blood, ruined my fortune, and seen all the fair things of life pass away like a dream. By heavens, I could cry as if I were a girl or a baby," and he dashed away a tear from his eye which he could not restrain; "and now," he continued, "and now if I do not prevent them they will put a damning seal to all their follies and crimes, which will render that holy and noble cause horrible in the eyes of all men, which will brand it for ever with infamy and shame, and leave it blighted and loathsome, so that men will shrink from the very thought thereof."

"But why not prevent them?" cried Wilton, "why not give up such traitors and villains to justice at once?" "Why not?" replied Green; "because there are men amongst them who have fought side by side with me in the day of battle; because there are some foolish when others are wicked; because that there are many who abhor their acts as much as I do, but who would be implicated in the consequences of their crimes. These are all strong reasons, Wilton, powerful, mighty reasons, and I find now, alas I--I find now, most bitterly--that he who seeks even the best ends, in dark and tortuous ways, is sure, sooner or later, to involve himself in circumstances where he can neither act nor refuse to act, neither speak nor be silent, without a crime, a danger and a punishment. In that situation I have placed myself; and I tell you that even now, since I have entered this room, I have determined to call upon my own head those dangers, if not that fate, which the mistake I have committed well deserves. I will frustrate these men's designs. They shall not commit the act they purpose. But yet I will betray no man; I will give no man up to death. They shall not wring it from me; but they shall be sufficiently warned. Now, however, let us leave all this, and only inquire how this girl can be saved from their hands. You, Wilton, must be the person to rescue her, for I feel sure that your fate and hers are bound up together. I feel sure, too," he added with a faint smile, "that she would rather it were your hand saved her than that of any one else. I have seen you together more than once, remember. But how it is to be done is the question. My time must be given to other things, for from tidings I have received not a moment is to be lost. They have taken such means that I find there are only two whom I can trust out of very many who were with me near London. I have no time to send either into Dorsetshire or Sussex, and the people there may have been tampered with also. Besides, as we cannot call in the power of the law upon our side, it would need a number to effect our purpose."

"But I will call in the power of the law," replied Wilton. "I have a Messenger with the Secretary of State's warrant at my command; and wherever this place may be, I can in a moment raise such a force in the neighbourhood as will enable me to rescue her, and capture those who have committed so daring an outrage.

"Ay, but that is what must not be, Wilton," replied Green. "There is not one of those men whom you would capture whose head would be worth ten days' purchase, were he within the walls of Newgate or the Tower. No, no! to that I cannot consent. Her freedom must be effected somehow, but their liberty not lost. I must think over it this night. Where can I find you to-morrow morning early?"

"At my own lodgings," replied Wilton, "not four streets off."

"No, no!" answered Green; "I never enter London in the day. I might risk much by doing so, and must not do it except in case of great need."

"Then let it be at Beaufort House," replied Wilton: "I sleep there to-night. But why should we not settle and determine the whole at once? Tell me but where is this place to which they have taken Lady Laura, and I will undertake to rescue her."

"You alone, Wilton?" said Green.

"Aided by none but the Messenger," replied Wilton: "armed with the force of the law, I fear not whom I encounter."

"Armed with the force of love!" answered Green, after looking at him for a moment with eyes in which affection and admiration were equally evident. "You want not the spirit of your race; and it will carry you through. If you will promise me to take none but the Messenger with you, you shall have some one to guide you to the house, and to aid you on my part. I need not tell you what you have to do. Demand the young lady's liberty simply and straightforwardly; say to all those who oppose you, that the task of investigating what have been the causes, and who the perpetrators of the outrage committed, must fall upon the Duke; that you have no authority to meddle with that part of the business. Say this, I repeat, and I doubt not that you will be fully successful. They dare not--I am sure they dare not--resist you, if you do not attempt to arrest any of their own number."

"I promise you most faithfully," replied Wilton, "to act as you have said. I will go with the Messenger and the person you send only. But where am I to meet this person? When, and how, and where, am I to find the house?"

"You would find it with difficulty," replied Green; "for it lies far off from the high road, not many miles from Rochester; and the lanes and woods about it are not arranged for the purpose of making it easily discovered. You must not, therefore, attempt to find your way alone. However, set out early to-morrow with strong fresh horses, and ride on till you come to the village of High Halstow. Should you reach that place before nightfall, remain there till it turns dusk. As it begins to become grey, ride out again, taking the way towards Cowley Castle. As you go along that road, you will find some one to show you the way. He will ask you what colour you are of. Answer him 'Brown,' but that 'Green' will do as well. I would be there myself if I could; but that, I fear, cannot be. Let me hear of you and of your success, however--though I will not doubt your success; and now, are you going back to Beaufort House? If so, I will bear you company on the way."

Wilton replied in the affirmative, and they accordingly left the house of the Earl of Sunbury. Wilton, however, had to procure his horse; and Green also was delayed, for a moment, by the same piece of business. When all was prepared, he seemed to hesitate and pause before he mounted; and while he yet remained speaking, with his foot in the stirrup, a boy ran up, saying, "I have just been down, sir, and seen him go in."

Green gave him a note which he had held in his hand during the whole conversation at Lord Sunbury's, saying, "Take him that note! Tell the servant to deliver it immediately. If Lord Sherbrooke asks who sent it, tell him it was the gentleman who wrote it, and who hopes to meet him at the appointed place." The boy ran off with the note as fast as he could go, and Wilton and his companion turned their horses' heads towards Chelsea.

What he had heard certainly did surprise Wilton a good deal; and he did not scruple to say, "You seem acquainted with every one, I think, and to have an acquaintance with many of whom I did not know you had the slightest knowledge."

"It is so," answered Green, in a grave and thoughtful tone, "and yet nothing wonderful. It is with a man like me as with nature," he added with a smile, "we both work secretly. Things seem extraordinary, strange, almost miraculous, when beheld only in their results, but when looked at near, they are found to be brought about by the simplest of all possible means. You, having lived but little in the world, and not being one half my age, yet know thousands of people in the highest ranks of life that I do not know, though I have mingled with that rank ten times as much as you have done: and I know many whom you would think the last to hold acquaintance with me in these changed times. You could go into any thronged assembly, a theatre, a ball-room, a house of parliament, and point me out, by hundreds, people with whose persons I am utterly unacquainted, and these would be the greatest men of the day.

"But I could lay my finger upon this wily statesman, or that great warrior, or the other stern philosopher, and could tell you secrets of those men's bosoms which would astonish you to hear, and make them shrink into the ground;--and yet there would be no magic in all this."

Wilton did not answer him in the same moralizing strain, but strove to obtain some farther information in regard to his proceedings proposed for the following day. But neither upon that, nor upon the subject of the note to Lord Sherbrooke, would Green speak another word, till, on arriving at the gates of Beaufort House, he said--

"Remember High Halstow."

CHAPTER XXI.

It was night, and the large assembly of persons who had thronged the palace at Kensington during the day had taken their departure. Silence had returned after the noise and bustle of the sunshine had subsided; scarcely a sound was heard throughout the whole building, except the porter snoring in the hall. The King himself had taken his frugal supper, and was sitting alone in his cabinet with merely a page at the door; his courtiers were scattered in their different apartments; and his immediate attendants were waiting in the distant chambers where he slept, for the hour of his retiring to rest.

Such had been the state of things for some little time, when the great bell rang, and the porter started up to open the door. A gentleman on horseback appeared without, accompanied by two others, apparently servants; and the principal personage demanded, in a tone of authority, "Is the Earl of Portland in the palace?"

The porter, though not well pleased to be roused, replied, with every sort of deference to the air and manner of the visitor, saying that the Earl was in the palace, but he believed was unwell.

"I am afraid I must disturb him," said the stranger. "My business is of too much importance to his lordship to wait till to-morrow morning."

The porter then gave the speaker another look: the dress, the demeanour, the horses, the attendants, were all such as commanded respect, although he did not recollect the stranger's face. "Well, sir," he said, "if you will come in, I will have his lordship informed."

The stranger nodded his head, and turning to his followers, bade them take away the horses. "I will walk back," he said, and then following the porter, entered the palace. The janitor led him onward through some large folding doors to a room where two or three servants were sitting, into whose hands he delivered him, bidding one of them conduct him to the page in waiting. This was speedily done; and the page, on being informed of the stranger's desire, again examined him somewhat curiously, and asked his name.

"That matters not," replied the stranger. "Tell him merely that it is a gentleman to whom he rendered great service many years ago, and who has now important intelligence to give him."

"I fear, sir," replied the page, "that my Lord Portland would not like to be disturbed without some clearer information than that."

"Do as you are ordered, sir," replied the gentleman, in a tone of stern authority, which seemed not a little to surprise his hearer. "Tell Lord Portland it is a gentleman whose life he saved at the battle of the Boyne."

The page retired with the air of one who would fain have been sullen if he had dared; and the stranger remained standing with his hand upon the table in the middle of the room, the doors closed round him on all sides, and no one apparently near.

His first thought was one not often indulged in that place, though by no means an unnatural one. It was a thought, for merely expressing which, not less than twelve people were once committed to a severe and lengthened imprisonment by a king of France. "How easy would it now be," the stranger said mentally, "to kill a king, were one so minded! Now, God forbid," he added, "that even the attempt of such an act should ever stain our loyalty to our legitimate sovereign! Those Romans, those splendid but most barbarous of barbarians, were certainly the greatest cheats of their own understandings that ever lived. There was scarcely a crime, a vice, or a folly upon earth, that they did not hug to their hearts, when they had once gilded it with a glorious name."

As he thus paused, moralizing, he laid down his hat upon the table, and brushing back his grey hair from his brow, pressed his hand upon his forehead as if his head ached, and then dropping it again, mused for several minutes with his eyes fixed upon the floor. He was only roused from this deep fit of thought by the door opening suddenly. A gentleman rather below the middle height, with strong marked features, and a keen but steadfast eye, entered the room with a paper in his hand. His eyes were fixed upon the ground as he came in, and he walked with a firm but somewhat heavy step, as if his limbs did not move very easily, though he was by no means a man far advanced in life.

The stranger gazed at him for a moment with a look of inquiry, and then advanced immediately towards him, bowing with a stately air, and saying, "My Lord of Portland, since I last saw you, you are somewhat changed, but perhaps not so much as I am, and therefore I may have to recall myself to your remembrance; especially as those who confer a benefit in a moment of haste and tumult, are more likely to forget the person they obliged, than that person to forget his benefactor."

He spoke in French, as it was generally known that Lord Portland was unwilling to speak English, though he understood it.

The other heard him out in perfect silence, and without the slightest change of countenance; but looked him in the face attentively, as if endeavouring to recollect his features.

"I have seen you somewhere before," he said at length, "but where I really do not know. It must have been a long time ago. Pray what do you want?"

"It is a long time ago, my lord," replied the visitor, "and the place where we met is far distant. It was upon the banks of the Boyne, just when the battle was over."

"Oh, I think I remember now," replied the other: "did I not come up just as one of our people had got his knee upon your throat, and was going to fire his pistol into your head, because you would ask no quarter, while another was wrenching your broken sword out of your band?"

"You did," answered the stranger, "you did: you saved my life; and when I jumped up and got to a horse, you would not let them fire after me. It was not to be forgotten, my lord; but--"

At that moment the door was again thrown open, and the page re-entered the room, speaking in a somewhat harsh and authoritative tone as he came in, so as to cut across what the stranger was about to say, with "My Lord of Portland--;" but the gentleman who had entered just before waved his hand, saying, in a stern voice, "Leave the room! and wait without."

The man obeyed immediately, and the other turning to the visitor, added, "I am at this moment not very well, and extremely busy--even pressed for a moment, so that I must leave you just now. If you will sit down and write what you wish, it shall have favourable attention, or if you would rather say it, and explain it more fully by word of mouth, I will send an intimate friend of mine to you to whom you can tell what you think proper. I will hear what it is, and give every attention to it; but at this moment it is impossible for me to remain. These papers in my hand require instant reply, and I was seeking for some one to answer them when I came here."

"What I have to say," answered the stranger, "requires also instant attention; that is to say, it must be told to your lordship before to-morrow morning, and I will therefore, if you will permit me, remain here till you are ready to hear. When once told to you, the burden of it will be off my shoulders."

"I could have wished to have gone to bed," replied the other, with a faint smile, "without any farther burden upon mine. But if it so please you to wait, do it; but I fear I shall be long."

The visitor, however, signified his acquiescence by bowing his head; and the other left him without saying anything more.

"Somewhat of the insolence of office!" he said to himself, as his acquaintance quitted the room: "however, I must not forget the obligation;" and seating himself, he fell into deep thought, which seemed of a painful kind; for the muscles of his face moved with the emotions of his mind, and one or two half-uttered words escaped him. At length, he seemed weary of his own thoughts, and turning round as if to look for some occupation for his thoughts, he said, "It matters not!"

There were no books in the room, nor any pictures; there was nothing that could attract the eye or amuse the mind, except the beautiful forms of some of the gilded panel-frames, and the spots of the carpet beneath his feet. The visitor began to grow weary, and to think that Lord Portland was very long in returning.

At length, however, when he had been there about half an hour, a somewhat younger man entered, splendidly dressed according to the costume of the day, and advancing directly towards the stranger, he said in very good English--

"My name is Keppel, sir, and I am directed to say that Lord Portland will really be hardly able to see you to-night, as he is anything but well; but as it would appear that what you have to say is important, I wish to know whether it is important to the King or to the Earl himself. If to the latter, the Earl will see you at two o'clock to-morrow; if to the King, I am directed to request that you would communicate it to me, by whom it shall be most faithfully reported, both to Lord Portland and to the King himself."

"Sir," replied the stranger, "the motive of my coming is on no private business. It is on business of importance to the state generally--of the very utmost importance. I had wished to communicate it to Lord Portland, because that gentleman once performed an act of great kindness and generosity towards me, and I wished to give him the means of rendering a great service to his master."

"The King and Lord Portland are both indebted to you, sir," replied Keppel, better known as the Earl of Albemarle, with a grave smile; "but in those circumstances, as the greatest favour to all parties, you will be pleased to communicate anything you have to say to me. From your whole tone and demeanour, I am perfectly sure that what you have to say is none of the unimportant things with which we are too often troubled here; and I may therefore confidently add, that, after you have given me a knowledge of the business, either the King or Lord Portland, as you may think fit, will see you to-morrow."

"Well, sir," replied the visitor, "I have no right to stand on ceremony, especially at such a moment as this. What I have to say would have been much more easily said to Lord Portland himself, as he knows under what circumstances we met, knows probably who I am, and would make allowances for my peculiar views. YOU may think it next to high treason for me to call that Personage, who was not long ago William Prince of Orange, by any other name than King of England"

"Oh no! oh no!" said Keppel with a smile--"names are but names, my good sir; and in this boisterous land of England we are accustomed to see things stripped of all ornaments. The difficulty you mention is easily obviated, by calling him of whom you just have spoken, 'The High Personage.'"

"Names, indeed, are nothing," said the other with a smile. "What I have got to say, sir, is this, that I have undoubted reason to know that the life of the High Personage we refer to is in hourly danger; that there are persons in this realm who have not only designed to kill him, but have laid with skill and accuracy their schemes for effecting that purpose. I have heard that he is very apt--for I have never seen the royal hunt--to go out to the chase nearly alone, or rather, I should say, very slightly attended; and I came to tell Lord Portland that if this were continued, that High Personage's life could not be counted upon from day to day. Let him be well guarded; let there be always some one near him as he rides; and, as far as possible, let some of his guards be ready to escort him home on his return."

"Your information," said Keppel, "is certainly very important, and the precaution you recommend wise and judicious; but yet I fear you must give us some more information to render it at all efficient--I say this, not at all from doubting you, but because we have had, especially of late, so many false reports of plots which never existed, that the King has become careless and somewhat rash. Nor would it be possible for either Lord Portland or myself to persuade him to take any precautions unless we had some more definite information. If you know that such a plot really exists, you must also know the names of those who laid it."

"But those names I will never give up," replied the other: "it is quite sufficient for me, sir, to satisfy my own heart and my own conscience, that I have given a full and timely warning of what is likely to ensue. It matters not to me whether that warning be taken or not; I have done what is right; I will tell no more. Lord Portland knows that I am neither a, coward, nor a low born man. I expect not--I ask not for favour, immunity, reward, or even thanks. All I do ask is, in the words of the poet, 'that Caesar would be a friend to Caesar.'"

"But you are doubtless aware," answered Keppel, after a pause, "that by concealing the names, and in any degree the purposes of persons guilty of high treason, you bring yourself under the same condemnation."

"I both know the fact, sir," replied the other, "and I knew before I came that it might be urged against me here; but I did not think that Lord Portland would urge it. However that may be, I came fully prepared to do what I think right, and as nothing, not even the cause to which I am most attached, would induce me to become an assassin or to wink at cold-blooded murder, so, sir, nothing on earth will induce me to betray others to the death which I do not fear myself. At all events, the truth of what I have told may be positively relied upon; and that I ask no reward or recompence of any kind, may well be received to show that the warning I have given is not vain."

Keppel again mused for a moment or two, and then said, "Well, sir, I must not urge you by any harsh menace, nor was such my intention in what I said. But there are other considerations which should induce you to tell me more than you have told. One is, the safety of the Great Personage we have mentioned himself. It is scarcely possible for him to guard against the evil you apprehend in the manner you propose. He is by far too fearless a man, as you well know, to shut himself up within the walls of his palace, or even to conceal himself in his carriage. If he rides out, he cannot always be surrounded by guards, nor can he have a troop galloping after him through the hunting field."

"Sir," replied the stranger, "to you and to his other friends and attendants I must leave the guardianship of his person--I neither know him nor his habits. I have done what I conceive to be my duty; I have done it to the extreme limit of what I judge right; and neither fear nor favour will make me go one step farther."

"These scruples are very extraordinary," replied Keppel--"indeed, I cannot understand them: but at all events I must beg you to remain a little, while I go and speak to Lord Portland upon the subject. Perhaps, if the King himself were to hear you, you might say more."

"I should say no more to the Personage you mention," replied the other, "than I should to Lord Portland--for to the one I am obliged, to the other, not."

"Well, wait a few minutes," replied Keppel, and quitted the room.

The other remained standing where the courtier had left him, though the thought crossed his mind, "My errand is now done. Why should I remain any longer? I should risk less by going now than by lingering."

But still be stayed; and in two minutes, or perhaps less, the door again opened, giving admission, not to Keppel, but to the elder personage with whom he had spoken before. Advancing into the middle of the room, he leaned upon the table, near which the other was standing, and said--

"Monsieur Keppel has told me all that you have said, and, moreover, what you have refused to say. First, let me tell you that I am much obliged to you for the intelligence you have brought; and next, let me exhort you to make it more full and complete to render it effectual."

"I have made it as complete, my lord," replied his visitor, "as it is possible for me to do without betraying men who were once my friends, and who have only lost my friendship by such schemes as these. I must not say any more even at your request; for I must not take from you the power of saying, that you saved the life of a man of honour. You must contrive means to secure the Great Personage we speak of, and I doubt not you will be able to do so. I had but one object in coming here, my lord, and that object was not a personal one; it was to tell you of the danger, and thereby enable you to guard against it; it was to tell you, that a body of rash and criminal men have conspired together, to assassinate a Personage who stands in the way of their schemes."

"Are there many of them?" demanded his companion.

"A great many," he replied--"enough to render their object perfectly secure, if means be not taken to frustrate it."

"But," said the other, "the men must be mad, for many of them must be taken and executed very soon."

"True," answered his visitor, "if we were to suppose the country would remain quiet all the while. But assassination might only be the prelude to insurrection and to civil war, and to the restoration of our old monarchs to the throne."

"Such was the purpose, was it?" replied his companion.

"Assassination is a pitiful help, and has never yet been called in to aid a great or good cause."

"Ay, my lord," replied his informant; "but in this instance it is a base adjunct affixed to the general scheme of insurrection by a few bloody-minded men, without the knowledge of thousands who would have joined the rising, and without the knowledge, I am sure, of King James himself."

"I really do not see," said the other, "what should have caused such hatred against the person they aim at--the post of King of England is no bed of roses; and a thousand, a thousand-fold happier was he, as Stadtholder of Holland, governing a willing people and fighting the battles of freedom throughout the world, than monarch of this great kingdom, left without a moment's peace, by divisions and factions in the mass of the nation, which called him to the throne, and seeing union nowhere but in that small minority of the people who oppose his authority, and even attempt his life. His is no happy fate."

"Sir, there are some men," replied the other, "in whom certain humours and desires are so strong, that the gratification thereof is worth the whole of the rest of a life's happiness, and gratified ambition may be sufficient in this case to compensate for the sacrifice of peace. I mean not to speak one word against the master that you serve. He has, as you say, fought the battles of liberty for many years: he is a brave and gallant soldier, too, as ever lived: I doubt not he is a kind friend and a good master"

"Stay, stay," replied the other, holding up his hand "before you go farther, let me tell you that you are under a mistake. I am the personage of whom you speak--I am the King. When I prevented the soldiers from killing you, Bentinek was near me. He is taller than I am: the Dutch guards saw him before me, and shouted his name, which led to your error."

The effect of these words upon the other can hardly be imagined. He turned pale--he turned red; but he yielded to the first impulse both of gratitude and respect, and without taking time to think or hesitate, he bent his knee and kissed the King's hand.

"Rise, rise!" said William--"I ask nothing of you, sir, but to speak to me as you would have done if I had really been Lord Portland. I could not let you go on without explanation, for you had said all that could be pleasant to a king's ears to hear; and you seemed about to say those things which you might not have been well pleased to remember, when you discovered my real situation."

"I thank you, sir, most deeply," replied the other, "for that act of kindness, as well as for that which went before. I have hitherto, as I need scarcely say, been a strenuous and eager supporter of King James. I have served him with all my ability, and had he at any time returned to this country, would have served him with my sword. That sword, sir, however, can never now be drawn against the man who has saved my life; and, indeed, though I have known many changes and chances, yet I remember no one moment of joy and satisfaction greater than this, when I think that, spontaneously, I have refused to take a share in criminal designs against my benefactor, though I knew him not to be so, and have revealed the schemes against his life, who generously spared my own."

"I intended," said the King, "in the character of Lord Portland, to press you to farther explanations; but now that you know who I am, I may feel a greater difficulty in so doing. I must leave it to yourself, then, to tell me all that you may think necessary for my safety."

The other put his hand to his head, and for a few minutes seemed embarrassed and pained. "The discovery, sir," he said, at length, "alters my situation also; and yet I pray and beseech you, do not press me to perform an act that is base and dishonourable; grant me but one or two conditions, and I will go to the very verge of what I ought to do, towards you."

"I will press you to nothing, sir," replied William; "what are the conditions?"

"First," replied the other, "that I may not be asked to name any names; secondly, that I may never be called upon to give any evidence upon this subject in a court of justice."

"The names, of course, are important," said William, "as by having them we are placed most upon our guard. However, you have come voluntarily to render me a service, and I will not press hard upon you. The conditions you ask shall be granted. The names shall not be required of you, and you shall not be called upon to give evidence. Call in Keppel! Arnold!" he added, raising his voice; and immediately the door was opened, and Keppel entered, bowing low as he did so.

"I have promised this gentleman two things, Keppel," said the King. "First, that he shall not be pressed to give up the names of the conspirators; and, secondly, that he shall not be called upon to give evidence against them."

"Your majesty is very gracious," replied Keppel: "without the names of the persons, I scarcely think--"

William made a sign with his hand, saying, "That is decided. Now, sir, what more have you to add?"

"Merely this, sir," replied the other: "it is not much, indeed, but it will enable you to take greater measures for your safety. The design to assassinate you has existed some time, but the period for putting it in execution was formerly fixed for the month of April. My opposition to the bloody design, and to the purpose of bringing French troops into Great Britain, has deranged all the plans of these base men. I had fancied that such opposition, and the falling away of many others on whom the assassins counted, would have induced them to abandon the whole design. Last night, however, I received intelligence that, instead of so doing, their purpose was but strengthened, and their design only hastened; that instead of April, the assassination was to take place whenever it could be accomplished; that even tomorrow, when it is believed you dine with the Lord Romney, if it were found possible absolutely to surround the house so as to prevent escape, the deed was to be attempted there; or as you went; or as you came back. If none of these occasions suited, you were to be assailed the first time that you went out to hunt; and dresses such as those worn by many of your attendants in the chase are already ordered for the purpose of facilitating the execution of the murder, and the escape of the assassins. It has been calculated, I find, that on the night of next Saturday you are likely to pass across Turnham Green towards ten o'clock, and that is one of the occasions which is to be made use of, if others fail."

William looked at Lord Albemarle, and Albemarle at the King; but the latter remained silent for a minute or two, as if to give his informant time to go on. The other, however, added nothing more; and the King, after this long pause, said, "I must not conceal from you, sir, that we have heard something of this matter, and may probably soon have farther tidings."

"It is high time, sir," replied the other, "that you should have farther tidings, for the first attempt will certainly be to-morrow night."

"Perhaps we have acted somewhat rashly," said Keppel; "but to say truth, there have been so many reports of plots, that we thought it but right to discourage the matter; his Majesty justly observing, that if he were to give attention to everything of the kind, he would have nothing to do but to examine into the truth of stories composed for the purpose of obtaining rewards. We therefore gave this matter not so much attention as it would seem to require."

"It requires every attention, sir," replied their visitor; "and from whomsoever you may have obtained the information, if possible, obtain more from him immediately. If he tell you what I have told, he tells you truth; and if so, it is probable that any farther information he may give will be true likewise. Did I know his name, perhaps I could say more."

"Suppose his name were Johnstone?" said the King.

"I know of none such," replied the other, "who could give you much information. There are many persons, whom men call Jacobites, of that name, and many very gallant gentlemen who would sooner die than become assassins. But none that I know of, in this business."

"What would you say, then," the King continued, "to the name of Williamson, or Carter, or Porter?"

"Porter!" replied the other, gazing in the King's face--"Porter!--I believe, sir," he added, "you are too generous to attempt to wring from me the names of persons connected with this business in any underhand manner; and therefore I reply to you straightforwardly, that if Captain Porter should give you any information upon this matter consistent with the tidings that I have given, or in explanation thereof, you may believe him. He is not a gentleman I either very much respect or esteem;

but I do not believe that he is one who would willingly take a part in assassination, or who would falsify the truth knowingly."

"Sir, you confirm my good opinion of you," replied the King: "we have intimation of some of these proceedings from Porter, and have had intimation from other quarters also, but none such as could be relied upon till the information that you have given us to-night. Porter's, indeed, might have proved more satisfactory; but he does not bear a good reputation, and it was judged better to discourage the thing altogether. He shall now be heard, and very likely the whole will be explained. On the complete discovery of the plot, I need hardly say that any reward within reason which you may require shall be given you."

The stranger waved his hand somewhat indignantly. "There was a man found, sir," he said, "to sell the blood of Christ himself for thirty pieces of silver; and therefore it can scarcely be considered as insulting to any of the sons of men to suppose that they would follow that example. I, however, do not trade in such things, and I require no reward whatsoever for that which I have done. I trust and see now that it will prove effectual, and I am perfectly satisfied. If these men fall into your hands by other means than mine, and incur the punishment they have justly deserved, I have not a word to say for them, but I have only to beseech you, sir, to separate the innocent from the guilty; to be careful--oh! most careful, in a moment of excitement and just indignation--not to confound the two, and to make a just distinction between fair and open enemies of your government, and base and treacherous assassins."

"I shall strive to do so, sir," answered the King, "and would always rather lean towards mercy than cruelty. And now, as it grows late, I would fain know your name, and would gladly see you again."

"My name, sir," replied the other, "must either be kept secret, or revealed to your Majesty alone. I have long been a nameless man, having lost all, and spent all, in behalf of that family opposed to your dynasty."

"Who have, doubtless, shown you no gratitude," said William.

"They have had no means, sir," replied the Jacobite, "and I have made no demand upon them."

"It is but right, however," said the King, changing the subject, "that I should know your name. When I inquired who you were when we last met--the only time, indeed, we have met, till now--they gave me a name which I now see must have been a mistaken one. Do you object to give it before this gentleman?"

"To give my real name, sir," replied the other, "I do. But I have no objection to give it to you yourself in private."

"Leave us, Arnold," said the King; and Lord Albemarle immediately quitted the presence.

CHAPTER XXII.

The day which we have just seen terminate at Kensington we must now conduct to a close in another quarter, where events very nearly as much affecting the peace and safety of this realm, and far more affecting the peace of various personages mentioned in this history than the events which took place at the palace, were going on at the same time. It was a bright, clear, frosty day, with everything sparkling in the sunshine, the last dry leaves of the preceding year still lingering in many places on the branches of the trees, and clothing the form of nature in the russet livery of decay.

Wilton Brown was up long before daylight, and ready to set out by the first streak of dawn in the east. Not having seen the Duke on the preceding night--as that nobleman, worn with anxiety and grief, had fallen ill and retired to seek repose--he sat down and wrote him a note, while waiting for the Messenger, informing him that he had obtained information concerning Lady Laura's situation, and doubted not to be enabled to set her free in the course of the following day. The Messenger was somewhat later up than himself, and Wilton sent twice to hasten his movements. When he did appear, he had to be informed of the young gentleman's purposes, and of the information he had obtained the night before; and this information Wilton could of course communicate only in part. When told in this mysterious manner, however, and warned that there might be some danger in the enterprise which they were about to undertake, he seemed to hesitate, as if he did not at all approve of the affair. As soon as Wilton remarked this, he said, in a stern tone, "Now, Mr. Arden, are you or are you not willing to go through this business with me? If you are not, let me know at once, that I may send for another messenger who has more determination and spirit."

"That you wont easily find," replied the Messenger, a good deal hurt. "It was not at any danger that I hesitated at all, for I never have in my life, and I wont begin now, when I dare say there is not half so much danger as in things that I do every day.--Did not I apprehend Tom Lambton, who fired two pistols at my head? No, no, it is not danger; but what I thought was, that the Earl very likely might not like any of these bargains about not taking up the folks that we find there, and all that. However, as he told me to obey your orders in everything, I suppose that must be sufficient."

"It must, indeed," answered Wilton; "for I have no time to stop for explanations or anything else; and if you hesitate, I must instantly send for another messenger."

"Oh, I shall not hesitate, sir," replied the Messenger; "but you must take all the burden of the business on yourself. I shall do exactly as you order me, neither more nor less; so that if there comes blame anywhere, it must rest at your door."

"Come. come, Arden," said Wilton, seeing that he was likely to have a luke-warm companion where a very ardent and energetic one was much wanted, "you must exert yourself now as usual, and I am sure you will do so. Let us get to our horses as fast as possible."

Wilton tried to soothe the Messenger out of his ill-humour as they rode along, but he did not succeed in any great degree. The man remained sullen; being one of those who like, when clothed with a little brief authority, to rule all around them rather than be directed by any. So long as he had conducted the search himself, it had been pleasant enough to him to have one of the minister's secretaries with him, following his suggestions, listening to his advice, and showing deference to his experience; but when the young gentleman took the business into his own hands, conducted the whole proceedings, and did not make him acquainted even with all the particulars, his vanity was mortified, and he resolved to assist as little as possible, though he could not refuse to act according to the directions which he received. This determination was so evident, that, before they had reached Gravesend, Wilton felt cause to regret that he had not put his threat in execution, and sent for another messenger. His companion's horse must needs be spared, though he was strong, quick, and needed nothing but the spur; he must be fed here, he must be watered there; and the young gentleman began to fear that delays which were evidently made on purpose, might cause them to be late ere they arrived at the place of their destination. He had remarked, however, that the Messenger was somewhat proud of the beast that carried him, and he thought it in no degree wrong to make use of a stratagem in order to hurry his follower's pace.

After looking at the horse for some time with a marking and critical eye, he said, "That is a fine, powerful horse of yours, Mr. Arden. It is a pity he's so heavy in the shoulder."

"Heavy in the shoulder, Mr. Brown!" said Arden--"I don't think he can be called that, sir, any how; for a really strong, serviceable horse, he's as free in the shoulder as any horse in England."

"I did not exactly mean," replied Wilton, "to say that he was heavy; I only meant that he could not be a speedy horse with that shoulder."

"I don't know that, sir; I can't say that," replied the Messenger, evidently much piqued: "you reckon your horse a swift horse, I should think, Mr. Brown, and yet I'll bet you money, that at any pace you like, for a couple of miles, mine wont be a yard behind."

"Oh, trotting will do, trotting will do," replied Wilton--"there's no such made horse as mine in England. Let him once get to his full pace, and he will out-trot any horse I ever saw."

"Well, sir," replied his companion, "let us put to our spurs and see."

"With all my heart," answered Wilton, and away they accordingly went, trotting as hard as they could go for the next four or five miles. Nevertheless, although the scheme was so far successful, Wilton and the Messenger did not reach the village of High Halstow above an hour before sunset. The horses were by this time tired, and the riders somewhat hungry. Provisions were procured in haste to satisfy the appetite of the travellers, and the horses, too, were fed. It was some time, however, before the tired animals would take their food, and Wilton and his companion at length determined to proceed on foot. Before they did so, as both were perfectly ignorant of the way, application was made to the host for directions, and the reply, "Why, there are three roads you can take!" somewhat puzzled the inquirers, especially when it was followed by a demand of where they were going exactly.

"When I know that," said the landlord, "I shall be able to tell you which is the best road."

"Why, I asked the way to Cowley Castle," said Wilton, both embarrassed and annoyed; for the Messenger stood coolly by, without any attempt to aid him, and, in truth, enjoying a little difficulty.

"But you are not going to Cowley Castle at this time of night," said the man: "why, the only house there is the great house, and that is empty."

"My good friend," said Wilton, "I suppose the next question you will ask me is, what is my business there? I ask you the way to Cowley Castle, and pray, if you can, give me a straightforward answer."

"I beg your pardon, sir," replied the man, with a determined air--"I have given you a straightforward answer. There are three roads, all of them very good ones, and there is, besides, a footpath."

As he spoke, he stared into Wilton's face with a look half dogged, half jocular; but in the end, he added,--

"Come, come, sir--you might as well tell me the matter at once. If you are going to Master Plessis's--the mountseer, as we call him here--I'll put you upon your road in a minute: I mean the gentleman that, folks think, has some dealings with France."

It struck Wilton, instantly, that this gentleman, who was supposed to have dealings with France, must have something to do with the detention of Laura, and he therefore replied, "Perhaps it may be as you suppose, my good friend. At all events, put me upon the principal horse-road towards Cowley Castle."

"Well, sir, well," replied the host, "you have nothing to do but to turn to the right when you go out of the door, and then you will find a road to the left; then take the first road to the right, which will lead you straight down to Cowley Church. Now, if you're going to Master Plessis's, you had better not go farther than that."

"That way will not be difficult to find," replied Wilton; and followed by the Messenger, he quitted the little inn, or rather public-house, for it was no better, and traced accurately the road the landlord had pointed out.

"He had better go no farther than Cowley Church, indeed," said a man who was sitting in the bar, as soon as he was gone; "for if he be going to Master Plessis's, he'll be half a mile beyond the turning by that time."

"Jenkin, Jenkin!" cried the landlord, not minding what his guest said, but addressing a boy who was cleaning some pewter stoups in a kitchen at the end of the passage--"come here, my man. Run down by the lanes as fast as you can go, and tell Master Plessis that there are two gentlemen coming to his house, whose looks

I don't like at all. One is a state messenger, if I'm not much mistaken. I've seen his face before, I'm sure enough, and I think it was when Evans the coiner was taken up at Stroud. You can get there half an hour before them, if you run away straight by the lanes."

The boy lost not a moment, very sure that any one who brought Monsieur Plessis intelligence of importance would get something at least for his pains.

In the meantime, Wilton and his companion walked on. The sky was clear above, but it had already become very dark, and a doubt occurred, both at the first and second turning, as to whether they were right. Wilton and the Messenger had furnished themselves with pistols, besides their swords; and the young gentleman paused for a moment to ascertain that the priming had not fallen out; but nothing would induce the Messenger to do so likewise; for his sullen mood had seized upon him again more strongly than ever, and he merely replied that his pistols would do very well, and that it would be lucky if Mr. Brown were as sure of his way as he was of his pistols.

"I should like you to give me my orders, Mr. Brown," he added, in the same dogged tone, "for I am always glad to know beforehand what it is I am to do, that I may be ready to do it."

"I shall of course give orders," replied Wilton, somewhat sharply, "when they are required, Mr. Arden. At the present moment, however, I have only to tell you that I expect every minute to meet a person who will lead us to the house where Lady Laura is detained. At that house, we shall have to encounter, I understand, a number of persons whose interest and design is to carry her off, probably to the coast of France. I intend to demand her in a peaceable and tranquil manner, and in case they refuse to give her up, must act according to circumstances. I expect your support on all the legal points of the case, such as the due notice of our authority, et cetera; and, in case it should become necessary or prudent either to menace or to use force, I will tell you at the time."

The Messenger made no reply, but sunk again into sullen silence; and Wilton clearly saw that little help, and indeed little advantage, was to be derived from the presence of his self-sufficient attendant, except in as much as the appearance of such a person in his company was likely to produce a moral effect upon those to whom he might be opposed. Messengers of state were in those days very awful people, and employed in general in the arrest of such criminals as were very unlikely to escape the axe if taken. Yet it seldom if ever happened that any resistance was offered to them; and we are told that at the appearance of a single individual of this redoubted species, it often happened three or four traitors, murderers, spies, or pirates, whose fate if taken was perfectly certain, would seem to give up all hope, and surrendering without resistance, would suffer themselves to be led quietly to the shambles.

Thus if Arden did but his mere duty, Wilton knew that the effect of his presence would be great; but as he walked on, he began to entertain new apprehensions. For nearly two miles, no one appeared to guide them to the place of their destination; at length a church, with some cottages gathered round it, announced that they had reached the little hamlet of Cowley, where, as several roads and paths branched off in different directions, he found it advisable to follow the counsel of the landlord, and not go any farther.

He consequently turned back again; but a thin white fog was now beginning to come on--a visitation to which that part of the country near the junction of the Thames and the Medway is very often subject. The cloud rolled forward, and Wilton and the Messenger advanced directly into it; so that at length the hedge could only be distinguished on one side of the road, and beyond it, on either side, nothing could be seen farther than the distance of five or six yards.

The Messenger lingered somewhat behind, muttering, "This is pleasant;" but ere long, as they were approaching the top of a narrow lane which Wilton had before remarked, as they passed, he thought he heard people speaking at a distance, and stopped to listen. The tones were those of a male and a female voice conversing evidently with eagerness, though with slow and measured words and long pauses. Wilton thought that the sound of one voice was familiar to him, though the speaker was at such a distance that he could not catch any of the words.

Not doubting at all, however, that one of the interlocutors was the person who was to guide him on his way, Wilton paused, determined to wait till they came up.

A loud "So be it then!" was at length uttered; and the next moment steps were heard advancing rapidly towards him, and the figure of a man made its appearance through the mist, first like one of the fabled shades upon the dim shores of the gloomy river, but growing into solidity as it came near.

CHAPTER XXIII.

For the right understanding of all that is to follow--strange as it may appear to the reader, we are only just at the beginning of the story--it may be necessary to go back to the house of Monsieur Plessis, and to trace the events of the past day, till we have brought them exactly down to that precise time Wilton was walking, as we have described, with a mist around him both moral and physical, upon the road between High Halstow and Cowley. We must even go beyond that, and introduce the reader into a lady's bedchamber, on the morning of that day, as she was dressing herself after the night's repose; though, indeed, repose it could scarcely be called, for those bright eyes had closed but for a short period during the darkness, and anxiety and grief had been the companions of her pillow. Yet it is not Lady Laura of whom we speak, but of that gentle-looking and beautiful lady whom we have described as sitting in the saloon of Plessis's house, shortly before the conspirators assembled there.

Without any of the aids of dress or ornament, she was certainly a very beautiful being, and as, sitting before the glass, she drew out with her taper fingers the glossy curls of her rich dark hair, nothing could be more graceful than the attitudes into which the whole form was cast. Often as she did so, she would pause and meditate, leaning her head upon her hand for a moment or two. Sometimes she would raise her eyes imploringly towards Heaven, and once those eyes became full of tears. She wiped them away hastily, however, as if angry with herself for giving way, and then proceeded eagerly with the task of the toilet.

While she was thus engaged, some one knocked at the door, which she unlocked, and the next instant, another lady, to whom the reader has been already introduced, entered the chamber. It was the same person whom we have called the Lady Helen, in her interview with Wilton Brown; and there was still in the expression of her countenance that same look of tender melancholy which is generally left upon the face by long grief acting upon an amiable heart. It was, indeed, less the expression of a settled gloom on her own part, than of sympathy with the sorrows of others, rendered more active by sorrows endured herself. On the present occasion she had a note in her hand, which she held out towards the fair girl whom she had interrupted at her toilet, saying, with a faint smile, "There, Caroline--I hope it may bring you good news, dear girl." The other took it eagerly, and broke the seal, with hands that trembled so much that they almost let the paper drop.

"Oh, Lady Helen," cried the younger lady, while the colour came and went in her cheek, and her eyes sparkled, and then again nearly overflowed, "we must, indeed, we must stay over to-day. He says he will come down to see me this afternoon. Indeed we must stay; for it is my last chance, Helen dear, my last chance of happiness in life."

"We will stay, of course, Caroline," replied the other; "but I trust, my poor girl, that if you see him, you will act both wisely and firmly. Let him not move you to yield any farther than you have done; left him not move you, my sweet Caroline, to remain in a degrading and painful state of doubt. Act firmly, and as you proposed but yesterday, in order, at least, if you do no more, not to be, as it were, an accomplice in his ill-treatment of yourself."

"Oh no!" replied the other--"oh no! Fear not, dear lady, that I will deal with him otherwise than firmly. But yet you know he is my husband, Helen, and I cannot refuse to obey his will, except where he requires of me a breach of higher duties."

"Ay," replied the Lady Helen. "When he claims you openly as his wife, Caroline, then he has a right to command, and no one can blame you for obeying; but he must not take the whole advantage of his situation as your husband, without giving you the name and station, or suffering you to assume the character of his wife. Let him now do you justice in these respects, or else, dear Caroline, leave him! fly from him! strive to forget him! Look upon yourself as widowed, and try to bear your sorrow as an infliction from the hand of Heaven, for having committed this action without your father's knowledge and consent."

"Oh, Helen!" replied the other, mournfully, "you know my father was upon the bed of death; you know that Henry was obliged to depart in three weeks; you know that I loved him, and that if I had parted with him then, without giving him the hand I had promised, it might have been years before I saw him again; for then I should have had no title to seek him as his wife, and the ports of France were not likely to be opened to him again. Would you have had me agitate my father at that moment? Could I refuse to be his, under such circumstances, when I believed every word that he said, when I thought that if he departed without being my husband, I might not behold him for many years to come?"

"Forgive me for glancing at the past, poor child," replied her friend--"I meant not to imply a reproach, Caroline; but all I wish is to counsel you to firmness. Let not love get the better of your judgment. But tell him your determination at once, and abide by it when it is told. If you would ever obtain justice for yourself, Caroline, now is the moment. He himself will love and respect you more for it hereafter. He assigns no reason for farther delay; and his letters, hitherto, have certainly suggested no motives which could lead either your judgment or your affection to consent to that which is degrading to yourself. I have seen enough of these things, Caroline, and I know that they always end in misery."

"Misery!" replied the younger lady, "alas! Helen, what have I to expect but misery? Oh, Helen, it is not that he does not openly acknowledge our marriage, and forbids me to proclaim it--it is not that which makes me unhappy. Heaven knows, were that all, I could willingly go on without the acknowledgment. I could shut myself from the day, devote myself to him alone, forswear rank, and station, and the pleasures of affluence, for nothing but his love; so long that, knowing I myself was virtuous, I also knew that he continued to love me well. It is not that, Helen, it is not that; but all which I have heard assures me, that notwithstanding every vow of amendment, of changed life, of constant affection towards me, he is faithless to me in a thousand instances; that his wish of longer concealment proceeds, not from necessity, but from a libertine spirit; in short, Helen, that I have been for a week the creature of his pleasure, but that he never really loved me; that his heart rested with me for an hour, and has now gone on to others."

As she spoke, she sank again into her chair, and clasping her hands together as they rested on her knee, fixed her eyes upon the ground during a moment or two of bitter thought.

The other lady advanced toward her, and after gazing at her for a minute, she kissed her beautiful brow affectionately, saying, "Nevertheless, Caroline, he does love you. He is a libertine by habit, Caroline, I trust not a libertine in heart; and I see in every line that he writes to you that he loves you still, and always will love you. It is my belief, dear Caroline, that if you behave well to him now, firmly, though kindly, gently, though decidedly; if you yield nothing, either to love, or importunity, or remonstrance, but tell him that you now bid him farewell for ever if he so chooses it, and that you will never either see him, or hear from him, or write to him, till he comes openly as your husband, and gives you the same vows and assurance of future affection and good conduct that he did at first--it is my firm conviction, I say, that the love for you which I see is still strong within him, the only good thing perhaps in his heart, will bring him back to you at last. Passion may lead him astray, folly may get the better of reason, evil habits may rule him for a time; but the memory of your sweetness, and your beauty, and your firmness, and your gentleness, will come back upon his mind, even in the society of the gay, the light, and the profligate, and will seem like a diamond beside false stones."

"Hush, hush, hush!" said the younger lady, blushing deeply--"I must not hear such praises, Helen: praises that I do not deserve."

"Nay, my dear child, I speak but what I mean," replied the Lady Helen--"I say that the recollection of you and your young fresh beauty, and your generous mind, will return to his remembrance, my Caroline, at all times and in all circumstances, even the most opposite: in the midst of various enjoyments, in the heated revel, and in the idle pageant; when lonely in his chamber, when suffering distress, or pain, or illness; amidst the reverses and the strife, as well as in the prosperity and the vanities, of the world, he will remember you and love you still. That memory will be to him as a sweet tune that we have loved in our youth, the recollection of which brings with it always visions of the only joys that we have known without alloy. But still, remember, Caroline, that the condition on which this is to be obtained, the condition on which his recollection of you is to be, as it were, a precious antidote to the evils of his heart, is, that you now act towards him with firmness and with dignity."

"But suppose, dear lady," said the other, "that he were to ask me to remain with him, still concealing our marriage. Nay, look not terrified--I am not going to do it. I have told you how I am going to act, and, on my honour, I will keep to my determination. I only ask you what you think would then be the consequences?"

"Destruction both to you and to him," replied the Lady Helen: "he would never look upon you entirely as his wife, he would never treat you entirely as such. You would dwell with him almost as a concubine.--Forgive me, but it must be spoken.--He would grow tired of your beauty, weary of your society; your virtues would be lost upon him, because he would see that firmness was not amongst them, and he would not respect you because you had not respected yourself. There is something, Caroline, in the state and dignity, if I may so call it, which surrounds a virtuous married woman, that has a great effect upon her husband, ay, and a great effect upon herself. There is not one man, Caroline, out of a million, who has genuine nobility of heart enough to stand the test of a long concealed private marriage. I never saw but one, Caroline, and I have mingled with almost every scene of human life, and seen the world with almost all its faces. However, here, there can be no cause which should justly induce you to consent to live with him under such circumstances, and there are a thousand causes to prevent you from so doing. If you were to do it, you would lose your respect for yourself, and how then could you expect that he would retain any for you?"

The conversation was some time protracted in the same tone, and nearly a whole hour was thus passed ere the younger lady was dressed and ready to accompany her friend to breakfast.

Monsieur Plessis was there to do the honours of his table, treating his fair guests not exactly as his equals, but yet behaving not at all as an Englishman, under such circumstances, could have demeaned himself He was polite, attentive, deferential; but he was still Monsieur Plessis in his own house. There can be no doubt that all he furnished them with was amply paid for; but yet he had an air of conferring a favour, and indeed felt that he did so when he received them into his dwelling at all. There was thus an air of gallantry mingled with his respectfulness, a sweet smile that bent his lips when he pressed either of them to their food, a courteous and affable look when he greeted them for the first time that day, all of which spoke that Monsieur Plessis felt that he was laying them under an obligation, and wished to do it in the most graceful manner possible. The breakfast table was beautifully laid out, with damask linen of the finest quality, and more silver than was usually displayed at that day even in families of distinction. Both the ladies seated themselves; and

Plessis was proceeding to recommend some of the most exquisite chocolate which had ever been brought from Portugal--at least so he assured them--when the elder lady interrupted its praises by saying, "Had we not better wait a little, Monsieur Plessis, for the young lady whom we saw yesterday?"

Plessis, however, put his finger on his large nose, saying, "Her breakfast will be taken to her in her chamber, Miladi. There are mysteries in all things, as you well know. Now here you are; and there are nine or ten gentlemen meet at my house every night, from whom I am obliged to hide that you are in the place at all. Here is this young lady, whom, it seems, I should have concealed from you in the same way: only I could not refuse to let you see her and speak to her yesterday, in order that you might be kind to her on board the ship; for she is to go in the ship with you, you know, and she seems quite helpless, and not accustomed to all these things. When the worthy gentlemen found that the ship was not to sail last night, they were in great embarrassment, and charged me strictly not to let her see any one till the ship sailed; and I find they have put a man to watch on both sides of the house, so that no one can go out or come in without being seen. They told me nothing about it; and that was uncivil; but, however, I must keep her to her own room; for the man that they left in the house, with my consent, to keep guard over her, watches sharply also."

The elder lady said nothing, but the colour of the younger heightened a good deal at this detail, and she started up indignantly as soon as Plessis had finished, exclaiming, "Nonsense, sir. I never heard of such a thing!--You, a man of honour and gallantry," she continued, with a gay smile, such as had once been common to her countenance, passing over it for a moment--"you, a man of honour and gallantry, Monsieur Plessis, consenting to see a lady discourteously used and maltreated in your house, and a stranger put as a spy upon you in your own dwelling. Fie! For shame! I never heard of such a thing! I shall go immediately to her, with your compliments, and ask her to come to breakfast. And let me see if this spy upon you will dare to stop me."

"Oh no, Miladi," replied Plessis, "he is not a spy upon me; but I said myself I would have nothing to do with the young lady being detained; that it was no part of my business, and should not be done by my people; that they might have the rooms at the west corner of the house if they liked, but that I would have nothing to do with it. I beseech you, dear lady," he continued, seeing Caroline moving towards the door--"I beseech you, do not meddle; for this is a very dangerous and bad business, and I fear it will end ill, Nay, nay!" and springing towards the door, he placed himself between it and the lady, bowing lowly, with his hand upon his heart, and exclaiming, "Humbly on my knees I kiss your beautiful feet, and beseech you not to meddle with this bad business."

"A very bad business, indeed," said Caroline; "and it is for that very reason that I am going to meddle, Monsieur Plessis. Do me the favour of getting out of my way. I thought you were a man of gallantry and spirit, Monsieur Plessis.--I am determined; so there is no use in opposing me."

Plessis shrugged up his shoulders, bowed his head low, and with a look which said as plainly as any look could say, "I see there is never any use of opposing a woman," he suffered the fair lady to pass out, while her friend remained sitting thoughtfully at the table.

The lady whom we have called Caroline walked quietly along one of the corridors of the house till she came to a spot where a man in the garb of a sailor was sitting on a large chest, with his elbows on his two knees, and his chin on his two hands, looking very much wearied with his watch, and swinging one of his feet backwards and forwards disconsolately. There was a door farther on, and towards it the lady walked, but found that it was locked, though the key was on the outside. The sailor personage had started up as she passed, and then gazed at her proceedings with no small surprise; but as she laid her hand upon the lock, he came forward, saying, "Ma'am, what do you want there?".

"I want," replied the lady, turning round, and looking at him from head to foot, "I merely to call this young lady to breakfast. Be so good as to open the door: the lock is rather stiff."

She spoke so completely with the tone of calm authority, that the man did not even hesitate, but opened the door wide, taking it for granted that she had some right to enter. The lady was about to go in; but suddenly a feeling of apprehension seized her, lest the man should shut the door and lock it upon her also; and pausing in the doorway, she addressed Lady Laura, who we need scarcely tell the reader was within,--"I have come to ask you," she said, "if you will go with me to breakfast."

"Oh gladly, gladly!" cried the poor girl, darting forward, and holding out her hands to her; and Caroline, drawing one fair arm through her own, led her onward to the room where she had left the Lady Helen.

The man paused and hesitated, and then followed the two ladies along the passage; but before he was near enough to hear what was said, Caroline had whispered to her companion, "It is already done: I have had an answer to my note, which went in the same packet, so that the place of your detention is now certainly known to those who will not fail to send you aid."

The bright joy that came up in the eyes of Laura might very well have betrayed to the man who guarded her, had he seen her face, that she has received more intelligence than his employers could have wished. He followed, however, at some distance, without taking any notice; and seeming to think it enough to watch her movements, and prevent her egress from the house, he seated himself again near the door of the chamber where breakfast had been prepared, while Laura and her fair companion entered the room.

They found the Lady Helen and Monsieur Plessis in eager conversation, the lady having just announced to him her intention of delaying their departure till another day; and he, who was in fact part proprietor of the vessel which was to bear them to France, and was actuated by very different views, urging her eagerly to follow her first intention of sailing that night. He made representations of all sorts of dangers and difficulties which were to arise from the delay; the two ladies were likely to be arrested; he was likely to be ruined; the master of the ship would sail without them; and in short, everything was represented as about to happen which could induce them to take their departure with all speed.

The Lady Helen, however, was resolute. She replied that, from what she had heard in London, she was convinced there was not the least chance whatsoever of their even being inquired after, and much less of their being arrested; that his ruin was only likely to be a consequence of the arrest, and therefore that was disposed of. Then again, in regard to the captain of the vessel sailing without them, she said that was improbable, inasmuch as he would thereby lose the large sum he was to receive, both for bringing them thither and taking them back.

Now, though Monsieur Plessis was, in his way, a very courageous and determined person, who in dealing with his fellow men could take his own part very vigorously, and, as we have shown, successfully, yet he was much feebler in the presence of a lady, and on the present occasion, with three to one, they certainly made him do anything they liked. The consequence was, that Laura was permitted to spend a great part of that day with the two accidental tenants of Monsieur Plessis's house; and not a little comfort, indeed, was that permission to her.

It was a moment when any society would have been a great consolation and relief. But there was in the two ladies with whom she was now associated for the time much more to interest and to please. The manners of each were of the highest tone; the person of each was highly pleasing; and when Laura turned to the Lady Helen, and marked the gentle pensiveness of her beautiful countenance, listened to the high, pure, noble words that hung upon her lips, and marked the deep feelings which existed beneath an exterior that people sometimes thought cold, the remembrance of her own mother rose up before her, and she felt a sort of clinging yearning towards a being who resembled her in so many respects.

With the younger lady, too, she had many a thought and many a feeling in common. Caroline was a few years older than herself, and evidently more acquainted with the world; but there were deep strong feelings apparent in every word she uttered--a thoughtfulness (if we may so express ourselves) which blended with an air of carelessness--a depth to be seen even through occasional lightness, which was only like a profound river rippled by a rapid breeze. Each had subjects for thought; each had more or less matter for grief or apprehension; but each found relief in the society of the other; and the day passed over more happily than Laura could have imagined it would have done in such circumstances.

Towards evening, indeed, she became anxious and apprehensive, for no attempt to deliver her had, apparently, been made, and she had been warned that she was to embark for France that night. From this apprehension, however, the Lady Helen speedily relieved her, by assuring her that there was no other ship to convey her but that which was hired to take herself and her young friend to France, and that they had determined upon putting off their departure till the succeeding night.

About the same hour, however, Caroline became uneasy and agitated. She rose often; she looked often at her watch; she gazed out froth the window; she turned her eyes to the sky; and in the end she retired for a time to her own chamber, and returned shortly after, dressed for going out, with a short black cloak, richly trimmed, cast over her shoulders, and a silk hood, stiffened with whalebone and deeply fringed with lace, covering her head and the greatest part of her face.

"Who are you going to take with you, my dear child, to show you the way?" said the Lady Helen.

"No one, sweet lady," replied the other. "While you were away from me in London I had plenty of opportunity to explore every path round this house, and the place is so distinctly marked, that neither he nor I can mistake it."

Lady Helen looked in her face for a moment with an expression somewhat sad as well as inquiring; and her beautiful companion, as if comprehending at once what she meant, advanced quietly towards her, knelt on the footstool at her feet, and putting her two hands in hers, she said, "I promise you most solemnly, dearest lady--most solemnly and firmly do I promise, not to suffer myself to be shaken in any one of the resolutions which I have taken with your advice."

"Thank you, my child, thank you," cried the elder lady, "thank you for giving me the prospect, Caroline, of seeing you ultimately happy. But oh, do not be late, my sweet child. Return to us soon. The country is in a distracted state--the hour is very late. You see it is already growing dusk."

"I will return as soon as I can," replied Caroline, and left the room.

The man who was still on watch in the passage looked at her attentively, but said nothing; and Plessis, who was at the door speaking to two ship-boys, said merely, "It is very cold and very late, madame. I wonder you don't get cold with such late walks."

She made no reply, but went on: and taking one or two turns through the tortuous lanes in the neighbourhood, arrived at a spot where a small obelisk, of no very graceful form or great dimensions, planted in the middle of the road, marked the boundary of four distinct parishes. She paused there for a moment, and leaned upon the landmark, as if from fatigue, weakness, or agitation. The light was now dim, but it was not yet dark; and in a moment or two she saw a figure appear suddenly in the lane before her.

It advanced rapidly towards her, and she pressed her hand tight upon her heart. One might have heard it throbbing. The gentleman came on with a pace like lightning, and held out his hand towards her. She gave him her hand, but turned away her head; and after gazing on her for a moment, he drew her gently to his bosom, saying, "One kiss at least, my Caroline."

She did not refuse it, and he pressed her warmly to his heart. There was a moment's silence, and then his arms relaxed their hold, and he exclaimed, "Oh Heaven!"

He then drew her arm within his, and walked on with her.

"Oh, Caroline," he said at length, "would that you did know how I love you!"

"If I did know, Sherbrooke," she replied, "that you really did love me, it would make me far, far happier than I am. But how can I believe it, Sherbrooke? how can I believe it?"

"Is it," he demanded, "is it because I have asked you to conceal our marriage a little longer? Is it for that reason that you doubt my love? Is it for that reason that you have come over to England, risking all and everything, affecting my fate in ways that you have no idea of? Is it for this, Caroline?"

There was a pause for several minutes, and at length she answered,--

"Not entirely. There may have been many reasons, Sherbrooke, joined therewith. There were many that I stated in my letters to you. There were others that you might have imagined. Was it unnatural that I should wish to see my husband? Was it unnatural I should believe that he would be glad to see me? As I told you, the circumstances were changed; my father was dead; I had none to protect me in France; the Lady Helen was coming to England. When she was gone, I was left quite alone. But oh, Sherbrooke, tell me, tell me, what cause have I had to believe that you love me? Have you not neglected me? Have you not forgotten me? Have you not----"

"Never, never, Caroline!" he cried, vehemently--"in my wildest follies, in my rashest acts, I have thought of you and loved you. I have remembered you with affection, and with grief, and with tenderness. Memory, sad memory, has come upon me in the midst of the maddest efforts for gaiety, and cast me into a fit of deep, anxious, sorrowful, repentant, remorseful thought, which I could not shake off: it seemed as if some vengeful spirit seized upon me for its prey, and dinned in my ears the name of love and Caroline, till my heart was nearly broken."

"And the moment after," she said, "what was it, Sherbrooke, that you did? Did you sit down and write to Caroline, to her who was giving every thought to you? or did you fly to the side of some gay coquette, to dissipate such painful thoughts in her society? or did you fly to worse, Sherbrooke?"

He was silent. "Sherbrooke," she added, after a time, "I wish not to reproach you. All I wish is to justify myself, and the firm unchangeable resolution which I have been obliged to take. I have always tried to close my ears against everything that might make me think less highly of him I love. But tales would reach me--tales most painful to hear; and at length I was told that you were absolutely on the eve of wedding another."

"They told you false!" exclaimed Lord Sherbrooke, wildly and vehemently-- "whoever said so, lied. I have been culpable, and am culpable, Caroline; but not to that extent. I never dreamed of wedding her. Did I not know it could not be? But you speak of your resolutions. Let me know what they are at once! To declare all, I suppose! Publicly to produce the proofs of our marriage! To announce to my father, already exasperated against me, that in this, too, I have offended him! To call down, even upon your own head, the revenge of a man who has never yet, in life, gone without it! To tell all--all, in short?"

"No, no, no, Sherbrooke!" she said--"I am going to do none of all these things. Angry and thwarted, you do not do that justice to your wife which you ought. You speak, Sherbrooke, as if you did not know me. I will do none of these things. You do not choose to acknowledge me as your wife. You are angry at my having come to England. I will not announce our marriage till the last moment. I will not publish it till my dying hour, unless I be driven to it by some terrible circumstance. I will return to France. I will live as the widow of a man that I have loved. But I will never see you more, Sherbrooke; I will never hear from you more; I will never write to you more; till you come openly and straightforwardly to claim me as your wife in the face of all the world. Whenever you declare me to be your wife, I will do all the duties of a wife: I will be obedient to your will, not alone from duty but from love; but till you do acknowledge me as your wife, you can plead no title to such submission."

"Ah, Caroline," replied Lord Sherbrooke, "you speak well and wisely, but coldly too. You can easily resign the man that you once loved. It costs you but little to give him over to his own course; to afford him no solace, no consolation, no advice; to deprive him of that communication, which, distant as it was, might have saved him from many an error. It costs you nothing to pronounce such words as you have spoken, and to sever our fate for ever."

"It is you that sever it," she replied, in a sad and reproachful tone. "Sherbrooke, Sherbrooke, you do me wrong--you know you do me wrong--Oh, how great wrong! Do you think I have shed no tears? Do you think my heart has not been wrung? Do you think my hours have not passed in anguish, my days in sadness, and my nights in weeping? Oh, Sherbrooke, since you left me, what has been my fate? To watch for some weeks the death-bed of a father, from whose mind the light had already departed; to sorrow over his tomb; to watch the long days for the coming of my husband--of the husband whom all had doubted, all had condemned, but my own weak heart, whose vows of amendment I had believed, to whose entreaties I had yielded, even to that rashest of all acts, a secret marriage; to find him delay his coming from day to day, and to see the sun that rose upon me in solitary sadness go down in grief; to lose the hope that cheered me; to look for his letters as the next boon; to read them and to weep over them; to remain in exile, not only from my native land, but also from him to whom I had given every feeling of my heart, to whom I had yielded all that a virtuous woman can yield; to remain in a strange court, to which I had no longer any tie, in which I had no longer any protector; and every time I heard his name mentioned, to hear it connected with some tale of scandal, or stigmatized for some new act of vice; and worse, worse than all, Sherbrooke, to be sought, idly sought, by men that I despised, or hated, or was indifferent to, and forbade to say the words which would have ended their pursuit at once, 'I am already a wife.' Sherbrooke, you have given me months and months of misery already. I weep not now, even with the thought of parting from you for ever; but it is, I believe, that the fountain of my tears is dried up and exhausted. Oh, Sherbrooke, when first I knew you, who was so blithe and joyous as myself? and now, what have you made me?"

He was much moved, and was about to speak; but she held up her hand beseechingly, and said, "Let me go on--let me go on. You said it costs me little to act as I proposed to act. Think, Sherbrooke, think what it does really cost me. Even were I all selfishness, how bitter is the part that I have assigned myself to play! To pass my time in solitude, without the pleasures of youth and gaiety; debarring myself from all the advantages of an unmarried woman, yet without the name, the blessings, the station, the dignity, of a wife; voluntarily depriving myself of every sort of consolation, relinquishing even hope. But if I am not altogether selfish, Sherbrooke--and you have no cause to say I am so--if, as you know too well, there is deep, and permanent, and pure and true affection for you at the bottom of my heart, judge what the after-hours of life will be, judge what a long dreary lapse lies before me, between the present instant and the grave."

Sherbrooke was moved, and again and again he assured her that he loved her more than any other being upon earth; and the conversation continued for nearly half an hour longer. He begged her to stay with him in England, still concealing their marriage; he pressed her in every way to break her resolution; he urged her, if it were but for one week, to remain with him, in order to see whether he could not make arrangements to render their marriage public. But she remembered her resolution, and held to it firmly, and even rejected that last proposal, fearing consequences equally dangerous to herself and to him. Opposition began to make him angry; he entered not into her reasons; he saw not the strength of her motives; he spoke some harsh and unkind words, which caused her to weep, and then again he was grieved at having pained her, and kissed the tears away, and urged and argued again. Still she remained firm, however, and again he became irritated.

At the end of half an hour, both Caroline and her husband heard the sound of feet approaching them on both sides; and though it seemed that the people who were coming from the direction of Plessis's house walked lightly and with caution, yet there were evidently many of them, and Caroline became alarmed for her husband.

"The people are coming from the house, Sherbrooke," she cried--"they must not, oh, they must not find you here!"

"Why not?" he demanded, sharply.

"Oh, because they are a dangerous and a desperate set," she said--"bent, I am sure, from what I have heard, upon bloody and terrible schemes. Me they will let pass, but I fear for you--the very name of your father would be sufficient to destroy you, with them. We must part, indeed we must part!"

"And can you, Caroline," he demanded, still lingering, but speaking in a bitter and irritated tone, angry alike with himself, and her, and with the interruption--"can you hold to your cold and cruel resolution, now?"

"I can, I must, Sherbrooke," she replied,--"nothing shall shake me."

"Well, then, be it so!" he answered sharply; and turning away, walked rapidly up the lane.

Caroline stood, for a single instant, on the spot where he left her; but then all the feelings with which she had struggled during the whole of that painful conversation with her husband, seemed to break loose upon her at once, and over-power her. Her head grew giddy, a weary faintness seemed to come over her heart, and she sank, unconscious, on the ground.

The next moment six or seven men came quickly up.

"Here's a woman murdered!" cried one--"and the fellow that did it is off up the lane."

A few hasty exclamations of surprise and pity followed, and then another man exclaimed, in a hasty and impatient tone, "Take her up in your arms, Jim, and bring her along. Perhaps we may find this Messenger the boy talked of, and the murderer together; but let us make haste, or we shall lose both."

"Mind," said another, speaking almost at the same time, "don't knock the Messenger's brains out. We will just take and plant him in the marsh, tie his arms, and put him up to the arm-pits. The boys will find him there, when they come to drive back the cattle.--The lady don't seem quite dead, I think."

"Bring her along! bring her along!" cried another voice--"we shall miss all, if you are so slow;" and thus speaking, the leader of the party quickened his pace, while the others, having raised the lady from the ground, bore her onward towards the end of the lane.

CHAPTER XXIV.

We have said that Wilton Brown paused and gazed through the mist at the figure of a man advancing towards him, and to the reader it need not be told who the person was that thus came forward. To Wilton, however, the conviction was brought more slowly; for though he had heard the sound of a familiar voice, yet it seemed so improbable that voice should be the voice of Lord Sherbrooke, that the idea never struck him, till the figure became so distinct as not to leave a doubt.

"Good God, Sherbrooke!" he exclaimed, advancing towards him at length--"can it be you?"

"And I may well ask, Wilton, if it be you," said Lord Sherbrooke, in a tone so sharp and angry, so unlike his usual voice and manner of speaking, that Wilton drew back astonished, imagining that he had given his friend some unknown offence. But Lord Sherbrooke grasped his arm, exclaiming, "Hark! There they are! They are close upon us, Wilton! I have fallen in with a nest of Jacobites, I fancy, ready for an outbreak, and they are after me. Have you any arms?"

"Here are plenty of pistols, my lord," said the Messenger, who knew him.

"Ah, Arden, is that you?" he exclaimed. "Give me a pistol!" and he took one from the Messenger's hand. "Here are three of us now, Wilton," he exclaimed, with a laugh, "and one of us a Messenger: enough surely for any dozen Jacobites in England."

There was something wild, hasty, and strange in Lord Sherbrooke's manner, which startled and alarmed Wilton a good deal.

"For Heaven's sake, Sherbrooke," he said, "do nothing rashly. Let us see who they are before you act."

"Oh, I will do nothing rash," replied Sherbrooke. "But here they come! just like Jacobites, gabbling at every step. Who goes there, my masters?" he exclaimed, at the same moment. "Don't advance, don't advance! We are armed! The first man that advances, I shoot upon the spot!"

"Those are the men! those are the men!" cried a loud voice from the other party, who were now seen coming up in a mass. "Rush upon them! Rush upon them, and tie the Messenger!"

"Oh, oh!" cried Arden. "They have found me out, have they! Stand by me, my lord! Stand by me, Mr. Brown! They are rushing on!"

"Then here's for the midst of them!" cried Lord Sherbrooke; and instantly levelling his pistol, he fired, though Wilton was in the very act of holding forth his hand to stop him.

The moment the fatal flash had taken place, there was a reel back amongst the advancing party, though they were at several yards' distance when the pistol was fired. A confusion, a gathering together, a murmur, succeeded; and while Lord Sherbrooke was in the very act of exclaiming, "Give me another pistol, Arden!" there was heard, from amongst the party who had been approaching, a loud voice, exclaiming, "By, he has shot the lady!--and she was only fainting, after all. See how the blood flows!"

The words were perfectly distinct. Lord Sherbrooke's hand, which had just seized the other pistol that the Messenger had held out to him, suddenly let it drop upon the ground. It was not possible to see the expression of his face fully, for his head was turned away; but Wilton felt him grasp his arm, as if for support, trembling in every limb.

"Good God! What have you done, Sherbrooke?" exclaimed his friend.

"I have killed her! I have killed her!" cried Lord Sherbrooke, gasping for breath--"I have killed the dear unfortunate girl!" and letting go Wilton's arm, he rushed forward at once into the midst of the other party, exclaiming, "Stand back! Let me forward! She is my wife! Stand out of my way! How, in the name of Heaven, did she--"

He left off, without concluding; and nobody answered. But the tone of bitter grief and agony in which Lord Sherbrooke spoke was not to be mistaken: there was in it the overpowering energy of passionate grief; and everybody made way for him. In a moment he bad snatched the form of the unhappy lady from the man who held her in his arms, and supporting her himself, partly on his knee, partly on his bosom, he kissed her again and again vehemently, eagerly, we may almost say frantically, exclaiming, "And I have killed thee, my Caroline! I have killed thee, my beloved, my wife, my own dear wife! I have killed thee, noble, and true, and kind! Oh, open your eyes, dear one, open your eyes and gaze upon me for a minute! She is living, she is living!" he added wildly--"she does open her eyes!--Quick, some one call a surgeon!--A hundred guineas to the first who brings me a surgeon!--God of Heaven! how has this happened?--Oh yes, she is living, she is reviving!--Wilton, for pity's sake, for mercy's sake, help me!"

Wilton Brown had followed Lord Sherbrooke rapidly; for a sudden apprehension had crossed his mind immediately the words were pronounced, "He has shot the lady," lest by some accident Lady Laura had fallen into the hands of the people who were approaching, and that she it was who had been wounded or killed by the rash act of his friend. The moment he came up, however, he perceived that the lady's face was unknown to him, and he saw also that the men who stood round, deprived of all power and activity by a horrible event, which they only vaguely comprehended, were anything but the persons he had expected to see. They seemed to be almost all common sailors; and though they were in general evidently Englishmen, they were habited more in the fashion of the Dutch seamen of that day. They were well armed, it is true, but still they bore not the slightest appearance of being connected with Sir John Fenwick and the party to which lie was attached; and the horror and consternation which seemed to have taken possession of them all, at the injury which had been inflicted on the unhappy lady, showed that they were anything but feelingless or hardened.

One rapid glance over the scene before his eyes had shown Wilton this; and he now stood beside Lord Sherbrooke, gazing with painful interest on a picture, the full horror of which he divined better than the others who surrounded them.

Almost as Lord Sherbrooke spoke, however, and before Wilton could reply, the lady made a slight movement of her hand, and raised her head. Her eyes were open, and she turned to Lord Sherbrooke, gazing on his face for a moment, as if to be certain who he was.

"Oh, Sherbrooke," she said at length, in a faint voice, "fly, fly!--I was very foolish to faint.--I am better now. The men will be upon you in a minute--Oh Heaven, they are all round us! Oh how weak it was to faint and keep you here till they have taken you.--I am better now," she said, in answer to a whispered inquiry of Lord Sherbrooke, as he pressed her to his heart. "But I must have hurt my shoulder in falling, for it pains me very much." And putting her hand towards it, she drew it suddenly away, exclaiming, "Good Heaven, it is blood!"

"Yes, dearest--yes, beloved," replied Lord Sherbrooke--"it is blood--blood shed by your husband's hand; but oh, inadvertently, clear girl. I rashly fired amongst the men that were pursuing me, and have killed the only woman that I ever loved!" And he struck his hand vehemently against his forehead, with a gesture of despair that could not be mistaken.

"Come, come, young gentleman," said a man who seemed the leader of the bluff sailors around him, "don't take on so. Some one has gone for a surgeon. There's a clever one at Halstow, I know, and mayhap the young lady is not so much hurt. At all events, you did not do it to hurt her, that's clear enough; and I rather fancy we've all been in a mistake together. For if you were flying from people looking out to take you, you were not the goods we were after--for we were looking for people that were coming to take us.

"They came down and said that a gentleman had come down with a Messenger to look after our little traffic, and have some of us up for it. Now we intended to plant the Messenger in the bog till we had got all things ready and the ship off, and it was him and his people we were after. But come along--bring down the lady to Master Plessis's. She will be taken good care of there, I warrant you. Here, Jack Vanoorst!--you're a bit of a surgeon yourself, for you doctored my head when the Frenchman broke my crown one day. See if you can't stop the blood, at least till we get the lady to old Plessis's, and the surgeon comes."

A broad-built elderly man advanced, and, with whatever materials could be obtained upon the spot, made a sort of bandage and compress by the dim light, and applied it dexterously enough, while Caroline lay with her head upon her husband's bosom, and her hand clasped in his.

Sherbrooke looked down in her face while this was done with agony depicted in his countenance; nor was that agony rendered the less by seeing a faint look of happiness come over her face as she thus rested, and by feeling her hand press gently upon his. It all seemed to say, "I could willingly die thus."

When the bandage had been applied, Lord Sherbrooke, though he shook in every limb with agitation and anxiety, took her in his arms and raised her, saying to the men, "Now show me the way."

But that way was long. The young nobleman put forth his strength too much at first in the effort to carry her quickly, and after bearing her on for about a mile, he paused and faltered.

"Let one of our people carry her," said the captain of the vessel, which was lying in the river at no great distance from Plessis's house--"there is near a mile to go yet."

Lord Sherbrooke turned and looked round. Wilton was close by his side.

"Wilton," he said, "Wilton, you take her. With the exception of herself, you are my best friend. Gently, oh gently! She is my wife, Wilton, and I know you will not mind the burden."

"Pardon me, lady," said Wilton, as he took her gently out of Lord Sherbrooke's arms, and she raised her head with a faint look of inquiry; "it is your husband's sincere friend, and I will bear you as carefully as if I were your brother."

She made no opposition; but no answer, only stretching forth her left arm, which was the unwounded one, to Lord Sherbrooke: she let her hand rest in his, as if she wished him to retain it; and Wilton remarked, but not displeased, that she suffered not her head to rest upon his bosom, as it had done upon that of his friend.

Considerably taller, and altogether of a more powerful frame than Lord Sherbrooke, he bore her with greater ease; but still anxiety made it seem an age till a glimmering light was seen through the trees at no great distance.

Lord Sherbrooke was then in the act of proposing to carry her again; but the good sailor who had spoken before interfered, saying, "No, no, let him carry her. It will only hurt her to change so. There's the house close by, and he's stronger than you are; and not knocked down with fright, you see, either, as you are, naturally enough.--Run on, boy, run on," he continued, somewhat sharply, to a lad who was with them--"run on, and tell old Plessis to get down a mattress to carry the lady up in."

The boy sped away to execute this kind and prudent order; and in a few minutes more, the whole party stood upon the little stone esplanade before the dwelling of Monsieur Plessis. That worthy personage himself was down, and already in a state of great anxiety and tribulation, being one of those who have an excessive dislike to anything which may bring upon them too much notice of any kind.

The mattress, too, had been brought down, but when Wilton gazed through the door, he turned quickly to his friend, saying, "I had better carry her up at once, Sherhrooke. I can do it easily, and it will save her the pain of changing her position more than once."

Without waiting for any one's consent, he accordingly began to mount the staircase, and had just reached the balustrade of the little sort of square vestibule at top, when the door of an opposite room opened, and the Lady Helen stood before him.

To Wilton, who knew nothing of all the secrets of Plessis's house, which the reader is already informed of, the sight was like that of an apparition; and to the Lady Helen herself, the sight of Wilton bearing Caroline in his arms, while the light of the lamp that Plessis carried before them shone upon the pale but still beautiful countenance of the poor girl, and showed her dress and that of Wilton both thickly stained and spotted with blood, was not less astounding.

"Oh, Wilton, Wilton," she cried--"what is this?--Caroline, my sweet Caroline, for Heaven's sake speak!--for Heaven's sake look at me!"

The next moment, however, her eyes fell upon Lord Sherbrooke; his countenance also as pale as death, his coat, and collar, and face also bloody.

"Oh young man, young man," she cried, "is it you that have done this?"

"Yes, Lady Helen," he answered, rather bitterly--"yes, after nearly killing her in another way, it is I who have shed her blood. But the first was the criminal act, not the last. The shot was unintentional: the wounds given by my words were the guilty ones."

"No, no, Sherbrooke!" said Caroline, raising her head faintly, and again stretching out her hand towards him--"No, no, dear Henry. You love me; that is enough!"

She could speak no more; and Plessis, whose senses were in a state of greater precision than those of any other person, exclaimed, eagerly, "Don't stand here talking about it, but carry the lady to her bedchamber.--This way, young gentleman; this way, this way!"

And passing by, he led onward to the room in which the unfortunate lady had received her husband's note that very morning. Wilton laid her gently on the bed; and closing her eyes for a moment, she gave a slight shudder, either with chilliness or pain. But a movement in the apartment caused her to look round again, and she said, eagerly, "Do not leave me, Sherbrooke! Do not leave me, my husband. You must stay with me NOW."

"Leave you, my Caroline!" he said, "oh no! I will never leave you more! I must atone for what I have done. Only promise me, promise me, Caroline, to live, to forgive, and to bless me."

"I do forgive you, I do bless you, Sherbrooke," she answered.

Before he could reply, a gentleman habited in a riding dress, and a large red roquelaure, entered the room hastily, threw off his hat and cloak, and advanced at once with a somewhat rough air to the bedside.

"What is this?" he said, quickly, but not in an ungentle tone. "Where is the lady hurt?--Bring me linen and water.--You may give her a little wine too.--She is faint from loss of blood;" and advancing to the bedside, he took Caroline's hand kindly in his own, saying, "Do not be alarmed, my dear. These things happen every day in battle; and women get well better than soldiers, for they are more patient and resigned. I see where the wound is. Do not be afraid;" and he put his hand upon her shoulder, running it round on both sides. The moment he had done so, he looked about him with a bright and beaming smile upon his lip, and the colour coming somewhat up into his cheek.

"She will do well," he said--"let no one alarm themselves: the ball has passed upon the right of the artery, and I feel it just above the scapula. She will do well!"

An audible "Thank God!" burst from every lip around; and Caroline herself, at the sudden change, from the apprehension of death to the hope of life, burst into silent tears.

"What are all these men doing here?" demanded the good surgeon, turning bluffly round. "Leave none but the women with me, and not too many of them."

The sailors began to move away at this command, and Wilton followed; but Lord Sherbrooke kept his place, saying, "I must remain!"

"And why should you remain, sir?" demanded the surgeon. "Who are you?"

"I am her husband, sir," replied Lord Sherbrooke, firmly and distinctly.

"Oh, sir, that makes a very great difference," replied the surgeon. "I make you a very low bow, and have nothing to say; only I hope you will behave quietly and rationally, and talk as little as possible."

"I will do everything, sir," replied Lord Sherbrooke, with a somewhat stately look--"I will do everything that may tend to promote the recovery of one I love so well."

At this moment, Wilton was in the doorway: but the Lady Helen laid her hand upon his arm, saying, "Wait for me in the neighbouring room, Wilton. I must speak with you before you go."

Wilton promised to remain, and quitted the chamber. He found at the top of the stairs the greater part of the sailors whom he had seen before, and with them Plessis himself and another man.

The sailors were talking with Plessis vehemently; and Wilton soon found that the worthy Frenchman was using all his powers of vituperation in various tongues--French and English, with a word or two of Dutch every now and then, and some quaint specimens of Portuguese--to express his indignation at the sailors for the unlucky business in which they had engaged.

The master of the vessel was defending himself stoutly, saying, "Why, didn't I meet the boy from the Blackamoor's Head at the very door of the place here? and didn't he tell me that there was a man coming down with a Messenger of State to seize the ship and the cargo, and you, and I, and every one else?"

"Poo! nonsense, nonsense!" cried Plessis: "all stuff and exaggeration. No Messenger, I dare say, at all. So be off, all of you, as fast as you can go; and get out of the way, for fear of any inquiries being made."

"Why here's the young gentleman himself!" cried the master: "he don't look like a Messenger, sure enough. But there was another man that ran away, he may have been the Messenger."

The man looked to Wilton as he spoke, who instantly replied, "You are right, sir. He was a Messenger; but neither he nor I came hither about anything referring to you. Indeed, neither of us even knew of your existence before we saw you."

At that moment, the stranger who was standing beside Plessis, and who was very different from the sailors in appearance, stepped forward to Wilton, and said in a low tone, "May I, sir, ask your name?"

The countersign that Green had given him immediately returned to Wilton's memory, and he replied, "My name is Brown, sir, but it might as well have been Green."

"Oh no, sir," replied the stranger, in the same tone, "every man should keep his right name, and be in his right place, which is the case with yourself in both respects at present;" and turning to Plessis, he said, "This is a friend of the Colonel's, Plessis. He sent me down to meet him and bring him here, because he could not come himself."

"Oh, oh!" said Plessis, looking wise, "that's all right, then. I saw that he spoke to the Lady Helen. Take him into the saloon, Captain, and I'll come to you in a minute, as soon as I've got the house clear, and everything quiet again. I expect some gentlemen to meet here to-night, to take their bowl of punch, you know."

"This way, sir," said the person whom the Frenchman had called Captain, turning to Wilton, and leading him on into the large room, which was now quite vacant. The moment that he was there, and the door closed, the stranger came close up to him, saying, "Where is the Messenger? Had you not a Messenger with you? I waited on the road for you three-quarters of an hour."

"I rather think," replied Wilton, "that I was misdirected by the landlord of the inn, and a series of unhappy mistakes has been the consequence."

"Which are not over yet," exclaimed the other; "for here are we, only two men, with very likely a dozen or two against us, with no power or authority to take the lady from out of their hands, and with nothing but our swords and pistols."

"Oh no!" answered Wilton--"you mistake. I have sufficient authority both from her father and from the Secretary of State."

"Ay, but not like the face of a Messenger!" replied the other--"that is the best authority in the world with people like these. By Heaven, the only way that we can act is to make a bold push for it at once, to get hold of the young lady, and carry her off before these men arrive. Plessis is sending away all the sailors: he'll not try much to oppose us himself. There is one man, I see, at the end of the other corridor, but we can surely manage him; and very likely we may get the start of the others by an hour or so."

"Let us lose not a moment," answered Wilton. "I will send for the Lady Helen, who may give us more information."

"Let me go and get it from Plessis himself," replied the man "I will be back in a minute. I know how to deal with the rogue of a Frenchman better than you do. If he comes back with me, take a high tone with him; determination is everything."

Thus saying, he quitted the room, and for about five minutes Wilton remained alone meditating over what had passed, if that could be called meditating, which was nothing but a confused series of indistinct images, all out of their proper form and order.

CHAPTER XXV.

THE first person that entered the room was the Lady Helen, who came forward towards her young friend with her eyes sparkling and a smile upon her lips.

"Oh, my dear boy," she cried, "this has been a terrible night, but she is better: there is every hope of her doing well. The ball has been extracted in a moment, the bleeding has ceased, and the comfort of her husband's love will be more to her--far more to her, than the best balm physician or surgeon could give. But now tell me, Wilton, what brings you here? Did you come with this gay gallant, or have you--though I trust and believe that you have not--have you taken any part in the wild schemes of these rash, intemperate, and vicious men?"

"I am taking part in no schemes, dear lady," replied Wilton. "I only come here to frustrate evil purposes. I came furnished with authority, and accompanied by a Messenger of State, to deliver Lady Laura Gaveston, who, I understand, is at this very moment in this house."

"That is most strange," said the Lady Helen--"I wrote to--to him who--who--whom you saw me with; in short, to tell him that they had brought the poor girl here, never thinking that you, my boy--"

"It was the person you speak of," interrupted Wilton, "who told me of her being here. One of his people is in the house with me at this present moment; but the Messenger has fled in the late affray. I understand that a number of the men who brought her hither are to be here to-night: we shall be then but two against many, if we delay; and it is absolutely necessary that we should find out where the lady is, and carry her off at once."

"Oh! I will find her in a moment," replied the Lady Helen. "But I know not whether they will suffer her to pass out of her chamber."

At that moment, however, Plessis, and the personage whom he called Captain, entered the room in eager conversation.

"It will be ruin and destruction to me," cried Plessis--"I cannot permit it! I cannot hear of it! nor can you manage it. There are three men here, one in the house, and one at each gate. You are only two."

"But we are two men together, and two strong men, too," replied the Captain, "and they are all separate. So I tell you we will do it."

"Oh, if you choose to use force, you may," replied Plessis; "but the consequence be upon your own head."

"Come, come, Plessis," replied the other--"you know you don't like a noise and a piece of work more than any one else. Do the matter cunningly, man, as you are accustomed to do. Get the fellow in the hall, there, down quietly out of the passage into the brandy cellar--I will follow him and lock him in. When that's done, all the rest is easy."

Plessis smiled at a trick exactly suited to his taste; but he hesitated, nevertheless, at putting it in execution, lest the fact of his having taken any part therein should come to the knowledge of men, from whom, at different times, he derived considerable advantage. Present evils, however, are always more formidable than distant ones, and Wilton bethought him of trying what a little intimidation would do with the good Frenchman.

"Listen to me, sir," he said, in a stern tone. "Instantly do what you are told, or take the consequences. Here is my authority from the Secretary of State, to demand the person of this young lady from the hands of any one with whom I may find her. A Messenger came down with me to High Halstow, with a warrant for the arrest of any person who may be found detaining her. It is, however, my wish to do all things quietly, if you will allow me. The Duke, her father, does not desire the business to be conducted with harshness--"

"A duke!" exclaimed Plessis, opening his eyes with astonishment. "A duke and peer! Why, they only told me that she was the daughter of some turncoat, who would betray them, they feared, if they had not his daughter in pawn."

"They deceived you!" replied Wilton--"she is the daughter of the Duke of Gaveston. But I have no time to discuss such points with you. Instantly do what you are told. Get the man out of the way quietly; give the lady up into my hands, as you are hereby formally required to do, or I immediately quit the house, raise the hue and cry, and in less than an hour this place shall be surrounded by a hundred men."

Plessis hesitated no longer. "Force majeure!" he cried. "Force majeure! No one can resist that. What am I to do? I will act exactly according to your bidding. You are witness, madam, that I yield to compulsion."

"Yes, Monsieur Plessis," replied the Lady Helen, "lawful compulsion."

"Well, Plessis, do as I bid you, at once," replied the Captain. "Get the man down into the brandy cellar, quickly!--I saw the door open as I passed--and either lock him in or let me do it."

"You are a tall man, and I am a small man," replied Plessis--"I have not the gift of turning keys, Captain. I'll send him down, however;" and taking a Venice glass from the mantelpiece, he went to the little vestibule at the top of the stairs, and called to the man who was sitting in the corridor beyond.

"Here, Harrison," he said--"I wish you'd go down and get the gentleman a glass of brandy out of the cellar. The door's open. Make haste, and don't drink any--there's a good fellow."

The tone in which Master Plassis spoke showed that he was no bad actor when well prompted. The man, who was completely deceived, came forward without the slightest hesitation, took the glass out of his hand, and went down stairs.

The moment he had passed, Plessis put in his head, and beckoned with his finger to the Captain, who ran down after the other in a moment, leaving the door open, and Plessis listening beyond, with some slight apprehension. That apprehension was increased, by hearing a word or two spoken sharply, a struggle, and the sound of glass falling and being broken. Wilton sprang out of the room to aid his companion; but at that moment there was the sound of a door banged sharply to, a key turned, and he met the Captain coming up the stairs laughing aloud.

"By Heaven, the fellow had nearly bolted," he said. "But there he is now, safe enough, and I dare say will find means to console himself with Master Plessis's brandy casks. He might have made himself quite comfortable if he hadn't dropped the glass, like a fool.--Now, Plessis," he continued, entering the room, "go for the lady as quick as lightning. Let us lose no time, but make sure of the business while we can; and I dare say, if you get yourself into any little scrape soon--as indubitably you will, for you never can expect to die unhanged--this gentleman will speak a good word for you to those who can get your neck out of the noose before it is drawn too tight. Come, make haste, man! or we may all get into trouble."

"I will go," said the Lady Helen, "I had better go. It will alarm her less, and she has been terrified and agitated too much already, poor thing."

Thus saying, she left them; but the lady returned alone in a moment after, saying, with some consternation, that the man had got the key of the door with him.

"Oh, that is nothing!" exclaimed Plessis, laughing; "I am never without my passe-partout;" and producing a key attached to a large ring, from his pocket, he gave it into the hands of the Lady Helen, who returned to her kind task once more.

Scarcely had she left the room when there came the sound of a man's step from the passage, and Plessis darted out. The footfall which he heard was that of Lord Sherbrooke, who was seeking Wilton; and as soon as the young nobleman saw him, he advanced towards him with both his hands extended, saying,--

"Oh, Wilton, dear friend, this has been a terrible night. But it is in the fiery furnace of such nights as this that hard hearts are melted and cast in a new mould. I feel that it is so with mine. But to the business that makes me seek you," he continued, in a low tone, seeing that there was another person in the room, and drawing Wilton on one side. "Listen to me! Quit this house as fast as possible. I find you are in a nest of furious Jacobites, and there may be great danger to you if found here. I remain with my poor Caroline; and far away from all the rest, have nothing to fear, although the warning that she gave was intended for me. You speed away to London as fast as possible. But remember, Wilton! remember: mention no word of this night's event to my father. He does not expect me in town for several days, and I must choose my own time and manner to give him the history of all this affair. He holds me by a chain you know not of--the chain of my heavy debts. I am at liberty but upon his sufferance, and one cold look from him to Jew or usurer would plunge me in a debtor's prison in an hour. The man who has debts he cannot pay, Wilton, is worse than any ordinary slave, for he is a slave to many masters. But I must away," he continued, in his rapid manner, "for I have left her with no one but the servant girl, and I must watch her till all danger be past."

"I trust she is better," said Wilton; "I trust there is no danger."

"They tell me not, they tell me not, Wilton," replied Lord Sherbrooke; "but now that I have been upon the very eve of losing a jewel, of which I was but too careless before, I feel all its value, and would fain hide it trembling in my heart, lest fate should snatch it from me. Say nothing of these things--remember, say nothing of them."

"But Arden, but Arden," said Wilton, as Lord Sherbrooke was turning away--"but the Messenger, Sherbrooke. May he not tell something?"

"The cowardly villain ran away so soon," replied Lord Sherbrooke, "he could hear nothing, and understand less. He is a cautious scoundrel, too, and will hold his tongue. Yet you may give him a warning, if you see him, Wilton."

"Here is the lady, sir," said Plessis, entering, and addressing Wilton. "I will go down stairs and see that all is safe below."

"He will not let the man out of the cellar?" demanded Wilton, as Plessis departed.

"I have taken care of that," replied the Captain, holding up a key; "but let us not lose time."

While these few words were passing, Lady Helen and Laura entered, the latter, pale, agitated, and trembling, less with actual apprehension than from all she had lately undergone. At that moment, she knew not with whom she was going, or what was the manner of escape proposed. All that the Lady Helen had told her was, that somebody had come to set her free, and that she must instantly prepare to depart. She had paused but for an instant, while the lady who brought her these glad tidings wrapped round her some of the garments which had been procured for her journey to France, by those who had carried her off; and all the agitation consequent upon a sudden revival of hopes that had been well nigh extinguished was still busy in her bosom, when, as we have said, she entered the room.

The first object, however, which her eye fell upon was the fine commanding form of Wilton Brown. It were scarcely fair to ask whether, in the long and weary hours of captivity, she had thought much of him. But one thing at least may be told, that with him, and with a hurried and timid examination of the feelings of her own bosom regarding him, her thoughts had been busied at the very moment when she had been dragged away from her own home. The sight of him, however, now, was both joyful and overpowering to her; the very idea of deliverance had been sufficient to agitate her, so that she shook in every limb as she entered the room; but when she saw in her deliverer the man whom, of all others, she would have chosen to protect her, manifold emotions, of a still more agitating kind, were added to all the rest. But joy--joy and increased hope--overcame all other feelings, and stretching out her hands towards him, she ran forward as he advanced to meet her, and clung with a look of deep confidence and gladness to his arm.

"Do not be frightened, do not be agitated," he said--"all will go quite well. Are you prepared to quit this place immediately?"

"Oh yes, yes, instantly!" she cried; but then her eyes turned upon Lord Sherbrooke, and the sight of him in company with Wilton seemed to cloud her happiness; for though she still looked up to Wilton's countenance with the same affectionate and confiding glance, yet there was evidently a degree of apprehension in her countenance, when, for a moment, she turned her eyes to Lord Sherbrooke. She bowed her head gracefully to him, however, and uttered some broken thanks to him and to Wilton, for coming to her deliverance.

"Pardon me, dear Lady Laura," replied Lord Sherbrooke. "I must accept no part of your thanks, for my being here is entirely accidental, and I cannot even offer to escort you on your departure. It is Wilton who has sought you bravely and perseveringly, and I doubt not you will go with him with perfect confidence."

"Anywhere, anywhere," said Lady Laura, with a tone and a look which at another moment might have called up a smile upon Lord Sherbrooke's countenance; but his own heart was also so full of deep feelings at that time, that he could not look upon them lightly enough even for a smile, when he detected them in another.

"I will go down and make sure that there is no trickery below," said the man called the Captain; "and when I call--Now! come down with the lady, Mr. Brown."

Lord Sherbrooke at the same moment took leave of them, and left the room; and Lady Laura, without quitting her position by Wilton's side, which she seemed to consider a place of sure refuge and support, held out her hand to the Lady Helen, saying, "Oh, how can I thank you, lady, for all your kindness? Had it not been for you, I should never have obtained this deliverance."

"I need no thanks, my sweet friend," replied the lady "the only things that give sunshine to the memories of a sad life are some few acts of kindness and sympathy which I have been able to perform towards others. But if you want to thank me," she added, looking with a smile upon Wilton, "thank him, Lady Laura, for he is the being dearest to me upon earth."

Lady Laura looked somewhat surprised; but Wilton held up his finger, thinking he heard their companion's call. It was not so, however, but only a quick step upon the stairs; and the next moment the Captain entered, with some marks of agitation on his countenance.

"By ---!" he said, "there seems to me to be a whole troop of horse before the house--such a clatter of iron-shod feet. I fear we have the enemy upon us, and Plessis has run to hide himself; frightened out of his wits. What can we do?"

"Come all into the lady's chamber, or into mine," said Lady Helen--"perhaps they may not think of searching for her. At all events, it gives us a chance, if we can but get across the vestibule before they come up. Quick, Wilton! come, quick!" and she was leading the way.

Before she got to the door, however, which the Captain had closed behind him, the tramp of heavy boots was heard upon the stairs, and a voice calling, "Plessis! Plessis! Where the devil are you? The whole house seems to be deserted! Why, what in Satan's name is here? Here's blood all the way down the stairs! By Heaven, it wouldn't surprise me if the Orangemen had got into the house. We must take care that there isn't a trap. Give me that lamp, Cranburne. You had better have your pistols ready, gentlemen. How can we manage now?--Two of you stay and guard each corridor, while we go in here."

There seemed now to take place a low-toned conversation amongst them, and the Lady Helen, with a pale countenance, drew back towards Wilton and Laura. The Captain, on his part, unbuttoned his coat, and drew out a pistol from the belt that he wore underneath: but Wilton said, "Put it up, my good friend, put it up. Do not let us set any example of violence. Where there are nine or ten against two, it is somewhat dangerous to begin the affray. We can always have recourse to resistance at last."

"Oh, not for my sake! not for my sake!" said Lady Laura, in a low voice. "For Heaven's sake, risk not your life for me!"

"Let us keep this deep window behind us," said Wilton, speaking to his companion, "for that will give us some advantage, at all events. Draw a little behind us, dear Lady Laura. We will manage all things as gently as we can."

"Let me speak to them, Wilton," said the Lady Helen--"from one circumstance or another, I must know them almost all."

As she spoke, the large heavy latch was lifted, and the door slowly and cautiously opened.

CHAPTER XXVI

A PAUSE of expectation, even if it be but for a minute, is sometimes the most painful thing in the world; and the heart of poor Laura at that moment, while the door was being slowly opened, and all their eyes were fixed eagerly upon it, felt as if the blood were stayed in it till it was nearly bursting. Wilton, who saw all that took place more calmly, judged by the careful opening of the door, that there was a good deal of timidity in the persons whom it hid from their view. But when it was at length opened, the sight that it presented was not well calculated to soothe any one's alarm.

In the doorway itself were three well-armed men, with each his sword drawn in his hand, while behind these again were seen the faces of several more. The countenance of the first, Sir George Barkley, which we have already described, was certainly not very prepossessing, and to the eyes of Laura, there was not one who had not the countenance of an assassin. It was evident that Sir George Barkley expected to see a much more formidable array than that presented to him and his companions, in the persons of two ladies and two armed gentlemen, for his eyes turned quickly from the right to the left round the room, to assure himself that it contained no one else. There was a momentary pause at the door; but when it was clear that very little was to be apprehended, the troop poured in with much more hasty and confident steps than those with which they had first approached.

Two or three of Sir George Barkley's party were advancing quickly to the spot where Wilton and the lady stood; but the young gentleman held up his right hand suddenly, putting his left upon one of the pistols which he carried, and saying, "Stand back, gentlemen! I do not permit men with swords drawn to come too close to me, till I know their purpose--Stand back, I say!" and he drew the pistol from his belt.

"We mean you no harm, sir," said Sir George Barkley, pausing with the rest. "But we must know who you are, and what you are doing here, and that immediately."

"Who I am, can be of no more consequence to you, sir," replied Wilton, "than who you are is to me--which, by your good leave, I would a great deal rather not know, if you will suffer me to be ignorant thereof;--and as to what I am doing here, I do not see that I am bound to explain that to anybody but the master of the house, or to some person authorized by law to inquire into such particulars."

"Mighty fine, sir," said the voice of Sir John Fenwick, as he advanced from behind--"Mighty fine! But this is a mere waste of time. In the first place, what are you doing with that lady, who, as her father's friend, I intend immediately to take under my protection."

"Her father, sir," replied Wilton, with a contemptuous smile, "judges that the lady has been somewhat too long under your careful but somewhat forcible protection already. I beg leave to give you notice, Sir John Fenwick, that I am fully authorized by the Duke of Gaveston, Lady Laura's father, by a writing under his own hand, to seek for and deliver her from those who have taken her away. I know you have been too wise and prudent to suffer yourself to be seen in this business hitherto, and if you will take my advice, you will not meddle with it now.--Stand back, sir; for as I live, I will shoot you through the head if you take one single step forward; and you know I will keep my word!"

"But there is more to be inquired into, sir," exclaimed Sir George Barkley-- "there is blood--blood upon the stairs, blood--"

"Hear me, Sir George," said Lady Helen, advancing. "You know me well, and must believe what I say."

"I have the pleasure of recollecting your ladyship very well," replied Sir George; "but I thought that you and Miss Villars had sailed back for France by this time."

"Alas! Sir George," replied the lady--"poor Caroline, I fear, will not be able to be moved. She has met with a severe accident to-night, and it is her blood, poor child, that you saw upon the stairs. This gentleman has had nothing farther to do with the matter, except inasmuch as he was accidentally present, and kindly carried her upstairs to the room where she now lies."

"That alters the case," said Sir George Barkley: "but who is he? We have heard reports by the way which give us alarm. Will he pledge his honour, as a gentleman, never to mention anything he has seen this night--or, at least, not for six months?"

"On that condition," demanded Wilton, "will you give me perfect freedom of egress with this lady and the gentleman who is with me?"

"Not with the lady!" exclaimed Sir George Barkley, sharply; and at the same moment Sir John Fenwick, Rookwood, and Parkyns all surrounded the Jacobite leader, speaking eagerly, but in a low tone, and evidently remonstrating against his permitting the departure of any of the party. He seemed puzzled how to act.

"Come out here again," he said--"come out here, where we can speak more at ease. They cannot get out of this room, if we keep the door."

"Not without breaking their neck from the window," replied Rookwood.

"What is that small door there at the side?" said Sir George Barkley. "Let some one see!"

"'Tis nothing but a cupboard," said Sir John Fenwick--"I examined it the other night, for fear of eavesdroppers. There is no way out."

"I shall consider your proposal, sir," said Sir George Barkley, turning to Wilton: "stay here quietly. We wish to offer no violence to any man; we are very harmless people in our way."

A grim smile hung upon his thin lip as he spoke; and looking from time to time behind him, as if he feared the use which Wilton might make of the pistol in his hand, he left the room with his companions. The moment after, the lock of the door was heard to turn, and a heavy bar that hung beside it clattered as it was drawn across.

"A few minutes gained is a great thing," cried Wilton. "I have heard of people defending themselves long, by forming a sort of temporary barricade. A single cavalier in the time of Cromwell kept at bay a large force for several hours. In this deep window we are defended on all sides but one. Let us do what we can to guard ourselves on that also."

The furniture was scanty; but still the large table in the middle of the room, and a sideboard which stood in one corner, together with chairs and various smaller articles, were speedily formed into a little fortress, as it were, which enclosed the opening of the window in such a manner as to leave a space open towards the enemy of not more than two feet in width. Wilton exerted himself to move all these without noise, and the Captain aided him zealously; while Laura clung to Lady Helen, and hid her eyes upon her new friend's bosom, anticipating every moment the return of the other party, and the commencement of a scene of strife and bloodshed.

It is to the proceedings of those without the room, however, that we must more particularly direct our attention.

"In the name of Heaven, Sir George," exclaimed both Rookwood and Fenwick, as soon as they were on the outside of the door--"do not let them go, on any account. Our whole plan is blasted, and ourselves ruined for ever, if such a thing is to take place!"

"Why," continued Fenwick, "this youth, this Wilton Brown, is secretary to the Earl of Byerdale, a natural son of Lord Sunbury, it is supposed, brought up from his infancy in the most violent Orange principles; and he will think himself justified in breaking his word with us the moment he is out of the house, and bringing upon us the troops from Hoo. He knows me well by sight, too; and if he be let loose, I shall not consider my life worth a moment's purchase."

"Even if you could trust him," said Rookwood, "there is the other, Captain Byerly as they call him, Green's great friend, who threw the money, which Lowick offered him to quit Green, in his face. If the tidings we just now heard, that the matter has taken some wind, be true, this fellow Byerly will bring down the soldiers upon us, and swear to us anywhere."

"But what am I to do?" demanded Sir George Barkley, hesitating. "We shall have bloodshed and much noise, depend upon it."

"Leave them all, locked in, where they are," said Sir William Parkyns--"they can do no harm there. Let us ourselves, like brave and determined men, carry into execution at once the resolution we have formed. Let us turn our horses' heads towards London; meet at Turnham Green, as was proposed; and while people are seeking for us here in vain, the usurper's life will be brought to an end, and his unsteady government overthrown for ever. Everything in the country will be in confusion; our friends will be rising in all quarters;--the Duke of Berwick, I know, was at Calais yesterday;--the army can land in two days; and the advantages of our situation will all be secured by one prompt and decided blow. I say, leave them where they are. Before they can make their escape, the whole thing will be over, and we shall be safe."

"Nonsense, Sir William," cried Fenwick, "nonsense, I say. Here is Plessis, has evidently played into their hands; the man we put to guard the girl has been bribed off his post; the window itself is not so high but that an active man might easily drop from it, if he could see clearly where to light below; ere noon, to-morrow, the tidings of our assemblies would reach Kensington. William of Orange would not stir out, and the whole plan would be frustrated. We should be hunted down through the country like wild beasts, and you would be one of the first to repent the advice you have given."

"But my good friend, Fenwick," said Sir George Barkley, "all this is very well. But still you do not say what is to be done. Every one objects to the plan which is proposed by another, and yet no one proposes anything that is not full of dangers."

"For my part," said Charnock, who had hitherto scarcely spoken at all--"for my part, if you were to ask my opinion, I should say, Let us walk in--we are here eleven or twelve in all; twelve, I think--and just quietly make a circle round, and give them a pistol-shot or two. If people WILL come prying into other persons' affairs, and meddling with things they have no business to concern themselves about, they must take the consequences."

"Not in cold blood! not in cold blood!" exclaimed Rookwood.

"And the women!" said Sir John Fenwick, "Remember the women!"

"I hope William of Orange won't have a woman with him to-morrow," said Charnock, coolly, "or if he has, that she'll not be upon my side of the carriage; I would never let a woman stand in the way when a great deed was to be done."

"Well, for my part," said Fenwick, "I agree with Sir William Parkyns, that no time is to be lost in the execution of this business; but I agree also with Captain Rookwood, that it would be horrible to cut these men's throats in cold blood. What I propose is this, that we at once demand that they lay down their arms, and that, pledging our word of honour no evil shall happen to them, we march them down one by one to the boat, and ship them off for France. It will be an affair of three hours to get them embarked; but that will be time well bestowed. We can then proceed to the execution of our scheme at once, and in far greater safety. If they make any resistance, the consequence be upon their own head."

"But," said Sir George Barkley, "depend upon it they will not go. There is a determination in that young fellow's look which is not to be mistaken. He will submit to no power but that of the law."

"Well, then," said Sir John Fenwick, "frighten him with the law! Declare that you will take them all before a magistrate, to give an account of the blood that has been shed here. There is blood on his collar, and his face too, for I saw it; and the whole stairs is spotted with blood. Tell them that both the men must surrender and go before a magistrate. The ladies, you can say, may go where they like, and do what they like, but the men must surrender. Let half of us go down with the men, and lead or force them to the ship, while the rest bring down the two women a few minutes after."

"That is not a bad plan at all, Fenwick," said Sir George Barkley. "Let us see what can be done by it. We can but come to blows at last."

While the latter part of this conversation had been going on between Fenwick and Barkley, the Jacobite called Charnock and a dull-looking man not unlike himself, but only shorter and more broadly made, had been speaking together in a low voice behind. At first their conversation was carried on in a whisper; but at length the man said somewhat louder, "Oh, I'll do it! That's the only way to settle it. You take the one, and I'll take the other. We don't readily miss our mark either of us."

"Let Sir George begin his story," replied Charnock. "There must be some talk at first, you know. Then get quietly up behind our timid friends here, and when I give a nod, we will both fire at once."

"I understand," answered the other. "You had better see that your pistols are primed, Charnock, and that the balls are not out, for you rode at a rate down that hill which would shake almost any ball into the holster."

"I looked just now," said Charnock--"it's all right. Let us keep pretty near Sir George;" and turning round, he came nearer to Sir George Barkley, who was just finishing his conversation with Fenwick, as we have described.

While holding this long consultation, the insurgents had not been many paces from the door, and they now turned and re entered the room. The state of defence in which Wilton and his companion had placed themselves showed a degree of determination that seemed to surprise and puzzle them a good deal; for Sir George Barkley again paused, and spoke to Sir John Fenwick, who was close behind him.

"The more reason for doing as we propose," replied Sir John to his friend's observation. "They will not resist going before a magistrate--at least, Wilton Brown will not, and we can easily manage the other."

Sir George Barkley then advanced another step, saying to Wilton, who, notwithstanding the barrier he had raised, was still quite visible as far as the waist, "We have consulted, sir, on what it is necessary to do with you, and if your own account of yourselves be true, you will readily acquiesce in our determination. If you resist it, you show that you know yourselves to be guilty of some crime, and we must deal with you accordingly."

"Pray, sir, what is your determination?" asked Wilton. "For my part, I require free permission to quit this place with this gentleman and Lady Laura Gaveston; and nothing shall prevent me from so doing at the risk of my life."

"You shall do so, sir," replied Sir George Barkley, "but you shall go before a magistrate in the first instance. Here are evident marks of violence having been committed upon the person of some one; the staircase, the vestibule, the corridors, are covered with blood; your coat, your collar, your face, are also bloody; and we feel ourselves bound, before we let you depart, to have this matter strictly inquired into."

"Oh, go before a magistrate at once," said Laura, in a low voice: "we have nothing to fear from that, and they have everything."

"Showing clearly that it is a pretence, dear lady," replied Wilton, in the same low tone. "Keep behind the barricade. I see one of those men creeping up from the door with a pistol in his hand.--Sir," he continued, addressing Sir George Barkley, "in those circumstances, the best plan for you to pursue will be to bring a magistrate here. I neither know who you are, nor what are your views; but I find this young lady, who has been carried off from her father's house, illegally brought hither, and detained. I know the house to be a suspected one; and although, as I have before said, I neither know who you are, nor what are your views, and do not by any means wish to know, yet the circumstances in which I find you are sufficiently doubtful to justify me in refusing to quit this spot, and place myself in your hands, unless every man present gives me his word of honour as a gentleman that I shall go free whithersoever I will. If, therefore, you think a magistrate requisite to inquire into this business, send for one. I think, however, that you would do much better to plight me your word at once, and let me go. I know no one but Sir John Fenwick here: therefore I can betray no one but him; and to Sir John Fenwick I pledge my word that I will not mention him."

It was evident that Sir John Fenwick put no trust in such assurances, and he was seen speaking vehemently with Sir George Barkley. At the same moment, however, a low conversation was carried on in a slow and careless sort of manner by Charnock and the other, who were just behind.

"I can't get a shot at the Captain," said Charnock, calmly. "His head is covered by that table they've set on end.--Stop a bit, stop a bit!"

"Better let me settle this young fellow first," said the other, "and then the stupid fools will be obliged to make a rush upon the Captain. When once blood is drawn, they must go on, you know."

"Very well," replied Charnock, "I don't care"--and there was the sudden click of a pistol-lock heard behind. "His eye is upon you," said Charnock. "Make haste! He is cocking his pistol!"

The man instantly raised the weapon that was in his hand, and was in the very act of firing over the shoulder of Sir George Barkley, when his arm was suddenly knocked up by a blow from behind, and the ball passed through the window, a yard and a half above Wilton's head.

Wilton instantly dropped the muzzle of his pistol, without returning the shot. But there was a cause for his so doing, which none of the conspirators themselves, who were all eagerly looking towards the spot where he stood, had yet perceived.

While Charnock and the other had been speaking, a young gentleman had suddenly entered the room, and pushing rapidly forward through the group in the doorway, he had advanced to the front and knocked up the hand of the assassin just as he was in the very act of firing. The new comer was dressed in dark-coloured clothes, and more in the French than in the English costume of that day, with a curious sort of cravat of red silk tied in a bow beneath the chin. He wore his hat, which was trimmed with feathers, and a large red bow of ribands, and in his hand he bore nothing but a small cane with an amber head, while his person displayed no arms whatever, except a small riding sword, which every gentleman wore in that day.

His figure was tall and commanding; his countenance open, noble, but somewhat stern; and there was to be remarked therein the peculiar expression which the pictures of Vandyke have handed down to us in the portraits of Charles I. It was a melancholy expression; but in Charles that melancholy seemed somewhat mingled with weakness; while on the stern brow and tightly-compressed lips of the young stranger, might be read, by the physiognomist, vigour and determination almost approaching to obstinacy.

The same, perhaps, might have been said of him which was said by the Roman sculptor when he beheld the picture of Charles, "That man will not die a natural death;" and in this instance, also, the prophecy would have been correct. But there was something that might have spoken, too, of death upon the battle-field, or in the deadly breach, or in some enterprise where daring courage needed to be supported by unshrinking pertinacity and resolution.

The sound of the pistol-shot fixed all eyes, for an instant, upon that particular point in the room towards which it had been fired; but the moment that the conspirators beheld the person who now stood amongst them, they instantly drew back in a circle. Every sword was thrust into its sheath, every hat was taken off, while, with a flashing eye and frowning brow, the young stranger turned to Sir George Barkley, exclaiming, "What is all this, sir? What is this, gentlemen? Are ye madmen? or fools? or villains?"

"Those are hard words, your grace," replied Sir George Barkley, "and hard to stomach."

"Not more than those persons deserve, sir," replied the stranger, "who betray the confidence of their King, when they know that he is powerless to punish them."

"We are serving our King, my lord duke," replied Sir John Fenwick, "and not betraying his confidence. Are we not here in arms, my Lord of Berwick, perilling our lives, prepared for any enterprise, and all on the King's behalf?"

"I say again, sir," replied the Duke of Berwick, "that those who abuse the trust reposed in them, so as to ruin their monarch's honour, his character, and his reputation, are tenfold greater traitors than those who have stripped him of his crown. There is but one excuse for your conduct, that you have acted with mistaken zeal rather than criminal intent. But you have aggravated the guilt of your plans by concealing them till the last moment, not only from your King, but from your Commander-in-chief. All here who hold commissions, or at least all but one or two, hold them under my hand as generalissimo of my father's forces. Those commissions authorize you to raise men for the service of your lawful sovereign, and to kill or take prisoner his enemies arrayed in arms against you, but to assassinate no man; and I feel heartily ashamed that any person leagued in this great cause with me, should not be able to distinguish between war and murder. However, on these subjects let us speak no more at present, for there are matters even more important to be thought of I heard of this but yesterday morning, and at the imminent peril of my life have come to England to stop such deeds. I sought you in London, Sir George Barkley, and have followed you hither; and from what I have heard, I have to tell you that your coming to England has been discovered, and that for the last four or five days a warrant has been out against you, without your knowing it. This I learned, beyond all doubt, from my Lady Middleton. There is reason, also, to believe that your whole designs are known, sirs, though it would seem all your names have not yet been obtained. My advice, therefore, is, that you instantly disperse to different parts of the country, or effect your escape to France. For you, Sir George, there is no chance but to retire to France at once, as the warrant is out."

"It most fortunately happens," said Sir George Barkley, "that a ship is on the point of sailing, and lies in the river here, under Dutch colours. Your grace will, of course, go back in her?"

"No, sir," replied the Duke--"I shall go as I came, in an open boat. But you have no time to lose, for I know that suspicion is attached to this spot. In the first place, however, tell me, what you have here. What new outrage is this that I have just seen attempted? If I had not entered at the very moment, cold and cowardly bloodshed would have taken place five minutes ago."

The Duke's eyes were fixed upon Wilton as he spoke; and that gentleman, now seeing and understanding whom he had to deal with, put back the pistol into his belt, and advanced, saying,--

"My lord, it is probable I owe my life to your inter-position; and to you the circumstances in which I am placed will be explained in a moment. In your honour and integrity, I have confidence; but the murderous purpose which you have just disappointed shows how well I was justified in doubting the intentions of the men by whom I was but now surrounded."

"Had you given them no offence, sir?" demanded the Duke of Berwick. "I can scarcely suppose that so dark and sanguinary an act would have been attempted had you not given some cause. I saw the pistol levelled over Sir George Barkley's shoulder, while he seemed speaking to you. That I considered a most unfair act, and stopped it. But you must surely have done something to provoke such deeds.--Good heavens! the Lady Helen Oswald!" he continued, as the elder lady advanced, with Laura clinging to her. "Madam, I fully thought you were at St. Germain.--Can you tell us anything of this strange affair?"

"But too much, my lord," replied the lady, speaking eagerly, "but too much for the honour of these men, who have thought fit to violate every principle of justice and humanity. This young lady beside me has been dragged from her father's house by the orders of some of these gentlemen here present, beyond all doubt. This young gentleman has traced her hither, legally authorized to carry her back to her father; and although he plighted his honour, and I pledged my word for him, that he would do nothing and say nothing to compromise any of the persons here present, they not only refused to let him depart, but have, as you saw yourself, most treacherously attempted to take his life while they were affecting to parley with him."

"Madam," said the Duke of Berwick, in a sorrowful tone, "I am deeply grieved and pained by all that has occurred. I confess I never felt despondency till I discovered that persons, pretending to be my father's friends, have made his cause the pretext for committing crimes and acts like these. I have already heard this young lady's story. All London is ringing with it; and the Earl of Aylesbury gave me this morning, what is probably the real explanation of the whole business. We will not enter upon it now, for there is no time to be spared. I feel and know--and I say it with bitter regret--that the deeds which these gentlemen have done, and the schemes which they have formed, will do more to injure the cause of their legitimate sovereign than the loss of twenty pitched battles. Sir George Barkley, I beg you would make no reply. Provide for your safety, sir. Your long services and sufferings are sufficient to make some atonement; and I will take care to conceal from the ears of the King, as far as possible, how you have misused his authority. Sir John Fenwick and the rest of you gentlemen must act as you think fit in regard to remaining in England, or going to the Continent. But I am inclined to recommend to you the latter, as the safest expedient. You will leave me to deal with this gentleman and his friends; for I need not tell you that I shall suffer no farther injury or insult to be offered to them. As to the personage who actually fired the pistol, I have merely to tell him, that should I ever meet with him in circumstances where I have the power to act, I will undoubtedly punish him for his conduct this night."

The conspirators whispered for a moment amongst themselves; and at length Sir William Parkyns took a step forward, saying, "Are we to understand your grace that you will give us no assistance from the French forces under your command?"

"You are so to understand me," replied the Duke of Berwick, sternly: "I will not, sir, allude distinctly to the schemes that you have formed. But you are all well aware of them; and I tell you that I will give no aid, support, or countenance what-soever, either to such schemes or to the men who have formed them. At the same time, let me say, that had there been--instead of such schemes--a general rising against the usurper--ay, or even a partial rising--nay, had I found twenty gentle-men in arms who needed my help in the straightforward, honest, upright intent of re-seating their sovereign on his lawful throne, I would not have hesitated for a moment to land the troops under my command, and to have made a last determined stand for honour and my father's rights. As it is, gentlemen, I have nothing farther to say, but take care of yourselves. I shall remain here for a couple of hours, and then return with all speed to France."

"But does not your grace run a great risk," said Sir George Barkley, "in remain-ing so long?"

"I fear no risk, sir," said the Duke of Berwick, "in a righteous cause; and I do not wish that any man should say I was amongst the first to fly after I had warned others. You have all time, gentlemen, if you make use of it wisely. Some, I see, are taking advantage of my caution already. Sir George, you had better not be left be-hind in the race. You say there is a ship in the river--get to her, and be gone with all speed."

"But the captain will not sail without the Lady Helen," said the conspirator, with some hesitation: "she, it seems, has hired the vessel, and he refused this morn-ing to go without her."

"That shall be no impediment," said the lady. "You may tell the captain that I set him free from his engagement, and I will give an order to his grace that the money may be paid which is the man's due. I told you before, Miss Villars had met with a severe accident, and I can neither quit her in such circumstances, nor go till she has recovered."

"Will you be kind enough, madam," replied Sir George, who always had thoughts for his own safety, "to write what you have said in these tablets? Here is a pencil."

The lady took the tablets and wrote; and while she did so, two or three, more of the conspirators dropped quietly out of the room. The Duke of Berwick at the same time advanced, and said a few kindly words to Lady Laura, and spoke for a moment to Wilton, with a familiar smile, in regard to the risk he had run.

"To tell the truth," he said, "I was almost afraid that I should myself meet with a shot between you; for I saw you had your pistol cocked in your hand, and expected that the next fire would have been upon your side."

"I saw you knock his arm up, sir," replied Wilton; "and though I was not aware of the name of the person who entered, I was not a little rejoiced to see, at least, one man of honour amongst them."

"Alas! sir," replied the Duke, in a lower tone, "they are all, more or less, men of honour; but you must remember that there is a fanaticism in politics as well as in religion, and men will think that a great end will justify any intermediate means. An oak, planted in the sand, sir, is as soon blown down as any other tree; and it is not every heart that is firm and strong enough constantly to support the honour that is originally implanted in it against the furious blasts of passion, interest, or ambition. You must remember, too, that those who are called Jacobites in this country have been hunted somewhat like wolves and wild beasts; and nothing drives zeal into fanaticism so soon as persecution."

"My lord, I am now ready to depart," said Sir George Barkley, approaching, "and doubt not to be able to make my views and motives good to my royal master."

"There is none, sir, who will abhor your views so much," replied the Duke of Berwick, proudly, "though he may applaud your motives. But you linger, Sir George. Can I do anything for you, or for those other gentlemen by the door?"

"Nothing, your grace," replied Sir George Barkley; "but we would fain see you provide for your own safety."

"Oh, no fear, no fear," replied the Duke. "Gentlemen, good night. I trust to hear, when in another land, that this bad affair has ended without evil consequences to yourselves. To the cause of your sovereign it may be a great detriment; but I pray God that no whisper of the matter may get abroad so as to affect his honour or bring suspicion on his name. Once more, good night!"

Sir George Barkley bowed his head, and followed by three others, who had still lingered, quitted the room.

CHAPTER XXVII.

There came a pause after the conspirators were gone, and the Duke of Berwick gazed down upon the floor for a moment or two, as if thinking of what was next to be done.

"I shall be obliged to stop," he said at length, "for an hour or so, till my horses can feed, for they want refreshment sadly. To say the truth, I want some myself, if I can obtain it. I must go down to the stable, and see; for though that is not exactly the place to procure food for a man, yet, in all probability, I shall get it nowhere else. I found the good master of the house, indeed, who is an old acquaintance of mine, hid in the farthest nook of his own stable, terrified out of his life, and assuring me that there would certainly be bloodshed up stairs."

"I will go down and look for him, your grace," replied Captain Byerly, coming more forward than he had hitherto done. "You will find no lack of provisions, depend upon it, in Monsieur Plessis's house."

"One moment, sir," said the Duke, stopping him as he was going: "have I not seen your face before?"

"Long ago, sir, long ago," replied the Captain. "I had the honour of commanding a troop, sir, in your regiment, during all that sad business in Ireland--Byerly is my name."

"I remember you well, sir," said the Duke, "and your good services. Should we meet in France, I may be able to repay them--especially if your views are still of a military kind."

Byerly bowed his head, without reply, but looked much gratified; and while lie proceeded to look for Plessis, the Duke once more turned to the Lady Helen.

"I am sorry," he said, "to hear, from your account, madam, that an accident has happened to Miss Villars. I have been so long absent from St. Germain myself, that it is not very long since I heard of her father's death. May I inquire if she is seriously hurt? for I should apprehend that, after what has occurred, persons holding our opinions would run considerable risks in this country, and be subjected to a persecution even more severe than heretofore."

The Lady Helen replied simply that her young friend was seriously hurt, and could not be removed; but she avoided carefully all reference to the nature of the injury she had received. The Duke then turned the conversation to indifferent subjects, spoke cheerfully and gaily with Lady Laura and Wilton, and showed that calm sort of equanimity in circumstances of danger and difficulty which is partly a gift of nature, and partly an acquisition wrung from many perils and evils endured. Ere long, Byerly returned with Plessis, and food and wine were speedily procured. The tables were set in order, and the Duke remained for about a quarter of an hour refreshing himself; while Wilton and the two ladies continued to converse with him, delaying their departure at his request, lest any of the more unscrupulous conspirators should still be lingering in the neighbourhood.

Plessis, however, was evidently uneasy; and he did not scruple at length to express his fear, that amongst all the events of that night, something might have happened to call the attention of the world at large upon what was going on in his dwelling.

Wilton's apprehensions, in regard to the Duke, were somewhat of the same nature; for he remembered that Arden, the Messenger, whom he now knew to be a thorough coward, had fled at the beginning of the whole business, and would most likely return accompanied by as large a force as he could raise in the neighbourhood.

These fears he failed not to communicate to the Duke of Berwick; but that nobleman looked up with a gay smile, replying, "My good sir, my horse can go no farther. I rode one to death yesterday, and this one, which I bought in London, is already knocked up: if I must be caught like a rat in a rat-trap, as well here as anywhere."

"But will it not be better," said Wilton, "to accompany me and the Lady Laura to High Halstow, where you can instantly procure a horse? We must proceed thither on foot. I suppose you are not likely to be known in this part of the country, and my being with you may shield you from some danger."

"By no means a bad plan," said the Duke, starting up--"let us go at once! When anything feasible is proposed, we should lose no time in executing it."

Wilton was ready to depart, and Lady Laura was eager to do so. Every moment, indeed, of their stay made her feel fresh apprehensions lest that night should not be destined to close without some more painful event still, than those which she had already witnessed.

She turned, however, to the Lady Helen before she went, and with the peculiar sort of quiet grace which distinguished her, approached her gently and kissed her cheek, saying, "I can never thank you sufficiently, dear lady, for the kindness you have shown me, or the deliverance which I owe, in the first place, to you; and I thank you for the kindness you have shown me here, as much as for my deliverance: for if it had not been for the comfort it gave me, I do believe I should have sunk under the sorrow, and agitation, and terror, which I felt when I was first brought hither. I hope and believe, however, that I do not leave you here never to see you again."

Lady Helen smiled, and laid her hand gently upon Wilton's arm.

"There is a link between him and me, lady," she said, "which can never be broken; and I shall often, I hope, hear of your welfare from him, for I trust that you will see him not infrequently."

Lady Laura blushed slightly, but she was not one to suffer any fine or noble feeling of the heart to be checked by such a thing as false shame.

"I trust I shall," she answered, raising her eyes to Wilton's face--" I trust I shall see him often, very often; and I shall never see him, certainly, without feelings of pleasure and gratitude. You do not know that this is the second time he has delivered me from great danger."

The Duke of Berwick smiled, not, indeed, at Lady Laura's words, but at the blush that came deeper and deeper into her cheek as she spoke. He made no observation, however, but changed the conversation by addressing Wilton, "Wherever I am to procure a horse under your good guidance, my dear sir," he said, "I must, I believe, take another name than my own; for though Berwick and London are very distant places, yet there might be compulsory means found of bringing them unpleasantly together. You must call me, therefore, Captain Churchill, if you please;--a name," he added, with a sigh, "which, very likely, the gentleman who now fills the throne of England might be very well inclined to bestow upon me himself. Lady Helen, I wish you good night, and take my leave. Master Plessis, I leave the horse with you: he never was worth ten pounds, and now he's not worth five; so you may sell him to pay for my entertainment."

Bowing to the very ground from various feelings of respect, French, English, and Jacobite, Plessis took a candle and lighted the Duke down stairs, while Wilton followed, accompanied by Laura and Captain Byerly. The outer door was then opened, and the whole party issued forth into the field which surrounded the house, finding themselves suddenly in the utter darkness of a moonless, starless, somewhat foggy night.

From the little stone esplanade, which we have mentioned, lay a winding road up to the gate in the walls, and along that Wilton and his companion turned their steps, keeping silence as they went, with the listening ear bent eagerly to catch a sound. It was not, indeed, a sense of general apprehension only which made Wilton listen so attentively, for, in truth, he had fancied at the very moment when they were issuing forth from the house, that he had heard a low murmur as if of people talking at some distance.

The same sound had met the ears of the Duke of Berwick, and had produced the same effect; but nothing farther was heard till they reached the gate, and Wilton's hand was stretched out to open it; when suddenly a loud "Who goes there?" was pronounced on the opposite side of the gate, and half-a-dozen men, who had been lying in the inside of the wall, surrounded the party on all sides.

Several persons now spoke at once. "Who goes there?" cried one voice again; but at the same time another exclaimed, "Call up the Messenger, call up the Messenger from the other gate."

These last words gave Wilton some satisfaction, though they were by no means pleasant to the ears of the Duke of Berwick.

The former, however, replied to the challenge, "A friend!" and instantly added, "God save King William!"

"God save King William!" cried one of the voices: "you cry that on compulsion, I've a notion. Pray, who are you that cry `God save King William'?"

"My name, sir, is Wilton Brown," replied the young gentleman, "private secretary to the Earl of Byerdale. Where is the Messenger who came down with me? Be so good as to call him up immediately."

"Oh! you are the young gentleman who came down with the Messenger, are you?" said one of the others: "he was in a great taking lest you should be murdered."

"It was not his fault," replied Brown, somewhat bitterly, "that I was not murdered; and if it had not been for Captain Churchill and this other gentleman, who came to my assistance at the risk of their lives, I certainly should have been assassinated by the troop of Jacobites and smugglers amongst whom I fell."

The Duke of Berwick could not refrain from a low laugh at the description given of the persons whom they had just seen; but Wilton spoke loud again, in order to cover the somewhat ill-timed merriment of his companion, asking of the person who had replied, "Pray, who are you, sir?"

"I am head constable of High Halstow," replied the man, "and I remained here with our party, while Master Arden and the rest, with the soldiers from Hoo, went round to the other gate."

"Why did not the cowardly rascal go in by this gate himself," demanded Wilton, "instead of putting you, my friend, at the post of danger?"

"Ay, it was shabby enough of him," replied the man; "but I don't fear anything; not I."

"I'm afraid, my good fellows, it is too late," replied Wilton. "All the gang have got off near an hour ago. If that stupid Messenger had known what he was about, this affair would have had a different result; but he ran away at the first shot that was fired--Have you sent for him?" he continued, after a moment's pause.

"Oh yes, sir, we've sent for him," said the man, "though it's not much use, if they are all gone, sir."

"Oh yes," replied Wilton, "you may as well make a good search amongst the grounds and in the hedges. It will say something for your activity, at all events. I shall go on to Halstow, but I wish one or two of you would just show us the way, and when Arden comes up, tell him to come after me immediately. I have a great mind to put him under arrest, and send him up to the Earl, for his bad conduct."

The tone in which Wilton spoke, and the very idea of his arresting the arrestor of all men, and sending up the Messenger of State as a common prisoner to London, proved so impressive with the personages he addressed, that they made not the slightest opposition to his purpose of proceeding, but sent one of their number to show him the way.

Accompanied, therefore, by Lady Laura, the Duke of Berwick, and Captain Byerly, Wilton proceeded as fast as possible up the lane. When they had gone about a hundred yards, however, he said, "Captain Churchill, will you have the kindness to give the lady your arm? I will follow you somewhat more slowly, for I want to speak a few words to this fellow Arden.--He must not see you, if it can be avoided," he added, in a low tone; "and I think I hear him coming."

It was indeed as Wilton imagined. Arden had come round with all speed, and joined the head constable of High Halstow, demanding eagerly, "Where is Mr. Brown?"

"He is gone on," replied the constable, "with the other gentlemen; and a mighty passion he is in, too, at you, Mr. Arden. He vows that you left him to be murdered, and that he would have been murdered too, if it had not been for that Captain Churchill that is with him."

"Captain Churchill!" cried the Messenger--"Captain Churchill! Why, Captain Churchill was sick in bed yesterday morning, to my certain knowledge!"

After a moment's thought, however, he concluded that the person who chose to assume that name might be Lord Sherbrooke, and he asked, "What sort of a man was he? Was he a slight young gentleman, about my height?"

"Oh bless you, no," replied the constable. "There wasn't one of them that was not three or four inches taller than you."

"Captain Churchill!" said the Messenger--"Captain Churchill!" and he added, in a lower voice, "I'll bet my life this is some d---d Jacobite, who has imposed himself upon this foolish boy for Captain Churchill. I'll be after them, and see."

Thus saying, he set off at full speed after Wilton and his party, and reached them within a minute after that gentleman had dropped behind.

"Is that you, Mr. Arden?" demanded Wilton, as he came up. "Stop a moment, I wish to speak to you."

"And I wish to go on, and see who you've got there, sir," said Arden, in a somewhat saucy tone, at the same time endeavouring to pass Wilton.

"Stop, sir!" cried the young gentleman, catching him by the collar. "Do you mean to say, that you will now disobey my orders, after having left me to provide for my own security, with the dastardly cowardice that you have displayed? Did not the Earl direct you to obey me in everything?"

"I will answer it all to the Earl," replied the man, in an insolent tone. "If he chooses to put me under a boy, I do not choose to be collared by one. Let me go, Mr. Brown, I say."

"I order you, sir," said Brown, without loosing his hold, "to go instantly back, and aid the people in searching the grounds of that house!--now, let me see if you will disobey!"

"I will search here first, though," said the man. "By, I believe that's Sir George Barkley, on before there. He's known to be in England. Let me go, Mr. Brown, I say, or worse will come of it!" and he put his hand to his belt, as if seeking for a pistol.

Without another word, Wilton instantly knocked him down with one blow of his clenched fist, and at the same moment he called out aloud, "Captain Byerly! and you constable, who are showing the way--come back here, and take this man into custody, and bear witness that he refuses to search for the Jacobites in the way I order him. Constable, I shall want you to take him to town in custody this night. I will show you my warrant for what I do when we get to the inn."

The two persons whom he addressed came back instantly at his call; and when the Messenger rose--considerably crest-fallen from Wilton's sudden application to measures which he had not expected--he found himself collared by two strong men, and led along unwillingly upon the road he had before been treading.

"Do not let him chatter, Captain," Wilton whispered to Captain Byerly, as he passed on; and then immediately walking forward, he joined the Duke and the Lady Laura. Byerly, who understood what he was about, kept the Messenger at some distance behind; but, nevertheless, some sharp words passing between them reached Wilton's ear during the first quarter of an hour of their journey; then came a dogged silence; but at length the voice of Byerly was again heard, exclaiming, "Mr. Brown, Mr. Arden says, that, if you will overlook what has passed, he will go back, and do as you order."

"I shall certainly not look over the business," replied Brown, aloud, "unless he promises not only to obey my orders at present, but also to make a full apology to me to-morrow."

"He says he will do what you please, sir," replied Byerly; and Wilton turning back, heard the sullen apologies of the Messenger.

"Mr. Arden," he said, "you have behaved extremely ill, well knowing, as you do know, that you were placed entirely under my orders. However, I shall pardon your conduct both upon the first occasion, and in regard to the present business, if you now do exactly as you are told. By your running away at the time you ought to have come forward to assist me, you have lost an opportunity of serving the state, in a manner which does not occur every day. In regard to the gentleman who has gone on, and whom you were foolish enough to think Sir George Barkley, I pledge you my honour that such is not the case. Sir George Barkley cannot be less than twenty years older than he is, and may be thirty."

"He's not Captain Churchill, though," replied the man, doggedly.

"Do not begin to speak impertinently again, sit!" said Wilton, in a sharp tone. "But go back, as I before ordered, with the constable: you know nothing of who that gentleman is, and my word ought to be sufficient for you, when I tell you that he has this very night not only aided me in setting free the Lady Laura, but absolutely saved my life at the risk of his own from the very gang of Jacobites in whose hands you most negligently left me. To drop this subject, however, I have one more caution to give you," he added, in a lower voice. "It is Lord Sherbrooke's wish that you should say not one syllable in regard to his share in the events of this night."

"Ay, sir, but I ought to ascertain whether he be safe or not. I know he has his wild pranks as well as most young men; but still one ought to know that he's safe."

"If my word for you is not sufficient on that score," replied Wilton, "you will find him at the house to which I directed you to go. It is now clear of all its obnoxious tenants, and I doubt not, Lord Sherbrooke will speak to you for a moment, if you wish it."

Thus saying, Wilton turned upon his heel, and walking quickly onward, soon overtook the Duke of Berwick and Lady Laura. They were now not far from High Halstow, and the rest of the way was soon accomplished. But as they passed into the door of the public-house, Captain Byerly, who came last, touched Wilton on the arm, and whispered, "Do you know that fellow is following you?"

"No, indeed," answered Wilton: "what can be done?"

"Go and speak to the master of the house," said Byerly, quickly. "I will wait here in the door, and take care he does not come in. The landlord will find means to get the Duke away by the back."

"I dare not trust him," replied Wilton, in the same low tone. "I feel sure he has betrayed me once to-night already."

"If he did," answered Byerly, hastily, "it was because he thought you on the wrong side of the question. He's a well-known man hereabouts, and you may trust him with any secrets on that side."

Wilton followed the Duke of Berwick and Laura as fast as possible, and found the landlord showing them into a small sanded parlour on the left hand, after passing a door which swung to and fro with a pulley.

"Come in here, landlord," he said, as he passed; "come in, and shut the door. Have you a horse saddled?" he continued.

"I have one that can be saddled in a minute," said the landlord, looking first at Berwick and then at Wilton.

"Have you any back way," continued Wilton, "by which this gentleman can get out of the town without going through the street?"

"Ay have I," answered the man; "through our stable, through the garden, lead the horse down the steps, and then away to Stroud. There's no missing the way."

"Well then, sir," said Wilton, grasping the Duke's hand, "this is your only chance for safety. That rascally Messenger has followed us to the door, and doubtless if there be any magistrates in the neighbourhood, or constables left in the place, we shall have them down upon us in ten minutes."

"Come with me, my lord, come with me!" cried the landlord, bursting into energy in a moment. "I know who you are well enough. But they shan't catch you here, I warrant you. Come into the stable: there's not a minute to be lost; for there's old Sir John Bulrush, and Parson Jeffreys, who's a magistrate too, drinking away up at the rectory till the people come back from Plessis's house." Berwick lingered not; but taking a quick leave of Lady Laura, and shaking Wilton's hand, he followed the landlord from the room. Laura and Wilton stood silent for a minute or two, listening to every sound, and calculating how long it might be before the horse was saddled and the Duke upon his way. Before they imagined it possible, however, the landlord returned, saying, in a low voice, but with an air of joyful triumph, "He is gone; and if they were after him this minute, the way through my garden gives him the start by half a mile."

"And now, landlord," said Wilton, "send off some one on horseback to get us a conveyance from Stroud to carry this young lady on the way to London. I suppose such a thing is not to be procured here."

"That there is not," replied the landlord; "and unless I send your horse, sir, or the Messenger's, or the Captain's, I have none to go."

"Send mine, then, send mine!" replied Wilton. "But here comes Captain Byerly himself, bringing us news, doubtless."

"No news," answered Byerly, "except that the rascal went up the street, and I followed him to the door of the parsonage. Your parson's a magistrate--isn't he, Wicks?"

The landlord gave a nod; and Byerly continued, "By Jove, I'll be off then, for I'm not fond of magistrates, and he'll be down here soon."

"You had better bid them bring down a chaise for the gentleman and lady from Stroud," said the landlord. "That will save me from sending some one on the gentleman's horse."

"No, no, landlord, no, no!" answered Byerly, "you are not up to a stratagem. Send your ostler with me on Mr. Brown's horse. We'll go clattering along the street like the devil, if we can but get off before the justices comedown, and they'll take it into their wise noddles that one of us is the gentleman who has just gone. Come, Wicks, there's no time to spare. We shall meet again, Mr. Brown; good night, good night. I shall tell the Colonel that we've done the business much more tidily than I could have expected." And without further ceremony he quitted the room.

Another pause ensued, during which but a few words passed between Wilton and Lady Laura, who sat gazing thoughtfully into the fire. Wilton stood by the window and listened, thinking he heard some distant sounds as of persons speaking, and loud tongues at the further end of the street. A minute after, however, there came the clatter of horses' feet upon the pavement of the yard; and in another instant Byerly's voice was heard, saying, "Come, put to your spurs," and two horses galloped away from the inn as hard as they could go.

CHAPTER XXVIII.

IT is wonderful how scenes of danger and difficulty--it is wonderful how scenes of great excitement of any kind, indeed--draw heart to heart, and bind together, in bonds indissoluble, the beings that have passed through them side by side. They are never to be broken, those bonds; for between us and the persons with whom we have trod such paths there is established a partnership in powerful memories, out of which we can never withdraw our interest. But it is not alone that they are permanent which renders them different from all lighter ties; it is that they bring us closer, more entirely to each other; that instead of sharing the mere thoughts of what we may call the outward heart, we enter into the deepest recesses, we see all the hidden treasures, we know the feelings and the ideas that are concealed from the general eye of day, we are no longer kept in the porch, but admitted into the temple itself.

Wilton was left alone in the small parlour of the inn with Lady Laura; and as soon as he heard the horses' feet gallop away, he turned towards her with a glad smile. But when he did so, he found that her beautiful eyes were now fixed upon him with a gaze deep and intense--a gaze which showed that the whole thoughts and feelings of her heart were abstracted from everything else on earth to meditate on all that she owed to him, and on the things alone that were connected therewith.

She dropped her eyes as soon as they met his; but that one look was overpowering to the man who now certainly loved her as deeply as it is possible for man to love woman. Many a difficulty and doubt had been removed from his mind by the words which Lord Sherbrooke had spoken while affecting to seek for the warrant; and there were vague hopes of high destinies in his heart. But it must be acknowledged, that if there had been none, he would have given way, even as he did.

He advanced towards her, he took her hand in his, he pressed it between both his own, he kissed it tenderly, passionately, and more than once. Lady Laura lifted up her eyes to his face, not blushing, but very pale.

"Oh, Wilton," she said, "what do I not owe you!" and she burst into tears. The words, the look, the very tears themselves, were all more than sufficient encouragement.

"You owe me nothing, Laura," Wilton said. "Would to God that I had such an opportunity of serving you as to make me forgive in myself the rash, the wild, the foolish feelings that, in spite of every struggle and every effort, have grown up in my heart towards you, and have taken possession of me altogether. But, oh, Laura, I cannot hope that you will forgive them, I cannot forgive them myself. They can- -I know they can, only produce anguish and sorrow to myself, and excite anger, perhaps indignation, in you."

"Oh no, no, no, Wilton!" she cried, eagerly, "not that, not that! neither anger, nor indignation, nor anything like it, but grief--and yet not grief either--oh no, not grief!--Some apprehension, perhaps, some anxiety both for your happiness and my own. But if you do feel all you say, as I believe and am sure you do, such feelings, so far as depends upon me, should produce you no anguish and no pain; but I must not conceal from you that I very much fear, my father would never--"

An increasing noise at the door of the house broke in upon what Laura was saying. There were cries, and loud tongues, and vociferations of many kinds; among which, one voice was heard, exclaiming, "Go round to the back door!"

Another person, apparently just under the window, shouted, "I am very sure that was not the man!" and then added, "Bring out my horse, however, bring out my horse! I'll catch them, and raise the hue and cry as I go!"

At the same time there were other voices speaking in the passage, and one loud sonorous tongue exclaiming, "Ah, Master Wicks, Master Wicks! I thought you would get yourself into a scrape one of these days, Master Wicks;" to which the low deep voice of the landlord was heard, replying--

"I have got myself into no scrape, your reverence. I don't know what you mean or what you wait.--Search? You may search any part of the house you like. I don't care! If there were twenty people here, I have nothing to do with it. I can't refuse gentlemen to put up their horses, or to give them a bowl of punch, or a mug of ale.

There, sir, there's a gentleman and lady in that parlour. Pray, sir, walk in, and see whether they are Jacobites or smugglers or what riots."

As these words sounded close to them, Lady Laura sunk down again into her chair; and Wilton, drawing a little back, hesitated, for a moment, whether he should go out himself and notice what was taking place, or not. The question, however, was decided for him by the door of the room being thrown suddenly open, and the rotund person of the clergyman of the parish, bearing, in the "fair round belly with fat capon lined," the sign and symbol affixed by Shakspeare to the "Justice of Peace," entered the apartment. He gazed with some surprise upon two persons, who, notwithstanding some slight disarray in their apparel from all the events which had lately taken place, still bore the appearance of belonging to the highest class of society.

The reverend justice had entered the room with a look of pompous importance, which was diminished, but not entirely done away, by evident surprise at the appearance of Laura and Wilton. The young gentleman, however, was not particularly well pleased with the interruption, and still less with this domineering air, which he hastened to extinguish as fast as possible.

"Pray, sir, what do you want?" he demanded, addressing the magistrate, "and who are you?"

"Nay, sir," answered the reverend gentleman, "what I want is, to know who you are. I have here information that there is in this house a notorious Jacobite malefactor, returned from beyond seas, contrary to law, named Sir George Barkley. I am a magistrate for the county, sir, and I have information, I say."

"Upon oath, sir?" demanded Wilton.

"No, sir, not upon oath, not upon oath," replied the clergyman, "but what is quite as good, upon the word of a Messenger of State, sir--of Mr. Arden, the Council Messenger, sir."

"Landlord!" exclaimed Wilton, seeing the face of Wicks amongst several others at the door, "be so good as to bring Mr. Arden, the Messenger, here. Bring him by the collar, if he does not come willingly. I will be answerable for the consequences."

The magistrate looked astounded; but the landlord came forward with a grin and a low bow, saying, "The gentleman has mounted his horse, sir, and ridden after those other two gentlemen who went away a quarter of an hour ago; but, Lord bless you, sir," he added, with a sly look, "he'll never catch them. Why, his horse is quite lame."

"The fact is," replied Wilton, "this man Arden did not choose to come in here, as he well knew I should certainly send him to London in custody, to answer for his bad conduct this night.--Sir, I beg to inform you, that I am private secretary to the Earl of Byerdale; and that this young lady, the daughter of the Duke of Gaveston, having been carried off from the terrace near his house by agents, it is supposed, of the late King James II., for the purpose of drawing over her father to support that faction, the Duke, who is pleased to repose some trust in me, authorized me, by this paper under his hand, to search for and deliver the lady, while at the same time the Earl of Byerdale intrusted me with this warrant for the purposes herein mentioned, and put this man Arden, the Messenger, under my direction and control. At the very first sight of danger the Messenger ran away, and by so doing left me with every chance of my being murdered by a gang of evil-disposed persons in this neighbourhood. On his return with a large body of constables and some military to the house of a person who is named Plessis, I understand, he refused to obey the orders I gave him, and followed me hither, alleging that one of two gentlemen who had come to my assistance, and to whom I owe my own life and the liberation of this lady, was the well-known personage called Sir George Barkley. Those gentlemen both departed, as soon as they saw us in safety, and I am ready to swear that neither of them was Sir George Barkley; the person this Messenger mistook for him being a young gentleman of four or five and twenty years of age."

"Phoo!" cried the magistrate, with a long sort of whistling sound--"Sir George Barkley is a man of fifty, with a great gash on his cheek. I remember him very well, when--"

But then seeming to recollect himself, he paused abruptly, adding, "But pray, who was this young gentleman who so came to your assistance, sir?"

"I never saw him in my life before," replied Wilton, "and the name he gave himself was Captain Churchill."

"To be sure, to be sure!" cried the clergyman; "a younger brother of my Lord of Marlborough's."

"Some relation of the Marlborough family, I believe," replied Wilton, dryly.

"However, I do not know the Earl's brother myself, nor am I aware whether there is any other Captain Churchill or not; but this was a young gentleman, evidently under thirty, and consequently he could not be Sir George Barkley."

"I have searched the house high and low," said the voice of another stout gentleman, who now pushed his way into the room; "and I can find nothing but a sick cat up in the garret."

"Ay, ay, Brother Bulrush, ay, ay!" replied the clergyman; "ay, ay, it is all explained. It is all that Messenger's fault, and he has now run away again. This worshipful young gentleman is secretary to the Earl of Byerdale, the great minister; and I'm sure we are both very sorry to have given him any trouble."

"You have given me no trouble at all, gentlemen," replied Wilton, "and I have only to beg that if the Messenger return after I am gone, you will send him up to town tomorrow morning in the custody of a constable. I shall not fail to report to Lord Byerdale your activity and zeal upon the present occasion; which, indeed, may be of some service, as I am sorry to say, that serious remonstrances have been made regarding this part of the country, it being intimated, that smuggling, coining, and even treasonable meetings and assemblies, are more common here than in any other part of Kent."

"Indeed, sir," replied one of the justices, somewhat alarmed, "indeed, it is not our fault. They are an unruly set, they are a most unruly set. We do the best we may, but cannot manage them.--But, sir, the young lady looks fatigued and tired. Had she not better come up to the parsonage, and rest there this night. She shall have a good warm bed, and Mrs. Jeffreys, who is a motherly sort of woman, will be quite delighted to take care of her ladyship."

"Or Lady Bulrush either, I am sure," said the other magistrate. "The manor-house is but half a mile."

Wilton turned to Laura, to inquire what she thought fit to do; but the young lady, not very much prepossessed in favour either of the motherly sort of clergyman's wife, or the more elevated Lady Bulrush, by the appearance and manners of their marital representatives, leaned both her hands upon Wilton's arm, feeling implicit confidence in him alone, and security with him only; and, raising her eyes imploringly to his face, she said in a low voice, "Indeed, indeed, Wilton, I would rather not--I would rather go home to Beaufort House at once, to relieve my poor father's anxiety."

"In truth," he replied, in the same tone, "I cannot but think it would be better for you to obtain a night's rest, if you can, rather than to take a long journey after such terrible agitation as you have undergone."

"Do not ask me--nay, do not ask me," she said; and then turning to the magistrates, who were conferring together, and settling in their own mind that a match was undoubtedly to take place between the Lady Laura and the Earl of Byerdale's secretary, she added, "I am very anxious to return to my father, gentlemen, and as a carriage has been already sent for from Stroud, I would certainly prefer going on to-night. I will very gratefully," she added--her apprehensions of some new dangers occurring at the little public-house coming back upon her mind--"I will very gratefully accept the shelter of the parsonage, till the carriage arrives from Stroud, if by so doing I shall not keep the lady up beyond her usual hour."

"Oh, not at all, madam, not at all," replied the clergyman: "Mrs. Jeffreys will be delighted to see you.--Let us lose no time.--Wicks, when the carriage comes, send it up to my house.--Ma'am, I will show your ladyship the way."

Laura, however, still clung to Wilton's arm, as her best support; and following the clergyman together, they proceeded to the parsonage, escorted by a number of footmen, farming servants, and people collected in haste, who had come to the examination of Wicks's house. On their arrival, they were ushered into a tall dining-room with carved panels, the atmosphere of which was strongly imbued with the mingled odour of punch and tobacco, an unsavoury but at that time very ordinary perfume in the dining-room of almost every country gentleman. The mistress of the mansion, however, proved, in point of manners and appearance, considerably superior to her lord and master, and did all that she could in a very kind and delicate manner to render the beautiful girl, cast for the time on her hospitality, as comfortable as the circumstances would admit.

It is not to be denied, indeed, that both Wilton and Laura could at that time have very well spared the presence of any other persons, for there were feelings in the hearts of both which eagerly longed for voice. There was much to be told; there was much to be explained; there was much to be determined between them. There was, indeed, the consciousness of mutual love, which is no slight blessing and comfort, under any circumstances; but that very consciousness produced the longing thirst for farther communion which nothing but love can give.

When all has been said, indeed--when the whole heart has been poured forth--when the first intense feelings of a new passion have worn away, or, having grown familiar to our bosoms, surprise us no longer, we can better bear the presence of others; for a look, an occasional word, even a tone, will convey to the mind of those we love, all that we could wish to say. But when love is fresh, and every feeling produced thereby is new and wonderful to our hearts; when we make hourly discoveries of new sensations in our own bosoms, and neither know how to express them, nor how to conceal them, the presence of others--cold, indifferent, strange--is no slight punishment and privation.

Laura endeavoured, as far as possible, to keep down such feelings, but yet she could not drive them from her bosom. The minutes seemed long, tedious, and heavy: from time to time she would fall into a fit of musing; from time to time she would answer wide from the question; but it fortunately so happened, that the events which had lately occurred, and her anxiety to rejoin her father, were causes sufficient to account for greater inequalities of conduct than these.

In the meantime, Wilton was subjected to the same, or even greater pain, from the impossibility of saying all that he could have wished to say; and he had, moreover, to contend both against the civility of his landlord, individually, and the curiosity of the two magistrates, conjointly, who did not fail, during the time that he remained, both to press hire to eat and drink, in spite of all denials and remonstrances, and to torment him with questions, many of them frivolous in the extreme, not only concerning the events in which he had been lately engaged, but also in regard to everything that was taking place in London.

Nearly two hours passed in this unpleasant manner; but at length the joyful sound of carriage-wheels announced that the man who had been sent to Stroud had returned. Laura was eager to set out; but the motherly care of good Mrs. Jeffreys detained her for some time longer, by insisting upon wrapping her warmly up in cloaks, and mantles, and hoods, to guard against the cold of the wintry night.

At length all was ready; and Wilton led her down to the carriage, which it seems had been procured with difficulty; the machines called post-chaises being not so common in those days as they became within fifty years afterwards. The two magistrates stood bowing low to the young lady as she entered the tall, long-backed, but really not uncomfortable vehicle. The landlord of the inn, too, and his ostler, were there; and Wilton failed not to pay them liberally for the services they had rendered. He then briefly gave his own address, and that of the Duke to his reverend entertainer, and entered the carriage beside the Lady Laura, with a heart beating high with the hope and expectation of saying all and hearing all that the voice of love could speak.

CHAPTER XXIX.

For once--perhaps the only time that ever such a thing happened in this world--hope and expectation were not disappointed. Wilton seated himself by the side of Laura, the postilion cracked his whip, which was then as common in England as it is now in France, the horses went forward, and the wheels rolling through the little street of High Halstow, were soon upon the road to Stroud.

There was a silent pause between Wilton and Laura for some minutes, neither of them could very well tell why; for both of them had been most anxious for the opportunity, and both of them had been not a little grieved that their former conversation had been interrupted. The truth is, however, that very interruption had rendered the conversation difficult to renew; for love--sometimes the most impudent of all powers--is at other times the most shy and bashful. Wilton, however, found that he must not let the silence go on much longer, and he gently took Laura's hand in his, saying, perhaps somewhat abruptly--

"Dear Laura, everything that we have to say to each other, must be said now."

"Oh, Wilton!--" was her only reply; but she left her hand in his, and he went on.

"You had just spoken, when we were interrupted," he said, "words that made me very, very happy, though they were coupled with expressions of fear and apprehension. I have nothing to tell you, dear Laura, that can altogether remove those fears and apprehensions, but I can say something, perhaps, that may mitigate them. You are not aware of the circumstances in which I have had the happiness of seeking you and finding you this night; but you doubtless heard me mention, that it was your father who intrusted me with the search; and surely, dear Laura, that must show no slight trust and confidence on his part--may I add, no slight regard."

"Oh, I am sure he feels that for you," replied Laura, "quite sure! but yet such a trust shows, indeed, far more regard than I knew he entertained, and that gives me some degree of hope. Still, I cannot judge, Wilton, unless I had seen the manner in which my father did it. You must tell me all that has been done and said in this unfortunate business: you must tell me everything that has occurred. Will you?-- and I will tell you, upon my word, exactly what the impression is that it all makes upon my mind."

Wilton had not spoken of their love; Laura had not mentioned the subject either; but they had done fully as much, they had referred to it as a thing known and acknowledged. Wilton had recalled words that had made him very happy, and Laura had spoken of hopes which could only apply to her union with himself.

He now, however, told her all that had occurred, briefly though clearly. He dwelt not, indeed, on his own feelings during the painful events lately past; but the few words that he did speak on that subject were of such a kind as to show Laura instantly the distress and anxiety which her disappearance had caused him, the agony that he had suffered when he thought that she was lost to him for ever. The whole of her father's conduct, as displayed by Wilton, seemed to her strange and unaccountable; and well it might do so! for her lover told her the terrible state of mind in which the Duke had been at first, and yet he did not think fit to explain, in any degree, the causes which he felt sure had prevented her father from joining in the search himself. Notwithstanding all that had taken place in the presence of Laura, he judged it far better to avoid any mention of the unfortunate hold which Sir John Fenwick had obtained over the Duke, by drawing him in to take a share, however small, in the great Jacobite conspiracy of the day.

Laura, then, was greatly surprised at all she heard; and that Wilton should be employed in the affair seemed to her not the least strange part of the whole business. An expression of this surprise, however, induced Wilton to add, what he still in some degree feared, and had long hesitated to say.

"I do not, indeed, believe, dear Laura," he said, "that your father would have trusted me so entirely in this business, if it had not been for some words concerning myself which were spoken to him by Lord Byerdale when I was not present. They were repeated to me afterwards by Sherbrooke, and were to the effect, that although, in consequence of some of the late unfortunate disturbances in the country--the rebellions, the revolutions, the changes of dynasties that have happened within the last twenty years--it was necessary to conceal my birth and station, yet my blood was as pure and ancient as that of your father himself. This, I think, made a change in all his feelings towards me."

Wilton felt the small rounded fingers of Laura's hand rest, for a single instant, more heavily in his own, while she drew a deep long breath, as if a weight had been taken from her bosom.

"Oh, Wilton!" she said, "it makes all the difference in his views. It will make all the difference in our fate. You know that it would make none to me; that the man I loved would be loved under any circumstances of fortune or station, but with him it is the first, the greatest consideration. There may be difficulties still; there may be opposition; for, as you know, I am an only child, and my father thinks that nothing can equal what I have a right to expect; but still that opposition will vanish when he sees that my happiness is concerned, if the great and predominant prejudice of his education is not arrayed against us. Oh! Wilton, Wilton, your words have made me very happy."

Her words certainly made Wilton happy in return;--indeed, most happy. His fate had suddenly brightened from all that was dark and cheerless, from a situation in which the sweet, early dream of love itself but rendered everything that was sombre, painful, and distressing in his course, more gloomy, more bitter, more full of despair, it had changed, to the possession and the hope of all that the most sanguine imagination could have pictured of glad, and joyful, and happy, to the prospect of wealth and station, to the hope of obtaining the being that he loved best on earth, and to the certainty of possessing her early, her first, her warm, her full affection.

Had Wilton given way to what he felt at that moment, he would have clasped her to his heart and sealed the covenant of their love on the sweet lips that gave him such assurance of happiness. But he remembered that she was there alone with him, in full confidence, under the safeguard of all his best feelings, and he would not for the world have done one thing that in open day could have called the colour into her cheek. He loved her deeply, fully, and nobly, and though, under other circumstances, he might scarcely have hesitated, he now forebore. But again and again he pressed his lips upon her hand, and thanked her again and again for all that she had said, and for all the hopes and glad tidings that her words implied.

Their conversation then turned to love, and to their feelings towards each other. How could it be helped? And Wilton told her all; how the passion had grown upon him, how he had struggled hard against it, how not even despair itself had been able to crush it; how it had gone on and increased in spite of himself; how intense, how ardent it had become. He could not tell her exactly, at least he would not, what he had felt on her account, when he believed that she was likely to become the bride of Lord Sherbrooke; but he told her fully, ay, and eloquently, what agony of mind he had endured when he thought of seeing her give her hand to any other man, without affording him an apparent chance of even making an effort for himself. In short, he gave her the whole picture of his personal feelings; and there is no woman that is not gratified at seeing such a picture displayed, when she is herself the object. But to a mind such as that of Lady Laura, and to feelings such as were in her bosom, the tale offered higher and nobler sources of delight. The love, the deep love, which she felt, and which was now acknowledged to her own heart, required every such assurance of full and ample return as his words afforded, to render it confident and happy. But from the display of his feelings which he now made, she felt, she saw, she knew that she was loved as she could wish to be--loved as fully, as intensely, as deeply, as she herself loved--loved with all those feelings, high, and bright, and sweet, which assured her beyond all question that the affection which she had inspired would be permanent as well as ardent.

Wilton won her, too, to speak upon the same subject as himself, though, of course, he could not expect her to dwell upon what she felt in the same manner. There was a great difference: on the one hand, all the sensations of his heart towards her were boldly avowed and minutely detailed; the history of his love was told in language straightforward, eager, and powerful. The love of her bosom, on the contrary, was shadowed forth rather than spoken, admitted rather than told, her feelings were referred to, but not depicted.

"You make me glad, Wilton," she said, "by telling me all this, for I almost feared--and was teasing my own heart about it at the rectory, lest I should have done the unwomanly thing of loving first--I will not call it, being too easily won; for I should certainly despise the woman who thought anything necessary to win her, when once she really loved, further than the conviction of her lover's sincerity, and honour, and nobility of spirit. But yet I thought, that even you might somewhat despise me, if you found that I had loved you before you loved me. And yet, Wilton," she added, after a momentary pause, "I cannot help thinking that even if it had been so, I should have been more pardonable than many people, on account of the very great services you have rendered me at various times, and the perils you have encountered in my behalf. How could I help loving a man who has twice risked his life for me?"

"Oh, dear Laura," replied Wilton, "those services have been very small ones, and not worthy of your naming. I certainly did strive to conceal my love," he continued; "but I believe that, let us struggle against our feelings as we will, there are always some signs and tokens which show to the eyes of those we love--if there be any sympathy between their hearts and ours--that which is passing in regard to themselves within the most secret places of our bosom. There is a cabalistic language in love, Laura--unknown to any but those who really do love, but learnt in a moment, when the mighty secret is communicated to our hearts. We speak it to each other without knowing it, dear Laura, and we are understood, without an effort, if there be sympathy between us."

In such conversation wore the night away, as the carriage wended slowly onward. Two changes of horses were required to carry Laura and her lover back to the metropolis, and bells had to be rung, ostlers and postilions wakened, horses brought slowly forth, and many another tedious process to be gone through, which had brought the night nearly to a close, before the carriage crossed the wide extent of Blackheath, and passed through a small part of the town of Greenwich, which had then never dreamt of the ambitious project that it has since achieved, of climbing up that long and heavy hill.

Wilton and Laura had sufficient matter for conversation during the whole way: for when they had said all that could be said of the present and the past, there still remained the future to be considered; and Laura entreated her lover by no precipitate eagerness to call down upon them opposition, which, if it showed itself of a vehement kind at first, might only strengthen, instead of diminishing with time. She besought him to let everything proceed as it had hitherto done, till his own fate was fully ascertained, and any doubt of his birth and station in society was entirely removed.

"Till that is the case," she said, "to make any display of our feelings towards each other might only bring great pain upon us both. My father might require me not to see you, might positively forbid our thinking of each other; whereas, were all difficulties on that one point removed, he might only express a regret that fortune had not been more favourable to you, or require a delay, to make him certain of our sincere and permanent attachment. After that point is made clear, let us be open as the day with him. In the meanwhile, he must receive you as a friend who has rendered him the greatest and deepest of services; and I shall ever receive you, Wilton, I need not tell you, as the only dear and valued friend that I possess."

"But suppose, dear Laura," said Wilton, "suppose I were to see you pressed to marry some one else; suppose I were to see some suitor in every respect qualified to hope for and expect your hand--"

"You do not doubt me, Wilton?" said Lady Laura.

"Oh no!" he replied. "Not for a moment, Laura. But it would be very painful."

"It would be so to us both," she replied; "but I would take care that the pain should soon be brought to an end. Depend upon it, Wilton, it will be better as I say; let us not, in order to avoid uncertain pains and dangers, run into certain ones."

Wilton at once yielded to her views, and promised to be entirely guided by her opinion.

The day broke upon them just as they were passing through London, on their way to Beaufort House; but the night which had just passed had left them with changed feelings in many respects. It had been one of those eventful periods which come in, from time to time, like revolutions in states, to change entirely the very constitution of our whole thoughts and feelings, to give a new character and entirely new combinations to the strange microcosm within us. That great change had been effected in Laura by that which is the great first mover of a woman's destinies. She loved and had avowed her love: she was married in spirit to the man beside her, and she felt that to a heart like hers eternity itself could not dissolve the tie which had that night been voluntarily established between them. She viewed not such things as many, nay, most other women view them; she looked not on such engagements, she looked not on such affections, as things to be taken up and dropped, to be worn to-day, in the gloss of novelty, and cast away to-morrow, like a fretted garment; she judged not that it was the standing before the altar and receiving the ring upon her finger, and promising to wear out earthly existence with another human being, that constitutes the union which must join woman to the man of her heart. But she regarded the avowal of mutual love, the promise of unchanging affection, as a bond binding for ever; as, in fact, what we have called it, the marriage of the spirit: as a thing never to be done away, which no time could break, no circumstances dissolve: it was the wedding of--forever. The other, the more earthly union, might be dear in prospect to her heart, gladdening to all her hopes, mingled with a thousand bright dreams of human joy, and tenderness, and sweet domestic peace: but if circumstances had separated her the next hour from Wilton for ever, she would have felt that she was still his wife in heart, and ended life with the hope of meeting him she had ever loved, in heaven. To take such ties upon herself, then, was in her estimation no light thing; and, as we have said, the period, the short period, of that night, was sufficient to effect a great, a total change in all the thoughts and feelings of her bosom.

The change in Wilton was of a different kind, but it was also very great. It was an epoch in man's destiny. His mind was naturally manly, powerful, and decided; but he was very young. The events of that night, however, swept away everything that was youthful or light from his character for ever. He had acted with vigour, and power, and determination, amongst men older, better tried, and more experienced than himself. He had taken a decided and a prominent part in a scene of strife, and danger, and difficulty, and he had (to make use of that most significant though schoolboy phrase) "placed himself." His character had gone through the ordeal: without any previous preparation, the iron had been hardened into steel; and if any part had remained up to that moment soft or weak, the softness was done away, the weakness no longer existed.

CHAPTER XXX.

If we were poets or fabulists, and could invest inanimate objects with all the qualities and feelings of animate ones; if, with all the magic of old AEsop, we could make pots and kettles talk, and endue barn-door fowls with the spirit of philosophy, we should be tempted to say that the great gates of Beaufort House, together with the stone Cupids on the tops of the piers, ay, and the vases of carved flowers which stood between those Cupids, turned up the nose as the antiquated, ungilt, dusty, and somewhat tattered vehicle containing the Lady Laura Gaveston and Wilton Brown rolled up.

The postboy got off his horse; Wilton descended from the vehicle, and applied his hand eagerly to the bell; and Laura, who had certainly thought no part of the journey tedious, did now think the minutes excessively long till the gates should be thrown open. In truth, the hour was still an early one; the morning cold and chilly, with a grey biting east wind, making the whole scene appear as if it were looked at through ground glass; and neither the porter nor the porter's wife had thought it expedient to venture forth from their snug bed at such an unpropitious moment. A second time Wilton applied his hand to the bell, and with more success than before, for in stays and petticoat, unlaced and half tied, forth rushed the grumbling porter's wife, with a murmured "Marry come up: people are in great haste: I wonder who is in such a hurry!"

The sight of Wilton, however, whom she had seen very lately with the Duke, but still more the sight of her young lady, instantly altered her tone and demeanour, and with a joyful swing she threw the gates wide open. The chaise was drawn round to the great doors of the house, and here a more ready entrance was gained.

"Is the Duke up?" demanded Wilton, as the servant opened the door.

"Oh yes, sir," replied the man: "he was up before day-break: but he is not out of his dressing-room yet."

Laura ran up the steps into the vestibule, to see her father, and to relieve his mind at once from all that she knew he was suffering on her account. She paused, however, for a moment at the top to see if Wilton followed; but he merely advanced a few steps, saying, "I will leave you to converse with your father; for, of course, I have very much to do; and he will be glad to spend some time with you alone, and hear all that you have to tell him."

"But you will come back," said Lady Laura, holding out her hand to him: "you will not be away long."

"Until the evening, perhaps," said Wilton, pressing that fair hand in his own: "I may have many things to do, and the Earl may also require my presence."

"Oh, but you must come to dinner--I insist," said Lady Laura. "You know I have a right to command now," she added, in a lower tone, "and therefore I will tell my father to expect you at dinner."

"I will come if I can," replied Wilton, "but--"

His sentence was interrupted, however, by the Duke's voice at the top of the stairs, exclaiming, "Surely that is Laura's voice? Laura, Laura! My child, my dear child!"

And the next moment, Lady Laura, darting on, was in her father's arms.

Wilton Brown turned away; and without waiting to press a third person upon a scene which should always be enacted between two alone, he got into the post-chaise, and bade the postilion drive him back into London, for it must be recollected that Beaufort House was out of the town. This was easily accomplished, as the reader may imagine; and having dressed himself, and removed the traces of blood and travel from his face, he hastened to the house of Lord Byerdale, to give hire an account of the success of his expedition.

The Earl had not been long up; but he had already gone to his cabinet to write letters, and take his chocolate at the same time. On entering, Wilton, without any surprise, found Arden, the Messenger, in the presence of the Earl; for the man, knowing that the situation in which he stood was a somewhat perilous one, was of course anxious to make the best of his story before the young gentleman appeared. What did very much surprise Wilton, however, was the gracious and even affectionate manner in which the Earl received him. He rose from his chair, advanced two or three steps to meet him, and shaking him warmly by the hand, exclaimed, "Welcome back, my dear Wilton. So you have been fully and gallantly successful, I find. But what is all this that Arden is telling me? He is making a terrible accusation against you here, of letting off Sir George Barkley, one of the most notorious Jacobites in Europe--a very dangerous person, indeed."

"My lord," replied Wilton, "Mr. Arden is repeating to you a falsehood which he devised last night. It is quite true, indeed, that if he had not been a most notorious coward, and run away at the first appearance of danger, there might have been a chance, though a very remote one, of our securing Sir George Barkley."

"Indeed!" exclaimed the Earl: "then you did meet with him?"

"Amongst the persons whom I had to encounter," replied Wilton, "there was a gentleman whom they called Sir George, and who, from his height, his age, and a deep scar upon his cheek, I have no earthly doubt, is Sir George Barkley: but he had been gone for an hour before this mighty brave gentleman, having collected forty or fifty people to keep his own head from harm, thought fit to come back and seek for me. The person who was with me when he did return was a tall fine-looking young man of five or six and twenty."

"Indeed!" said the Earl. "Who could that be?"

"He called himself Captain Churchill," replied Wilton. "I do not mean to say, my lord, that I believe such was his real name; for I do not: but I never saw Captain Churchill at all; and I never saw this gentleman till the moment when he came to my aid and rescued me, with the assistance of another, from the hands of as desperate a set of men as I ever met in my life, and who would certainly have murdered me had it not been for his arrival. I have a report to make to your lordship upon all Mr. Arden's proceedings, who, notwithstanding your most positive commands to obey me in all things, has refused to obey me in anything, and by the delays he has occasioned, and the obstructions he has thrown in my way, very nearly prevented me from effecting the liberation of Lady Laura at all."

"Your lordship will believe what you choose," replied Arden, in a saucy tone. "All I mean to say is, I am sure that gentleman was not Captain Churchill; and so you will find, if you inquire. Whoever he was, Mr. Brown aided his escape, and prevented me from doing my duty."

"Your duty, sir, was to obey Mr. Brown," replied the Earl, sternly; "for that I shall take care that you are punished; and if it should prove that this gentleman was really Captain Churchill, you shall be dismissed from your office. You will attend here again at two o'clock, by which time I shall have written to Captain Churchill, to know whether he was the person present or not.--Now leave the room."

Arden slunk doggedly away, seeing that Wilton's star happened to be in the ascendant. Had he known how much it was so, however, having often heard the Earl speak sharply and discourteously to the young gentleman, he would have been more surprised even than he was at the change which had taken place. The moment he was gone, and the door closed, the Earl again shook Wilton by the hand.

"You have accomplished your task most brilliantly, Wilton," he said, "and I shall take care that you reap the reward of your diligence and activity, by any effort that depends upon me; but from all that I have seen, and heard, and know, you are likely to obtain, from the very act itself, far higher recompences than any that I could bestow. You are indeed a fortunate young man."

"I am fortunate in your lordship's approbation," replied Wilton; "but I see not why you should call me so in any other respect, except, indeed, in being so fortunate as to effect this young lady's liberation."

"In that very respect," replied the Earl, with a look full of meaning. "Good heavens! my dear Wilton, are you blind? If you are so, I am not; and at your age, certainly I should not have been blind to my own advantage. You think, perhaps, that because Lady Laura has refused to marry Sherbrooke, and broken off the proposed alliance between our families, it would make me angry to find she had placed her affections anywhere else. But I tell you no, Wilton! Quite the contrary is the case. The discovery that she has done so, at once banished all the anger and indignation that I felt. If with a free heart she had so decidedly refused my son, I should have considered it as little less than an insult to my whole family, and, in fact, did consider it so till Sherbrooke himself expressed his belief that she was, and has been for some time, attached to you. His words instantly recalled to my memory all that I had remarked before, how the colour came up into her cheek whenever you approached her, how her eye brightened at every word you said. That made the matter very different. I could not expect the poor young lady to sacrifice her first affection to please me: nor could I wish her, as you may well imagine, to marry Sherbrooke, loving you. This is the reason that makes me say that you area most fortunate man; for the service that you have rendered her, the immense and important service, gives you such a claim upon her gratitude, as to make it easy for her at once to avow her attachment. It gives you an enormous claim upon the Duke, too; and I have one or two little holds upon that nobleman which he knows not of--by which, indeed, he might be not a little injured, if I were a revengeful man, but which I shall only use for your best interests."

"But, my lord," replied Wilton, "you seem totally to forget my humble birth and station. How--situated as I am--could I dare to ask the Duke for his daughter's hand, the only remaining child of such a house, the heiress of such immense wealth?"

"Fear not, fear not, Wilton," said the Earl, laying his hand upon his arm. "Fear not: your blood is as good as the Duke's own; your family, older and as noble."

"I have sometimes thought, my lord," replied Wilton, wishing to gain as much information as possible--"I have sometimes thought, in the utter ignorance wherein I have been left of my own history, that I am the son of one who has indeed been a father to me, Lord Sunbury,--the natural son, I mean."

"Oh no!" cried the Earl, with an air almost of indignation: "you are no relation of his whatsoever. I knew not who you were when you first came hither; but I have since discovered, and though at present I must not reveal anything farther to you, I tell you, without hesitation, to set your mind at ease, to pursue your suit towards Lady Laura, if you have really any regard for her, and to aspire to her hand. In a very few months more you shall know all."

Wilton cast down his eyes, and mused.

"This is not a little strange," he said; "but I know I may place implicit reliance on your lordship's word, and proceed in a matter where I own my heart is deeply engaged, without the risk of calling upon myself a charge of gross presumption."

"You may, you may," answered the Earl, eagerly; "and if the Duke should discover your mutual affection, and make any objection, merely refer him to me. But now let us hear more of your adventures of yesterday and last night."

Wilton would have been very well contented to muse for a few minutes over what the Earl said. Although his experience of the world was not great, yet he had a sufficient portion of good sense to supply experience in a high degree. This good sense told him, that a sudden and extraordinary change in the demeanour of any man, but more especially in that of a man both subtle and determined, was more or less to be suspected. He would fain, then, have obtained time to seek for the real motives and views of the Earl of Byerdale, in the extraordinary fit of kindness and condescension which had seized upon him; for he could almost fancy that the Earl was contriving his ruin, by engaging him in some rash endeavour to obtain the hand of Lady Laura.

Strong, however, in her love, he resolved to go on, to deal with her and with her father in all honour, and, supposing even that the Earl was endeavouring to play him false, to try whether straightforward and upright honesty, guided by a clear head, a firm heart, and a well prepared mind, might not win the game against subtilty and worldly cunning.

The Earl marked him as he mused for a minute, but saying nothing more upon the subject of his hopes, still pressed him to speak of the events of the preceding day. It was somewhat difficult for Wilton so to shape his words as not to mention Lord Sherbrooke, and not to involve himself in any such distinct account of the Jacobites and their proceedings as might lead to their arrest, and force him at some future period to become a witness against them. He succeeded tolerably well, however. He could not, and indeed he did not, think it right to conceal, that he was perfectly certain the men he met with were engaged in the most dark and dangerous designs. But he stated, at the same time, that such was merely the impression upon his mind, for that no distinct avowal of their purposes had been made in his presence, so as to justify him in charging them with treason.

"Nevertheless, my lord," he added, "I think it highly and absolutely necessary for you to take the same measures as if you knew that a general insurrection was contemplated, for I feel perfectly certain that something of the kind is in agitation."

The Earl smiled. "Now tell me, Wilton," he said, "amongst these worthy conspirators, did you see any one that was personally known to you?"

Wilton hesitated.

"Come, come, my young friend," said the Earl--"you must speak out. We will not make an evidence of you, I promise you; and, indeed, both the King himself and all his ministers would be very glad that these persons should get beyond sea, and relieve us of their troublesome presence, provided--mark me--provided, there does not exist the clearest and most distinct proof, not alone that they are conspiring to overthrow the present dynasty--for such conspiracies have been going on in every corner of the kingdom, and in the heart of every family, for the last ten years, so that we should only make them worse by meddling with them--but that these men are conspiring in a darker, a more dangerous, a more treasonable, or a more dishonourable manner, than has ever been clone before. I must explain this business to you, Wilton, and my views upon it. Politicians have adopted as a maxim that a plot discovered and frustrated always strengthens the hands of the existing government; but this maxim is far too general, and consequently often proves false and dangerous in application. The conditions under which the discovery and frustration of a plot do really strengthen the hands of government are peculiar. There must be circumstances attending upon the whole transaction which, when the plot is exposed, either destroy the means of future conspiracies formed upon the same basis, remove for ever the objects of the conspirators, or cause a great change in public feeling, in regard to their views and motives. If the discovery be so general, the frustration so complete, and the punishment so severe, as to raise the power and authority of the government in the eyes of the people, to awaken a wholesome fear in the disaffected, and to encourage and elevate the well disposed and the friends of the state, a very great object is certainly gained; and that which was intended to ruin a government or overthrow a dynasty, serves but to root it more firmly than before. There is another case, also, which is very applicable at the present moment. If there be something in the nature and designs of the conspiracy, so odious in its means, its character, and its objects, as to enlist against the conspirators sensations of horror, indignation, and contempt, one gains from public feeling very much more by its discovery and exposure, than even by the power of fear over the disaffected, and the elevation of triumph on the part of the well disposed. But in other circumstances, either when partial discoveries are made, when the success is not of the most absolute, general, and distinct kind, when the objects of the conspirators excite many sympathies, the errors they commit admit of easy palliation, the means they employ are noble, generous, and chivalrous, and the fate they undergo is likely to produce commiseration, the detection and crushing of them only tends to multiply and strengthen similar endeavours. With such conspiracies as these, no wise minister will ever meddle, if he can help it; the more quiet the means he can adopt to frustrate them, the better; the less he exposes them and brings them into light, the greater will be his success; for they are like the Lernwan serpent, whose heads multiplied as they were smitten off; and it is far more easy to smother them privately than to smite them in public. This is the view I myself take of the matter; this is the view the King takes of it; and you may have remarked that there has been no attempt made for many years to investigate or punish plots here and there, although we have bad the proofs that hundreds existed every year. In this instance, however, the matter is different. There is reason to believe that the present conspiracy is one of such a dark and horrible nature, as instantly to excite the indignation of the whole people, to make all the better part of the Jacobites ashamed of the deeds of their friends, and to rouse up universal feelings of loyalty throughout the land. The fact is, the thing is already discovered. Information has long been tendered to the government by various persons implicated: but acting upon the plan which we have generally pursued, such advances have been met coldly, till last night more distinct, and definite information was given by some one, who, instead of being actuated by motives of gain, or of fear, as we suspected in all other cases, came forward, it seems, from personal feelings of gratitude towards the King himself. His majesty promised this person not to bring him forward in the business at all, and has refused to give up his name, even to me. But his conviction of the truth of all that was told was so strong, that the previous informer was sent for last night at one o'clock to the palace at Kensington, to which place I also had been summoned. The whole facts, the names, the designs of everybody concerned, were then completely discovered, and I have been busying myself ever since I rose, in adopting the proper measures for arresting and punishing the persons directly implicated. Having explained to you these views, I must now put my question again. Did you see any one amongst these conspirators with whose person you were acquainted? I only ask for my own satisfaction, and on every account shall abstain from bringing your name forward, in the slightest degree."

"There was only one person, my lord," replied Wilton, who had listened with deep interest to this long detail; "there was only one person, my lord, that I had ever knowingly seen before, and that was Sir John Fenwick."

"I signed a warrant for his arrest half an hour ago," rejoined the Earl, "and there are two Messengers seeking him at this moment. I think you said you saw Sir George Barkley?"

"I cannot absolutely say that, my lord," replied Wilton; "but I certainly saw a gentleman whom I believed, and most firmly do still believe, to be him: he was a tall, thin, sinister-looking man, of a somewhat saturnine complexion, with a deep scar on his cheek."

"The same, the same," said the Earl, "undoubtedly the same. Listen, if you know any of these names;" and he read from a list--"Sir William Parkyns, Captain Rookwood, Captain Lowick, Sir John Friend, Charnock, Cranburne, the Earl of Aylesbury--"

"The Earl certainly was not there, my lord," replied Wilton; "for I know him well by sight, and I saw no one, I can assure you, whom I knew, but Sir John Fenwick."

"And this Plessis, at whose house you saw them," continued the Earl--"did he seem to be taking a share in the business with them? He is an old friend of mine, this Master Plessis; and obtains for me some of the best information that I ever get from abroad. I do not know what I should do without Plessis. He is the most useful man in the world. We must let him off, at all events; but it will be no bad thing to have a rope round his neck, either."

"I cannot say, my lord," replied Wilton, "that he took any part whatsoever in the business. In the matter of setting free Lady Laura, he showed himself more afraid of these good gentry than fond of them, and after their arrival, he ran away and hid himself."

"And yet," said the Earl, "he's a rank Jacobite, too. But that does not signify. He's an excellent creature, and the greatest rogue in Christendom. All this chocolate comes from him; there's nothing like it in Europe. Won't you take some, Wilton? I forgot to ask if you had broken your fast."--Wilton replied that he had not, and the Earl made him sit down and follow his example, of writing letters and taking his chocolate at the same time. One of the notes, however, which the Earl himself wrote, attracted his secretary's attention in some degree; for as soon as Lord Byerdale had concluded it, he rang the bell and gave it to a servant, saying, "Take that to Captain Churchill's lodgings. You know where he lives, just in Duke Street. Wait for an answer."

The man went away, and business proceeded. At the end of about an hour, however, the servant returned, saying, as an excuse for his long absence, that Captain Churchill was in bed when he reached his house, and that his valet had refused to wake him.

"When he did wake, however, my lord," added the man, "he said he would not detain me to write a note, as I had been kept so long already; but would wait upon your lordship at the hour you named."

Shortly after the return of the servant, the Earl took up his papers, and prepared to proceed to Whitehall. Before he went, however, he paused opposite to the table at which Wilton was writing, and looking at him for a moment with a smile, he said,--

"You are surprised, Wilton, and have been puzzling yourself with the reason why I take so much more interest in you than I used to do. I will explain it all to you, Wilton, in one word. I did not at first know who you were. I now do, as I have before hinted; and my conduct to one whom I believed to be a natural son of the Earl of Sunbury, and who was forced upon me somewhat against my own will, was of course very different from that which I show towards a young gentleman of a high and noble family, not very distantly related to myself.--Now are you satisfied?"

And with these words he left the room. Yet, strange to say, Wilton, though not a little surprised at what he heard, knew the Earl of Byerdale, and was NOT satisfied. But at all events, the words which had passed set his mind at ease, in regard to Laura. He now felt that he was committing no breach of confidence; that he was pursuing no presumptuous suit, in seeking the object of his dearest and his brightest hopes; that though fortune might still be adverse, and such wealth might never be his, as to place him in a position equal, in that respect, to herself, yet he had every right and title to strive for her hand with the noblest of the land.

Wilton did not, indeed, entertain the vain thought that he brought with him a treasury of distinguished talents, high and noble feelings, a generous spirit, and a gallant heart--qualities which many a competitor, if not most, would want:--he did not, indeed, so argue the matter with himself; but there was in his bosom the proud consciousness of deserving well, and the still more strengthening and emboldening confidence, of loving well, truly, nobly, as Laura deserved to be loved.

Still, however, he was not satisfied with the sudden change in the Earl of Byerdale: there was something in it that roused suspicion; and he resolved to watch all that noble man's proceedings steadily and keenly, and if possible never to be off his guard for a moment.

Before the time appointed for the return of Arden, the Messenger, the Earl himself came home, bearing a smile of dark satisfaction on his countenance.

"Four or five of these gentry," he said, as he entered, "are already in custody, and one or two have been brought before the council. A man of the name of Cook, and another, seem well inclined to become approvers. If so, the matter will be easily managed. I find the rumour is spreading all over the town, with various additions and improvements, of course. I even hear that there were reports of it all yesterday, though neither the King, nor I, nor any one else, knew aught of the matter then."

"Are any of the principals caught, my lord?" demanded Wilton. "I confess, I believe that man, Sir John Fenwick, to be as great a villain as any upon earth; nor do I look upon him as a man of much courage either."

"He is not caught," replied the Earl; "but we have got one poor foolish fellow, called Sir John Friend, who has shown himself a friend to anybody but himself;" and he laughed at his own joke. "I rather suspect," he continued, "that there are a good many people not a little anxious for Fenwick's escape. With the exception of Sir George Barkley, he is undoubtedly the man of most importance amongst them. He is nearly connected, you know, with all the Howards, and was very intimate with your good friend the Duke. He is well acquainted with Lord Aylesbury, too; and I can tell you there are a good many suspicions in that quarter. There is another noble lord, Lord Montgomery, implicated; and all these good folks are suspected," and he proceeded to read a list of some twenty or thirty names. "But there is no intention of dealing harshly," he added; "and a distinction will be made between the more culpable and the less. Pray has Captain Churchill been here?"

"Not yet that I have heard of, my lord," replied Wilton; "but I fairly tell your lordship that I do not think he was the man I saw, though that was the name given."

The Earl rang the bell which stood upon the table, and when a servant appeared, demanded if Captain Churchill had been there.

The servant replied in the negative, but added that Mr. Arden was waiting. The Earl ordered him to be sent in; and the Messenger accordingly entered, bearing on his face an air of triumph and insolence which provoked Wilton's anger a good deal.

"Well, my lord," he said, not waiting for the Earl of Byerdale to speak--"I have got proof positive now, for I have been at Captain Churchill's lodgings, pumping his servants, and they tell me that he was very ill all yesterday, as, indeed, I knew he was, and in bed the greater part of the day."

"Indeed!" said the Earl. "This is strange enough! But as you say, Wilton, that you do not think it was really Captain Churchill, the name might be given merely as a nom de guerre, and the person giving it might be a very honest man, too."

Before he could conclude, one of the servants announced that Captain Churchill waited without; and in a moment after he was admitted, presenting to Wilton's eyes a person not very unlike in size and form the Duke of Berwick, and somewhat resembling him in countenance, but several years older, and somewhat darker in complexion.

He entered with a gay and smiling air, and with a grace of carriage and demeanour which was common to himself and his brother, afterwards the famous Duke of Marlborough.

"Why, my lord," he said, advancing towards Lord Byerdale, and shaking him by the hand, "I am almost alarmed at your unexpected summons, especially after all the terrible doings which I hear have taken place. Why, they tell me that the gates of Newgate have never ceased turning upon their hinges all the morning, and that the Tower itself is full."

"Not quite so bad as that," replied the Earl: "but I am sure, my dear Captain, you have nothing to fear in such a matter."

"Not that I know of," answered Churchill, "and I would have come at once when you wrote; but, to say the truth, I was up late last night, and slept till nearly noon this morning.--But, bless my soul!" he continued, turning towards Wilton--to that gentleman's utter surprise and astonishment "is not this my good friend, Mr. Wilton Brown, your lordship's secretary?" and advancing a step or two, he shook Wilton heartily by the hand.

"How is the young lady?" he continued. "I hope you got quite safe to London with your fair charge?"

The countenance of Arden, the Messenger, presented a ludicrous picture of disappointment and consternation. Wilton was certainly even more surprised than himself; but he did not suffer his face to betray any expression of wonder, though, it must be owned, he felt a strong inclination to laugh. He replied, however, calmly to Churchill's question,--

"I thank you very much, sir: she got quite safe to London. At an early hour this morning I left her with her father."

"Then, Captain Churchill," said the Earl, "you are neither more nor less than the person who rendered my young friend Wilton, here, such very good assistance last night."

Churchill made a low and complimentary bow, replying, "Oh, my lord, you are too good! The assistance that I rendered him was little enough, I can assure you. His own gallantry and good conduct did much more than I could possibly do.--But I hope and trust my good friend, Arden, the Messenger, there, is not waiting for me; for I can assure your lordship that, though I was upon a little frolic last night, which I might not very well like to have inquired into, it was certainly nothing of a Jacobitical nature, as you may well suppose, and as my good friend, Mr. Brown, here, can testify."

"I do not in the slightest degree suspect you, Churchill," replied the Earl. "The only point was to ascertain whether it was you or Sir George Barkley who was with my friend Wilton, here, last night; Arden, the Messenger, who has behaved very ill throughout the whole business, positively swearing, this morning, that Wilton was accompanied along part of the road by Sir George Barkley, the well-known traitor, and that he, Wilton, my private secretary, connived at and aided his escape."

"I can assure your lordship," replied Churchill, in a perfectly grave tone, "on my honour as a gentleman, I have the most perfect certainty, and could prove, if necessary, that the charge is entirely and totally false; that Sir George Barkley did not accompany your young friend for a single step, and that he was only accompanied by a fair lady with very bright eyes, by another gentleman whom I understand to be a certain Captain Byerly--a very respectable man, only that he rides a little hard upon the King's Highway--and by a person, of perhaps less importance and repute, named Captain Churchill."

"That is quite satisfactory, my dear sir," replied the Earl. "You hear, Mr. Arden. Be so good as to quit the room, and to remember, that from this moment you are no longer a Messenger of State."

Wilton could almost have found it in his heart to interpose, knowing all that he did know; but when he recollected the whole course of the man's bad conduct, he felt that the retribution which had fallen upon him was but just, and he left the matter to take its course. Churchill then conversed for a few minutes with the Earl, in an under tone; and as the business of the day seemed over, Wilton prepared to take his departure.

"Wait one moment, Mr. Brown," said Churchill, "and if you are going my way, I will accompany you."

"You will not fail, my dear Wilton, I trust," said the Earl, "to visit the young lady, and inquire after her health. Pray present my most devoted homage to her, and assure her that I have been most uneasy at her situation, and grieved for all that she must have undergone. I shall certainly wait upon her to-morrow. In the mean-time," he added, in a lower tone, "do not entertain any apprehensions in regard to your situation. Go boldly forward, make sure of her heart, and all the rest will be rendered much more easy than you imagine. Nothing that I can do for you shall be wanting; and you have only to let me know when you have any engagement at Beaufort House, and I will find means to do without your attendance here.--I beg your pardon, Captain Churchill; I only wished to give this young gentleman a word of good advice before he left me."

"And I only waited till he was ready, my lord," replied Churchill, "to take my leave of your lordship, wishing you full success in dealing with the nest of vaga-bonds you have got hold of."

Thus saying, he took his leave, and quitting the house together with Wilton, put his arm through his, and walked on as familiarly as if they had been old ac-quaintances.

CHAPTER XXXI.

It may be made a question of very great doubt, whether the faculty--and it is indisputably a faculty of the mind in its first freshness--the faculty of wondering at anything extraordinary, or out of the common course of our knowledge, is or is not productive of advantage as well as pleasure to us. But there can be no question whatsoever, that very great advantages are attached to the power of concealing our wonder. Nothing, indeed, should surprise us in life, for we are surrounded by daily miracles; nothing should surprise, because the combination of means in the hand of Almighty Power must be infinite; and to permit our wonder to appear at anything, is but to confess ourselves inexperienced, or unobserving, or thoughtless; and yet with all that, it is a very pleasant sensation.

Wilton Brown, from his commerce with the world, and especially from the somewhat bard lessons which he had received in the house of the Earl of Byerdale, had been taught, in communicating with persons unknown and indifferent to him, to put a strong restraint upon the expression of his feelings. On the present occasion, not having the slightest knowledge or conception of Captain Churchill's character, he walked on beside him, as their way seemed to lie together, without the slightest inquiry or expression of surprise in regard to what had taken place; and Captain Churchill was almost inclined to believe that his young companion was dull, apathetic, and insensible, although he had good reason to know the contrary. The silence, however, did somewhat annoy him; for he was not without a certain share of good-humoured vanity; and he thought, and thought justly, that he had acted his part to admiration. He resolved, therefore, to say nothing upon the subject either, as far as he could avoid it; and thus, strange to say, after the extraordinary scene which had taken place, the two people who had borne a part therein had got as far as the door of Captain Churchill's house in Duke-street, without interchanging a word upon the subject. There, however, Wilton was about to take his leave; but Churchill stopped him, saying,--

"Do me the favour of coming in for a moment or two, Mr. Brown. I have something which I wish to give you."

Wilton followed him up stairs, with merely some reply in the common course of civility; and Churchill, opening a cabinet in the drawing-room, took out a handsome diamond ring, saying, "I have received a commission this morning from a near relation of mine, who considers that he owes his life to you, to beg your acceptance of this little token, to remember him by when you look upon it. He sent it to me by a messenger at the moment that he was embarking for France, together with a letter of instructions as to how he wished me to act in case of there being any question regarding the transactions of last night."

"I saw," replied Wilton, "that you must have got information some way; but in whatever way you did get that information, you certainly played your part as admirably as it was possible to conceive. I fear I did not play mine quite so well, for I was taken by surprise."

"Oh, quite well enough, quite well enough," replied Captain Churchill. "To say the truth, my task was somewhat of a delicate one, for in these days one might easily involve one's self in imputations difficult to be got rid of again. My family have chosen our parts so strongly and decidedly, that my young relation did not venture to see me when he was in London; not, indeed, from any fear of my betraying him, for that, of course, was out of the question,--but rather from the apprehension of committing me. He trusted me with this other matter, however, probably not knowing, first, that I was ill, and had been in bed all yesterday, and, next, that this diabolical plot for assassinating the King and admitting the enemy into the heart of the land has been discovered. The letter came about an hour after Lord Byerdale's, and just in time to save me from denying that I was out of my own house all yesterday. But you do not take the ring, Mr. Brown: pray accept it as a mere token of gratitude and esteem on the part of the Duke. His esteem, I can assure you, is worth having."

"I doubt it not in the least, my dear sir," replied Wilton; "but yet I must beg to decline his gift: in the first place, because I am entitled to no gratitude; and in the next, because the Duke must be considered as an enemy of the government I serve. He certainly saved my life; for I do not suppose the man who was in the act of firing at me would have missed his mark, if his hand had not been knocked up. After that I could not, of course, suffer the Duke to be arrested by my side, if I could help it, and therefore I did what I could to assist him, but that was little."

Churchill endeavoured, by various arguments, to persuade his young companion to receive the ring; but Wilton would not suffer himself to be moved upon the subject; and had, at all events, the satisfaction of hearing Churchill himself acknowledge, as he was taking his leave, "Well, after all, I believe you are right."

Their conference was not very long; for it may be easily imagined, that one of the party, at least, was anxious to proceed on his way in another direction; and leaving Captain Churchill as soon as he decently could, Wilton returned to his house, changed his dress, and entered one of those vehicles called hackney coaches, which, in the days of King William III, were as rumbling and crazy, and even more slow, than at present.

Before he reached Beaufort House, Wilton's patience was well nigh exhausted; but if we may tell the truth, there was one as impatient. as himself. When they had arrived that morning at Beaufort House, Laura's thoughts had been divided. Her anxiety to see her father, to tell him she was safe, to give joy to the heart of one she loved with the fullest feelings of filial affection, had a strong share in all her sensations; but that was over, and her mind turned to Wilton again. In telling her father all that had occurred, in recounting everything that Wilton had done, in hearing from the Duke himself all her lover's exertions and anxiety, till he obtained some clue to the place where she was detained, vivid images were continually brought up before her mind of things that were most sweet to contemplate. When she retired to her own chamber, although she strove, at her father's request, to obtain sleep, those sweet but agitating images followed her still, and every word, and tone, and look of him she loved, returned to her memory, and banished slumber altogether from her pillow.

On whatever part of his conduct memory rested, to the eyes of affection it seemed all that could be desired. If she thought of him standing boldly in the presence of superior numbers--calm, cool, unintimidated, decided; or if she recalled his conduct to the Duke of Berwick, generously risking all rather than not repay that nobleman's gallant interposition in his favour by similar efforts in his behalf; or if she recollected his behaviour to herself; when alone under his care and guidance, the tenderness, the gentleness, the delicate forbearance, the consideration for all her feelings, and for every difficult point of her situation which he had displayed--each part of his behaviour seemed to her partial eyes all that she could have dreamed of excellent and good, and each part stood out in bright apposition with the other; the gentle kindness contrasting strongly with the firm and courageous determination; the generous and unhesitating protection of an upright and gallant enemy, seeming but the more bright from his calm and prudent bearing towards a body of low-minded and ill-designing traitors.

Thus, during the time that she remained alone, her thoughts were all of him, and those thoughts were all sweet. Gratitude, it is true, might derive a great portion of its brightness from love: but Laura fancied that she had not said half enough in return for all that he had done in her behalf: she fancied that she had scarcely spoken her thanks sufficiently warmly, and she longed to see him again, to talk over all that had taken place, to assure him of her deep, deep gratitude, and, perhaps--though she did not acknowledge that purpose to her own heart--to assure him also still more fully of her unchanging affection. Laura had never felt, even in the least degree, what love is before. She was not one of the many who trifle away their heart's brightest affections piece by piece. She had given her love all at once, and the sensation was the more overpowering.

At length, then, as the hour approached when she supposed he might be likely to return, she rose and dressed herself, and perhaps that day she thought more of her beauty than she had ever done before in life; but it was not with any vain pleasure; for she thought of it only inasmuch as it might please another whom she loved. We can all surely remember how, when in the days of our childhood we have had some present to give to a dear friend, we have looked at it and considered it, and fancied it even more valuable and delightful than it really was, with the bright hope of its appearing so to the person for whom it was destined. Thus with her toilet, Laura let her maid take as much pains as she would; and when she saw in the glass as lovely a face and form as that instrument of vanity ever reflected, and could not help acknowledging that it was so, she smiled with a pleasure that she had never felt before, to think that beauty also was a part of the dowry of bright things which she was to bring to him she loved.

Though the maid was somewhat longer with her mistress's toilet than usual, delaying it for a little, perhaps, with a view of obtaining farther information than Lady Laura was inclined to give her, upon all the events of the two or three days preceding, yet Laura was down in the saloon some time before the dinner-hour, and she looked not a little anxiously for the coming of Wilton. She was not inclined to chide him for delay, for she knew that it would be no fault of his if he were not there early. The Duke, not knowing that she had risen, had gone out; but he, too, had left her heart happy in the morning when they parted, by answering her, when she told him of the invitation she had given, with such encomiums of her deliverer, of his manner, of his character, of his person, and of his mind, that Laura was almost tempted into hopes more bright than the reality.

Notwithstanding all delays Wilton did at length arrive, and that, too, before the Duke returned, so that Laura had time to tell him how happy her father's praises of him had made her, and to insinuate hopes, though she did not venture absolutely to express them. Her words, and her manner, and her look, in consequence of all that had been passing in her mind during the morning, were more warm, more tender than they had even been before; and who could blame Wilton, or say that he presumed, if he, too, gave way somewhat more to the warm and passionate love of his own heart, than he had dared to venture during their preceding intercourse?

Laura did not blame him. She blushed, indeed, as he pressed her to his heart, though he was the man whom she loved best on earth; but yet, though she blushed, she felt no wrong: she felt, on the contrary, the same pure and endearing affection towards him that he felt for her, and knew that gentle pressure to be but an expression, on his part, of the same high, holy, and noble love with which she could have clung to his bosom in any moment of danger, difficulty or distress.

At length the Duke made his appearance; and eagerly grasped Wilton's hand in both his own, thanking him a thousand and a thousand times for restoring to him his beloved child, and telling him that no words or deeds could ever express his gratitude. Indeed, so much more eager, so much more demonstrative, was his whole demeanour, than that of his daughter, that he blamed Laura for coldness in expressing what she felt only too warmly for words; and until dinner was announced, he continued talking over all that had occurred, and inquiring again and again into each particular.

As they went into the dining-room, however, he made a sign to his daughter, whom he had cautioned before, and whispered to Wilton, "Of course, we must not talk of these things before the servants."

All that had passed placed Wilton now in a far different situation with the Duke and his daughter from that in which he had ever stood before. His mind was perfectly at ease with them, and the relief had its natural effect on his conversation: all the treasures of his mind, all the high feelings of his heart, he knew might be displayed fearlessly. He did not, indeed, seek to bring those treasured feelings forward; he did not strive to shine, as it is called, for that striving must in itself always give a want of ease. But poor, indeed, must be the mind, dull and slow the imagination, which, out of the ordinary things of life--ay! even out of the every-day conversation of beings inferior to itself--does not naturally and easily derive immense, unfathomable currents of thought, combinations of fancy, of feeling, and of reflection, which only want the licence of the will to flow on and sparkle as they go. It is, that the Will refuses that licence when we are with those that we despise or dislike: it is, that we voluntarily shut the flood-gates, and will not allow the streams to rush forth. But with Wilton it was very, very different now: he was in the presence of one whose eye was sunshine to him, whose mind was of an equal tone with his own; and there was besides in his bosom that strong passion in its strongest form which gives to everything it mingles with its own depth, and intensity, and power--which, like a mountain torrent, suddenly poured into the bed of some summer rivulet, changes it at once in force, in speed, in depth--that passion which has made dumb men eloquent, and cowards brave.

Thus, though the conversation began with ordinary subjects, touched but upon matters of taste and amusement, and approached deeper feelings only as a deviation from its regular course, yet at every turn it took, Wilton's mind displayed its richness and its power; till the Duke, who had considerable taste and natural feeling, as well as high cultivation of mind, looked with surprise and admiration towards his daughter; and every now and then Laura herself, almost breathless with mingled feelings of pleasure, pride, and affection, turned her eyes upon her father, and marked his sensations with a happy smile.

And yet it was all so natural, so easy, so unaffected, that one felt there was neither effort nor presumption. There was nothing of what the vulgar mass of common society call eloquence about it; but there was the true eloquence, which by a single touch wakes the sound that we desire to produce in the heart of another: which by one bright instantaneous flash lights up, to the perception of every one around, each point that we wish them to behold. Eloquence consists not in many words, but in few words: the thoughts, the associations, the images, may be many, but the acme of eloquence is in the rapidity of their expression.

Wilton, then, did not in any degree presume. He discoursed upon nothing; he did not even attempt to lead. The Duke led the conversation, and he followed: but it was like that famous entry of the Roman emperor, where an eagle was seen hovering round and round his head: the royal bird followed, indeed, the monarch; but in his flight took ten times a wider scope: the people hailed with loud gratulations the approach of Caesar, but in the attendant bird they recognised Jove. The Duke, however, who had taste, as we have said, and feeling, and who, in regard to conversational powers, was not a vain roan, was delighted with his guest, and laid himself out to lead Wilton on towards subjects on which he thought he would shine: but there was one very extraordinary thing in the history of that afternoon. There was not a servant in the hall--no, neither the laced and ribanded lackey lately hired in London, the old blue bottles from the country mansion, the stately butler and his understrapper of the cellaret, nor the Duke's own French gentleman, who stood very close to his master's elbow during the whole of dinner time--there was not one that did not clearly and perfectly perceive that their young lady was in love with her hand some deliverer, and did not comment upon it in their several spheres, when they quitted the room. Every one felt positive that the matter was all arranged, and the wedding was soon to take place; and, to say the truth, so much had Wilton in general won upon their esteem by one means or another, that the only objection urged against him, in the various councils which were held upon the subject, was, that his name was Brown, that he had not a vis-a-vis, and that he kept only two horses.

The two or three last sentences, it must be owned, are lamentable digressions; for we have not yet stated what the extraordinary thing was. It was not in the least degree extraordinary that the servants should all find out the secret of Laura's heart; for her eyes told it every time that she looked at Wilton; but it is very extraordinary, indeed, that her father should never find it out, when every one else that was present did. Is it that there is a magic haze which surrounds love, that can never be penetrated by the eyes of parents or guardians, till some particular allotted moment is arrived? I cannot tell; so, however, has it always proved, and so in all probability it ever will.

Such was the case with the Duke at the present moment. Although there was every opportunity for his daughter and Wilton falling in love with each other; although there was every reasonable cause thereunto them moving--youth, and beauty, and warm hearts, and gratitude, and interesting situations: although there was every probability that time, place, and circumstance could afford; although there was every indication, sign, symptom, and appearance, that it was absolutely the case at that very moment, yet the Duke saw nothing of it, did not believe it existed, did not imagine that it was likely ever to exist, and was quite prepared to be astonished, surprised, and mortified, at whatever period the fact, by the will of fate, should be forced upon his understanding.

Such was the state of all parties at the time when Laura rose from the table, and left her father and Wilton alone. Now the bad custom of men sitting together and drinking immense and detrimental quantities of various kinds of wine, was at that time at its very acme; so much so, indeed, that there is more than one recorded instance, in the years 1695 and 1696, of gentlemen--yes, reader; actually gentlemen, that is to say, persons who had had every advantage of birth, for time, and education--killing themselves with intoxication, exactly in the manner which a noble but most unhappy bard of our own days has described, in--

--"the Irish peer
Who kill'd himself for love, with wine, last year."

On this subject, however, we shall not dwell, as we may be fated, perhaps, in the very beginning of the next chapter, to touch upon some of the other peculiar habits of those days.

Now neither Wilton nor the Duke were at all addicted to the vice we have mentioned; and Wilton had certainly much stronger attractions in another room of that house than any that the Duke's cellar could afford him. The Duke, too, had small inclination usually to sit long at table; but on the pre sent occasion he had an object in detaining his young friend in the dining-room after Lady Laura had departed. Wilton's eyes saw him turn towards him several times, while the servants were busy about the table, and had, indeed, even during dinner, remarked a certain sort of restlessness, which he attributed, and rightly, to an anxiety regarding the plots of the Jacobites, in which the peer had so nearly involved himself.

At length, when the room was cleared and the door closed, the Duke drew round his chair towards the fire, begging his young friend to do the same, and mingling the matter of alarm even with his invitation to the first glass of wine, "My dear Wilton," he said--"you must permit me to call you so, for I can now look upon you as little less than a son--I wish you to give me a fuller account of all this business than poor Laura can, for there is news current about the town to-day which somewhat alarms me, though I do not think there is any need of alarm either. But surely, Wilton, they could not bring me in as at all accessory to a plot which I would have nothing to do with."

"Oh no, my lord, I should think not," replied Wilton, without much consideration. "I know it is the wish of the government only to punish the chief offenders."

"Then you think it is really all discovered, as they say?" demanded the Duke.

"I know it is," replied Wilton. "Several of the conspirators are already in custody, and warrants are issued, I understand, against the rest. As far as I can judge, two or three will turn King's evidence, and the rest will be executed."

"Good God!" exclaimed the Duke. "I heard something of the business when I was out, but scarcely gave it credit. It seemed so suddenly discovered."

"I believe the government have had the clue in their hands for some time," replied Wilton, "but have only availed themselves of it lately."

"Have you heard any one named, Wilton?" demanded the Duke again; "any of those who are taken, or any of those who are suspected?"

"Sir John Friend has been arrested this morning," replied Wilton; "a person named Cranburne, and another called Rookwood. I heard the names of those who are suspected also read over."

"Then I adjure you, my dear young friend," cried the Duke, starting up, and grasping his hand in great agitation--"I adjure you, by all the regard that exists between us, and all that you have done for me and my poor child, to tell me if my name was amongst the rest."

"No, it certainly was not," replied Wilton; and as he spoke, the Duke suffered himself to sink back into his chair again, with a long and relieved sigh.

The moment Wilton had uttered his reply, however, he recollected that there was one name in the list at which Lord Byerdale had hesitated; and he then feared that he might be leading the Duke into error. Knowing, however, that Laura's father had been but at one of the meetings of the conspirators, and being perfectly sure, that, startled and dismayed by what he had heard of their plans, he had instantly withdrawn from all association with them, he did not doubt that no serious danger could exist in his case, and therefore thought it unnecessary to agitate his mind, by suggesting the doubt which had suddenly come into his own.

He knew, indeed, that any alarm which the Duke might feel, would but make Laura's father lean more entirely day by day upon him, who, with the exception of the conspirators themselves, was the only person who possessed the dangerous secret which caused him so much agitation. But Wilton was not a man to consider his own interests in any such matter, and he determined, after a moment's consideration, to say nothing of the doubts which had just arisen. A pause had ensued, however, for the Duke, busied with his own feelings, had suffered his thoughts to run back into the past; and, as is the case with every human being whose mind dwells upon the acts that are irrevocable, he found matter for sorrow and regret. After about five minutes' silence, during which they both continued to gaze thoughtfully into the fire, the Duke returned to the matter before them by saying--

"I wish to heavens, my dear young friend, I had taken your advice, and not gone to this meeting at all; or that you had given me a fuller intimation of what was intended."

"I could not, indeed, my lord," replied Wilton, "for I had no fuller knowledge myself; I only conveyed to you a message I had received."

The Duke shook his head doubtingly. "Oh! Wilton, Wilton!" he said, "you are training for a statesman! You have much better information of all these things than you will suffer to appear. Did you not warn me of this before any one else knew anything of it? Did you not in a very short time find out where Laura was when nobody else could?"

It was in vain that Wilton denied any superior knowledge. The Duke had so completely made up his mind that his young friend had been in possession of all the secret information obtained by the ministers, and, indeed, of more and earlier information than they had possessed, that nothing would remove the impression from his mind; and when he at length rose, finding that Wilton would drink no more wine, he said--

"Well, Wilton, remember, I depend entirely upon you, with the fullest and most implicit confidence. No one possesses my secret but you, and one or two of these men, who will have enough to do in thinking of themselves without implicating others, I trust. Most of those who were present--for the meeting was very large--did not know who I was, and the rest who did know, must know also very well, that I strenuously objected to their whole proceedings, and quitted them as soon as I discovered what were their real objects. A word said upon the subject, however, might ruin me; for rank and fortune in this world, Wilton, though they bear their own inconveniences with them, are always objects of envy to those who do not possess them; and malice as surely treads upon the steps of envy as night follows day. I trust to you, as I have said, entirely, and I trust to you even with the more confidence, because I find that you have been wise and prudent enough not even to communicate to Laura the fact of my having attended any of these meetings at all. While all this is taking place, however, my dear Wilton--as of course the matter will be a very agitating one to me, when the trials come on (for fear any of the traitors should name me)--let me see you frequently, constantly, every day, if you can, and bring me what tidings you can gain of all that passes."

Wilton easily promised to do that which the Duke desired, in this respect at least, and they then joined her he loved, with whom he passed one of those calm, sweet evenings, the tranquil happiness of which admits of no description.

CHAPTER XXXII.

Amongst all the curious changes that have taken place in the world--by which expression I mean, upon the world, for the great round ball on which we roll through space is the only part of the whole that remains but little altered--amongst all the changes, then, which have taken place in the world, moral, political, and social, there has been none more extraordinary, perhaps, than the rise, progress, extension, and dominion of that strong power called Decorum. I have heard it asserted by a very clever man, that there was nothing of the kind known in England before the commencement of the reign of George III., and that decorum was, in fact, a mere decent cloak to cover the nakedness of vice. I think he was mistaken: the word was known long before; and there has been at all times a feeling of decorum in the English nation, which has shown itself in gradually rooting out from the ordinary commerce of society everything that is coarse in expression, or doubtful in conduct. The natural tendency of this is to mark more strongly the limits of the realms of vice and virtue; and vice, as a matter of course, in order to obviate the detrimental effect which such a clear definition of her boundaries must produce, loses no opportunity of travelling over into the marches or debateable land which is left under the warden ship of decorum.

The name was not, perhaps, applied as now it is, in former years, but still the spirit existed, as may be seen by any one who takes up and reads the works of one of our purest but coldest of writers, Addison, who, about the time of the peace, which took place in the beginning of the eighteenth century, laments the loss of much of the delicacy (or, in other terns, decorum) of English society which was likely to ensue from a free intercourse with France. It must, indeed, be admitted that at that period the reign of decorum had not made nearly so great a progress as it has at present. It was then a constitutional monarchy, where it is now a despotism, but was probably not a bit less powerful from being decidedly more free. People in those days did certainly speak of things that we now speak not of at all. They called things by their plain straightforward names, for which we have since invented terms perhaps less definite and not more decent. But people of refined minds and tastes were refined then as now, and loved and cultivated all those amenities, graces, and proprieties, which form not alone the greatest safeguards, but also the greatest charms of human existence. Perhaps the difference was more in the thoughts than in the expressions, and that the refined of those days bound themselves to think more purely in the first place, so that there was less need of guarding their words so strictly.

We shall not pause to investigate whether it was that greater purity of thought, or any other cause, which produced a far more extensive liberty of action, especially in the female part of society, than that which is admitted at present. It is certain, however, that it was so, and that there was something in virtue and innocence which in those days was a very strong safeguard against the attacks of scandal, calumny, and malice. In the present day, even the servants of virtue are found to be the absolute slaves of decorum; but in those days, so long as they obeyed the high commands of their rightful mistress, they had but little occasion to apprehend that the scourge of calumny, or the fear thereof, would drive them continually back into one narrow and beaten path.

It is, indeed, the greatest satire upon human nature which the world has ever produced, that acts perfectly innocent, high, and pure as God's holy light, cannot be permitted to persons even of tried virtue, simply because they would afford the opportunity of doing ill. It is, in fact, to say, that no one is to be trusted; that there is nothing which keeps man or woman virtuous but want of opportunity. It is a terrible satire; it is more than a satire; it is a foul libel, aimed by the vicious against those who are better than themselves.

Such things did not exist in the days whereof I write, or existed in a very, very small degree. It is true, from time to time, a woman's reputation might suffer falsely; but it was in general from her having approached very near the confines of evil, and the punishment that ensued, though perhaps even then disproportioned to the fault, had no tendency whatever to diminish the innocent liberty of others. We find from all the writers who painted the manners of those days--Addison, Swift, Steele, and others--that a lady, especially an unmarried lady, feared no risk to her reputation in going hither or thither, either perfectly alone, or with any friend with whom she was known to be intimate. She might venture upon an excursion into the country, a party of pleasure, nay, a journey itself in many instances, with any gentleman of honour and reputation, without either friends or enemies casting an imputation upon her character, or the world immediately giving her over to him in marriage.

It was left indeed to her own judgment whom she would choose for her companion, and the most innocent girl might have gone anywhere unreproved with a man of known honour and virtue, who would have ruined her own character had she placed herself in the power of a Rochester or a Bucking ham. These were rational boundaries; but perhaps the liberty of those days went somewhat beyond even that. In the early part of the eighteenth century, many of the habits of the Continent were introduced into England at a time that continental society was so corrupt as to require licence instead of liberty, and so far from attending to propriety, to give way to indecency itself. It became common in the highest circles of society for ladies, married and single alike, to dispense almost entirely with a female attendant, and following that most indecent and beastly of all continental habits, to permit all the offices of a waiting woman to be performed for them by men. The visits of male acquaintances were continually received in their bed-rooms, and that, also, before they had risen in the morning. This, perhaps, was too much, though certainly far less indecent than the other most revolting of all immodest practices which I have just mentioned. Others, again, admitted no visitors further than their dressing-room, and thought themselves very scrupulous; but there were others, as there must be at all times, who, with feelings of true modesty and perfect delicacy, hesitated not to use all proper and rational liberty, yet shrunk instinctively from the least coarseness of thought or language, and never yielded to aught that was immodest in custom or demeanour.

Of these was Lady Laura Gaveston; and though she had no fear of becoming the talk of the town, or losing the slightest particle of a bright and pure reputation, by treating one who had rendered her important services in all respects as she would a brother, by being seen with him often and often alone, by showing herself with him in public places, or by any other act of the kind that her heart prompted her to, she in no way gave in to the evil practices which the English had learned from their continental neighbours, and, indeed, never thought or reasoned upon the subject, feeling that decency as well as morality is a matter of sentiment and not of custom.

The peculiar situation in which the Duke and Wilton were placed towards each other; the Duke's repeated entreaties that Wilton would see him every day, if possible; the intimacy that had arisen from services rendered and received, produced that constant and continual intercourse which was necessary to the happiness of two people who loved as Wilton and Laura did; not a day passed without their seeing each other, scarcely a day passed without their being alone together, sometimes even for hours; and every moment that they thus spent in each other's society increased their feelings of love and tenderness for each other, their hopes, their confidence, their esteem.

Not a secret of Laura's bosom was now concealed from him she loved, not a thought, not a feeling. She delighted to tell him all: with whatever subject her mind was employed, with whatever bright thing her fancy sported, Wilton was always made the sharer; and it was the same with him. The course that their thoughts pursued was certainly not always alike, but they generally arrived at the same conclusion, she by a longer and a softer way, he by a more rapid, vigorous, and direct one. It was like the passing of a hill by two different roads; the one, for the bold climber, over the steepest brow; the other, for gentler steps, more easy round the side.

In the meantime, the Duke proceeded with his young friend even as he had commenced. He treated him as his most intimate and dearest confidant; he gradually went on to consult and trust him, not alone with regard to the immediate subject of his situation, as affected by the conspiracy, but upon a thousand other matters; and as Wilton's advice, clear-sighted and vigorous, was always judicious, and generally successful, the Duke, one of whose greatest weaknesses was the habit of putting his own judgment under the guidance of others, learned to lean upon his young companion, as he had at first done upon his wife, and then upon his daughter.

The various changes and events of the day, as they kept the Duke's mind in a state of frequent suspense and anxiety, made him more often recur to Wilton than otherwise would have been the case. London was filled with rumours of every kind regarding the discovery of the plot, and the persons implicated. The report of Lady Laura's having been carried off by the Jacobites, for the purpose of inducing her father to join in their schemes, spread far and wide, and filled Beaufort House, during a great part of the morning, with a crowd of visitors, all anxious to hear the facts, and to retail them with what colouring they thought fit.

Some argued, that though the Duke had always been thought somewhat of a Jacobite, at least he had now proved his adherence to the existing dynasty, beyond all manner of dispute, by what he and his daughter had suffered from their resistance to the Jacobites. Others, again, curled the malicious lip, and declared that the Duke must have given the conspirators some encouragement, or they would never have ventured upon such deeds. All, however, to the Duke himself, affected to look upon him and his family as marked by the enmity of the other faction; and he, on his part, perhaps, did feel his importance in a little degree increased by the sort of notoriety which he had acquired.

If there was any pleasure in this--and when is not in creased importance pleasurable?--it was speedily brought to an end, as soon as the trials of the conspirators began, and intelligence of more and more traitors being arrested in different parts, and increased rumours of the number suspected, or actually implicated, reaching the ears of the Duke. Persons who one day appeared perfectly free and stainless, were the next marked out as having a share in the conspiracy. Fear fell upon all men: the times of Titus Oates and his famous plot presented themselves to everybody's imagination, and the Duke's head lay more and more uneasy on his pillow every night.

Sir John Fenwick, however, was not yet taken: Sir William Parkyns and Sir John Friend died with firmness and with honour, compromising no man. Sir George Barkley had escaped; the Earl of Aylesbury, though implicated by the testimony of several witnesses in the lesser offences of the conspiracy, was not arrested; and not a word had yet been spoken of the Duke's name.

It was about this period, however, that Laura's father suddenly received a note from Lord Aylesbury to the following effect:--

"Your grace and I being somewhat similarly situated in
several respects, I think fit to give you intimation of my
views at the present moment. While gentlemen, and men of
honour, were the only individuals made to suffer in

consequence of the late lamentable events, people, who knew themselves to be innocent of any bloody or treasonable designs, might feel themselves tolerably safe, even though they were well acquainted with some of the persons accused. I hear now, however, that there is a certain Rookwood, together with men named Cranburne, Lowick, Knightly, and others, some of them small gentry of no repute, and others merely vulgar and inferior persons, who are about to be brought to immediate trial; and I have it from a sure hand, that some of these persons, for the purpose of saving their own miserable lives, intend to charge men of much higher rank than themselves with crimes of which they never had any thought, simply because they were acquainted with some of the unfortunate gentlemen by whom these evil and foolish things were designed. Such being the case, and knowing myself to be somewhat obnoxious to many persons in power, I have determined to remove from London for the time, that my presence may not excite attention, and perhaps call upon my head an accusation which may be levelled at any other if I should not be here. I by no means purpose to quit the kingdom, and would rather, indeed, surrender myself, and endeavour to prove my innocence, even against the torrent of prejudice, and all the wild and raging outcry which this business has produced, both in the parliament and in the nation. At the same time, I think it best to inform you of these facts, as an old friend, well knowing that your grace has a house ready to receive you in Hampshire, within thirty-five miles of the city of London, in case your presence should be wanted, and about the same distance from the sea-coast. I will beg your grace to read this, and then instantly to burn it, believing that it comes with a very good intent, from

"Your humble servant, "AYLESBURY."

This letter once more excited all the apprehensions of the Duke, who well knew that Lord Aylesbury would never have written such an epistle without intending to imply much more than he directly said.

His recourse was immediately to Wilton, who was engaged to dine with him on that day, together with a large party. As Wilton's engagements, however, were always made with a proviso, that his official duties under the Earl of Byerdale permitted his fulfilling them, the Duke sent off a special messenger with a note beseeching him not to fail. The dinner hour, however, arrived; the various guests made their appearance; the cook began to fret, and to declare to his understrappers that the Duke always spoilt the dinner; but Wilton had not yet come, and the Duke was anxious, if but to obtain five words with him.

At length, however, the young gentleman arrived; and it was not a little to the surprise of all the guests, and to the indignation of some, that they saw who was the person for whom the meal had been delayed. Wilton, though always well dressed, and in any circumstances bearing the aspect of a gentleman, had evidently made his toilet hastily and imperfectly; and notwithstanding the distance he had come, bore about his person distinct traces of heat and excitement.

"I have not failed to obey your summons, my lord," he said, following the Duke into the opening of one of the windows, "though it was scarcely possible for me to do so. But I have much that I wish to say to you."

"And I to you," replied the Duke; and he told him the contents of the letter he had received from Lord Aylesbury that morning.

"The Earl says true, my lord," replied Wilton. "But I have this very day seen Cook myself--I mean Peter Cook, the person that it is supposed will be permitted to turn king's evidence. He did certainly slightly glance at your grace; but I believe that the orders of Lord Byerdale will prevent him from implicating any persons but those who were actually engaged in the worst designs of the conspirators."

"Had I not better go into the country at once?" demanded the Duke, eagerly.

"Far from it, far from it, my lord," replied Wilton: "the way, of all others, I should think, to cause yourself to be arrested. On the contrary, if you would take my advice, you would immediately sit down and write a note to Lord Byerdale, saying that I had told you--for he did not forbid me to mention it--that Cook had made some allusion to you. Tell him that it was, and is, your intention to go out of town within a few days, but that knowing your own innocence of every design against the government, you will put off your journey, or even surrender yourself at the Tower, should he judge, from any information that he possesses, that even a shade of suspicion is likely to be cast upon you by any of the persons about to be tried. I will answer for the success, if your grace follows my advice. A bold step of this kind disarms suspicion. Lord Byerdale will, in all probability, intimate to Cook, that nothing at all is to be said in regard to you, feeling sure that you are innocent of any great offence; whereas, if the charge were once brought forward, the set of low-minded villains concerned in this business might think it absolutely necessary to work it up into a serious affair, from which your grace would find a difficulty in extricating yourself."

"You are right, Wilton, you are right," replied the Duke: "I see you are right, although I judged it hazardous at first. You shall see what confidence I have in you. I will write the letter directly;" and he turned away with him from the window.

Laura had watched the conference with some anxiety, and the Duke's guests with some surprise; but when the Duke ended by saying aloud, "I fear I must beg your pardon, ladies, for two minutes, but I must write a short note of immediate importance; Wilton, my dear young friend, be kind enough to order dinner, and help Laura to entertain my friends here till I return, which will be before they have covered the table," every one looked in the face of the other; and they all mentally said, "The matter is clearly settled, and the hand of this rich and beautiful heiress is promised to an unknown man of no rank whatever."

Knowing the feelings that were in his own heart, being quite sure of the interpretation that would be put upon the Duke's words, and yet having some doubts still whether the Duke himself had the slightest intention of giving them such a meaning, Wilton cast down his eyes and coloured slightly. But Laura, to whom those words were anything but painful--though she blushed a little too, which but confirmed the opinion of those who remarked it--could not restrain altogether the smile of pleasure that played upon her lips, as she turned her happy eyes for a moment to the countenance of the man she loved.

There was not an old lady or gentleman, of high rank, in the room, possessed of a marriageable son, who would not at that moment have willingly raised Wilton to the final elevation of Haman, by the same process which that envious person

underwent; and yet it is wonderful how courteous and cordial, and even affectionate, they all were towards the young gentleman whom, for the time, they mortally
hated. Wilton felt himself awkwardly situated for the next few minutes, not choosing fully to assume the position in which the Duke's words had placed him. He
well knew that if he did enact to the full the part of that nobleman's representative,
every one would charge him with gross and shameful presumption, and would most
likely talk of it, each in his separate circle, during the whole of the following day.

He was soon relieved, however, by the return of the Duke, who had sent the
letter, but who continued evidently anxious and thoughtful during the whole of
dinner. Wilton was also a little disturbed, and showed himself rather silent and
retiring than otherwise. But before dinner was over--for such meals were long protracted in those days--one of the servants brought a note to the Duke, who, begging pardon for so far violating all proprieties, opened, read it, and, while the cloud
vanished from his countenance, placed it on the salver again, saying to the servant,
"Take that to Mr. Brown."

The note was in the hand of Lord Byerdale, and to the following effect:--

"MY DEAR LORD DUKE,
"Your grace's attachment to the government is far too
well known to be affected by anything that such a person as
Peter Cook could say. I permitted our dear young friend
Wilton to tell you what the man had mentioned, more as a
mark of our full confidence than anything else. But I doubt
not that he will forbear to repeat the calumny in court; and
if he does, it will receive no attention. Go out of town, then,
whenever you think fit, and to whatsoever place you please,
feeling quite sure that in Wilton you have a strenuous
advocate, and a sincere friend in
"Your grace's most humble and
"most obedient servant,
"BYERDALE."

CHAPTER XXXIII.

For nearly ten days after the events which we have recorded in the thirtieth chapter of this volume, and while the principal part of the events were taking place of which we have just spoken, Lord Sherbrooke remained absent from London. Knowing the circumstances in which he was placed, Wilton felt anxious lest the delay of his return might attract the attention of Lord Byerdale, and lead him to suspect some evil. No suspicion, however, seemed to cross the mind of the Earl, who was more accustomed than Wilton knew to find his son absent without knowing where he was, or how employed.

At length, however, one morning Lord Sherbrooke made his appearance again; and Wilton saw that he was on perfect good terms with his father, who never quarrelled with his vices, or interfered with his pursuits, when there was any veil of decency thrown over the one, or the Earl's own views were not openly opposed by the other.

When Wilton entered the room where the father and son were seated at breakfast, he found Lord Sherbrooke descanting learnedly upon the fancy of damask table-cloths and napkins. He vowed that his father was behind all the world, especially the world of France, and that it was absolutely necessary, in order to make himself like other men of station and fashion, that he should have his coronet and cipher embroidered with gold in the corners, and his arms, in the same manner, made conspicuous in the centre.

"And pray, my good son," said Lord Byerdale to him, "as your intimacy with washerwomen is doubtless as great as your intimacy with embroiderers and sempstresses, pray tell me how these gilded napkins are to be washed?"

"Washed, my lord!" exclaimed Lord Sherbrooke in a tone of horror. "Do you ever have your napkins washed? I did not know there was a statesman in Europe whose fingers were so clean as to leave his napkin in such a state that the stains could ever be taken out, after he had once used it."

"I am afraid, my dear boy," replied Lord Byerdale, "that, if you had not--as many men of sharp wit do--confounded a figure with a reality, for the purpose of playing with both, and if there were in truth such a thing as a moral napkin, what you say would be very true. But as far as I can judge, my dear Sherbrooke, yours would not bear washing any better than mine."

"It would be very presumptuous of me if it did, my dear father," replied Lord Sherbrooke, "and would argue that precept and example had done nothing for me. Come, Wilton," he added, "come in to my help, for here are father and son flinging so hard at each other, that I shall get my teeth dashed down my throat before I've done. Now tell me, did you ever see such a napkin as that in the house of a nobleman, a gentleman, or a man of taste, three states, by the way, seldom united in the same person?"

"Oh yes," replied Wilton, "often; and, to tell the truth, I think them in much better taste than if they were all covered with gold."

"Surely not for the fingers of a statesman?" said Lord Sherbrooke. "However, I abominate them; and I will instantly sit down and write to a good friend of mine in France, to smuggle me over a few dozens as a present to my respectable parent."

"A present which he will have to pay for," replied the Earl, somewhat bitterly. "My dear Sherbrooke, your presents to other people cost your father so much one way, that I beg you will make none to him, and get him into the scrape the other way also."

"Do not be alarmed, my dear and most amiable parent," replied Lord Sherbrooke: "the sweet discussion which we had some time ago, in regard to debts and expenses, has had its effect: though it is a very stupid plan of a son ever to let his father see that what he says has any effect upon him at all; but I intend to contract my expenses."

"Intentions are very excellent things, my dear Sherbrooke," replied his father. "But I am afraid we generally treat them as gardeners do celery,--cut them down as soon as they sprout above ground."

"I have let mine grow, my lord, already," replied Sherbrooke. "I last night gave an order for selling five of my horses, and now keep only two."

"And how many mistresses, Sherbrooke?" demanded his father.

"None, my lord," replied Sherbrooke.

Not a change came over Lord Byerdale's countenance; but ringing the bell which stood before him on the table, he said to the servant, "Bring me the book marked 'Ephemeris' from my dressing-room, with a pen and ink.--We will put that down," continued he; and when the servant brought the book he wrote for a moment, reading aloud as he did so, "Great annular eclipse of the sun--slight shock of an earthquake felt in Cardigan--Sherbrooke talks of contracting his expenses."

Wilton could not help smiling; but he believed and trusted, from all that he knew of Lord Sherbrooke's situation, that new motives and nobler ones than those which had ever influenced him before, produced his present resolution, and would support him in it.

The business which he had to transact with the Earl proved very brief; and after it was over, he sought Lord Sherbrooke again, with feelings of real and deep interest in all that concerned him. He found the young nobleman seated with his feet on the fire-place, and a light book in his hand, sometimes letting it drop upon his knee, and falling into a fit of thought, sometimes reading a few lines attentively, sometimes gazing upon the page, evidently without attending to its contents.

He suffered Wilton to be in the room several minutes without speaking to him; and his friend, knowing the eccentricities that occasionally took possession of him, was about to quit the room and leave him, when he started up, threw the book into the midst of the fire, and said, "Where are you going, Wilton? I will walk with you."

They issued forth together into the streets, and entering St. James's Park, took their way round by the head of the decoy towards the side of the river. While in the streets they both kept silence; but as soon as they had passed the ever-moving crowds that swarm in the thoroughfares of the great metropolis, Wilton began the conversation, by inquiring eagerly after his friend's wife.

"She is nearly well," replied Lord Sherbrooke, coldly--"out of all danger, at least. It is I that am sick, Wilton--sick at heart."

"I hope not cold at heart, Sherbrooke," replied Wilton, somewhat pained by the tone in which the other spoke. "I should think such a being as I saw with you might well warm you to constancy as well as love. I hope, Sherbrooke, those feelings I beheld excited in you have not, in this instance, evaporated as soon as in others."

Lord Sherbrooke turned and gazed in his friend's face for a moment intently, even sternly, and then replied, "Love her, Wilton? I love her better than anything in earth or in heaven! It is for her sake I am sad; and yet she is so noble, that why should I fear to bear what she will never shrink from."

"Nay, my dear Sherbrooke," replied Wilton. "The very resolution which I see you have taken to shake yourself free of the trammels of your debts ought to give you joy and confidence."

"Debts!" said Lord Sherbrooke--"debts! Do you think that it was debts I had in view when I ordered my horses to be sold, and my carriages to follow them, and kicked my Italian valet down stairs, and dismissed my mistresses, and got rid of half-a-dozen other blood-suckers?--My debts had nothing to do with it. By Heaven, Wilton, if it had been for nothing but that, I would have spent twenty thousand pounds more before the year was over; for when one has a mind to enrage one's father, or go to gaol, or anything of that kind, one had better do it for a large sum at once, in a gentleman- like way. Oh no, I have other things in my head, Wilton, that you know nothing about."

"I will not try to press into your confidence, Sherbrooke," replied Wilton, "though I think in some things I have shown myself deserving of it. But I need hardly tell you, that if I can serve you, I am always most willing to do so, and you need but command me."

"Alas! my dear Wilton," replied Lord Sherbrooke--"this is a matter in which you can do nothing. It is like one man trying to lift Paul's church upon his back, and another coming tip and offering to help him. If I did what was right, and according to the best prescribed practice, I should repay your kind wishes and offers by turning round and cutting your throat."

"Nay, nay, my dear Sherbrooke," replied Wilton, "you are in one of your misanthropical fits, and carry it even further than ordinary. The world is bad enough, but not so bad as to present us with many instances of people cutting each other's throats as a reward for offers of service."

"You are very wise, Wilton," replied Lord Sherbrooke, "but nevertheless you will find out that at present I am right and you are wrong. However, let us talk of something else;" and he dashed off at once into a wild gay strain of merriment, as unaccountable as the grave and gloomy tone with which he had entered into the conversation.

This morning's interview formed the type of Lord Sherbrooke's conduct during the whole time of his stay in town. Continual fluctuations, not only in his own spirits, but in his demeanour towards Wilton himself; evidently showed his friend that he was agitated internally by some great grief or terrible anxiety. Indeed, from time to time, his words suffered it to appear, though not, perhaps, in the same manner that the words of other men would have done in similar circumstances. The only thing in which he seemed to take pleasure was in attending the trials of the various conspirators; and when any of them displayed any fear or want of firmness, he found therein a vast source of merriment, and would come home laughing to Wilton, and telling him how the beggarly wretch had showed his pale fright at the block and axe.

"That villain Knightly," he said, one day, "who was as deep or deeper in the plot than any of the others, and surveyed the ground for the King's assassination, came into court the colour of an old woman's green calamanco petticoat, gaping and trembling in every limb like a boar's head in aspic jelly; and Heaven knows that I, who stood looking and laughing at him, would have taken his place for a dollar."

The perfect conviction that some very serious cause existed for this despondency induced Wilton to deviate from the line of conduct he had laid down for himself, and to urge Lord Sherbrooke at various times to make him acquainted with the particulars of his situation, and to give him the opportunity of assisting him if possible. Lord Sherbrooke resisted pertinaciously. He sometimes answered his friend kindly and feelingly, sometimes sullenly, sometimes angrily. But he never yielded; and on one occasion he expressed himself so harshly and ungratefully, that Wilton turned round and left him in the park. They were on horseback at the time; and Lord Sherbrooke rode on a little way, without taking the slightest notice of his companion's departure. He then suddenly turned his horse, however, and galloping after him at full speed, he held out his hand to him, saying, "Wilton, you must either fight me or forgive me, for this state must not last five minutes."

Wilton took his hand, replying, "I forgive you with all my heart, Sherbrooke, and let me once more explain that my only view, my only wish, is to be of assistance to you. I see, Sherbrooke, that you are melancholy, wretched, anxious. I wish much to do anything that I can to relieve that state of mind; and though I have no power, and very little interest, yet there do occasionally occur opportunities to me, which, as you have seen in the case of Lady Laura, afford me means of doing things which might not be expected from my situation."

"You can neither help me, nor relieve me, nor assist me in the least, Wilton," replied Lord Sherbrooke, "unless, indeed, you could entirely change beings with me; unless you become me, and I become you. But it cannot be, and I cannot even explain to you any part of my situation. Therefore ask me nothing more upon the subject, and only be contented that it is from no want of confidence in you that I hold my tongue."

"I hope and trust that it is not," replied Wilton; "but now that we are speaking upon the subject, let me still say one word more. I can conceive, from various reasons, that you may not think fit to confide in me. I am a man of your own age, with less wit, less experience, less knowledge of the world than you have--"

"You have more wit in your little finger, more knowledge of the world, and experience--Heaven knows how you got it--more common sense, ay, and uncommon sense too, than ever I shall have in my life," replied Lord Sherbrooke, hastily.

"But hear me, Sherbrooke, hear me," said Wilton--"whatever may be the cause, it does not suit you to take my advice and assistance. Now there is one person in whom you may fully rely, who will never betray your confidence, who will give you the very best advice, and I am sure will, if it be in his power, render you still more important assistance--I mean Lord Sunbury. He is now at Geneva, on his way home, waiting for passports from France. In his last letter, lie mentioned you with much interest, and desired me--"

"Good God!" cried Lord Sherbrooke, "that I should ever create any interest in anybody! However, Wilton, your suggestion is not a bad one. Perhaps you have pointed out the only man in Europe in whom I could confide with propriety, strange as that may seem. But in the first place, I must consult with others.--Have you seen your friend Green lately?"

"Not since the night before all that business in Kent," replied Wilton. "I have sought to see him, but have never been able; and I begin to apprehend that he must have taken a part in this conspiracy, different from that I imagined, and has absented himself on that account."

"Not he, not he!" replied Lord Sherbrooke; "I saw him but two days ago. But who have we here, coming up on foot? One of the King's servants, it would seem, and with him that cowardly rascal Arden. They are snaking towards us, Wilton, doubtless not recognising us. Suppose we take Master Arden, and horsewhip him out of the park."

"No, no," replied Wilton, "no such violent counsels for me, my dear Sherbrooke. The man is punished more than I wished already."

The two men directed their course at once towards Lord Sherbrooke and his companion; and as they approached, the King's servant advanced before the other, and with a respectful bow addressed Wilton, saying, "I have the King's commands, sir, to require your presence at Kensington immediately. I was even now about to seek you in St. James's Square, and then at Whitehall. But I presume Mr. Arden has informed me rightly, that you are that Mr. Brown who is private secretary to Lord Byerdale."

"The same, sir," replied Wilton. "Am I to present myself to his majesty in my riding dress?"

"His majesty's commands were for your immediate attendance, sir," replied the servant: "the council must be over by this time, and then he expects you."

"Then I will lose no time," replied Wilton, "but ride to the palace at once."

"What can be the meaning of this, Wilton?" said Lord Sherbrooke, as he put his horse into a quick pace, to keep up with that of his friend.

"On my word, I cannot tell," replied Wilton. "I trust for no evil, though I know not that any good can be in store."

"Well, I will leave you at the palace gates," replied Lord Sherbrooke, "and ride about in the neighbourhood till I see you come out. I hope it will not be in custody."

"I trust not, indeed," replied Wilton. "I know of no good reason why it should be so: but in these days of suspicion, and I must say of guilt and treason also, no one can tell who may be the next person destined for abode in Newgate."

In such speculations the two young gentlemen continued till they reached the palace, where Lord Sherbrooke turned and left his friend; and Wilton, if the truth must be confessed, with an anxious and beating heart, applied to the porter for admittance.

The moment that his name was given, he was led by a page to a small waiting room on the ground floor. The carriages which had surrounded the entrance seemed to indicate that the council was not yet over; but in a few minutes after, the sound of many feet and of various people talking was heard in the neighbouring passage; and then came the roll of carriages followed by a dead silence. To the mind of Wilton the silence continued for an exceedingly long time; but at length a voice was heard, apparently at some distance, pronouncing a name indistinctly; but Wilton imagined that it sounded like his own name.

The next instant, another voice took it up, and it was now distinctly, "Mr. Brown to the King." The door then opened, and a page appeared, saying, "Mr. Brown, the King commands your presence."

CHAPTER XXXIV.

William III. was seated in a small cabinet, with a table to his right hand on which his elbow rested; an inkstand and paper were beside him; and on the other hand, a step behind, stood a gentleman of good mien, with his hand upon the back of the King's chair, in an attitude familiar, but not disrespectful. The harsh and somewhat coarse features of the monarch, which abstractedly seemed calculated to display strong passions, were in their habitual state of cold immobility; and Wilton, though he knew his person well, and had seen him often, could not derive from the King's face the slightest intimation of what was passing in his mind. There was no trace of anger, it is true; the brow was sufficiently contracted to appear thoughtful, but no more; and, at the same time, there was not one touch even of courteous affability to be seen in those rigid lines to tell that the young gentleman had been sent for upon some pleasurable occasion. Dignity, to a certain extent, there must have been in his demeanour, that sort of dignity which is communicated to the body by great powers of mind, and great decision of character--in fact, dignity divested of grace. Nobody could have taken him for a vulgar man, although his person, as far as mere lines and colouring go, might have been that of the lowest artizan; but what is more, no one could see him, however simple might be his dress, without feeling that there sat a distinguished man of some kind.

Wilton had been accustomed too much and too long to mingle with the first people in the first country of the world, to suffer himself to be much affected by any of the external pomp and circumstance of courts, or even by the vague sensations of respect with which fancy invests royalty; but he could not help feeling, as he entered the presence of William, that he was approaching a man of vast mind as well as vast power.

William looked at him quietly for several minutes, letting him approach within two steps, and gazing at him still, even after he had stopped, without uttering a single word. Wilton bowed, and then stood erect before the King, feeling a little embarrassed, it is true, but determined not to suffer his embarrassment to appear.

At length, the King addressed him in a harsh tone of voice, saying, "Well, sir, what have you to say?"

"May it please your majesty," replied Wilton, "I do not know on what subject your majesty wishes me to speak. I met one of the royal servants in the Park who commanded me to present myself here immediately, and I came hither accordingly, without waiting to inquire for what purpose."

"Oh! then you do not know?" said the King. "I thought you did know, and most likely were prepared. But it is as well as it is. I doubt not you will answer me truly. Where were you on Friday, the 22d of February last?"

"I cannot exactly say where I was, Sire," replied Wilton; "for during the greater part of that day I was continually changing my place. Having set out for a small town or village called High Halstow, in Kent, at an early hour in the day, I arrived there just before nightfall, and remained in that place or in the neighbourhood for several hours, indeed, till nearly or past midnight."

"Pray what was your business there?" demanded the King.

"I fear," replied Wilton, "I must trouble your majesty with some long details to enable you to understand the object of my going."

"Go on," was William's laconic reply; and the young gentleman proceeded to tell him, that having been employed in recovering Lady Laura from those who had carried her off, he had learned in the course of his inquiries in London that she was likely to be heard of in that neighbourhood.

"I judged it likely to be so myself, sire," continued Wilton, "because I believed her to have been carried off by some persons belonging to a party of Jacobites who were known to be caballing against the government, though to what extent was not then ascertained."

"And what made you judge," demanded the King, "that she had been carried off by these men?"

"Because, sire," replied Wilton, "the lady's father had been an acquaintance of Sir John Fenwick, one of the most notorious of the persons now implicated in the present foul plot against your majesty's life and crown. With him the Duke of Gaveston, I found, had quarrelled some time previously, and I suspected, though I had no proof thereof, that this quarrel had been occasioned by the Duke strongly differing from Sir John Fenwick in his political views, and refusing to take any part in any designs against the government."

"I am glad to hear this of the Duke, sir," replied the King. "Then it was out of revenge, you believe, they carried away the young lady?"

"Rather out of a desire to have a hold upon the Duke," replied Wilton. "I found afterwards, your majesty, that their intention was to send the young lady to France, and I judged throughout that their design was to force the Duke into an intrigue which they found he would not meddle with willingly."

William III., though he was himself of a very taciturn character, and not fond of loquacity in others, was yet fond of full explanations, always sitting in judgment, as it were, upon what was said to him, and passing sentence in his own breast. He now made Wilton go over again the particulars of Lady Laura's being taken away, though it was evident that he had heard all the facts before, and obliged him to enter into every minute detail which in any way affected the question.

When this was done, without any other comment than a look to the gentleman on his left hand, he fixed his eyes again upon Wilton, and asked,--"Now, where did you learn that these conspirators were likely to be found in Kent?"

"I heard it from a gentleman named Green," replied Wilton, "whom I met with at a tavern in St. James's-street."

"Green is a very common name," said the King.

"I do not believe that it is his real name," replied Wilton; "but what his real name is I do not know. I had not seen him often before; but he informed me of these facts, and I followed his advice and directions."

"That was rash," said the King. "You are sure you do not know his real name?"

"I cannot even guess it, sire," replied Wilton; and the King, after exchanging a mute glance with his attendant, went on,--"Well, when you had discovered the place of meeting of these conspirators, and reached it, what happened then?"

"I did not go, may it please your majesty, to discover their place of meeting, but to discover the place where Lady Laura was detained, which, when I had done, aided by a person I had got to assist me--after Arden, formerly Messenger of State, had fled from me in a most dastardly manner, in a casual rencounter with some peo-ple--smugglers, I believe--I made the master of the house and some other persons whom we found there, set the Lady Laura at liberty. I informed her of the authority that her father had given me, and she was but too glad to accept the assistance of any friend with whom she was acquainted."

"So, so; stop!" said the King. "So, then, Arden was not with you at this time?"

"No, sire," replied Wilton--"he had run away an hour before."

"That was not like a brave man," said William.

"No, indeed, sire," replied Wilton, "nor like one of your majesty's friends, for it is your enemies that generally run away."

A faint smile came upon William's countenance, and he said, "Go on. What happened next?"

"Before we could make our escape from the house," replied Wilton, "we were stopped by a large party of men, who entered; and, principally instigated by Sir John Fenwick, who was one of them, they opposed, in a violent manner, our de-parture."

Hitherto Wilton had been very careful of his speech, unwilling to compromise any one, and especially unwilling to mention the name of Lord Sherbrooke, the Lady Helen Oswald, or anybody else except the conspirators who had taken a part in the events of that night. Now, however, when he had to dwell principally upon the conduct of the conspirators and himself; he did so more boldly, and gave a full account of all that had been said and done till the entrance of the Duke of Berwick. He knew, or rather divined, from what had already passed, that this was in reality the point to which the examination he underwent principally tended. But yet he spoke with more ease, for, notwithstanding the danger which existed at that mo-ment in acknowledging any communication whatsoever with Jacobites, he well knew that the conduct of the Duke of Berwick himself only required to be truly reported, to be admired by every noble and generous mind; and he felt conscious that in his own behaviour he had only acted as became an upright and an honour-able heart. He detailed then, particularly, the fact of his having seen one of his op-ponents in the act of pointing a pistol at him over the shoulder of their principal spokesman: he mentioned his having cocked his own pistol to fire in return, and he stated that at the time he felt perfectly sure his life was about to be made a sacrifice to apprehensions of discovery on the part of the conspirators; and he then related to the King how he had seen a stranger enter and strike up the muzzle of the pistol pointed at him, at the very moment the other was in the act of firing.

"The ball," he said, "passed through the window above my head, and seeing that new assistance had come to my aid, I did not fire."

"Stay, stay!" said the King. "Let me ask you a question or two first. Did you see, in the course of all this time, the person called Sir George Barkley amongst these conspirators?"

"I saw a person, sire," replied Wilton, "whom I believed at the time to be Sir George Barkley, and have every reason to believe so still."

"And this person who came to your assistance so opportunely was not the same?" demanded the King.

"Not the least like him, sire," replied Wilton. "He was a young gentleman, of six or seven and twenty, I imagine, but certainly no more than thirty."

"What was his name?" demanded the King.

"The name he gave," replied Wilton, "was Captain Churchill."

"Go on," said William, and Wilton proceeded.

Avoiding all names as far as possible, he told briefly, but accurately, the severe and striking reprehension that the Duke of Berwick had bestowed upon Sir George Barkley and the rest of the conspirators: he dwelt upon the hatred he had displayed of the crime they were about to commit, and of the noble and upright tendency of every word that he had spoken. William's eyes glistened slightly, and a glow came up in his pale cheek, but he made no comment till Wilton seemed inclined to stop. He then bade him again go on, and made him tell all that had happened till he and Lady Laura had quitted the house, to make the best of their way to Halstow. He then said--

"Three questions. Why did you not give instant information of this conspiracy when you came to town?"

"May it please your majesty," replied Wilton, "I found immediately on my arrival that the conspiracy was discovered, and warrants issued against the conspirators. Nothing, therefore, remained for me to do, but to explain to Lord Byerdale the facts, which I did."

"If your majesty remembers," said the gentleman on the King's left, mingling in the conversation for the first time, "Lord Byerdale said so."

"Secondly," said the King, "Is it true that this gentleman who came to your assistance went with you, and under your protection, to the inn at Halstow, and thence, by your connivance, effected his escape?"

The King's brow was somewhat dark and ominous, and his tone stern, as he pronounced these words: but Wilton could not evade the question so put without telling a lie, and he consequently replied at once, "Sire, he did."

"Now for the third question," said the King,--"What was his real name?"

Wilton hesitated. He believed he had done right in every respect; that he had done what he was bound to do in honour; that he had done what was in reality the best for the King's own service; but yet he knew not by any means how this act might be looked upon. The minds of all men were excited, at that moment, to a pitch of indignation against the whole Jacobite faction, which made the slightest connivance with any of their practices, the slightest favour shown to any of their number, a high crime in the eyes of every one. But Wilton knew that he was, moreover, actually and absolutely punishable by law as a traitor for what he had done: what he was called upon to confess was, in the strict letter of the law, quite sufficient to send him to the Tower, and to bring his neck under the axe; for in treason all are principals, and he had aided and abetted one marked as a traitor. But, nevertheless, though he hesitated for a moment whether he should speak at all, yet he had resolved to do so, and of course to do so truly, when the King, seeing him pause, and mistaking the motives, added,--

"You had better tell the truth, sir. Captain Churchill has confessed, that though out of consideration for you he had admitted that he was present on this occasion, yet that in reality he had never quitted his house during the whole of the day in question."

"Sire," replied Wilton, looking him full in the face, with a calm, but not disrespectful air, "your majesty may have seen by my answers hitherto that whatever I do say will be the truth, plain and undisguised. I only hesitated whether I should not beg your majesty to excuse my answering at all, as you know by the laws of England no man can be forced to criminate himself; but as I acted in a manner that became a man of honour, and also in a manner which I believed at the time to be fitted to promote your majesty's interests, and to be in every respect such as you yourself could wish, I will answer the question, though, perhaps, my answer might in some circumstances be used against myself."

The slightest possible shade of displeasure had come over the King's countenance, when Wilton expressed a doubt as to answering the question at all; but whether it was from his natural command over his features, the coldness of a phlegmatic constitution, or that he really was not seriously angry, the cloud upon his brow was certainly not a hundredth part so heavy as it would probably have been with any other sovereign in Europe. He contented himself, then, when Wilton had come to the end of the sentence, by merely saying, with evident marks of impatience and curiosity, "Go on. What was his real name?"

"The name, sire, by which he is generally known," replied Wilton, "is the Duke of Berwick."

For once the King was moved. He started in his chair, and turning round, looked at the gentleman by his side, exclaiming, "It was not Drummond, then!"

"No, sire," replied Wilton; "although he never expressly stated his name to me, yet from all that was said by every one around, I must admit that I knew perfectly it was the Duke of Berwick. But, sire, whoever it was, he had saved my life: he had said not one word disrespectful to your Majesty's person: he had reprobated in the most severe and cutting terms those conspirators, some of whom have already bowed the head to the sword of justice; and he had stigmatized the acts they proposed to commit with scorn, contempt, and horror. All this he had done in my presence to ten or twelve armed men, whose conduct to myself, and schemes against you, showed them capable of any daring villany. These, sire, may be called my excuses for aiding a person, known to be an enemy of your crown, to escape from your dominions; but, if I may so far presume to say--it, there was a reason as well as an excuse which suggested itself to my mind at the time, and in which your majesty's interests were concerned."

The King had listened attentively: the frown had gone from his brow; and he had so far given a sign of approbation, as, when Wilton mentioned the conduct of the Duke of Berwick, to make a slight inclination of the head. When the young gentleman concluded, however, he paused in order to let him go on, always more willing that others should proceed, than say a single word to bid them do so.

"What is your reason?" he said at last, finding that nothing was added.

"It was this, sire," replied Wilton; "that I knew the Duke of Berwick was connected with your majesty's own family; that he was one person of high character and reputation amongst a vast number of low and infamous conspirators; that he was perfectly innocent of the dark and horrible crimes of which they were guilty; and yet, that he must be considered by the law of the land as a traitor even for setting his foot upon these shores, and must be concluded by the law and its ministers under the same punishment and condemnation as all those assassins and traitors who are now expiating their evil purposes on the scaffold. In these circumstances, sire, I judged that it would be much more agreeable to your majesty that he should escape, than that he should be taken; that you would be very much embarrassed, indeed, what to do with him, if any indiscreet person were to stop him in his flight; and that you would not disapprove of that conduct, the first motive of which, I openly confess, was gratitude towards the man who had saved my life."

"Sir, you did very right," said William, with scarcely a change of countenance. "You did very right, and I am much obliged to you."

At the same time, he held out his hand. Wilton bent his knee, and kissed it; and as he rose, William added, "I don't know what I can do for you; but if at any time you want anything, let me know, for I think you have done well--and judged well. My Lord of Portland here, on application to him, will procure you audience of me."

With those few words, which, however, from William III., conveyed a great deal of meaning, the King bowed his head to signify that Wilton's audience was over; and the young gentleman withdrew from his presence, very well satisfied with the termination of an affair, which certainly, in some hands, might have ended in evil instead of good.

CHAPTER XXXV.

Wilton Brown, on quitting the King, did not find Lord Sherbrooke where he expected; but little doubting that he should have to encounter a full torrent of wrath from the Earl of Byerdale, on account of his having concealed the fact of the Duke of Berwick's visit to England, he set spurs to his horse to meet the storm at once, and proceeded as rapidly as possible to the Earl's office at Whitehall. His expectations were destined to be disappointed, however. Lord Byerdale was all smiles, although as yet he knew nothing more than the simple fact that Captain Churchill had acknowledged his presence at a scene in which he had certainly played no part. His whole wrath seemed to turn upon Arden, the Messenger, against whom he vowed and afterwards executed, signal vengeance, prosecuting him for various acts of neglect in points of duty, and for some small peculations which the man had committed, till he reduced him to beggary and a miserable death.

He received Wilton, however, without a word of censure; listened to all that passed between him and the King, appeared delighted with the result; and although, to tell the truth, Wilton had no excuse to offer for not having communicated the facts to him before, which h-; had abstained from doing simply from utter want of confidence in the Earl, yet his lordship found an excuse himself, saying,--

"I'm sure, Wilton, I am more obliged to you even than the King must be, for not implicating me in your secret at all. I should not have known how to have acted in the least. It would have placed me in the most embarrassing situation that it is possible to conceive, and by taking the responsibility on yourself you have spared me, and, as you see, done your self no harm."

Wilton was puzzled; and though he certainly was not a suspicious man, he could not help doubting the perfect sincerity of the noble lord. All his civility, all his kindness, which was so unlike his character in general, but made his secretary doubt the more, and the more firmly resolve to watch his conduct accurately.

A few days after the events which we have just related, the Duke of Gaveston and Lady Laura left Beaufort House for the Earl's seat in Hampshire, which Lord Aylesbury had pointed out as the best suited to the occasion. It was pain ful for Wilton to part from Laura; but yet he could not divest his mind of the idea that Lord Byerdale did not mean altogether so kindly by the Duke as he professed to do, and he was not sorry the latter nobleman, now that he could do so without giving the slightest handle to suspicion, should follow the advice of Lord Aylesbury.

By this time Wilton had become really attached to the Duke; the kindness that nobleman had shown to him; the confidence he had placed in him; the leaning to his opinions which he had always displayed, would naturally have excited kindly and affectionate feelings in such a heart as Wilton's, even had the Duke not been the father of her he loved best on earth. But in the relative situation in which they now stood, he had gradually grown more and more attached to the old nobleman, and perhaps even the very weaknesses of his character made Wilton feel more like a son towards him.

To insure, therefore, his absence from scenes of political strife, to guard against his meddling with transactions which he was unfitted to guide, was a great satisfaction to Wilton, and a compensation for the loss of Laura's daily society. Another compensation, also, was found in a general invitation to come down whenever it was possible to Somersbury Court, and a pressing request, that at all events he would spend the Sunday of every week at that place. In regard to all his affairs in London, and more especially to everything that concerned Sir John Fenwick and the conspiracy, the Duke trusted implicitly to Wilton; and the constant correspondence which was thus likely to take place afforded him also the means of hearing continually of Laura.

He was not long without seeing her again, however; for it was evident that Lord Byerdale had determined to give his secretary every sort of opportunity of pursuing his suit with the daughter of the Duke.

"Did you not tell me, Wilton," he said one day, "that your good friend the Duke of Gaveston had invited you to come down and stay with him at Somersbury?"

"He has invited me repeatedly, my lord," replied Wilton, "and in a letter I received yesterday, pressed his request again; but seeing you so overwhelmed with business, I did not like to be absent for any length of time. I should have gone down, indeed, as I had promised, on Saturday last, to have come up on Monday morning again; but if you remember, on Saturday you were occupied till nearly twelve at night with all this business of Cook."

"Who, by the way, you see, Wilton, has said nothing against your friend," said the Earl.

"So I see, indeed, my lord," replied Wilton. "What will be done with the man?"

"Oh, we shall keep the matter over his head," said the Earl, "and make use of him as an evidence. But to return to your visit to the Duke--I can very well spare you for the next week, if you like to go down on Monday; and now that I know your arrangements, will contrive that you shall always have your Saturday evenings and Monday mornings, so as to be able to go down and return on those days, till you become his grace's son-in-law, though I am afraid fair Lady Laura will think you but a cold lover."

Wilton smiled, well knowing that there was no such danger. The Earl's offer, however, was too tempting to be resisted, and accordingly he lost no time in bearing down, in person, to Somersbury Court the happy intelligence that Cook, who was to be the conspirator most feared, it seemed, had said nothing at his trial to inculpate the Duke.

His journey, as was not uncommon in those days, was performed on horseback with a servant charged with his valise behind him, and it was late in the day before he reached Somersbury; but it was a bright evening in May; the world was all clad in young green; the calm rich purple of the sunset spread over the whole scene; and as Wilton rode down a winding yellow road, amidst rich woods and gentle slopes of land, into the fine old park that surrounded the mansion, he could see enough to show him that all the picturesque beauty, which was far more congenial to his heart and his feelings than even the finest works of art, was there in store for him on the morrow.

On his arrival, he found the Duke delighted to receive him, though somewhat suffering from a slight attack of gout. He was more delighted still, however, when he heard the news his young friend brought; and when, after a few moments, Laura joined him and the Duke, her eyes sparkled with double brightness, both from the feelings of her own heart at meeting again the man she loved best on earth, and from the pleasure that she saw on her father's countenance, which told her in a moment that all the news Wilton had brought was favourable.

The result to the Duke, however, was not so satisfactory as it might have been. In the joy of his heart he gave way somewhat more to his appetite at supper than was prudent, ate all those things that Sir George Millington, his good physician, forbade him to eat, and drank two or three glasses of wine more than his usual portion. At the time, all this seemed to do him no harm, and he spoke somewhat crossly to his own servant who reminded him of the physician's regulations. He even shook his finger playfully at Laura for her grave looks upon the occasion, and during the rest of the evening was as gay as gay could be. The consequence, however, was, that about a quarter of an hour after Wilton had descended to the breakfast-room on the following morning, Laura came down alone.

"I am sorry to say, Wilton," she said, with a slight smile, "that my dear father has greatly increased his pain by exceeding a little last night. He has scarcely slept at all, I find, and begs you will excuse him till dinner-time. He leaves me to entertain you, Wilton. Do you think I can do it?"

Wilton's answer was easily found; and Laura passed the whole morning with him alone.

Certainly neither of the two would have purchased the pleasure at the expense of the Duke's suffering; but yet that pleasure of being alone together was, indeed, intense and bright. They were both very young, both fitted for high enjoyment, both loving as ardently and deeply as it is possible for human beings to love. Through the rich and beautiful woods of the park, over the sunny lawns and grassy savannas--where the wild deer, nested in the tall fern, raising its dark eyes and antlered head to gaze above the feathery green at the passers by--Wilton and Laura wandered on, pouring forth the tale of affection into each other's hearts, gazing in each other's eyes, and seeming, through that clear window lighted up with life, to see into the deepest chambers of each other's bosom, and there behold a treasury of joy and mutual tenderness for years to come.

In the midst of that beautiful scene their love seemed in its proper place--everything appeared to harmonize with it--whereas, in the crowded city, all had jarred. Here the voices of the birds poured forth the sweetest harmony upon their ear as they went by; everything that the eye rested upon spoke softness, and peace, and beauty, and happy days; everything refreshed the sight and made the bosom expand; everything breathed of joy or imaged tranquillity.

The words, too, the words of affection, seemed more easily to find utterance; all the objects around suggested that imagery which passion, and tenderness, and imagination, can revel in at ease; the fanciful clouds, as they flitted over the sky, the waving branches of the woods, the gay sparkling of the bright stream, the wide-extending prospect here and there, with the hills, only appearing warmer and more glowing still, as the eye traced them into the distance--all furnished to fancy some new means of shadowing forth bright hopes, and wishes, and purposes. Each was an enthusiastic admirer of nature; each had often and often stood, and pondered and gazed, and admired scenes of similar loveliness; each, too, had felt deep and ardent affection for the other in other places; and each had believed that nothing could exceed the joy that they experienced in their occasional solitary interviews; but neither had ever before known the same sensations of delight in the beautiful aspect of unrivalled nature, neither had tasted the joy which two hearts that love each other can feel in pouring forth their thoughts together in scenes that both are worthy to admire.

Nature had acquired tenfold charms to their eyes; and the secret of it was, that the spirit of love within their hearts pervaded and brightened it all. Love itself seemed to have gained an intensity and brightness in those scenes that it had never known before, because the great spirit of nature, the inspiring, the expanding genius of the scene, answered the spirit within their hearts, and seemed to witness and applaud their affection.

Oh, how happily the hours went by in those sweet words and caresses, innocent but dear! oh, how glad, how unlike the world's joys in general, were the feelings in each of those young hearts, while they wandered on alone, with none but love and nature for their companions on the way! On that first day, at least to Laura, the feeling was altogether overpowering: she might have had a faint and misty dream that such things could exist, but nothing more; but now that she felt them, they seemed to absorb every other sensation for the time, to make her heart beat as it had never beat before, to cast her thoughts into strange but bright confusion, so that when she returned with Wilton, and found that her father had come down, she ran to her own room, to pause for a few moments, and to collect her ideas into some sort of order once more.

Day after day, during Wilton's stay, the same bright round of happy hours succeeded. During the whole of the first part of his sojourn, the Duke was unable to go out, and Wilton and Lady Laura were left very much alone. Wilton felt no hesitation in regard to his conduct. He could not believe, he scarcely even feared, that the Duke was blind to the mutual love which existed between Laura and himself; and he only waited till his own fate was cleared up, to speak to her father upon the subject openly.

Thus passed his visit; and we could pause upon it long, could paint many a scene of sweet and sunshiny happiness, warm, and soft, and beautiful, like the pictures of Claude de Lorraine: but we have other things to do, and scenes far less joyous to dwell upon. The time of his stay at length expired, and of course seemed all the more brief for being happy.

If the sojourn of Wilton at Somersbury Court had given pleasure to Laura, it gave scarcely less to the Duke himself, though in a different way; and when his young visitor was gone, he felt a want and a vacancy which made the days seem tedious. Thus, shortly after Wilton's arrival in town, he received a letter from the Duke, begging him not to forget his promise of another speedy visit of longer duration, nor neglect the opportunity of each week's close to spend at least one day with him and Laura. The origin of these feelings towards his young friend was certainly to be traced to the somewhat forced confidence which he had been obliged to place in him, in regard to Sir John Fenwick; but the feelings survived the cause; and during six weeks which followed, although Sir John Fenwick was universally supposed to have made his escape from England, and the Duke felt himself quite safe, Wilton experienced no change of manner, but was greeted with gladness and smiles whenever he presented himself.

On every occasion, too, the Earl of Byerdale showed him self as kind as it was possible for him to be; and in one instance, in the middle of the year, spoke to him more seriously than usual, in regard to his marriage with Lady Laura. The tone he took was considerate and thoughtful, and Wilton found that he could no longer give a vague reply upon the subject.

"I need not say to your lordship," he said, "how grateful I feel to you in this business; but I really can tell you no more than you see. I am received by the Duke and Lady Laura, upon all occasions, with the greatest kindness and every testimony of regard. I am received, indeed, when no one else is received, and I have every reason to believe that the Duke regards me almost as a son; but of course I cannot presume, so long as I can give no information of who I am, what is my family, what are the circumstances and history of my birth, to seek the Duke's approbation to my marriage with his daughter. Fortuneless and portionless as I must be, the proposal may seem presumptuous enough at any time; and though the legend told us, my lord, to 'be bold, and bold, and everywhere be bold,' it told us also to 'be not too bold.'"

"You are right, you are right, Wilton," replied the Earl. "But leave it to me: I myself will write to the Duke upon the subject, and doubt not shall find means to satisfy him, though I cannot flatter you, Wilton--and I tell you so at once--I cannot flatter you with the idea of any unexpected wealth. Your blood is your only posses-sion; but that is enough. I will write myself in a few days."

"I trust, my lord, you will not do so immediately," replied Wilton. "You were kind enough to promise me explanations regarding my birth. Others have done so, too." (The Earl started.) "Lord Sunbury," continued Wilton, "promised me the same explanation, and to give me the papers which he possesses regarding me, even be-fore the present period; but he returns in September or October, and then they will of course be mine."

"Ha!" said the Earl, musing. "Ha! does he? But why does he not send you over the papers? he is no farther off than Paris now; for I know he obtained a passport the other day, and promised to look into the negotiations which are going on for peace."

"I fancy, my lord," replied Wilton, "that in the distracted state of both coun-tries he fears to send over the papers by any ordinary messenger."

"Oh, but from time to time there are council messengers," replied the Earl. "There is not a petit maitre in the whole land who does not contrive, notwithstand-ing the war, to get over his embroidery from France, nor any old lady to furnish herself with bon-bons."

"I suppose he thinks, too," replied Wilton, "that, as he is coming so soon, it is scarcely worth while, and, perhaps, the papers may need explanations from his own mouth."

"Ah! but the papers, the papers, are the most important," replied the Earl, thoughtfully. "In September or October does he come? Well, I will tell you all before that my self, Wilton. I thought I should have been able to do it ere now; but there is one link in the chain incomplete, and before I say anything, it must be rendered perfect. However, things are happening every day which no one anticipates; and though I do not expect the paper that I mentioned for a fortnight, it may come to-morrow, perhaps."

About ten days after this period, Wilton, as he went to the house of the Earl of Byerdale, remarked all those external signs and symptoms of agitation amongst the people, which may always be seen more or less by an observing eye, when any event of importance takes place in a great city. They were, perhaps, more apparent than usual on the present occasion; for in the short distance he had to go he saw two hawkers of halfpenny sheets bawling down unintelligible tidings to maids in the areas, and two or three groups gathered together in the sunshiny morning at the corners of the streets.

When he reached the Earl's house, he found him more excited than he usually suffered himself to be, and holding up a letter, he exclaimed,--

"Here's an account of this great event of the day, which of course you heard as you came here. This is a proof how things are brought about unexpectedly. Not a man in England, statesman or mechanic, could have imagined, for the last six weeks, that this dark, cold-blooded plotter, Sir John Fenwick, had failed to effect his escape."

"And has he not?" exclaimed Wilton, eagerly. "Is he in England? Has he been found?"

"He has not escaped," replied the Earl, dryly. "He is in England; and he is at the present moment safe in Newgate. Some spies or other officers of the Duke of Shrewsbury dis covered him lingering about in Kent and Sussex, and he has since been apprehended, in attempting to escape into France."

"This is indeed great intelligence," replied Wilton. "I suppose there is no chance whatever of his being acquitted."

"None," answered the Earl; "none whatever, if they manage the matter rightly, though he is more subtle than all the rest of the men put together. It seems likely that the whole business will fall upon me, and I shall see him in a few days; for he already talks of giving information against great persons, on condition that his life be spared."

Wilton concealed any curiosity he might feel as well as he could, and went on with the usual occupations of the day, not remarking as anything particular, that the Earl wrote a long and seemingly tedious letter, and gave it to one of the porters, with orders to send it off by a special messenger.

On going out afterwards, he found that the tidings of Sir John Fenwick's arrest had spread over the whole town; and the rumour, agitation, and anxiety which had been caused by the plot, and had since subsided, was, for the time, revived with more activity than ever. As no one, however, was mentioned in any of the rumours but Sir John Fenwick himself, Wilton did not think it worth while to make the mind of the Duke anxious upon the subject till he could obtain farther information; and he therefore refrained from writing, as it was now the middle of the week, and his visit was to be renewed on the Saturday following. A day passed by without the matter being any farther cleared up; but on the Friday, when Wilton visited the Earl at his own house, he found him reading his letters with a very cloudy brow, which however, grew brighter soon after he appeared.

Wilton found that some painful conversation must have taken place between the Earl and his son; for Lord Sherbrooke was seated in the opposite chair, with one of those listless and indifferent looks upon his countenance which he often assumed during grave discussions, to cover, perhaps, deeper matter within his own breast. The Earl, though a little irritable, seemed not angry; and after he had concluded the reading of his letters, he said, "I must answer all these tiresome epistles myself, Wilton: for the good people who wrote them have so contrived it, in order, I suppose, to spare you, and make me work myself. I shall not need your aid to-day, then; and, indeed, I do not see why you should not go down to Somersbury at once, if you like it; only be up at an early hour on Monday morning.--Sherbrooke, I wish you would take yourself away: it makes me angry to see you twisting that paper up into a thousand forms like a mountebank at a fair."

"Dear papa," replied Lord Sherbrooke, in a childish tone, "you ought to have given me something better to do, then. If you had taught me an honest trade, I should not have been so given to making penny whistles and cutting cockades out of foolscap paper. Nay, don't look so black, and mutter, 'Fool's cap paper, indeed!' between your teeth. I'll go, I'll go," and he accordingly quitted the room.

"Wilton," said the Earl, as soon as his son was gone, "I have one word more to say to you. When you are down at Somersbury, lose not your opportunity--confer with the Duke about your marriage at once. The political sky is darkening. No one can tell what another hour may bring. Now leave me."

Wilton obeyed, and passed through the ante-room into the hall. The moment he appeared there, however, Lord Sherbrooke darted out of the opposite room and caught him by the arm, almost overturning the fat porter in the way.

"Come hither, Wilton," he said, "come hither. I want to speak to you a moment. I want to show you a present that I've got for you."

Wilton followed him, and to his surprise found lying upon the table a pair of handsome spurs, which Lord Sherbrooke instantly put in his hand, saying, "There, Wilton! there. Use them to-night as you go to Somersbury; and, amongst other pretty things that you may have to say to the Duke, you may tell him that Sir John Fenwick has accused him of high treason. My father is going to write to him this very night, to ask him civilly to come up to town to confer with him on business of importance. You yourself may be the bait to the trap, Wilton, for aught I know. So to your horse's back and away, and have all your plans settled with the Duke before the post arrives to-morrow morning."

The earnestness of Sherbrooke's manner convinced his friend that what he said was serious and true, and thanking him eagerly, he left him, and again passed through the hall. Lord Byerdale was speaking at that moment to the porter; but he did not appear to notice Wilton, who passed on without pausing, sought his own lodgings with all speed, mounted his horse, and set out for Somersbury.

CHAPTER XXXVI.

The world was in all its summer beauty, nature smiling with her brightest smiles, the glorious sunshine just departing from the sky, and glowing with double brightness in its dying hour, the woods still green and fresh, the blackbird tuning his evening song, and everything speaking peace and promising joy, as Wilton rode through the gates of Somersbury park.

When he dismounted from his horse and rang the bell, his own servant took the tired beast and led it round towards the stable with the air of one who felt himself quite at home in the Duke's house. But the attendant who opened the doors to him, and who was not the ordinary porter, bore a certain degree of sadness and gravity in his demeanour, which caused Wilton instantly to ask after the health of the Duke and Lady Laura.

"My young lady is quite well, sir," replied the servant; "but the Duke has had another bad fit of the gout in the beginning of the week--which has made him wonderfully cross," he added, lowering his voice and giving a marked look in Wilton's face, which made the young gentleman feel that he intended his words as a sort of warning.

"I am afraid," thought Wilton, "what I have to tell him will not diminish his crossness."

But he said nothing aloud, and followed the servant to wards the Duke's own particular sitting room. He found that nobleman alone, with his foot upon a stool. He had calculated as he went thither how he might best soften the tidings he had to bring; but the Duke began the conversation himself, and in a manner which instantly put all other thoughts to flight, and, to say the truth, banished Sir John Fenwick and his whole concerns from his young companion's mind in a moment.

"So, sir, so," he began, using none of the friendly and familiar terms that he generally applied to Wilton, "so you have really had the goodness to come down here again."

"My lord duke," replied Wilton, "your invitation to me was not only so general but so pressing, that always having found you a man of sincerity and truth, I took it for granted that you wished to see me, or you would not have asked me."

"So I am, sir, so I am," replied the Duke; "I am a man of sincerity and truth, and you shall find I am one, too. But from your manner, I suppose my Lord of Byerdale has not told you the contents of my letter to him this morning."

"He never told me," replied Wilton, "that your grace had written to him at all; but so far from even hinting that my visit could be disagreeable to you, he told me that as he did not require my assistance I had better come down here."

"He did, he did?" said the Duke. "He is marvellous kind to send guests to my house, whom he knows that I do not wish to see."

Wilton now began to divine the cause of the Duke's present behaviour. It was evident that Lord Byerdale, without letting him know anything about it, had interfered to demand for him the hand of Lady Laura. How or in what terms he had done so, Wilton was somewhat anxious to ascertain, but he was so completely thunderstruck and surprised by his pre sent reception, that he could scarcely play the difficult game in which he was engaged with anything like calmness or forethought.

"My lord," he replied, "it is probable that the Earl of Byerdale was more moved by kindness towards me than consideration for your grace. As you do not tell me what was the nature of your correspondence, I can but guess at Lord Byerdale's motives--"

"Which were, sir," interrupted the Duke, "to give you a farther opportunity of engaging my daughter's affections against her father's wishes and consent. I suppose this was his object, at least."

"I should think not, my lord," replied Wilton, resolved not to yield his point so easily. "I should rather imagine that Lord Byerdale's view was to give me an opportunity, on the contrary, of pleading my own cause with the Duke of Gaveston--to give me an opportunity of recalling all those feelings of kindness, friendship, and generosity which the Duke has constantly displayed towards me, and of urging him by all those high feelings, which I know he possesses, not to crush an attachment which has grown up under his eyes, and been fostered by his kindness."

The Duke was a little moved by Wilton's words and his manner; but he had taken his resolution to make the present discussion between himself and Wilton final, and he seized instantly upon the latter words of his reply.

"Grown up under my eye, and fostered by my kindness!" he exclaimed. "You do not mean to say, sir, I trust, that I gave you any encouragement in this mad pursuit. You do not mean to say that I saw and connived at your attachment to my daughter?"

Wilton might very well have said that he certainly did give such encouragement and opportunity that the result could scarcely have been by any possibility otherwise than that which it actually was. But he knew that to show him in fault would only irritate the Duke more, and he was silent.

"Good God!" continued the peer, "such a thing never entered into my head. It was so preposterous, so insane, so out of all reasonable calculation, that I might just as well have been afraid of building my house under a hill for fear the hill should walk out of its place and crush it. I could never have dreamed of or fancied such a thing, sir, as that you should forget the difference between my daughter, Lady Laura Gaveston, and yourself, and presume to seek the hand of one so much above you. It shows how kindness and con descension may be mistaken. Lord Byerdale, indeed, talks some vague nonsense about your having good blood in your veins; but what are your titles, sir? what is your rank? where are your estates? Show me your rent-rolls. I have never known anything of Mr. Wilton Brown but as the private secretary of the Earl of Byerdale--HIS CLERK he called him to me one day--who has nothing but a good person, a good coat, and two or three hundred a year. Mr. Wilton Brown to be the suitor for the only child of one of the first peers in the land, the heiress of a hundred thousand per annum! My dear sir, the thing was too ridiculous to be thought of. If people had told me I should have my eyes picked out by a sparrow I should have believed them as much;" and he laughed aloud at his own joke, not with the laugh of merriment, but of anger and scorn.

Wilton felt cut to the heart, but still he recollected that it was Laura's father who spoke; and he was resolved that no pro vocation whatsoever should induce him to say one word which he himself might repent at an after period, or with which she might justly reproach him. He felt that from the Duke he must bear what he would have borne from no other man on earth; that to the Duke he must use a tone different from that which he would have employed to any other man. He paused a moment, both to let the Duke's laugh subside, and the first angry feelings of his own heart wear off: but he then answered,--

"Perhaps, my lord, you attribute to me other feelings and greater presumption than I have in reality been actuated by. Will you allow me, before you utterly condemn me--will you allow me, I say, not to point out any cause why you should have seen, or known, or countenanced my attachment to your daughter, but merely to recall to your remembrance the circumstances in which I have been placed, and in which it was scarcely possible for me to resist those feelings of love and attachment which I will not attempt to disown, which I never will cast off, and which I will retain and cherish to the last hour of my life, whatever may be your grace's ultimate decision, whatever may be my fate, fortune, happiness, or misery, in other respects?"

The Duke was better pleased with Wilton's tone, and, to say the truth, though his resolution was in no degree shaken, yet the anger which he had called up, in order to drown every word of opposition, had by this time nearly exhausted itself.

"My ultimate decision!" said the Duke; "sir, there is no decision to be made: the matter is decided.--But go on, sir, go on--I am perfectly willing to hear. I am not so unreasonable as not to hear anything that you may wish to say, without giving you the slightest hope that I may be shaken by words: which cannot be. What is it you wish to say?"

"Merely this, your grace," replied Wilton. "The first time I had the honour of meeting your grace, I rendered yourself, and more particularly the Lady Laura, a slight service, a very slight one, it is true, but yet sufficient to make you think, yourself, that I was entitled to claim your after-acquaintance, and to justify your reproach for not coming to your box at the theatre. You must admit then, certainly, that I did not press myself into the society of the Lady Laura."

"Oh, certainly not, certainly not," replied the Duke--"I never accused you of that, sir. Your conduct, your external demeanour, has always been most correct. It is not of any presumption of manners that I accuse you."

"Well, my lord," continued Wilton, "it so happened that an accidental circumstance, not worth noticing now, induced your lordship to place much confidence in me, and to render me a familiar visitor at your house. You on one occasion called me to your daughter your best friend, and I was more than once left in Lady Laura's society for a considerable period alone. Now, my lord, none can know better than yourself the charms of that society, or how much it is calculated to win and engage the heart of any one whose bosom was totally free, and had never beheld before a woman equal in the slightest degree to his ideas of perfection. I will confess, my lord, that I struggled very hard against the feelings which I found growing up in my own bosom. At that time I struggled the more and with the firmer determination, because I had always entertained an erroneous impression with regard to my own birth, an impression which, had it continued, would have prevented my dreaming it possible that Lady Laura could ever be mine--"

"It is a pity that it did not continue," said the Duke, dryly; but Wilton took no notice, and went on.

"At that time, however," he said, "I learned, through the Earl of Byerdale, that I had been in error in regard to my own situation--though the distance between your grace and myself might still be great, it was diminished; and you may easily imagine that such joyful tidings naturally carried hope and expectation to a higher pitch than perhaps was reasonable."

"To a very unreasonable pitch, it would seem, indeed, sir," answered the Duke.

"It may be so, my lord," replied Wilton, "but the punishment upon myself is very severe. However, not even then--although I had the fairest prospects from the interest and promises of the Earl of Byerdale, and from the whole interest of the Earl of Sunbury, who has ever treated me as a son--although I might believe that a bright political career was open before me, and that I might perhaps raise myself to the highest stations in the state--not even then did I presume to think of Lady Laura with anything like immediate hopes. Just at this same period, however, the daring attempt to mix your grace with the plans of the conspirators by carrying off your daughter took place, and you were pleased to intrust to me the delicate and somewhat dangerous task of discovering the place to which she had been carried, and setting her free from the hands of the bold and in famous men who had obtained possession of her person. Now, my lord--feeling every inclination to love her, I may indeed say loving her before--you can easily feel how much such an attachment must have been increased; how much every feeling of tenderness and affection must have been augmented by the interest, the powerful interest of that pursuit; how everything must have combined to confirm my love for her for ever, while all my thoughts were bent upon saving her and restoring her to your arms; while the whole feelings of my heart and energies of my mind were busy with her, and her fate alone. Then, my lord, when I came to defend her, at the hazard of my life; when I came to contend for her with those who withheld her from you; when we had to pass together several hours of danger and apprehension, with her clinging to my arm, and with my arm only for her support and protection, and when, at length, all my efforts proved successful, and she was set free, was it wonderful, was it at all extraordinary, that I loved her, or that she felt some slight interest and regard for me? Since then, my lord, reflect on all that has taken place; how constantly we have been together; how she has been accustomed to treat me as the most intimate and dearest of her friends; how you your self have said you looked upon me as your son--"

"But never in that sense, sir, never in that sense!" ex claimed the Duke, glad to catch at any word to cut short a detail which was telling somewhat strongly against him. "A son, sir, I said, a son, not a son-in-law. But, however, to end the whole matter at once, Mr. Wilton Brown, I am very willing to acknowledge the various services you have rendered me, and which you have recapitulated somewhat at length, and to acknowledge that there might be a great many motives for falling in love with my daughter, without my attributing to you any mercenary or ambitious motives. It is not that I blame you at all for falling in love with her; that was but a folly for which you must suffer your own punishment: but I do blame you very much, sir, for trying to make her fall in love with you, when you must have known perfectly well that her so doing would meet with the most decided disapprobation from her father, and that your marriage was altogether out of the question. I think that this very grave error might well cancel all obligations between us; but, nevertheless, I am very willing to recompense those services--" Wilton waved his hand indignantly--"to recompense those services," continued the Duke; "to testify my sense of them, in short, in any way that you will point out."

"My lord, my lord," replied Wilton, "you surely must wish to give me more pain than that which I feel already. The services which I have rendered were freely rendered. They have been repaid already, not by your grace, but by my own heart and feelings. The only recompence I ever proposed to myself was to know that they were really serviceable and beneficial to those for whom they were done. I ask nothing of your grace but that which you will not grant. But the time will come, my lord,--"

"Do not flatter yourself, to your own disappointment!" interrupted the Duke: "the time will never come when I shall change in this respect. I grant my daughter a veto, as I promised her dear mother I would, and she shall never marry a man she does not love; but I claim a veto, too, Mr. Wilton Brown, and will not see her cast herself away, even though she should wish it. The matter, sir, is altogether at an end: it is out of the question, impossible, and it shall never be."

The Duke rose from his chair as he spoke; and then went on, in a cold tone:-- "I certainly expected that you might come to-morrow, sir, but not to-night, and I should have made in the morning such preparations as would have prevented any unpleasant meeting between my daughter and yourself in these circumstances. I must now give orders for her to keep her room, as I cannot consent to your meeting, and of course must not treat you inhospitably; but you will understand that the circumstances prevent me from requesting you to protract your visit beyond an early hour to-morrow morning."

"Your grace, I believe, mistakes my character a good deal," replied Wilton: "I remain not an hour in a house where I am not welcome, and I shall beg instantly to take my leave, as Somersbury must not be my abode to-night."

His utterance was difficult, for his heart was too full to admit of his speaking freely, and it required a great effort to prevent his own feelings from bursting forth.

"But your horse must be tired," said the Duke, feeling somewhat ashamed of the part he was acting.

"Not too tired, my lord," replied Wilton, "to bear his master from a house where he is unwillingly received. Were it necessary, my lord, I would walk, rather than force your grace to make any change in your domestic arrangements. You will permit me to tell the porter to call round my groom;" and going out for a moment, he bade the porter in a loud clear voice order his horses to be saddled again, and his groom to come round. He then returned to the chamber where the Duke remained, and both continued silent and embarrassed. It was some time, indeed, before Wilton's orders could be obeyed, for his valise had been carried up to his usual apartments. At length, however, the horse was announced, and Wilton went towards the door,--

"I now take my leave of you, my lord," he said, "and in doing so, shall endeavour to bear with me all the bright memories of much kindness experienced at your hands, and forgetfulness of one night's unkindness, which I trust and believe I have deserved even less than I did your former goodness towards me. For yourself I shall ever retain feelings of the deepest regard and esteem; for your daughter, undying love and attachment."

The Duke was somewhat moved, and very much embarrassed; and whether from habit, embarrassment, or real feelings of regard, he held out his hand to Wilton as they parted. Wilton took it, and pressed it in his own. A single bright drop rose in his eye, and feeling that if he remained another moment his self-command would give way, he left the Duke, and sprang upon his horse's back.

Two or three of the old servants were in the hall as he passed, witnessing, with evident marks of consternation and grief, his sudden departure from Somersbury. The Duke's head groom kept his stirrup, and to his surprise he saw the old butler himself holding the rein.

As Wilton thanked him and took it, however, the man slipped a note into his hand, saying in a low voice, "From my young lady." Wilton clasped his fingers tight upon it, and with one consolation, at least, rode away from the house where he had known so much happiness.

CHAPTER XXXVII.

The light was fading away as Wilton took his path through the thick trees of the park up towards the lodge at the gates; but at the first opening where the last rays of the evening streamed through, he opened Laura's note, and found light enough to read it, though perhaps no other eyes than those of love could have accomplished half so much; and oh, what a joy and what a satisfaction it was to him when he did read it! though he found afterwards, that note had been written while the eyes were dropping fast with tears.

"Fear not, dear Wilton," it said: "I have only time to
bid you not to fear. I am yours, ever yours; and whatever
you may be told, never believe that I give even one thought
to any other man.
"LAURA GAVESTON."

She signed her name at full, as if she felt that it was a solemn act--not exactly a pledge, that would bind her in the least, more than her own resolutions had already bound her--but a pledge to Wilton's heart--a pledge to which in after years she could always refer, if at any time the hand of another man should be proposed to her.

She had wept while she had written it, but it had given her deep satisfaction to do that act; for she figured to her self the balm, the consolation, the support which it would be to him that she loved best on earth--yes, best on earth; for though she loved her father deeply, she loved Wilton more.

When the high command went forth, "Thou shalt leave all on earth and cleave unto thy husband or thy wife," the God that made the ordinance fashioned the human heart for its accomplishment. It would seem treating a high subject somewhat lightly, perhaps, to say that it may even be by the will of God that parents so very frequently behave ill or unkindly to their children in the matter of their marriage, in order to lessen the breaking of that great tie--in order that the scion may be stripped from the stem more easily. But it were well if parents thought of the effect that they produce in their children's affection towards them by such conduct; for youth is tenacious of the memories of unkindness, and often retains the unpleasant impression that it makes, when the prejudices that produced it have passed away.

However that might be, Laura loved Wilton, as we have said, best on earth; she had a duty to perform to him, and she had a duty to perform to her father, and she determined to perform them both; for she believed--and she was right--that no two duties are ever incompatible: the greater must swallow up the less; and to let it do so, is a duty in itself; but in the present instance there were two duties which were perfectly compatible. She would never marry Wilton while her father opposed; but she would never marry any one else; for she felt that in heart she was already wedded unto him.

The words that she wrote gave Wilton that assurance, and it was a bright and happy assurance to him: for so long as there is nothing irrevocable in the future, the space which it affords gives room for Hope to spread her wings; and though he might feel bitterly and deeply depressed by the conduct of the Duke, and the stern determination which he had displayed, yet with love--with mutual love, and firmness of heart on both sides, he thought that happiness might be in deed delayed, but was not permanently lost.

Meditating on these things, he rode on for about a couple of miles; but then suddenly recollected that in all the agitation of the moment, and the painful discussion he had under gone, he had totally forgotten to tell the Duke either the arrest of Sir John Fenwick, or the tidings which he had heard more immediately affecting himself. He again checked his weary horse, and asked himself, "Shall I ride back?" But then he thought, "No, I will not. I will stop at the first farm-house or inn that I may find, where I can get shelter for myself and food for my horses during the night, and thence I will write him the intelligence, take it how he will. I will not expose myself to fresh contumely by going back this night."

He accordingly rode on upon his way, full of sad and melancholy thoughts, and with the bright but unsubstantial hopes which Laura's letter had given him fading away again rapidly under causes of despondency that were but too real. It was an hour in which gloom was triumphant over all other feelings; one of those hours when even the heart of youth seems to lose its elastic bound; when hope itself, like some faint light upon a dark night, makes the sombre colours of our fate look even blacker than before, and when we feel like mariners who see the day close upon them in the midst of a storm, as if the sun of happiness had sunk from view for ever. Such feelings and such thoughts absorbed him entirely as he rode along, and he marked not at all how far he went, though, from the natural impulse of humanity, he spared the tired horse which carried him, and proceeded at a slow pace.

About three miles from the Duke's gates, his servant rode up, saying, "I see a light there, sir. I should not wonder if that were the little inn of the village which one passes on the right."

"We had better keep our straight-forward way," replied Wilton. "We cannot be very far from the Three Cups, which, though a poor place enough, may serve me for a night's lodging."

The man fell back again, and Wilton was proceeding slowly when he perceived three men riding towards him at an easy pace. The night was clear and fine, and the hour was so early, that he anticipated no evil, though he had come unarmed, expecting to reach Somersbury, as he did, before dark.

He rode on quietly, then, till he met them, when he was forced suddenly to stop, one of the three presenting a pistol at his breast, and exclaiming, "Stand! Who are you?"

"Is it my money you want, gentlemen?" demanded Wilton; "for if it be, there is but little of it: but as much as I have is at your service."

"I ask, who are you?" replied the other. "I did not ask you for your money. Are you a King's officer? And which King's?"

"I am no King's officer," replied Wilton, "but a true subject of King William."

"Pass on," replied the other man, dropping his pistol "you are not the person we want."

Wilton rode forward, very well contented to have escaped so easily; but he remarked that his servant was likewise stopped, and that the same questions were put to him also. He, too, was allowed to pass, however, without any molestation, and for the next half mile they went on without any further interruption. Then, however, they were met by a single horseman, riding at the same leisurely pace as the others; but he suffered Wilton to pass without speaking, and merely stopped the servant to ask, "Who is that gentleman?"

No sooner had the man given his name than the horseman turned round and rode after him, exclaiming, "Mr. Brown! Mr. Brown!"

Wilton checked his horse, and in a moment after, to his surprise, he found no other but the worthy Captain Byerly by his side.

"How do you do, Mr. Brown?" said the Captain, as he came up. "I have but a moment to speak to you, for I have business on before; but I wanted to tell you, that if you keep straight on for half a mile farther, and taking the road to the right, where you will see a finger-post, go into a cottage--that cottage there, where you can just see a light twinkling in the window over the moor--you will find some old friends of yours, whom you and I saw together the last time we met, and another one, too, who will be glad enough to see you."

"Who do you mean?" demanded Wilton, somewhat anxiously.

"I mean the Colonel," replied Captain Byerly.

"Indeed!" said Wilton. "I wish to see him very much."

"You will find him there, then," replied the other. "But he is sadly changed, poor fellow, sadly changed, indeed!"

"How so?" said Wilton. "Do you mean that he has been ill?"

"No, not exactly ill," answered Byerly, "and I don't well know what it is makes him so.--At all events, I can't stop to talk about it at present; but if you go on you will see him, and hear more about it from himself. Good night, Mr. Brown, good night: those fellows will get too far ahead of me, if I don't mind." And thus saying, he rode on.

Wilton, for his part, proceeded on his way, musing over what had occurred. It seemed to him, indeed, not a little strange, that a party of men, whose general business was hardly doubtful, should suffer him, without any knowledge of his person or any private motives for so doing, to pass them thus quietly on his way, and he was led to imagine that they must have in view some very peculiar object to account for such conduct. That object, however, was evidently considered by themselves of very great importance, and to require extraordinary precautions; for before Wilton reached the direction-post to which Byerly had referred, he passed two more horsemen, one of whom was singing as he came up, but stopped immediately on perceiving the wayfarer, and demanded in a civil tone--

"Pray, sir, did you meet some gentlemen on before?"

"Yes," replied Wilton, "I did: three, and then one."

"Did they speak to you?" demanded the other.

"Yes," replied Wilton, "they asked me some questions."

"Oh, was that all?" said the man. "Good night, sir;" and on the two rode.

At the finger-post, Wilton turned from the highway; but for some time he was inclined to fancy, either that he had mistaken the direction, or that the light had been put out in the cottage window, for not the least glimmering ray could he now see. At length, on suddenly turning a belt of young planting, he found himself in front of a low but extensive and very pretty cottage, or rather perhaps it might be called two cottages joined together by a centre somewhat lower than themselves. It was more like a building of the present day than one of that epoch; and though the beautiful China rose, the sweetest ornament of our cottage doors at present, was not then known in this country, a rich spreading vine covered every part of the front with its luxuriant foliage. The light was still in the window, having only been hidden by the trees; and throwing his rein to the groom, Wilton said,--

"Perhaps we may find shelter here for the night; but I must first go in, and see."

Thus saying, he advanced and rang a bell, the handle of which he found hanging down by the door-post, and after having waited a minute or two, he heard the sound of steps coming along the passage. The door was opened by a pretty, neat, servant girl, with a candle in her hand; but behind her stood a woman considerably advanced in life, bowed in the back, and with a stick in her hand, presenting so much altogether the same appearance which the Lady Helen Oswald had thought fit to assume in her first interview with him, that for an instant Wilton doubted whether it was or was not herself. A second glance, however, at the old woman's face, showed the withering hand of time too strongly for him to doubt any farther.

The momentary suspense had made him gaze at the old woman intently, and she had certainly done the same with regard to him. There was an expression of wonder, of doubt, and yet of joy, in her countenance, which he did not at all understand; and his surprise was still more increased, when, upon his asking whether he could there obtain shelter during the night, the woman exclaimed with a strong Irish accent, "Oh, that you shall, and welcome a thousand times!"

"But I have two horses and my groom here," replied Wilton.

"Oh, for the horses and the groom," replied the woman, "I fear me, boy, we can't take them in for ye; but he can go away up to the high road, and in half a mile he'll come to the Three Cups, where he will find good warm stabling enough."

"That will be the best way, I believe," replied Wilton; and turning back to speak with the man for a moment, he gave him directions to go to the little public house, to put up the horses, to get some repose, and to be ready to return to London at four o'clock on the following morning.

As soon as he had so done, he turned back again, and found the old lady with her head thrust into the doorway of a room on the right-hand side, saying in a loud tone--"It's himself, sure enough, though!"

The moment she had spoken, he heard an exclamation, apparently in the voice of Lord Sherbrooke; and, following a sign from the girl who had opened the door, he went in, and found the room tenanted by four persons, who had been brought together in intimate association, by one of the strangest of those strange combinations in which fate some times indulges.

Seated in a large arm-chair, with her cheek much paler than it had been before, but still extremely beautiful, was the lady whom we must now call Lady Sherbrooke. Her large dark eyes, full of light and lustre, though somewhat shaded by a languid fall of the upper eyelid, were turned towards the door as Wilton entered, and her fair beautiful hand lay in that of her husband as he sat beside her.

On the opposite side of the room, with her fine face bearing but very few traces of time's withering power, and her beautiful figure falling into a line of exquisitely easy grace, sat the Lady Helen, gazing on the other two, with her arm resting on a small work-table, and her cheek supported by her hand.

Cast with apparent listlessness into a chair, somewhat behind the Lady Helen Oswald, and shaded by her figure from the light upon the table, was the powerful form of our old acquaintance Green. But there was in the whole attitude which he had assumed an apathy, a weary sort of thought fulness, which struck Wilton very much the moment he beheld him. Green's eyes, indeed, were raised to mark the opening door, but still there was a gloomy want of interest in their glance which was utterly unlike the quick and sparkling vivacity which had characterized them in former times.

The first who spoke was Lord Sherbrooke, who, still holding Caroline's hand in his, held out the other to his friend, saying, in a tone of some feeling, but at the same time of feeling decidedly melancholy, "This is a sight that will give you pleasure, Wilton."

"It is, indeed, my dear Sherbrooke," replied Wilton; "only I do wish that it had been rendered more pleasant still, by seeing no remaining trace of illness in this lady's face."

"I am better, sir, much better," she said; "for my recovery has been certain and uninterrupted, though somewhat long. If I could but teach your friend to bear a little adversity as unrepining as I have borne sickness, we might be very happy. I am very glad, indeed, to see you, sir," she continued; "for you must know, that this is my house that you are in," and she smiled gaily as she spoke: "but though I should always have been happy to welcome you as Sherbrooke's friend, yet I do so more gladly now, as it gives me the opportunity of thanking you for all the care and kindness that you showed me upon a late occasion."

Though Wilton had his heart too full of painful memories to speak cheerfully upon any subject, yet he said all that was courteous, and all that was kind; and, as it were to force himself to show an interest, which he would more really have experienced at another moment, he added, "I often wished to know how the sad adventures of that night ended."

The lady coloured; but he instantly continued, "I mean what was the result, when the constables, and other people, visited the house. I knew that Sherbrooke's very name was sufficient to protect him, and all in whom he had an interest, and therefore I took no steps in the matter; but I much wished to hear what followed after I had left the place, though, as Sherbrooke said nothing, I did not like to question him."

"You have questioned me on deeper subjects than that, Wilton," replied Lord Sherbrooke.--"But the matter that you speak of was easily settled. The constables found no one in the house but Plessis, myself, these two ladies, and some humbler women. It so happened, however, that I was known to one of the men, who had been a coachman in my father's service, and had thriven, till he had grown--into a baker, of all earthly things. As to Plessis, no inquiries were made, as there was not a constable amongst them who had not an occasional advantage, by his I 'little commerce,' as he calls it; and the ladies of course passed unscathed, though the searching of the house, which at the time we could not rightly account for, till Plessis afterwards explained the whole, alarmed my poor Caroline, and, I think, did her no small harm. But look you, Wilton, there is your good friend, and mine, on the other side of the room, rousing himself from his reverie, to speak with you. Ay! and one who must have a share in your greetings, also, though, with the unrivalled patience which has marked her life, she waits till all have done."

Wilton crossed over the room, and spoke a few words to the Lady Helen Oswald; and then turning to Green, he held out his hand to him; but the greeting of the latter was still somewhat abstracted and gloomy.

"Ha! Wilton," he said. "What brought you hither this night, my good boy? You are on your way to Somersbury, I suppose,"

"No," replied Wilton; "I have just come thence."

"Indeed!" said Green. "Indeed! How happens that, I wonder? Did you meet any of my men? Indeed you must have met them, if you come from Somersbury."

"I met several men on horseback," replied Wilton; "one party of whom, three in number, stopped me, and asked me several questions."

"They offered no violence? They offered no violence?" repeated Green, eagerly.

"None," answered Wilton; "though I suppose, if I had not answered their questions satisfactorily, they would have done so, as they seemed very fit persons for such proceedings. But I was in hopes," he continued, "that all this had gone by with you, and that such dangerous adventures were no more thought of."

"I wish I had never thought of any still more dangerous," replied Green; "I should not have the faces looking at me that now disturb my sleep. But this is not my adventure," he continued, "but his--his sitting opposite there. I have nothing to do with it, but assisting him."

"Yes, indeed, my dear Wilton," replied Lord Sherbrooke, "the adventure is mine. All other trades failing, and having exhausted every other mad prank but that, I am taking a turn upon the King's Highway, which has become far more fashionable now-a-days than the Park, the puppet-show, or even Constitution Hill."

"Nay, nay, Henry!" exclaimed his wife, interrupting him, "I will not hear you malign yourself in that way. He is not taking a turn upon the King's Highway, sir, for here he sits, bodily, I trust, beside his wife; and if the spirit have anything to do with the adventure that he talks of, the motive is a noble one--the object is not what he says."

"Hush, hush, Caroline," replied Lord Sherbrooke; "you will make Wilton believe, first, that I am sane; next, that I am virtuous; and, lastly, that I love any woman sufficiently to submit to her contradicting me; things which I have been labouring hard for months to make him think impossible."

"He knows, sir," said Green, interrupting him, "that you are generous, and that you are kind, though he does not yet know to what extent."

"I believe he knows me better than any man now living," replied Lord Sherbrooke; "but it happens somewhat inopportunely that he should be here to-night.--Hark, Colonel! There is even now the galloping of a horse round to the back of the house. Let you and I go into the other room, and see what booty our comrade has brought back."

He spoke with one of his gay but uncertain smiles, while Green's eyes sparkled with some of the brightness of former times, as he listened eagerly, to make sure that Lord Sherbrooke's ear had not deceived him.

"You are right, you are right, sir," he said; "and then, I hear Byerly's voice speaking to the old woman."

But before he could proceed to put Lord Sherbrooke's suggestion in execution, Byerly was in the room, holding up a large leathern bag, and exclaiming, "Here it is! here it is!"

"Alas!" said Caroline--"I fear dangerously obtained."

"Not in the least, madam," replied Byerly: "if the man dies, let it be remarked, he dies of fright, and nothing else; not a finger has been laid, in the way of violence, upon his person; but he would have given up anything to any one who asked him. We made him promise and vow that he would ride back to the town he came from; and tying his feet under his horse's belly, we sent him off as hard as he could go. I, indeed, kept at a distance watching all, but the others gave me the bag as soon as it was obtained, and then scattered over the moor, every man his own way. I am back to London with all speed, and not a point of this will be ever known."

"Come hither, then, come hither, Byerly," said Green, leading him away; "we must see the contents of the bag, take what we want, and dispose of the rest. You had better come with me too, sir," he added, addressing Lord Sherbrooke; "for as good Don Quixote would have said, 'The adventure is yours, and it is now happily achieved.'"

Thus saying, the three left the room together, and were absent for nearly half an hour.

CHAPTER XXXVIII.

It was evident to Wilton, that whatever was the enterprise in which Lord Sherbrooke and Green were engaged, it was one which, without absolutely wanting confidence in him, they were anxious to conceal from his knowledge; and, to say truth, he was by no means sorry that such should be the case.

He knew Lord Sherbrooke too well to hope that any remonstrance would affect him, and he was therefore glad not to be made a partaker of any secret regarding transactions which he believed to be dangerous, and yet could not prevent. In regard to Green too, there were particular feelings in his bosom which made him anxious to avoid any further knowledge of that most hazardous course of life in which he was evidently engaged; for he could not shut his eyes to what that course of life really was. Although, as we have already said, at that period the resource of the King's Highway had been adopted by very different people from those who even ten or twenty years afterwards trafficked thereon: though many a man of high education, gallant courage, and polished manners, ay, even of high birth, cast from his station by the changes and misfortunes of the day--like parts of a fine building thrown down by an earthquake, and turned to viler purposes--sought the midnight road as their only means of support: nay, though there were even some names afterwards restored to the peerage, which are supposed to have been well known amongst the august body of traffickers in powder and lead: yet Wilton could not but feel grieved that any one in whom he felt an interest should be tempted or driven to such an expedient, and at all events, he thought that the less he knew upon the subject the better.

That, however, which struck him as the most strange, was to find two beings such as those who were now left alone with him, graceful, beautiful, gentle, high-toned in manners, distinguished in appearance, fitted to mingle with the highest society, and adorn the highest rank, cognizant of, if not taking part in, things so dangerous and reprehensible.

A momentary silence ensued when he was left alone with the two ladies, and the first words that he spoke evidently showed to the Lady Helen what was passing in Wilton's mind. She looked at him for a moment with a grave smile, and after she had herself alluded more directly to the subject, he expressed plainly the regret that he felt at what he witnessed.

"I regret likewise, my dear boy," she said, "much that has gone before, nay, almost everything that has taken place in the conduct of him you speak of for many years past. I regret it all deeply, and regret it far more than I do the present transaction. You will think it strange, but I see not well how this was to be avoided. Not that I believe," she added, thoughtfully, "that we ought to frustrate bad men by bad means; but nevertheless, Wilton, here was a very great and high object to be attained: utter destruction to all our hopes would have been the consequence of missing that object; and there was but one way of securing it. This is to be the last enterprise of the kind ever undertaken; and it was that very fact which made me so fearful, for I know how treacherously fate deals with us in regard to any rash or evil acts. How very often do we see that the last time--the very last time--men who have long gone on with impunity, are to commit anything that is wrong, punishment and discovery overtake them, and vengeance steps in before reformation."

Wilton did not, of course, press the subject, as it was one, in regard to which he would have been forced to converse on abstract principles, while the others spoke from particular knowledge. Nor was his mind attuned at that moment to much conversation of any kind, nor to any thoughts but those of his own grief.

The conversation lingered then till Green and Lord Sherbrooke returned. Captain Byerly was now no longer with them, and not another word was said of the transactions of that night. Green relapsed into gloomy silence, and very shortly after, the two ladies retired to rest.

The moment they were gone, Lord Sherbrooke grasped Wilton's hand, saying, "What is the matter, Wilton? You are evidently ill at ease."

Wilton smiled.

"You give me none of your confidence, Sherbrooke," he said, "and yet you demand mine. However, I will tell you in one word what I might well have expected has occurred. An explanation has taken place between the Duke and myself, and that bright vision has faded away."

"Indeed!" said Lord Sherbrooke, thoughtfully. "Have you, too, met with a reverse, Wilton? I thought that you were one of the exempt, that everything was to smile upon you, that prosperity was to attend your footsteps even to the close of life. But fear not, fear not, Wilton--this is only a momentary frown of the capricious goddess. She will smile again, and all be bright. It is not in your fate to be un fortunate!"

"Nay, nay, Sherbrooke, this is cruel jesting," said Wilton. "Surely my lot is no very enviable one."

"It is one of those that mend, Wilton," replied Sherbrooke, sadly. "I live but to lose."

He spoke with a tone of deep and bitter melancholy; and Green, who had hitherto scarcely uttered a word, chimed in with feelings of as sad a kind; adding, as an observation upon what Lord Sherbrooke had said, "Who is there that lives past twenty that may not say the same? Who is there that does not live to lose?--First goes by youth, down into that deep, deep sea, which gives us back none of all the treasures that it swallows up. Youth goes down and innocence goes with it, and peace is then drowned too. Some sweet and happy feelings that belonged to youth, like the strong swimmers from some shipwrecked bark, struggle a while upon the surface, but are engulfed at last. Strength, vigour, power of enjoyment, disappear one by one. Hope, buoyant hope, snatching at straws to keep herself afloat, sinks also in the end. Then life itself goes down, and the broad sea of events, which has just swallowed up another argosy, flows on, as if no such thing had been; and myriads cross and re-cross on the same voyage the spot where others perished scarce a day before. It is all loss, nothing but loss," and he again fell into a fit of bitter musing.

"Come, Wilton," said Lord Sherbrooke, after a moment's thought, "I will show you a room where you can sleep. These are but melancholy subjects, and your fancies are grave enough already. They will be brighter soon--fear not, Wilton, they will be brighter soon."

"I know not what should brighten them," replied Wilton. "But I will willingly go and seek sleep for an hour or two, as I must depart by daylight to-morrow. In the meanwhile, Sherbrooke, I will ask you to let me write a brief note to the Duke, and trust to you to send it as early as may be; for to say the truth, in the bitter disappointment I have met with, and the harsh language which he used towards me, I forgot altogether to mention what you told me this morning."

The materials for writing were soon furnished, although Lord Sherbrooke declared, that were he in Wilton's situation, he would let the proud peer take his own course, as he had shown himself so ungrateful for previous services.

Wilton, however, only replied, "He is Laura's father, Sherbrooke," and the note was accordingly written.

"It shall be delivered early," said Lord Sherbrooke, as soon as it was ready. "Give it to me, Wilton; and now let us go."

Ere he quitted the room, however, Wilton turned to Green, and held out his hand, saying, "I am grieved to see you so sad. Can I by no means aid you or give you comfort?"

Green grasped his hand eagerly and tightly in his own, and replied, "No, my boy, no; nothing can give me comfort. I have done that which calmly and deliberately I would do again to-morrow, were I so called upon, and which yet, in the doing it, has deprived my mind of peace. There may be yet one ray of comfort reach me, and it will reach me from you, Wilton; but it may be that you may wish to speak with me from time to time; if so, you will hear of me here, for I go no more to London. I have seen bloody heads and human quarters enow. Seek me here; and if you want anything, ask me: for though powerless to cure the bitterness of my own heart, I have more power to serve others than ever I had."

"I have tried more than once in vain to see you," replied Wilton; "not that I wanted anything, but that I was anxious to hear tidings of you, and to thank you for what you had already done. I will now, however, bid you good night, and trust that time, at least, may prove an alleviation of your burdens as well as those of others."

Green shook his head with a look of utter despondency, and Wilton quitted him, seeing that further words were vain. Lord Sherbrooke then conducted him to a small neat room, and left him to lie down to rest, saying--

"I know not, Wilton, whether I can conquer my bad habits so much as to be up before you go. If not, I may not see you for many days, for I have leave of absence," he added, with one of his light laughs, "from my most honoured and respected parent. Should you need me, you will find me here; and I would fain have you tell me if anything of import befals you. I shall hear, however--I shall hear."

Thus saying, he left him, and at an early hour on the following day Wilton was on his way homeward. He reached London before the time at which it was usual for him to present himself at the house of Lord Byerdale; but when, after pulling off his riding dress, he went thither, he found that the Earl had already gone to Whitehall, and consequently he followed him to that place.

The statesman seemed not a little surprised to see him, and instantly questioned him in regard to his interview with the Duke. That interview was soon told by Wilton, who loved not to dwell upon the particulars, and consequently related the whole as briefly as possible.

He told enough, however, to move the Earl a good deal, but in a different manner from what might have been expected. Once or twice he coloured and frowned heavily, and then laughed loud and bitterly.

"His pride is almost more absurd than I had fancied, Wilton," he said, at length; "but to tell you the truth, I have in some degree foreseen all this, though not quite to this extent. If he had willingly consented to your marriage with his daughter, he might have saved himself, perhaps, some pain, for he must consent in the end, and it would not surprise me some day to see him suing you to the alliance that he now refuses you. His grace is certainly a very great and haughty peer, but nevertheless he may some day find you quite a fitting match for his daughter."

"I trust it may be so, my lord," replied Wilton; "but yet I see not very well how it can be so."

"You will see, you will see, Wilton," replied Lord Byerdale: "it matters not at present to talk of it. But now sit down and write me a letter to the Lord Lieutenant of Hampshire, telling him that I must beg he and the Sheriff would take prompt measures for restoring peace and security in the county. Let him know that one of the government couriers was stopped and plundered on the road last night. Luckily the bag of despatches has been found upon the highway unopened, but still the act was a most daring one. The same sort of thing has been of frequent occurrence in that county: it is evident that a large troop of these gentry of the road make that part of the world their field, and we must put a stop to it."

Wilton sat down and did as he was bid, feeling, it is true, that he could give a good deal more information upon the subject than the Earl possessed, if he thought fit to do so. This, of course, he did not choose to do; and after the letter to the Lord Lieutenant was written, the Earl allowed him to depart, saying--"Our business is somewhat light to-day, Wilton; but do not be the least afraid on account of this fair lady. The Duke's foolish pride will come down when he hears more."

Wilton departed, in a meditative mood; for notwithstanding every assurance given him, he could not but feel apprehensive, sad, and despondent. He might ask himself, in deed--for the Earl's words naturally led to such a mistaken question--"Who, then, am I? Who is it they would have me believe myself, that so proud a man should seek the alliance which he now scorns, as soon as he knows who I am?" But there seemed to him a sort of mockery in the very idea, which made him cast it from him as a vain delusion.

Though freed from ordinary business, and at liberty to go where he liked, with a thousand refined tastes which he was accustomed to gratify in his own dwelling, yet Wilton felt not the slightest inclination to turn his steps homeward on the present occasion. Music, he knew full well, was by no means calculated to soothe his mind under the first effects of bitter disappointment. Had it been but the disappointment of seeing Laura at the time he expected to do so--had circumstances compelled him to be absent from her for a week or a month longer than he had expected--had the bright dreams which he always conjured up of pleasant hours and happy days, and warm smiles and sweet words, when he proposed to go down to Somersbury, been left unrealized by the interposition of some unexpected event--the disappointment would certainly have been great; but nevertheless he might have then found a plea-sure, a consolation in music, in singing the songs, in playing the airs, of which Laura was fond; in calling up from memory the joys that were denied to hope, which can never so well be done, so powerfully, as by the magic voice of song.

But now all was uncertain: his heart was too full of despondency and grief to find relief by re-awakening even the brightest memories of the past: he could not gaze upon the days gone by, like the painter or the poet looking upon some beau-tiful landscape, for his situation he felt to be that rather of some unhappy exile looking back upon a bright land that he loved, when quitting it, perhaps never to return. Neither could books afford him relief; for his own sorrowful feelings were now too actively present to suffer him to rove with the gay imagination of others, or to meditate on abstracted subjects with the thoughtful and the grave.

To fly from the crowds that at that time thronged the streets--to seek solitary thought--to wander on, changing his place continually--to suffer and give way to all the many strange and confused ideas and feelings of grief, and disappointment, and bitterness of heart, and burning indignation, at ill-merited scorn, and surprise and curiosity in regard to the hopes that were held out to him, and despairing rejection of those hopes, even while the voice of the never-dying prophetess of blessings was whispering in his heart that those very hopes might be true--was all that Wilton could do at that moment.

The country, however, was sooner reached in those days than it is at present; and after leaving Whitehall, he was in a few minutes in the sweet fields, with their shady rows of tall elms, which lay to the westward of St. James's-street. Here he wandered on, musing, as we have said, for several hours, with his arms crossed upon his chest, and his eyes scanning the ground. At length he turned his steps home ward, thinking that it was a weakness thus to give way; but still as he went, the same feelings and the same thoughts pursued him; and that black care, which in the days of the Latin poet sat behind the horseman, was his companion, also, by the way.

On reaching his lodgings, the door was opened by the servant of the house, and he was passing on, but the girl stopped him, saying--"There is a lady, sir, up stairs, who has been waiting for you near an hour."

"A lady!" exclaimed Wilton, with no slight surprise; for though such a visit in those days might have passed without scandal, he knew no one who was likely to call upon him, unless, indeed, it were the Lady Helen Oswald, whose interest in him seemed to be of such a kind as might well produce a visit upon any extraordinary occasion.

He mounted the stairs with a rapid step, however, for he knew that it must be something out of the common course of events which had brought her, and opening the door quickly, entered his small sitting-room. But what was his surprise to behold, seated on the opposite side of the room, and watching eagerly the door, none other but Lady Laura Gaveston herself.

Astonishment certainly was the first sensation, but joy was the second; and advancing quickly to her, he took her in his arms and held her to his heart, and kissed her cheek again and again. For several moments he asked no question. It was sufficient that she was there, pressed to his bosom, returning his affection, and whatever might be the consequences, for the tine at least he was happy. The joy that was in his countenance--the tenderness--the deep devoted love of his whole manner--gave as much happiness to Laura herself as she was capable of receiving from anything at that moment.

Her thoughts, also, for a minute or two, were all given up to love and happiness; but it was evident from the tears on her cheeks that she had been weeping bitterly ever since she had been there; and the moment that he had recovered him self a little, Wilton led her back to her seat, and placing himself beside her, still holding her hand, he said--"Dear, dear Laura! I fear that something very painful, I may say very terrible, has driven you to this step; but indeed, dear girl, you have not placed your confidence wrongly; and I shall value this dear hand only the more, should your love for me have deprived you of that wealth which you have been taught to expect. I will labour for you, dear Laura, with redoubled energy, and I fear not to obtain such a competence as may make you happy, though I can never give you that affluence which you have a right to claim."

The tears had again run over Laura's cheek; but as she returned the pressure of his hand, she replied--"Thank you, dear Wilton--thank you: I know you would willingly do all for me, but you mistake, and I think cannot have heard what has happened."

Those words instantly guided Wilton's mind back to the right point, though for a moment thought hovered round it vaguely. He recollected all that Lord Sherbrooke had said with regard to Sir John Fenwick, and the charge against the Duke, and he replied, "I had mistaken, Laura--I had mistaken. But what has happened? I have been out wander ing long in the fields, thinking of but one subject, and melancholy enough, dear girl."

"I know it, dear Wilton--oh, I know it!" she replied, leaning her head upon his shoulder; "and I, too, have passed a wretched night, thinking of you. Not that I ever feared all would not in the end go right, but I knew how miserable what had occurred would make you; and I knew how angrily my father sometimes speaks, how much more he says than he really means, and what pain he gives with out intending it. The night was miserable enough, clear Wilton; but I knew not indeed how much more miserable the morning was to be.--You have not heard, then, what has taken place?"

"I have heard nothing, dearest Laura," replied Wilton; "I have heard nothing of any consequence since I came to town: but I fear for your father, Laura; for I heard yesterday that some accusation had been brought against him by Sir John Fenwick; and though last night, in the agitation and pain of the moment, I forgot to tell him, I wrote a note, and sent it early this morning."

"He got it before eight this morning," replied Laura, "and sent to call me down in haste. I found him partly angry, partly frightened, partly suspicious, and hesitating what to do. I besought him, Wilton, to fly with all speed. I pledged my word that Wilton, however ill-treated he might have been, and however he might feel that the services which he had rendered had been undervalued, would say nothing but that which was actually true, and absolutely necessary for the safety of those he loved."

"Surely," said Wilton, "he did not suspect me of falsifying the truth to give myself greater importance in his eyes?"

"Whatever were his suspicions, dear Wilton," replied Lady Laura, "they were too soon painfully removed; for he had scarcely given orders to have breakfast immediately, and the carriage prepared without loss of time, when two Messengers arrived with a warrant for his committal to the Tower. They treated us with all kindness," continued Lady Laura, "waited till our preparations were made, permitted me to accompany him, and have promised that to-morrow or the day after--as soon, in short, as a proper order can be made for it--I shall be permitted to be with him, and have a room near his. But oh, Wilton, you cannot imagine how my father's mind is overthrown. It seems, though I never knew it before, that he has really had some dealings with this Sir John Fenwick, and his whole reliance now appears to be upon you, Wilton."

"Oh, I trust, dearest Laura, that this charge will prove nothing," replied Wilton. "As far as I know, though he acted imprudently, there was not anything in the slightest degree criminal in his conduct. The days, I trust, are gone by when fictitious plots might be got up, and the blood of the innocent be sold for its weight of gold. It may have been judged necessary to secure his person, and yet there may not be the slightest probability of his being condemned or even tried."

"I do not know, Wilton," replied Lady Laura, sadly--"I do not know. He seems in very great terror and agitation. Are you sure he has told you all, Wilton?"

"On that subject, of course, I cannot be sure," replied Wilton. "But I do not feel at all sure, Laura, that this charge and this imprisonment may not have its origin in personal revenge. If so, perhaps we may frustrate the plotter, though we be weak and he is strong. Who was the warrant against your father signed by?--Was it--?"

"Not by Lord Byerdale," replied Laura, laying her hand upon his and gazing into his face, and thus showing Wilton that she instantly divined his suspicions.--"It was by the Duke of Shrewsbury."

"That looks ill, dearest Laura," replied Wilton, thoughtfully. "The Duke of Shrewsbury is one above all suspicion, high, noble, independent, serving the state only for the love of his country, abhorring office and the task of governing, but wise and prudent, neither to be led by any art or trickery to do what is not just, nor even to entertain base suspicions of another, without some very specious cause to give them credibility. This is strange, Laura, and I do not understand it. Did your father express a wish that you should see me, so that I may act openly in the business without offending him?"

"He not only told me to consult with you," replied Laura, "but he sent me direct from the Tower in the chair which you saw standing at the door, desiring me not to go to Beaufort House till I had seen you; to beseech you to come to him immediately, in order that he might advise with and consult you upon his situation. Indeed, he seems to have no hope in any one but in you."

Wilton mused for a minute or two.

"I do not think, my clear Laura," he said, "that the Earl of Byerdale knew anything of your father's arrest this morning when I saw him. I believe I must have done him wrong in my first suspicions. I will now, however, go to him at once, and endeavour to ascertain the precise nature of Sir John Fenwick's charge."

"Might it not be better," said Laura, anxiously, "to see my father first?"

"I must obtain an order of admission, dear Laura," replied Wilton. "What are the orders respecting your father's confinement I cannot tell, but I know that Sir John Fenwick is permitted to see no one but the ministers of the crown or somebody appointed by them. At all events, I think it will be better to converse with the Earl, and get the order at the same time. I will then hasten to your father with all speed, give him what comfort and consolation I can, and afterwards come for a few minutes to Beaufort House to see my Laura, and tell her the result--that is to say, if I may."

"If you may! dear Wilton," said Lady Laura, casting herself upon his bosom, "if you could see my poor father now with all his pride subdued, you would not ask if you may."

"But we must lose no time, dear Laura," replied Wilton. "You shall go on to Beaufort House with all speed. But where are your servants? I saw none in the hall."

"Oh, I have none with me," replied Lady Laura; "there was but one with the carriage: the others were left with orders to follow quickly to town; and I am sure in the agitation of the moment neither my father nor I thought of servants at all."

"Nay, dear Laura," replied Wilton, "my own servant shall go with you then; for after having once lost my treasure and found it again, I will not trust you with two strange chairmen such a distance, and alone."

This arrangement was soon made; and with a mind comforted and relieved, even from this short interview with him she loved, Lady Laura left him, and took her way to her solitary home.

CHAPTER XXXIX.

Wilton was sincerely pained and grieved for the Duke; and the moment that he had seen Laura safely on her way towards Beaufort House, he hastened to seek the Earl of Byerdale, supposing that he had returned to his own dwelling, which was near at hand. He was still at Whitehall, however, and thither Wilton accordingly went. He was admitted immediately to the Earl's presence, and found him with a number of written letters before him, folded up and ready for the departure of the courier. Not knowing that there was anything in the mere addresses of the letters that was not intended for him to see, Wilton suffered his eye to rest upon them for a moment. The Earl hastily gathered them together, but not before Wilton had remarked that one of them was addressed to the Earl of Sunbury; and the very haste with which the statesman removed them from his sight naturally gave rise to a suspicion of something being wrong, though Wilton could form no definite idea of what was the motive for this concealment.

"Have you heard that the Duke is arrested, Wilton?" was the Earl's first question, before Wilton himself could speak.

"Yes, my lord," replied Wilton. "I have heard, and was somewhat surprised, as your lordship did not speak to me on the subject in the morning."

"I knew nothing about it," replied the Earl, "except that I thought it likely. It was his grace of Shrewsbury's doing, and I do not doubt that he was very right, for one cannot punish mean offenders and let high ones pass."

"Certainly not, my lord," replied Wilton; "but from what I know of the Duke, I should think that he was the last man on earth to do any treasonable act. I have come to ask your lordship's permission to visit him in the Tower, and to obtain an order to that effect, hoping, too, that you may tell me the particulars of the charge against him, for he is now very anxious to see me."

"Oh ho!" exclaimed the Duke. "What! is his pride come down so soon? What! in one single day does he send for the man that he maltreated the night before? Such is human pride and human weakness. Well, well, Wilton, we will not mar your young fortunes. You shall have every opportunity, and perhaps may serve the Duke; although, I very much fear," he added, in a graver tone, "from the Duke of Shrewsbury having signed the warrant, that your good friend has been led much farther into these matters than you are aware of. Make out an order to see him, and I will sign it."

"But cannot I, my lord, obtain any information," said Wilton, as he wrote the order, "concerning the real charges against the Duke?"

"I really am not aware of them," replied Lord Byerdale. "The business has not been done through this office. I have seen Fenwick, indeed, but he only spoke generally, and seemed inclined to accuse everybody indiscriminately. However, I will send to Lord Shrewsbury, and ask all the particulars; but, by the way, Shrewsbury went out of town to-day. I must write to Vernon, his secretary, instead;" and sitting down, he wrote and despatched a note to a neighbouring ministerial office. An answer was almost immediately returned in the following terms:--

"MY LORD,-I have been honoured with your lordship's
note, and beg to inform you that the charge against the Duke
of Gaveston is for high treason, in having heard and connived
at the projected assassination of the King in the beginning
of this year, together with various other counts, such as
that of levying war, holding treasonable correspondence with
the enemy, and concealing the designs of traitors, &c. Your
lordship's order will admit Mr. Brown immediately to the
Tower, as no particular directions have been given in regard
to keeping the Duke a close prisoner. His grace of Shrewsbury
went out of town to Eyford at eleven this morning.--
I have the honour to be, your lordship's obedient servant,"
&c.

"There, Wilton," said the Earl, putting over the note to his secretary, "there is all the information that I can obtain on the subject; and here, take the order, and go and see your friend the Duke. Tell him I will come and see him to-morrow, and give him what consolation you can; but yet do not act like a silly boy, and make too light of the business, for two reasons: first, because the matter is really serious--the good folks of London have an appetite for blood upon them just now, and will not be satisfied unless they see a head struck off every now and then; and next, because, if his lordship do escape the abbreviating process of Tower Hill, we shall have to bring down his pride still farther than it is, to make him give ready consent to your marriage with his daughter."

"I would rather win his consent by good services, my lord," replied Wilton, "than drive him to give it by any harsh means."

"Pshaw! you are a silly boy," replied the Earl: "there is nothing so tiresome to a man of experience as the false generosity with which young men set out in the world. Here, when you have the opportunity in your power of inducing the Duke easily to give his consent to that which is most for his own interests, for yours, and for everybody's, you would let it slip, remain miserable yourself, and see Laura made miserable too, from the mere idle fancy of not taking advantage of misfortunes which the Duke has brought upon himself; but I will consent to no such idle folly, Wilton. I am determined to take care of your interests, if you do not take care of them for yourself, and I have a right to do so, as I believe I am your nearest living relation. And now, my good youth, mark my words, and remember that I am one who will keep them to the letter. The Duke, I know, has so far committed himself as to be really criminal. How far his crime may be aggravated I do not know. If he have brought his own head to the block I cannot help it, and then all matters will be clear, for Lady Laura will be free to do as she pleases; but as his pardon for the offences he has really committed must pass through my hands, if it should be found that his errors are not of a very deep dye, I give you fair warning, that he shall not set his foot beyond the doors of the Tower till Lady Laura is your bride. Say not a word, for my determination is taken, and he shall find me somewhat firmer in my purpose than he has shown himself towards you."

"I suppose your lordship means," replied Wilton, "till he has given his consent to the marriage. The Duke is too honourable a man to revoke it when once it is granted."

"No, by Heaven!" answered Lord Byerdale: "she shall be yours, fully, irrevocably your wife, ere he sets his foot forth. There are such things, I tell you, Wilton, as quarrels about marriage-settlements. I will have none of that. I will be a better friend to you than you would be to yourself. However, on second thoughts, say nothing about it to the Duke. I will take it all upon myself, which will spare you pain. You shall see that the proposal will come from the Duke himself."

Wilton smiled; and we cannot think that he was much to blame if there was some pleasure mingled in his feelings at the thought of soon and easily obtaining her he loved, even though he experienced repugnance to the means which the Earl proposed to employ. He resolved, therefore, to let the matter take its course, feeling very sure that the result of the Duke's present situation would be much affected, and his liberation greatly facilitated, by suffering the Earl to manage the matter in his own way.

He took the order, then, and proceeded at once to the Tower, where, through walls, and palisades, and courts, he was led to that part of the building reserved for the confinement of state prisoners. There was nothing very formidable or very gloomy in the appearance of the rooms and corridors through which he passed; but the sentry at the gates, the locked doors, the turning of keys, announced that he was in a place from which ever-smiling liberty was excluded; and the very first aspect of the Duke, when his young friend was admitted to the apartments assigned to that nobleman, showed how deeply he felt the loss of freedom. In the few hours that had passed since Wilton last saw him, he lead turned very pale; and though still slightly lame, he was walking up and down the room with hasty and irregular steps. The sound of the opening door made him start and turn round with a look of nervous apprehension; and when he beheld the countenance that presented itself, his face, indeed, lighted up with a smile, but that smile was so mingled with an expression of melancholy and agitation, that it seemed as if he were about to burst into tears.

"This is very kind of you, indeed, Wilton!" he exclaimed, stretching out his hand towards him: "pray let us forget all that took place last night. Indeed, your kindness in coming now must make a very great difference in my feelings towards you: not only that, indeed, but your note, which reached me early this morning, and which had already made such a difference, that I should certainly have sent for you to talk over all matters more calmly, if this terrible misfortune had not happened to me."

Was the Duke endeavouring to deceive Wilton?--No, indeed, he was not! Though there can be scarcely a doubt that, had he not been very much brought down by fear and anxiety, he would not have sent for Wilton at all. The truth was, he had first deceived himself, and at that moment he firmly believed that he would have done everything that was kind and considerate towards Wilton and his daughter, even had he not been arrested.

"We will not think of any of these things, your grace," replied Wilton. "I need not tell you that I was both overjoyed to see Lady Laura, and terribly grieved to hear the cause of her coming. As soon as I had heard from her your grace's situation and wishes, I sent my servant to accompany her to Beaufort House."

"Ay," said the Duke, interrupting him, "in the agitation of the moment, poor girl, I forgot to send any one with her I kept my man here. But what then, Wilton, what then?-You are always kind and considerate.--What did you do then?"

"I went immediately to Lord Byerdale," replied Wilton, "who seemed just to have heard of your arrest. From him I obtained an order to see you; and he was kind enough also to write to his grace of Shrewsbury's secretary to know upon what charge you had been arrested."

"Ay, that is the point! that is the point!" exclaimed the Duke, eagerly. "When we hear what is the charge, we can better judge what danger there is; in short, how one is situated altogether."

"Why, I grieve to say, my lord," replied Wilton, "that the charge is heavy."

"Good God!" exclaimed the Duke, "what is it, Wilton, what is it? Do not keep me in suspense, but tell me quickly. What does the villain charge me with? He first spoke upon the subject to me, and he knows that I am as innocent as the child unborn."

"It would seem, your grace," replied Wilton, "that he levels charges at many persons most likely as innocent as you are; and that he wishes to save his own life by endangering the lives of other people. He charges you with neither more nor less than high treason, for having been cognisant of, if not consenting to, the plan for assassinating the King--"

"I never consented to such a thing!" exclaimed the Duke, interrupting him. "I abhorred the very idea. I never heard of it--I--I--I never heard it distinctly proposed. Some one, indeed, said it would be better; but there was no distinct proposal of the kind; and I went away directly, saying, that I would have no farther part in their counsels."

Wilton's countenance fell at hearing this admission; for he now for the first time saw fully how terrible was the situation in which the Duke had placed himself. That nobleman, then, had, in fact, heard and had concealed the design against the King's life. The simple law of high treason, therefore, held him completely within its grasp. That law declared a person concealing treason to be as guilty as the actual deviser or perpetrator thereof, and doomed them to the same penalty. There was no hope, there was no resource, but in the clemency of the government; and the words used by Lord Byerdale rang in Wilton's ears, in regard to the bloody appetite of the times for executions. He turned very pale, then, and remained silent for a moment or two, while the Duke clasped his hands, and gazed in his face.

"For Heaven's sake, my lord," he said, at length, "withhold such admission from anybody else, for I fear very much a bad use might be made of it."

"I see that you think that the case goes ill with me," said the Duke. "But I give you my word of honour, my dear Wilton, that the moment I heard of the designs of these men I left the place in indignation."

"It is necessary, my lord," replied Wilton, "that your grace should know how you stand; and I fear very much that if this business can be proved at all, the best view of the case that can be taken will be, that you have committed misprision of treason, which may subject you to long imprisonment and forfeiture. If the government deals leniently with you, such may be the case; but if the strict law be urged, I fear that your having gone to this meeting at all, and consented to designs against the government of the King, and afterwards concealing the plans for introducing foreign forces, and for compassing the death of the King, must be considered by the peers as nothing short of paramount treason itself. Let me beseech you, therefore, my lord, to be most careful and guarded in your speech; to content yourself with simply denying all treasonable intentions, and to leave me, and any other friends whom you may think fit to employ, to endeavour, by using all extraordinary means, to save you even from the pain and risk of trial. Our greatest hope and the greatest security for you, is the fact--which is so generally reported that I fancy it must be true--that Sir John Fenwick has charged a number of persons in the highest stations, and some even near to the King's person and counsels. It will be for every one's interest, therefore, to cast discredit upon all his accusations, and amongst the rest, perhaps, this also may fall to the ground."

"Could you not see him, Wilton, could you not see him?" demanded the Duke, eagerly. "Perhaps he might be persuaded to mitigate his charge; to withdraw it; or to add some account of the abhorrence I expressed at the plans and purposes I heard."

"I see no way by which I could gain admittance, my lord," replied Wilton. "He is a close prisoner in Newgate. I know no one who even is acquainted with him; and I believe none but his wife and various members of the government are admitted to see him alone. However, I will do my best, my lord, and if I can gain admission, I will."

The Duke cast himself in deep despondency into a chair, and mused for several minutes without reply, seeing evidently, from Wilton's words and manner, that he thought his case a desperate one. After a moment, however, a momentary ray of hope crossed his countenance again.

"Cannot you see the Lady Mary Fenwick?" he said. "She could surely gain you admission to her husband. She is a distant relation of my own, too, for my grandfather married Lady Carlisle's aunt. Beseech her, Wilton, to gain you admittance; and try also--try, by all means--to make her use her influence with her husband in my behalf. Perhaps at her entreaty he would modify the charge, or retract a part of it. It can do him no good--it may ruin me."

"I will do my best, my lord," replied Wilton, "and in the meantime my Lord of Byerdale desired me to tell your grace that he would visit you to-morrow. He comes, indeed, merely as a friend; but I would beg your grace to remember that he is also a minister of the crown, bound by his office to give intimation of everything affecting the welfare of the state."

"Oh, I will be careful, I will be careful!" replied the Duke. "But can you think of nothing else, Wilton? can we fall upon no means? Would to Heaven I had always taken your advice! I should not now be here. Should I ever escape, you will find me a different being, Wilton. I will not forget your kindness, nor be ungrateful for it;" and he fell into a somewhat sad and feeble commentary upon his own conduct, briefly expressing regret for what he had done, partly alleging excuses for it, but still evidently speaking under the overpowering influence of fear; while pride, that weakest and most enfeebling of all evil passions, gave him no support under affliction, no strength and vigour in the moment of danger. In his heart Wilton could not respect him; but still he had nourished in his bosom feelings of affectionate regard towards him: he knew that Laura's happiness was not to be separated from her father's safety, and he resolved once more to exert every energy of mind and body in the service of the Duke.

For about half an hour more their conversation was protracted in the same strain, and then Wilton took his leave, telling the prisoner that he feared he should not be able to visit him on the following day. The Duke pressed him much to do so; but when he heard that every spare moment of Wilton's time was to be devoted to his service, he readily agreed, for that object, to lose the consolation of seeing him.

According to his promise, Wilton sped as fast as possible to Beaufort House; and though the brief conversation which ensued between him and Laura was mingled with much that was sad, yet the very fact of being together--of pouring out every thought of the heart to each other--of consulting with each other upon the welfare of one who was now an object of the deepest interest to both--was in itself a happiness, to Wilton powerful and intense; to Laura, sweet, soothing, and supporting. During the short time that Wilton stayed, the conversation turned entirely upon the Duke. At that moment, and with but little cheering hope to give, Wilton could not mingle the subject of his own feelings with the sadder ones which brought him thither. Love, indeed, pervaded every word he spoke; love, indeed, gave its colouring to all his feelings and to all his thoughts; but that very love was of a kind which prevented him from making it the subject of discourse at such an hour as that. Nor was his visit long, for it was now dark; and after one whole day, which he knew had been spent in anxiety, care, and fatigue, and after a night which he likewise knew had gone by in sorrow and anguish, he felt that Laura would require repose, and hoped, though but faintly, that she would obtain it.

He left her, then, in less than an hour, and took his way homeward, meditating over what might be done for the Duke, but seeing no hope, no chance, but in the exertions of the Earl of Byerdale, or the merciful interposition of the Duke of Shrewsbury. He was not without hope that the Earl would exert himself; though when he asked his own mind the question, "Upon what motives, and to what effect, will the Earl exert himself?" he was obliged to pause in doubt--ay, and in suspicion. He could not divest his own heart of a conviction that the Earl was acting insincerely; that there was some object in view which it was impossible for him to divine; some purpose more than mere kindness to a relation whom he had never known or acknowledged for so many years of their mutual life.

CHAPTER XL.

It was the ninth hour of the evening on the following day when a carriage stopped at the gates of Newgate, and a lady got out and entered the prison. It was by this time dark, for the year was already beginning to show a slight diminution in the length of the days; and there were few people just at that moment in the streets to remark that she left a male companion behind her in the vehicle, who, with his arms crossed upon his chest, and his eyes bent thoughtfully upon the other side of the carriage, remained buried in deep and seemingly gloomy meditation.

After the lapse of about ten minutes the lady returned, and said, "You may come; but the governor says your visit must not be long, and on no account must be mentioned."[6]

Wilton instantly stepped out of the carriage as Lady Mary Fenwick spoke, and followed her into the prison. A turnkey was in waiting with a light, and led them round the outer court and through one or two dark and narrow passages to the cell in which Sir John Fenwick was confined. There was another turnkey waiting without; and Wilton, being admitted, found the wretched man whose crimes had brought him thither, and whose cowardly treachery was even then preparing to make his end disgraceful, sitting pale, haggard, and worn, with his elbow resting on the small table in the middle of the cell, and his anxious eye fixed upon that door from which he was never more to go forth but to trial, to shame, and to death.

Lady Mary Fenwick, his unfortunate wife, whose eager and strenuous exertions in her husband's behalf were sufficient to atone in some degree for the error of countenancing those calumnies by which he hoped to escape his well-deserved

---

6 It is an undoubted historical fact, that more persons visited and conversed long with Fenwick in prison than the court was at all aware of.

fate, accompanied or rather followed Wilton into the cell; and as she did so, remarking the haggard glance with which Sir John regarded the visitor, she held up her finger with a meaning look, as if to entreat him to assume more calmness, at least in his demeanour.

Sir John Fenwick made an effort to do so; and, with one of those painful smiles wherewith wretchedness often attempts to cover its own misery, he said, "Good evening, Mr. Brown. This is a poor place for me to receive you in. I could have done better, if you had honoured me by a visit in Northumberland."

"I grieve much, Sir John, to see you in it," replied Wilton, "and trust that you may be enabled to free yourself speedily."

A look of anguish came over Sir John Fenwick's countenance; but Wilton went on, saying, "When last we met, Sir John, it was not, perhaps, on the best of terms, and I certainly thought that you treated me ill; but let all that be forgotten in the present circumstances."

"Do you mean," asked Sir John Fenwick, with a cynical look, "that we are both to forget it, or that I am to forget the whole business, and you to recollect it at my trial for the benefit of my accusers?"

"I meant for us both, of course, to forget it," replied Wilton; "or, rather, I should say, I meant merely that we should forget all feelings of enmity; for to see you here deprives me of all such sensations towards you."

"Ay, sir," said Sir John Fenwick, eagerly. "But let us keep to the other point, if you please. Do you intend to forget our former meeting, or to give evidence in regard to it?"

Wilton paused, and thought for a moment; and then a sudden idea struck him that that very interview to which Fenwick alluded might, perhaps, prove the means of making him modify his charge against the Duke.

"I cannot, of course," he said, "promise you, Sir John Fenwick, not to give evidence against you, if I am called upon, for you know that I can be compelled to do so; but I do not see that my evidence could do you the slightest harm in regard to your trial for treason, as I heard you utter no treasonable sentiments, and saw you perform no treasonable act."

"True, true!" cried Sir John Fenwick, gladly. "True, you can have nothing to say."

"So shall I tell any one who asks me," said Wilton. "I can give no pertinent evidence whatsoever, and therefore can easily keep out of court--unless, indeed," he added, with particular emphasis, "the charges which you have brought against the Duke of Gaveston should compel me to come forward as one of his witnesses, especially as his trial is likely to take place before your own."

"But how can that affect me?" demanded Sir John Fenwick, looking sharply in his face. "How can the Duke's trial have any effect upon mine?"

"Merely by bringing forward my evidence," replied Wilton.

"But how, why, wherefore?" said Sir John Fenwick, eagerly. "You have yourself admitted that you saw nothing, heard nothing at all treasonable--you cannot dally with a man whose life is in jeopardy. What evidence can you give with regard to the Duke that can at all affect me?"

"Only in this way," answered Wilton. "The Duke must be tried upon your accusation. He will call me to prove that you and he were at enmity together, and that therefore your charge is likely to be a calumny. He will also call me to prove that it was both my opinion and his, expressed to each other at the very time, that you carried off his daughter for the purpose of forcing him into a plot against the state, or at all events to prevent his revealing what he knew of your proceedings, from the fear of some injury happening to his child. I shall then have to prove that I found her absolutely in your power: that you refused to give her up at my request; that you were at that time in company with and acting in concert with various persons, five or six of whom have since been executed; that from amongst you a shot was fired at me, showing that the Duke's apprehensions regarding his daughter were well founded; and I shall also have to declare, that before the Duke could have any assurance of his daughter's safety, the conspiracy was itself discovered, so that he had no time or opportunity to reveal the plot, unless at a period when his so doing might have endangered, perhaps, the life of Lady Laura. All this, my good sir, I shall have to prove, if the Duke's trial is forced on. To sum the matter up, it must be shown upon that trial that you and the Duke were at bitter enmity, and that therefore your charge is likely to be malicious; that you carried off his daughter as a sort of hostage; and that he was under reasonable apprehensions on her account, in case he should tell what he knew of the conspiracy; that I found you associating intimately with all the condemned traitors the very day before the arrest of some of them, and that the

Duke did not recover his daughter by my means, till the plot itself was discovered. Now you will judge, Sir John, how this may affect your own trial. I warn you of the matter, because I have a promise, a positive promise, that I shall not be brought forward to give evidence in this business without my own consent; but once having proffered my testimony in favour of the Duke, I cannot refuse it, should any link in the chain of evidence be wanting against you which I can supply."

Sir John Fenwick had listened to every word that Wilton said in bitter silence; and when he had done, he gnashed his teeth one against the other, saying, with a look of hatred, "You should have been a lawyer, young sir, you should have been a lawyer. You have missed your vocation."

"Lawyers, Sir John Fenwick," replied Wilton, "are often, even against their will, obliged to support falsehood; but I merely tell you the truth. You have brought a charge against the Duke, as far as I can understand, of which he is virtually innocent, to all intents and purposes--"

"Who told you I had brought a charge against him at all?" demanded Sir John Fenwick. "Who told you what that charge was? It must be all guess-work, upon your part. Depend upon it, if I have brought a charge at all, it is one that I can prove."

"I may have been mistaken," replied Wilton, "and I hope I am, Sir John. I hope that you have brought no charge, and that if you have, it is not of the nature that I supposed; for as I have shown you, it would be most unwise and imprudent of you so to do. You would not injure the Duke in any other way than by a long imprisonment, and you would, in all probability, insure your own condemnation, while you were uselessly attempting to do evil to another. At all events, Sir John, you must not take it ill of me that I point this out to you, and if you will take the warning I have given, it may be of great benefit to you."

"How should I take it?" demanded Sir John Fenwick, still frowning upon him from under his bent brows. "What I have said I have said, and I shall not go back from it. There may be other witnesses, too, against the Duke, that you know not of. What think you of Smith? What think you of Cook?"

"I know not, really," replied Wilton. "In fact, I know nothing upon the subject, except that the Duke is virtually innocent of the crime with which you would charge him. You made him listen to designs which he abhorred; and because he did not betray you, you charge him with participating in them. As for the witnesses Cook and Smith, I have heard from the Earl of Byerdale that neither the one nor the other have anything to say against the Duke."

Sir John Fenwick had listened with a bitter smile to what Wilton said; but he replied almost fiercely, "You know nothing of what you are talking. Are you blind enough or foolish enough to fancy that the Earl of Byerdale is a friend of the Duke?"

"I really do not know," replied Wilton, calmly. "I suppose he is neither very much his friend nor his enemy."

"And there, too, you are mistaken," answered Sir John Fenwick: "for an envoy, you know marvellous little of the sender's situation."

"I only know," replied Wilton, "thus much, which you yourself cannot deny, that to accuse the Duke, so as to bring him to trial for this unfortunate affair, will be to produce your certain condemnation; to cut you off from all chance of hope."

Lady Mary Fenwick had hitherto stood silent a step or two behind Wilton; but now advancing a little, she said, "Indeed, Sir John, you had better think of it. It seems to me that what Mr. Brown says is reasonable, and that it would be much better so to state or modify your charge against the Duke as not to hazard his life."

"Nonsense, Lady Mary!" exclaimed Fenwick; "neither you nor be know anything of what my charges are, or in what my hopes consist. My charge against the Duke shall stand as I have given it; and you may tell him, that it is not on my evidence alone he will be condemned; so that yours, young man, will not tend much to save him."

Wilton saw that it would be useless to urge the matter any farther at that moment, though, notwithstanding the perverse determination shown by the prisoner, he was not without hope that their conversation might ultimately produce some effect upon his mind.

"Well, Sir John," he said, "I will keep you no longer from conversation with your lady. I grieve for you on every account. I grieve to see you here, I grieve for the situation in which you have placed yourself, and I still more grieve to see you struggling to deliver yourself from that situation by means which MAY PRODUCE the destruction of others, and will certainly PRODUCE your own."

"I neither want your grief, nor care for it, sir," replied the prisoner. "Good night, good night."

Wilton then turned and left him; but Lady Mary Fenwick accompanied the young gentleman into the passage, saying in a low voice, "The Earl of Byerdale has seen him twice. You will do well to be upon your guard there."

"Thank you, lady, thank you," replied Wilton. "I am upon my guard, and am most grateful for what you have done."

Thus saying, he left her: and as it was too late, at that hour, to visit the prisoner in the Tower, he turned towards his own home; but ere he reached it, he bethought him of seeking some farther information from the public reports of the day, which were only to be met with in their highest perfection in the several different resorts of wits and politicians which have become familiar to our minds in the writings of Steele and Addison. Will's and the Chocolate-house, and other places of the same kind, supplied in a very great degree the places of the Times, the Herald, the Globe, or the Courier; and though the Postman and several other papers gave a scanty share of information, yet the inner room of the St. James's Coffee-house might be considered as representing the leading article to the newspaper of the day.

To one or two of these houses, then, Wilton repaired, and found the whole town still busy with the arrest of Sir John Fenwick, and with the names of persons he was said to have accused. If the rumours were to be believed, he had brought charges of one kind or another against half the high nobility and statesmen of the land. The King's servants and most familiar friends, many who were still actually employed by him, and many who had aided to seat him on the throne, were all said to be accused of treasonable communications with the court of St. Germain; and Wilton had the satisfaction of thinking, that if there were, indeed, any safety in numbers, the Duke had that security at least.

When he had satisfied himself on this point, he returned to his own house, to meditate upon the best defence which could be set up for the noble prisoner. None, however, suggested itself better than that which he had sketched out in his conversation with Sir John Fenwick; and without loss of time he put it down in writing, in order to take the Duke's opinion upon it. There was one flaw, indeed, in the chain which he could not but see, and which he feared might be used by an enemy to the Duke's disadvantage. He could prove, that after Lady Laura had been carried away the Duke had no opportunity whatever of disclosing the plot until it was already discovered; but unfortunately, between the time of the meeting in Leadenhall-street and the period at which the conspirators so daringly bore off the lady from the terrace there had been a lapse of some time, during which her father might have made any communication to the government that he liked. There was a hope, however, that this might pass unremarked; and at all events what he proposed was the only defence that could be set up.

On the following morning, when he saw the Earl of Byerdale, he inquired if he had seen the Duke; but found that such was not the case, business being the excuse for having failed in his promise. Wilton, however, proceeded to the Tower as soon as he was free, and found Laura now sharing the apartments assigned to her father, and striving to support and comfort him, but apparently in vain. The Duke's mind was still in a terrible state of depression; and the want of all certain intelligence, the failure of the Earl of Byerdale's promise, and the absence of Wilton, had caused his anxiety apparently to increase rather than to diminish, since the first day of his imprisonment.

We must not pause upon the various interviews which succeeded, and were painful enough. Wilton had little to tell that could give the Duke any comfort. The determined adherence of Sir John Fenwick to his charge, the sort of indifference which the Earl of Byerdale displayed in regard to the prisoner's situation, neglecting to see him, though repeatedly promising to do so, all served to depress his spirits day by day, and to render him altogether insensible to the voice of comfort. Towards Wilton himself the Earl resumed a portion of his reserve and gravity; and though he still called him, "My dear Wilton," and "My dear boy," when he addressed him, he spoke to him very little upon any subject, except mere matters of business, and checked every approach to the topic on which Wilton would most willingly have entered.

On the seventh or eighth day of the Duke's imprisonment, however, Lord Sherbrooke again appeared in town; but the Earl employed Wilton constantly, during the whole of that day; so much so, indeed, that his secretary could not help believing that there was effort apparent in it, in order to prevent his holding any private communication with his friend. At length, however, he suffered him to return home, but not till nearly ten at night, by which time Lord Sherbrooke had left the house, to go to some great entertainment.

Scarcely had Wilton passed the door, when he found some one take hold of his arm, and to his surprise found the young nobleman by his side.

"I have been watching for you eagerly, Wilton," he said, "for it seems to me, that the game is going against you, and I see the faces of the cards."

"I am very anxious indeed about the Duke, if such be your meaning, Sherbrooke," replied Wilton.

"And I am so also," answered Lord Sherbrooke. "What my father intends, I do not well see; but I should think, that to make the poor man lose his head on Tower-hill would be somewhat too severe a punishment, too bitter a revenge, for Lady Laura refusing to wed so worshipful a person as I am."

"I hope and trust," replied Wilton, "that there is no chance of such a consummation."

"On my word, I do not know," replied Lord Sherbrooke. "My father, when he is hungry for anything, has a great appetite; I don't think the Duke's head would much more than dine him. However, take my advice; depend not upon him in the least; go to the Duke of Shrewsbury at once, if he be in town, and if not, to Vernon. Try to interest them in favour of the Duke; see what you can allege in his favour. The King has just returned from Holland, you know, and any application made to him now may perhaps be received graciously. Have you anything that you can state in the Duke's favour?"

Wilton recapitulated all that could be said to palliate the error which Laura's father had committed, and Lord Sherbrooke answered eagerly, "That is enough, surely that is enough. At least," he added, "it ought to be enough, and would be enough, if there were no under-influence going on. At all events, Wilton, I would go decidedly to his grace of Shrewsbury, or to Vernon, for I believe the Duke is absent. Represent all these facts, and induce him to lay them before the King. This is the best and most straightforward course, and you will speedily learn more upon the subject. But there is another thing which I have to tell you--though I put no great reliance upon the result being as effectual as we could wish--I was speaking a few nights ago with our friend the Colonel, upon the situation of the Duke, and upon your anxiety regarding him, all of which I have heard from my good rascally valet, who--considering that he is one of the greatest scoundrels that ever was un-hung--is a very honest fellow in his way, and finds out everything for me, Heaven knows how, and lets me know it truly. The Colonel seemed to laugh at the idea of anything being done to the Duke, saying, 'No, no; he is safe enough.' But after a while he added, 'If Wilton have any difficulty about the business, he had better speak to me:' and then he fell into one of his long sullen fits of thought; after which he said, 'Tell him to ride out hitherward on Saturday night next, just as it is turning dark--I should like to speak with him about it.'"

"I will not fail," replied Wilton; "for there is something about that man that interests, nay, attaches me, in spite of all I know and all I guess concerning his desperate habits. It is evident that he has had a high education, and possesses a noble heart; in fact, that he was fitted for better things than the criminal and disgraceful course he has pursued."

"Hush, hush!" cried Lord Sherbrooke, laughing; "speak more respectfully of the worthy Colonel, I beg. You are not aware that he is a near relation of mine."

Wilton started, and turned round as if he would have gazed in his companion's face, but the darkness of the night prevented him from well seeing what was passing there. As he recalled, however, his first interview with Green, his look, his manner, and the jesting tone in which he sometimes spoke, he could not but acknowledge that there was something in the whole resembling Lord Sherbrooke not a little, although Green was a much taller and more powerful man.

"This is strange enough, Sherbrooke," he replied, "if you are not joking; and, indeed, I think you are not, for there is a certain likeness between you and him, though more in the manner than in the person."

"It is quite true," replied Lord Sherbrooke; "he is a near relation. But, however, in regard to the Duke, I see not how he can help you, though he certainly does very wonderful things sometimes, which nobody expects or can account for. I would hear all he has to say, then; but at the same time, Wilton, I would not neglect the other business with Vernon, for, you see, the Colonel names Saturday. This is Monday, and before that time the Duke's head may be upon a pole, for aught we know. They make short work with trials and executions in these days."

"I will not fail," answered Wilton, "I will not fail. In such a case as this it is scarcely possible to do too much, and very possible to do too little. I trust your father will not detain me the whole day to-morrow."

"Oh no!" replied Lord Sherbrooke: "I am going to remove the cause, Wilton. As soon as ever I arrived last night, I perceived that the Earl was delicately working at some grand scheme regarding the Duke, and I very soon perceived, too, that he was determined you and I should not have an opportunity of talking the matter over, for fear we should spoil proceedings. I was obliged to watch my opportunity to-night with great nicety, but to-morrow I go back, that is to say, if my sweet Caroline is ready to go with me, for I am the most obedient and loving of husbands, as all reformed rakes are, you know, Wilton."

"But is the lady in town, and at your father's?" demanded Wilton, with surprise.

"She is in town, dearly beloved," replied Lord Sherbrooke, "but certainly not at my father's; and now, Wilton, ask me no more upon the subject, for, between you and me, I know little or nothing more myself. I know not what brings her into London; who she comes to see here, or who the note was from that called her so suddenly up to this great den of iniquity. It is a very horrible thing, Wilton, a very horrible thing, indeed," he continued, in the same jesting tone, "that any woman should have secrets from her husband. I have heard many matrons say so, and I believe them from my whole heart; but I've heard the same matrons say that there should be perfect reciprocity, which, perhaps, might mean that the wife and the husband were to have no secrets from each other, which, I am afraid, in my case, would never do, so I am fain to let her have this secret of her own, especially as she promises to tell me what it is in a few days. Reciprocity is a fine thing, Wilton; but it is wonderful what a number of different sorts of reciprocity there are in this world. Look there. Do you know there is something that puzzles me about that house."

"Why, that is Lord Sunbury's," replied Wilton; "but there are lights up in the drawing-room apparently."

"Ay, that's one part of the story that puzzles me," said Lord Sherbrooke. "I think the old housekeeper must be giving a drum. My valet tells me that on Saturday morning last there was a hackney coach stopped at that house, and two men went into it: one seemed a gentleman wrapped in a long cloak, the other looked like a valet, and stayed to get a number of packages out of the coach. Now I cannot suspect that same old housekeeper, who, as far as I recollect, is much like one of the daughters of Erebus and Nox, of carrying on an amorous correspondence with any gentleman; and it is somewhat strange that she should have lent the use of her master's house, either for love or money. I should not wonder if the Earl himself had come to London before his baggage."

"I should think not," replied Wilton; "I should certainly think not. I had a letter from him not long ago, dated from Paris, and I think he certainly would have written to inform me if he had been coming."

"I am not so sure of that, by any means, Wilton," replied his friend. "I can tell you, that two or three things have happened to his good lordship lately, which, with all his kindness and benevolence, might make him wish to see two or three other people before he saw you. There is a report even now busy about town that he is corresponding from Paris privately and directly with the King, and that his arrival in England will be followed by a change of ministry, if he will consent to take office again, which seems to be very doubtful."

These tidings interested Wilton not a little; and perhaps he felt a curiosity to ascertain whether Lord Sherbrooke's suspicion was or was not correct. His mind, however, was too high and delicate to admit of his taking any steps for that purpose, and after some more conversation on the same subject, he and his friend parted.

On the following morning Wilton had an opportunity of visiting the Duke of Shrewsbury's office, and found Mr. Vernon disengaged. To him he communicated all that he had to say in defence of the Duke, and found Vernon mild in his manners and expressions, but naturally cautious in either promising anything or in giving any information. He heard all that Wilton had to say, however, and assured him that he would lay the statement he made before the King on the ensuing morning, adding, that if he would call upon him in the course of the next day he would tell him the result. He smiled when Wilton requested him to keep his visit and its object secret, and nodded his head, merely replying, "I understand."

On the following day Wilton did not fail to visit him again, and waited for nearly an hour till he was ready to receive him.

"I am sorry," said Vernon, when he did admit him, "that I cannot give you greater satisfaction, Mr. Brown; but the King's reply, upon my application, was, that he had already spoken with the Earl of Byerdale on the subject. However, it may be some comfort to you to know that his grace of Shrewsbury takes an interest in the situation of the Duke, and has himself written to the King upon the subject."

CHAPTER XLI.

It was about the hour of noon, and the day was dull and oppressive. Though the apartments assigned to the Duke were high up, and in themselves anything but gloomy, yet no cheering ray of sunshine had visited them, and the air, which was extremely warm, seemed loaded with vapour. The spirits of the prisoner were depressed in proportion, and since the first hour of his imprisonment he had never, perhaps, felt so much as at that moment, all the leaden weight of dull captivity, the anguish of uncertainty, and the delay of hope, which, ever from the time of the prophet king down to the present day, has made the heart sick and the soul weary. It was in vain that his daughter, with the tenderest, the kindest, the most assiduous care, strove to raise his expectations or support his resolution; it was in vain that she strove to wean his thoughts away from his own painful situation by music, or by reading, or by conversation. Grief, like the dull adder, stops its ear that it may not hear the song of the charmer; and while she sang to him or played to him upon the lute, at that time an instrument still extremely common in England, or read to him from the books which she thought best calculated to attract his attention, she could see by the vacant eye that sometimes filled with tears, and the lips that from time to time murmured a word or two of impatience and complaint, that his thoughts were all still bent either upon the sad subject of his captivity, or upon the apprehension of what the future might bring.

At the hour of noon, then, the servant whom the Duke had chosen to wait upon him, and who was freely admitted to the prison, as well as a maid to attend upon the Lady Laura, entered the apartment in which the Duke sat, and announced that the Earl of Byerdale was in the antechamber. The Duke started up with an expression of joy, ordering him to be admitted instantly; and the Earl entered, assuming even an unusual parade of dignity in his step, and contriving to make his countenance look more than commonly severe and sneering, even though there was a marked smile upon it, as if he would imply that no slight pleasure attended his visit to the Duke.

"My dear lord," he said, "I really have to apologize for not having waited upon you before, but it has been quite impossible. Since the King's return I have been called upon daily to attend his majesty, besides having all the usual routine of my office to go through; otherwise I can assure your grace that I should have been with you long ago, as both duty and inclination would have prompted me to wait upon you. I am happy to see you so comfortably lodged here. I was afraid that, considering the circumstances, they might have judged it right to debar you of some indulgences; but my lord the governor is a good-hearted, kindly man.--Lady Laura, how are you? I hope you are quite well. I grieve, indeed, to see you and your father in this place; but alas! I had no power to prevent it, and indeed, I fear, I have very little power to serve you now."

"From your lordship's words," said the Duke, after having habitually performed the civilities of the apartment--"from your lordship's words, I fear that you take a bad view of the case, and do not anticipate my speedy deliverance."

"Oh, you know," answered the Earl, "that the trial must take place before we can at all judge what the King's mercy may incline him to do; but I fear, my lord, I fear that a strong prejudice prevails against your grace. The King, as well may be, is terribly indignant at all persons concerned with this plot."

"He may well be, indeed," said the Duke; "for nothing ever made me more indignant than when I first heard of the purposed assassination and invasion myself. With that I had nothing on earth to do. I should have hoped that his majesty's indignation on other points would have subsided by this time, and that clemency would have resumed her sway towards those who may have acted imprudently but not criminally."

"Not yet, not yet, I fear, my lord," replied the Earl; "six months, or a year longer, indeed, would have made all the difference. If your grace had but taken the advice and warning given you by my wise and virtuous young friend, Wilton, and made your escape at once to Flanders, or any neutral ground. I am sure I gave you opportunity enough."

"But, my lord," replied the Duke, "Wilton never gave me any warning till the very morning that I was arrested. It is true, indeed," he added, recollecting the circumstances, "poor Wilton and I unfortunately had a little quarrel on the preceding night, and he left me very much offended, I believe, and hurt, as I dare say he told you, my lord."

"Oh, he told me nothing, your grace," replied Lord Byerdale. "Wilton, knowing my feeling on the subject, very wisely acted as he knew I should like, or, at least, INTENDED TO ACT as he knew I should like, without saying anything to me upon the subject. I might very well remain somewhat wilfully ignorant of what was going on, but I must not openly connive, you know.--Then it was not really," he continued, "that your grace refused to go?"

"Oh, not in the least, not in the least!" replied the Duke. "I received his note early on the next morning, after he left me, and was consulting with my dear child here as to the necessary arrangements for going, when the Messengers arrived."

"Most unfortunate, indeed," said the Earl. "I had concluded, judging from your letter to me on the preceding day, that your grace that afternoon, notwithstanding all I had said regarding the young gentleman's family, refused him the honour to which he aspired, and would not follow the advice he gave."

Lady Laura rose, and moved towards one of the windows; and her father, with his colour a little heightened, and his manner somewhat agitated, replied, but in a low tone, "I did indeed refuse him Laura's hand, and, I am afraid, somewhat harshly and angrily; but I never refused to take his advice or warning."

"Ay, but the two subjects are so mingled up together," said the Earl, "that the one may be considered to imply the other."

"I see not how, my lord, I see not how they are so mingled," said the Duke.

"Ay, it may be difficult to explain," answered the Earl, "and I cannot do it myself; but so it is. It might not indeed be too late now, if it were not for this unfortunate prejudice of yourself or Lady Laura against my young friend, who, I must say, has served you both well."

"How not too late, my lord?" demanded the Duke, eagerly: "all prejudices may be removed, you know; and if there were any prejudice, it was mine."

"Still it would be an obstacle," answered the Earl; "and the whole matter would of course be rendered much more difficult now. There might be still more prejudices to be overcome at present.--May I ask," he added, abruptly, "if you have still got the note which Wilton sent you?"

"No," answered the Duke, "no. I destroyed it immediately, out of regard for his safety."

"It was a wise precaution," answered the Earl, "but unnecessary in his case. He has friends who will manage to justify whatever he does of that kind. Humble as he is in all his deportment, he can do many things that I could not venture to do. I have heard the King himself say, in presence of one half of his council, that he is under great personal obligations to Wilton Brown."

"Indeed!" exclaimed the Duke; "but may I request your lordship to inform me what it was you meant just now? You said it might not be yet too late."

"I fear, my lord, I must not talk to your grace on the subject," said the Earl; "there might be conditions you would not comply with. You might not like even the idea of flying from prison at all."

"I do not see why, my lord," exclaimed the Duke, "I really do not see why. But pray, may I ask what are the conditions?"

"Nay, I make neither any suggestions nor conditions," replied the Earl, who saw that the Duke was fully worked up to the pitch he wished, "I only spoke of such a thing as escape being very possible, if Wilton chose to arrange it; and then of course the conditions he might require for his services struck my mind."

"Why as yet, my lord," answered the Duke, "our noble young friend has not even named any condition as the price of his services."

"Perhaps, your grace," replied the Earl, "he may have become wiser by experience. If I have understood you both right, his hopes were disappointed, and hopes which he imagined he entertained with great reason."

"No, my lord, no!" cried the Duke. "He had no reason for entertaining such hopes. I cannot admit for a moment that I gave him any cause for such expectations."

"Nay, then, my lord duke," replied the Earl, with an offended look, "if such be your view of a case which everybody in London sees differently, the more reason why Wilton should make sure of what grounds he stands upon before he acts further in this business. However, I have nothing to do with the affair farther than as his sincere friend, and as having the honour of being his distant relation, which of course makes me resolute in saying that I will not see his feelings sported with and his happiness destroyed. Therefore, your grace, as we shan't agree, I see, upon these matters, I will humbly take my leave of you." And he rose, as if to depart.

"Nay, nay, my lord--you are too hasty," replied the Duke. "I beseech you, do not leave me in this way. I may in former instances have given Wilton hopes without intending it; but the matter is very much altered now, when he has done so much more for me in every way. I do not scruple at all to say that those objections are removed."

"Perhaps, my lord," said the Earl, sitting down again, and speaking in a low voice, "we had better discuss the matter in private. Could I not speak to you apart for a moment or two? Suppose we go into the anteroom."

"Nay, nay," said the Duke, "Laura will leave us.--Go to your room, my love," he added, raising his voice. "I would fain have a few minutes conversation with my noble friend alone."

"Very wrong of you, Lord Byerdale," she said, with a smile, as she walked towards the door, "to turn me out of the room in this way."

Lord Byerdale smiled, and bowed, and apologized, all with an air of courtier-like mockery. The moment she was gone, however, he turned to the Duke, saying, "Now, my lord duke, we are alone, and I will beg your grace to give me your honour that no part of our present conversation transpires in any circumstances. I can then hold much more free communication with you. I can lay before you what is possible, and what is probable, and you can choose whatever path you like."

"Most solemnly I pledge my honour," replied the Duke, "and I can assure your lordship that I fully appreciate Mr. Brown's merits and his services to me. He has not only talents and genius, but a princely person and most distinguished manners, and I could not have the slightest objection, as soon as his birth is clearly ascertained and acknowledged--"

"My lord duke," replied the Earl, interrupting him, "I fear your lordship is somewhat deceiving yourself as to your own situation and his. Wilton, I tell you, can easily find the means of effecting your escape from this prison, and can insure your safe arrival in any continental port you may think fit to name. I do not mean to say that I must not shut my eyes; but for his sake and for yours I am very willing to do so, if I see his happiness made sure thereby."

The Duke's eyes sparkled with joy and hope, and the Earl went on.

"Your situation, my lord, at the present moment, you see, is a very unfortunate one, or such a step would in no degree be advisable. But at this period, when the passions of the people and the indignation of the King are both excited to the highest pitch; when there is, as I may call it, an appetite for blood afloat; when the three witnesses, Sir John Fenwick, Smith, and Cook, to say nothing of the corroborative evidence of Goodman, establish beyond doubt that you were accessorily, though perhaps not actively, guilty of high treason--at this period, I say, there can be little doubt that if you were brought to trial--that is, in the course of next week, as I have heard it rumoured--the result would be fatal, such, in short, as we should all deplore."

The Duke listened, with a face as white as a sheet, but only replied, in a tremulous tone, "But the escape, my lord! the escape!"

"Is quite possible and quite sure," replied the Earl. "I must shut my eyes, as I have said, and Wilton must act energetically; but I cannot either shut my eyes or suffer him to do so, except upon the following precise condition, which is indeed absolutely necessary to success. It is, that the Lady Laura, your daughter, be his wife before you set your foot from without these walls."

"But, good heavens, my lord!" exclaimed the Duke--"how is that possible? I believe that Laura would do anything to save her father's life; but she is not prepared for such a thing. Then the marriage must be celebrated with unbecoming haste. No, my lord, oh no! This is quite impossible. I am very willing to promise that I will give my consent to their marriage afterwards; but for their marriage to take place before we go is quite impossible--especially while I am a prisoner in the Tower of London--quite impossible!"

"I am sorry your grace thinks so," replied the Earl, drily; "for under those circumstances I fear that your escape from the Tower will be found impossible also."

A momentary spirit of resistance was raised in the Duke's breast by feelings of indignation, and he tried for an instant to persuade himself that his case might not be so desperate as the Earl depicted it; that in some points of view it might be better to remain and stand his trial, and that the King's mercy would very likely be obtained even if he were condemned. But that spirit died away in a moment, and the more rapidly, because the Earl of Byerdale employed not the slightest argument to induce him to follow the plan proposed.

"My lord, this is a very painful case," he said, "a very painful case, indeed."

"It is, Duke," replied the Earl, "it is a painful case; a choice of difficulties, which none can decide but yourself. Pray do not let anything that I can say affect you. I thought it right, as an old friend, to lay before you a means of saving yourself; and no one can judge whether that means be too painful to you to be adopted, as nobody can tell at what rate you value life. But you will remember, also, that forfeiture accompanies the sentence of death in matters of high treason, and that Lady Laura will therefore be left in a painful situation."

"Nay, my lord, nay," said the Duke, "if it must come to that, of course I must consent to any terms, rather than sacrifice everything. But I did not think Wilton would have proposed such conditions to me."

"Nor does he, my lord," replied the Earl: "he is totally ignorant of the whole matter. He has never, even, that I know of, contemplated your escape as possible. One word from me, however, whispered in his ear, will open his eyes in a minute. But, my lord, it must be upon the condition that I mention. Wilton's father-in-law may go forth from this prison before twelve to-morrow night, but no other prisoner within it shall, or indeed can."

"Well, my lord, well," replied the Duke, somewhat impatiently, "I will throw no obstacle in the way. Laura and Wilton must settle it between them. But I do not see how the matter can be managed here in a prison."

"Oh, that is easily arranged," replied the Earl--"nothing can be more easy. There is a chaplain to the Tower, you know. The place has its own privileges likewise, and all the rest shall be done by me. Am I to understand your grace, that you consider yourself pledged upon this subject?"

The Duke thought for a moment, and the images of the trial by his peers, the block and the axe, came up before his sight, making the private marriage of his daughter with Wilton, and the escape to France or Flanders, appear bright in the comparison.

"Well, my lord, well," he said, "I not only pledge myself, but pledge myself willingly. I always liked Wilton, I always esteemed him highly; and I suppose he would have had Laura at last, if he did not have her now."

"I congratulate you on your approaching freedom, Duke," said the Earl, "and as to the rest, I have told you perfectly true, in saying that it is not Wilton who makes any conditions with you. He knows nothing of the matter, and is as eager to set you at liberty without any terms at all, as you could be yourself to obtain it. You had better, therefore, let me speak with him on the subject altogether. Should he come here before he sees me, only tell him that the marriage is to take place to-morrow evening, that it is all settled between you and me, and that as to the means of setting you free, he must talk with me upon the subject. You must then furnish him with your consent to the immediate marriage under your own hand. After that is done, he and I will arrange all the rest."

The Duke acquiesced in all that was proposed to him, having once given his consent to the only step which was repugnant to him to take. Nay more, that point being overcome, and his mind elevated by the hope of escape, he even went before Lord Byerdale in suggesting arrangements which would facilitate the whole business.

"I will tell Laura after you are gone, my lord," he said, "and her consent will be easily obtained, I am sure, both because I know she would do anything to save my life, and because I shrewdly believe--indeed she has not scrupled to admit--that she loves this young man already. I will manage all that with her, and then I will leave her and Wilton, and Wilton and your lordship, to make all the rest of the arrangements."

"Do so, do so," said the Earl, rising, "and I will not fail, my lord, as soon as you are safe, to use every influence in my power for the purpose of obtaining your pardon, which will be much more easily gained when you are beyond the power of the English law, than while you are actually within its gripe."

The Earl was now about to take his departure, and some more ceremonious words passed between him and the Duke, in regard to their leave-taking. Just as the Earl had reached the door, however, a sudden apprehension seemed to seize the prisoner, who exclaimed, "Stay, my good lord, stay, one moment more! Of course your lordship is upon honour with me, as I am with you? There is no possibility, no probability, of my escape being prevented after my daughter's hand is given?"

Nothing more mortified the Earl of Byerdale than to find, that, notwithstanding all his skill, there was still a something of insincerity penetrated through the veil he cast over his conduct, and made many persons, even the most easily deceived, doubtful of his professions and advances.

"I trust your grace does not suspect me of treachery," he said, in a sharp and offended tone.

"Not in the least, not in the least, my lord," replied the Duke; "but I understood your lordship to say, that my escape by the means proposed would be rendered quite certain, and I wish to ascertain whether I had not mistaken you."

"Not in the slightest degree, my lord duke," replied the Earl. "I pledge you my honour, that under the proposed arrangements you shall be beyond the doors of this prison, and at perfect liberty, before the dawn of day on Monday morning. I pledge myself to you in every respect, and if it be not so, I will be ready to take your place. Does this satisfy you?"

"Quite, quite," answered the Duke. "I could desire nothing more." And the Earl, with a formal bow, opened the door and left him.

CHAPTER XLII.

As soon as the Earl of Byerdale was gone, the Duke called Laura from her room, and told her what had been proposed. "Laura," he said, as he concluded, "you do not answer me: but I took upon me to reply at once, that you would be well pleased to lay aside pride and every other feeling of the kind, to save your father from this torturing suspense--to save perhaps his life itself."

Laura's cheeks had not regained their natural colour since the first words respecting such a sudden marriage were spoken to her. That her father had consented to her union with Wilton was of course most joyful; but the early period fixed for such an important, such an overwhelming change in her condition, was startling; and to think that Wilton could have made it the condition of his using all his exertions in her father's cause would have been painful--terrible, if she could have believed it. We must not, indeed, say, that even if it had been really so, she would have hesitated to give him her hand, not only for her father's sake, but because she loved him, because, as we have said before, she already looked upon herself as plighted to him beyond all recall. She would have tried to fancy that he had good motives which she did not know; she would have tried, in short, to find any palliation for such conduct; but still it would have been very painful to her--still it might, in a degree, have shaken her confidence in high and upright generosity of feeling, it might have made her doubt whether, in all respects, she had found a heart perfectly responsive to her own.

"My dear father," she replied, gazing tenderly upon him, and laying her two hands on his, with a faint smile, "what is there that I would not do for such objects as you mention, were it ten thousand times more than marrying the man I love best, even with such terrible suddenness.--It is very sudden, indeed, I must say; and I do wonder that Wilton required it."

"Why, my dear Laura," replied the Duke, "it was not exactly Wilton himself. It was Lord Byerdale took it all on his own shoulders: but of course Wilton prompted it; and in such circumstances as these I could not hesitate to consent."

Lady Laura looked down while her father spoke; and when her first agitation was over, she could not but think, that perhaps, considering her father's character, Wilton was right; and that the means he had taken, though apparently ungenerous, were the only ones to secure her own happiness and his, and her father's safety also. The next instant, however, as she recollected a thousand different traits in her lover's conduct, and combined those recollections with what her father said concerning Lord Byerdale, she became convinced that Wilton had not made such conditions, and that rather than have made them he would have risked everything, even if the Duke were certain to deny him her hand the moment after his liberation.

"I do not think, my dear father," she replied, as this conviction came strong upon her--"I do not think that Wilton did prompt the Earl of Byerdale. I do not think he would make such conditions, on any account."

"Well, it does not matter, my dear Laura," replied her father, whose mind was totally taken up with his own escape. "It comes to the same thing. The Earl has made them, if Wilton has not, and I have pledged my word for your consent. But hark, Laura, I hear Wilton's step in the outer room. I will leave you two together to make all your arrangements, and to enter into every explanation," and he turned hurriedly towards the door which led to his bedroom.

Ere he reached it, however, he paused for a moment, with a sudden fear coming over him that Laura might by some means put an end to all the plans on which he founded his hopes of liberty.

"Laura," he said, "Laura--for heaven's sake show no repugnance, my dear child. Remember, your father's safety depends upon it." And turning away, he entered his bedroom just as Wilton opened the opposite door.

Laura gazed upon her lover, as he came in; and asked herself, while she marked that noble and open countenance, "Is it possible he could make any unworthy condition?"

Wilton's face was grave, and even sad, for he had again applied to Vernon, and received a still less satisfactory reply than before; but he was glad to find Laura alone, for this was the first time that he had obtained any opportunity of seeing her in private, since she had been permitted to join her father in the Tower. His greeting, then, was as tender and as affectionate as the circumstances in which they stood towards each other might warrant; but he did not forget, even then, that subject which he knew was of the deepest interest to her --her father's situation.

"Oh, dearest Laura," he said, "I have longed to speak with you for a few minutes alone, and yet, now that I have the opportunity, I have nothing but sad subjects to entertain you with."

His words confirmed Laura's confidence in his generosity. She saw clearly that he knew not what had been proposed by the Earl; the very conviction gave her joy, and she replied, looking up playfully and affectionately in his face,--

"I thought, Wilton, that you had come to measure my finger for the ring," and she held out her small fair hand towards him.

"Oh, would to Heaven, dear Laura," he answered, pressing the hand that she had given to his lips--"would to Heaven, that we had arrived at that point!--But, Laura, you are smiling still. You have heard some good news: your father is pardoned: is it not so?"

"No, Wilton, no," she said, "not quite such good news as that. But still the news I have heard is good news; but it is odd enough, Wilton, that I should have to tell it to you; and yet I am glad that it is so."

She then detailed to him all that had occurred, as far as she had learned it from her father. Wilton listened with surprise and astonishment; but, though at the joyful tidings of the Duke's consent, and at the prospect of her so soon becoming his irrevocably, he could not restrain his joy, but clasped her in rapture to his heart, yet there was a feeling of indignation, ay, and of doubt and suspicion also, in regard to Lord Byerdale's conduct, and his purposes, which mingled strangely with his satisfaction.

"Although, dear Laura," he said, "although this is a blessed hope for ourselves, and also a blessed hope for your father, I cannot help saying that Lord Byerdale has acted very strangely in this business, and very ill. It may be out of regard for me; but it is a sort of regard I do not understand; and, were it not that I am sure my dear Laura has never for a moment doubted me, I should say that he in some degree compromised my honour, by making that consent a condition of your father's safety, which should only be granted to affection and esteem."

Laura coloured slightly, to think that she had even doubted for an instant: but Wilton went on, relaxing the graver look that had come over his countenance, and saying, "We must not, however, my dear Laura, refuse to take the happiness that is offered to us, unless, indeed, you should think it very, very terrible to give me this dear hand so soon; and even then I think my Laura would overcome such feelings, when they are to benefit her father."

"I do not feel it so terrible, Wilton," replied Lady Laura, "as I did ten minutes ago. If I thought that you had made the condition, it would seem so much more as if you were a stranger to me, that it might be terrible. But when I hear you speak as you do now, Wilton, I feel that I could trust myself with you anywhere, that I could go away with you at any moment, perfectly secure of my future happiness; and so I reply, Wilton, that I am not only willing, but very willing."

"We must lose no time, then, dear Laura," replied Wilton, "in making all our arrangements. I must now, indeed, have the measure of that small finger, and I must speed away to Lord Byerdale with all haste, in order to learn the means that are to be employed for your father's escape. I must inquire a little, too, into his motives, Laura, and add some reproaches for his having so compromised me."

"For Heaven's sake, do not--for Heaven's sake, do not!" cried Laura. "My father would never forgive me, if, in consequence of anything I had said, you and Lord Byerdale were to have any dispute upon the matter, and the business were to fail."

"Oh, fear not, fear not, Laura," replied Wilton, smiling at her eagerness: "there is no fear of any dispute."

"Nay, but promise me," she said--"promise me, Wilton."

"I do promise you, dear Laura," he replied, "that nothing on earth which depends upon me, for your father's liberation or escape, shall be wanting, and I promise you more, my beloved Laura, that I will not quarrel with the means, because my Laura's hand is to be mine at once."

"Well, Wilton," continued Laura, still fearful that something might make the scheme go wrong, "I trust to you, and only beg you to remember, that if this does not succeed, my father will never forgive either you or me."

Some farther conversation upon these subjects ensued, and all the arrangements of Laura and Wilton were made as far as it was possible. There were feelings in the mind of Wilton--that doubt of ultimate success, in fact, which we all feel when a prospect of bright and extraordinary happiness is suddenly presented to us, after many struggles with difficulties and dangers--which led him to linger and enjoy the present hour. But after a time, as he heard the clock chime two, and knew that every moment was now of importance, he hastened away to seek the Earl of Byerdale, and hear farther what was to be done for the escape of the Duke.

The Earl was not at home, however, nor at his office, and Wilton occupied himself for another hour in various preparations for the events that were likely to ensue. At the end of that time he returned to the Earl of Byerdale's house, and was immediately admitted.

"Well, Wilton!" exclaimed the Earl, as soon as he saw him, with a cheerful smile, in which there was, nevertheless, something sarcastic--"have I not done well for you? I think this proud Duke's stomach is brought down sufficiently."

"I am only grieved, my lord," replied Wilton, "that either the Duke or Lady Laura should have cause to think that I made it a condition she should give me her hand before I aided in her father's escape. There seemed to me something degrading in such a course."

The Earl's brow, for a moment, grew as dark as a thunder-cloud, but it passed away in a sneer, and he contented himself with saying, "Are you so proud, also, my young sir?--It matters not, however. What did the Duke say to you? He showed no reluctance, I trust. We will bring his pride down farther, if he did."

"I did not see the Duke, my lord," replied Wilton, a good deal mortified at the tone the Earl assumed--"I only saw Lady Laura."

"And what said she?" demanded the Earl. "Is she as proud as her father?"

"She showed no repugnance, my lord," replied Wilton, "to do what was necessary for her father's safety; and when she saw how much pained I was it should be thought that I would make such a condition with her, she only seemed apprehensive that such feelings might lead to any derangement of your lordship's plan."

"What?" said the Earl. "You were very indignant, indeed, I suppose, and abused me heartily for doing the very thing that is to secure you happiness, rank, station, and independence. But she conquered, no doubt. You promised to concur in my terrible scheme? Is it not so, Wilton?"

"Yes, my lord, I did," replied Wilton.

"Upon my word, you are a pretty gentleman, to make ladies sue you thus," continued the Earl, in a jeering tone. "I dare say she made you vow all sorts of things?"

"I pledged myself solemnly, my lord," replied Wilton, "to do all that depended upon me to forward your lordship's plan for the Duke's escape, and she knows me too well to entertain a doubt of my keeping that promise to the letter."

"Not my plan, not my plan, Wilton," said the Earl, in a more pleasant tone. "It must be your plan, my young friend; for I might put my head in danger, remember. It is a different thing with you, who are not yet sworn of the privy council. I will take care, also, that no harm shall happen to you. The Duke was talking of some valet that he has, whom he wishes to send out of the prison to-morrow night. Now, what I propose, in order to facilitate all your arrangements with regard to Lady Laura, is to give you an order upon the governor of the Tower to suffer you and Lady Laura, and one man-servant and one maid, to pass out any time to-morrow before twelve o'clock at night. I write a little note to the Governor at the same time, telling him that, with the consent of all parties, you and Lady Laura are to be married privately in the Tower, to-morrow evening, by the chaplain, and I have provided you with all the necessary authorizations for the chaplain. You will find them there in that paper.--My note will not at all surprise the Governor, because it has been the common talk of the town for the last two months that you were going to be married to Lady Laura, and most likely the good Governor has not heard of the Duke's whims at Somersbury. The note will therefore only serve as a reason for your wishing to go out late at night, which is contrary to rules, you know. The Governor will give orders about it to his subordinates, as he is going down to spend a day or two at Hampton Court, and testify his duty to the King. If, therefore, you go away with your attendants towards midnight, you will find nobody up who knows the Duke, and a livery jacket and badge may cover whomsoever you like. A carriage can be waiting for you on Tower Hill, and a small brig called the Skimmer is lying with papers sealed and everything prepared a little below Greenwich.--Now, Wilton," he added, "if this does not succeed in your hands, it is your fault. Do you agree to every part of this as I have laid it before you?"

"Most assuredly, my lord," replied Wilton, with eager gladness; "and I can easily show Laura now, that there is a sufficient motive for our marriage taking place so rapidly and so secretly."

"I did not think of that," said the Earl, much to Wilton's surprise. "However, I shall leave to you entirely the execution of this scheme, Wilton. You understand that my name is never to be mentioned, however, and I take it as a matter of honour, that whatever be the result, you say not one word whatsoever to inculpate me."

"None, my lord--none, upon my honour!" replied Wilton.

"Is there anything else I can do for you, Wilton?" demanded the Earl. "If not, just be good enough to copy out that letter for me against my return, for the carriage is at the door, and I must go in haste to Kensington, to see the King depart for Hampton Court. The papers are all there in that packet I have given you--the order, the note, the special licence, and everything. Is there anything more?"

"Nothing, my lord. I thank you most sincerely," replied Wilton, sitting down to copy the letter, while the Earl took up his hat and cane, and walked a step or two towards the door. The Earl paused, however, before he reached it, and then turned again towards Wilton, gazing upon him with a cold, unpleasant sort of smile.

"By the way, Wilton," he said, "I promised to tell you part of your own history, but did not intend to do it for some little time. As we are likely however to be separated for a month or two by this marriage trip of yours, there is one thing that I may as well tell you. But you must, in the first place, promise me, upon your honour as a gentleman, and by all you hold most sacred, not to reveal one word thereof to any one, till the safety of the Duke is quite secured--do you promise me in that solemn manner?"

"I do, indeed, my lord," replied Wilton, "and feel most sincerely grateful to your lordship for relieving my mind on the subject at once."

"Well, then, Wilton," continued the Earl, "you may recollect I said to the Duke that there was as ancient and good blood in your veins as in his own or in mine. Now, Wilton, my uncle, the last Earl of Byerdale, had two other nephews besides myself, and you are the son of one of them, who, espousing the cause of the late King James, was killed at the battle of the Boyne, and all he had confiscated. Little enough it was. You are his son, I say, Wilton. Do you hear?--His natural son, by a very pretty lady called Miss Harriet Oswald!--But upon my honour I must go, or I shall miss the King."

And turning round with an air of perfect coolness and composure, the Earl quitted the room, leaving Wilton thunderstruck and overwhelmed with grief.

CHAPTER XLIII.

The whole of the Earl's dark scheme was cleared up to Wilton's eyes in a moment; and the secret of his own fate was only given to him in conjunction with an insight into that black and base transaction, of which he had been made an unwitting tool.

Horrible, most horrible to himself was the disappointment of all his hopes. The bright dreams that he had entertained, the visions of gay things which he had suffered the enchanter Imagination to call forth from the former obscurity of his fate, were all dispelled by the words that he had just heard spoken; and everything dark, and painful and agonising, was spread out around him in its stead. He was as one who, having fallen asleep in a desert, has dreamt sweet dreams, and then suddenly wakes with the rising sun, to find nothing but arid desolation around him.

Thus, painful indeed would have been his feelings if he had only had to contemplate his situation in reference to himself alone; but when he recollected how his position bore upon the Duke and Laura, the thought thereof almost drove him mad. The deceit which had been practised upon him had taught him to entertain hopes, and to pursue objects which he never would have dreamed of, had it not been for that deceit. It had made him throw open his heart to the strongest of all affections, it had made him give himself up entirely to ardent and passionate love, from which he would have fled as from his bane, had he known what was now told to him. He had been made also the instrument of basely deceiving others. He knew that the Duke would never have heard of such a thing as his marriage with Lady Laura; he, knew that in all probability he would never have admitted him into any extraordinary intimacy with his family, if he had not firmly believed that he was anything but that which he was now proved to be. He did not know, but he doubted much whether Laura, knowing her father's feelings upon such a subject, would ever have thought of him otherwise than as an ordinary acquaintance. He knew not, he could not tell, whether she herself might not upon that subject entertain the same feelings as the Duke. But what would be their sensations, what their astonishment, what their indignation, when they found that they had been so basely deceived, when they found that he had been apparently a sharer in such deceit! Would they ever believe that he had acted unwittingly, when the whole transaction was evidently to the advantage of none but himself; when he was to reap the whole of the solid benefit, and the Earl of Byerdale had only to indulge a revengeful caprice? Would anybody believe it? he asked himself: and, clasping his hands together, he stood overpowered by the feeling of having lost all hope in his own fate, of having lost her he loved for ever, and, perhaps, of having lost also her love and esteem, and the honourable name which he had hitherto borne.

For a few minutes he thus remained, as it were, utterly confounded, with no thought but the mere consciousness of so many evils, and with the cold sneering tone of the Earl of Byerdale still ringing in his ears, announcing to him plainly, that the treacherous statesman enjoyed the wound which he had inflicted upon him, almost as much as the humiliation to which he had doomed the Duke.

Wilton's mind, however, as we have endeavoured to show throughout this book, was not of a character to succumb under a sense of any evils that affected him. All the painful feelings that assailed him might, it is true, remain indelibly impressed upon his mind for long years. It was not that the effect wore out, it was only that the mind gained strength, and bore the burden that was cast upon it; and thus, in the present instance, he shook off, in a very short space of time, the thought of his sorrows themselves, to consider more clearly how he should act under them.

But new difficulties presented themselves with this consideration. He had solemnly pledged himself not to reveal what the Earl had told him till the Duke was placed in safety. He had pledged himself to Laura to throw no obstacle whatever in the way of her father's escape by the means which the Earl had proposed. Neither was there a way of evading any part of the plan as the Earl had arranged it. Otherwise he would undoubtedly have attempted to postpone the marriage till after the Duke was free, and then, having placed his own honour beyond all question, to tell Laura and her father the whole truth. But as the Earl had taken care to inform the governor of the Tower that he was to go out with Lady Laura and the attendants after his private marriage to her, there could be no pretence for his staying in the Tower after the usual hour, and making use of the Earl's order, if the marriage did not take place.

He saw that the wily politician had entangled him on all sides. He saw that he had left him scarcely a possibility of escape. He had either to commit an action which he felt would be dishonourable in the highest degree towards Laura, or to break the solemn pledge that he had made, and at the same time leave himself still under the imputation of dishonour; for he had nothing else to propose to Laura or her father but her instant marriage with himself, notwithstanding the circumstances of his birth, or the imminent risk of her father's total ruin.

"She may think," he said to himself, "and the Duke certainly will think, that I have never told this fact till the very last moment, when I have so entangled her that there was no receding. Thus I shall violate my word to the Earl, which his baseness, perhaps, would justify me in doing, but shall yet derive scarcely any benefit either to the Duke, or Laura, or myself."

It was all agony, and clasping his hands together once more, he remained gazing upon the ground in absolute despair. Which way, he asked himself, could he turn for help or advice? His mind rested for a moment on Lord Sunbury. There were many strong reasons to believe that he was in London, but incognito; but as Wilton thus thought, he recollected his pledge not to mention either the plans the Earl had laid out, or the facts concerning his own birth which had been told him. And again he was at sea, but the next moment came the thought of Lord Sherbrooke and his strange acquaintance Green: he recollected that on that very night he was to meet the Colonel; he recollected that the very object of that meeting was to be the Duke; he remembered that Green's words had been, "to apply to him in any difficulty, for that he had more power to do him a service than ever;" he recollected that the very person he was to see possessed some knowledge of his own history; and hope, out of these materials, however incoherent, strange, and unpromising they might be, contrived to elicit at least one ray of light.

"I will meet him," he thought; "I will meet him, and will do the best that I can when I do see him. I must not allude to what I have heard; but he may have power that I do not know of, he may even aid me in some other plan for the Duke's escape. I will set out as soon as it is dusk."

As he thus thought, he turned towards the door, nearly forgetting the letter which the Earl had given him to copy; but his eye chanced to fall upon it as he passed, and saying aloud, "This man shall not see how he has shaken me," he sat down, and copied it clearly and accurately. He then left the house, went home, ordered his horse, and made preparations for his journey. The sun was just touching the horizon as he put his foot in the stirrup, and he rode forward at a quick pace on the road towards Somersbury.

It was a beautiful clear evening, and many people were abroad; but for the first six miles he saw nobody but strangers, all hurrying to their several destinations for the night, travellers wending their way into the great metropolis, and carts carrying to its devouring maw the food for the next day. Between the sixth and seventh milestone, however, where the moon was just seen raising her yellow horn beside the village spire, he beheld a man mounted upon a powerful horse, riding towards him, who by his military aspect, broad shoulders, powerful frame, and erect seat upon his horse, he recognised, while still at some distance, as Green.

"Ah Wilton, my boy," cried the Colonel, as he rode up, "I am glad to see you.--You are not behind your time, but there is an impatience upon me now that made me set off early. I am glad I did, for I have not been on my horse's back for a fortnight; and there is something in poor Barbary's motion that gives me back a part of my former lightness of heart."

"I wish to Heaven that you could get it all back," replied Wilton. "But I fear when it is lost it is not to be regained--I feel that it is so, but too bitterly, at this moment."

"What you!" exclaimed the Colonel. "What is the matter, Wilton? What have you done? for a man never loses his lightness of heart for ever, but by his own act?"

"I think," said Wilton, "from what I have heard you say, that you can feel for my situation, when I tell you, that, by the entanglements of one I do not scruple to call a most accursed villain, I can neither go on with honour in the course that is before me, nor retreat without dishonour; and even if I could do either, there would still be absolute and perpetual misery for me in life."

"Who is the villain?" demanded Green, abruptly.

"The Earl of Byerdale," replied Wilton.

"Ha, ha, ha!" shouted Green aloud. "He is a cursed villain; he always was, and ever will be. But we will frustrate the Earl of Byerdale, Wilton. I tell you, that, with my right hand on his collar, the Earl of Byerdale is no more than a lackey."

"But you cannot frustrate him," replied Wilton, "so as to relieve me, unless you can find means to set the Duke of Gaveston at liberty; and even then--but it matters not. I can bear unhappiness, but not dishonour."

"Set the Duke at liberty!" said Green, thoughtfully. "He ought to have been at liberty already. He has committed no crime, but only folly. He has been stupid, not wicked; and besides, I had heard--but that may be a mistake. Let us ride on, Wilton," he continued, turning his horse; "and as we go, tell me gill that has happened."

"Alas!" replied Wilton, riding on beside him, "that is of all things what I cannot and must not do. If I could speak, if I could open my mouth to any one on the subject, one half of my difficulties, one half of my grief; would be relieved at once. But that I am pledged and bound not to do, in a manner which leaves me no relief, which affords me no means of escape."

"Well, then, Wilton," said his companion, "I know there are situations in which, to aid a friend at all, we must aid him upon his own showing, and without inquiry. We must do what he asks us to do without explanation, or sacrifice his service to our pride. Such shall not be the case with me. I will do what I can to serve you, even to the last, altogether without explanation. Let me ask you, however, one or two questions."

"I will answer them, if I can," replied Wilton. "But remember always, there is much that I am pledged not to reveal at present."

"They will be very easily answered, my boy," replied Green. "Have you seen the Earl of Sunbury?"

"I have not," replied Wilton, "though I believe he is in England. To him I should have applied, certainly, if I had been able to explain to him, in any degree, my situation."

"He is in England," replied Green: "I saw him two days ago; but I leave him to smart for a time under the consequences of an imprudence he has committed. In the next place, I have but the one general question to put,--What can I do for you?"

"I know not, indeed," replied Wilton, "though I sought you with a vague hope, that you might be able to do something. But the only thing that could in any degree relieve me would be, either to effect the escape of the Duke from the Tower--"

"That is impossible!" said Green, "utterly impossible! What was the alternative?"

"To obtain from the King a warrant for his liberation," said Wilton, in a despairing tone, "which is impossible also; for how can I expect you to do what neither Vernon nor the Duke of Shrewsbury has been able to accomplish? The King's only answer to all applications is, that he has spoken to the Earl of Byerdale; and in the Earl of Byerdale we have no hope. So that is out of the question."

"Not so much as you imagine, Wilton," replied Green. "I will do it if it is to be done, though I would fain have avoided the act which I must now perform. Come to me on Monday, Wilton, here upon this road where we now ride, and I think I will put the order in your hand."

"Alas!" replied Wilton, "Monday will not do. The liberation must be for to-morrow night to answer the intended purpose. I have lately thought to do the bold, and perhaps the rash, act of going to the King myself--telling him all I know--and beseeching him to set the Duke at liberty. He even told me once, that I had done him good service, and that he would favour me. But, alas! kings forget such words as soon as spoken."

"He has a long memory, this William," replied Green; "but you shall go with me, Wilton. If it must be to-morrow, to-morrow it shall be. Meet me then at twelve o'clock exactly, at the little inn by the water, called the Swan, near Kingston Bridge. I will be there waiting for you. It is a likely hour to find the King after he comes from chapel; but I will apply beforehand both in your name and in mine; for I heard some time ago, from Harry Sherbrooke, that you had won such praises from William as he seldom bestows on any one."

"At twelve to-morrow!" said Wilton, thoughtfully. "I was to have been at the Tower at twelve to-morrow. But it matters not. That engagement I at least may break without losing my honour, or wounding her heart. But tell me, tell me, Green, is there any hope, is there any chance of our being successful?"

"There is great hope, there is great chance," replied Green. "I will not, indeed, say that it is by any means sure; for what is there we can rely upon on earth? Have I not seen everything break down beneath me like mere reeds, and shall I now put my faith in any man? But still, Wilton, I will ask this thing. I will see William of

Orange--I will call him King at once--for King he is in fact; and far more kingly in his courage and his nature than the weak man who never will wear the crown of these realms again. We will both urge our petition to the throne; and even if he have forgotten the last words that he said to me, those which you have to speak perhaps may prove sufficient. He is not a cruel or a bloody-minded man; and I do believe he forgets his enmities more easily than he does his friendships. If we could have said the same of the race of Stuart, the crown of England would never have rested on the brow of the Prince of Orange. I thought to have led you to other scenes and other conferences to-night," he added, "but this matter changes all, and we will now part. I will to my task, and prepare the way for to-morrow. You to yours; but fail not, Wilton, fail not. Be rather before than after the hour."

"I will not fail," replied Wilton; and after this short conference, he turned his rein and rode back to London.

As he went, he meditated on the hopes which his conference with Green had raised up again; but the brightness of those hopes faded away beneath the light of thought. Yet, though such was the case, the determination remained, and grew firmer and stronger, perhaps from the want of any very great expectation. He determined to appeal to the King, as the last act in his power; to do so firmly and resolutely; and if the King refused his petition, and gave him no reason to hope, to apply, as the next greatest favour, for a memorandum in writing of his having so appealed, in order that he might prove to Laura and her father that he had done all in his power to give the Duke an opportunity of rejecting that means of escape, which could only be obtained by uniting his daughter to one, from whom, in any other circumstances, he would have withheld her.

"It is strange," he said to himself, "it is strange and sad, that I can scarcely move a step in any way without the risk of dishonour; and that the only means to avoid it requires every exertion to deprive myself of peace, and happiness, and love for ever."

Thus he thought as he went along; and imagination pictured his next parting from her he loved, and all that was to follow it--the grief that she would suffer as well as himself--the long dreary lapse of sad and cheerless hours that was to fill up the remainder of existence for him, with all happy hopes at an end, and fortune, station, love, gone away like visions of the night.

Early on the ensuing morning, he despatched a note to the Tower, telling Laura that business, affecting her father's safety, would keep him away from her at the hour he had promised to visit her. He would be with her, he said, at all events before nightfall; and he added every term of love and affection that his heart suggested; but at the same time he could not prevent a tone of sadness spreading through his letter, which communicated to Laura a fear lest her father's hopes of escape should be frustrated.

By eleven o'clock Wilton was at the door of the small inn named for the meeting; and two handsome horses which were standing there, held by a servant, announced that Green had arrived before him. On going in, he found his strange friend far more splendidly dressed than he had ever seen him, apparently waiting for his coming. His fine person told to much advantage, his upright carriage and somewhat proud and stern demeanour, the grave and thoughtful look of his eye, all gave him the appearance of one of high mind and high station, accustomed to action and command. A certain sort of gay and dissipated look, which he had previously borne, was altogether gone: within the last few months he had become paler and thinner, and his countenance had assumed an air of gloom which did not even leave it when he laughed.

As Wilton now advanced towards him, he could not but feel that there was something dignified and imposing in his aspect; and yet it caused him a strange sensation, to think that he was going into the King's presence in company with a man whom he had actually first met upon the King's Highway.

"I am glad you have come early, Wilton," said Green. "The King returns from the chapel at a quarter past twelve, and expects us to be in waiting at that hour, when he will see us. This is no slight favour, I find, Wilton," he added, "for the palace is full of courtiers, all eager and pressing for royal attention. Let us go immediately, then, and ride slowly up to the palace."

They mounted their horses accordingly, and rode on, speaking a few words from time to time, but not, indeed, absolutely conversing, for both were far too thoughtful, and too much impressed with the importance of the act they were about to perform, to leave the tongue free and unfettered.

On their arrival at the palace, they found that the King had not yet returned from the chapel; but on being asked whether they came by appointment or not, and giving their names, they were admitted into a waiting-room where two or three other people were already assembled. The moments passed slowly, and it seemed as if the King would never return.

At length, however, a distant flourish of drums and trumpets was heard, together with the sounds of many people passing to and fro in the courts and passages. Buzzing conversation, manifold footfalls, gay laughter, announced that the morning service was over, and the congregation of the royal chapel dispersed.

CHAPTER XLIV.

In the royal closet, at the palace of Hampton Court, stood King William III. leaning against a gilt railing, placed round some ornamental objects, near one of the windows. The famous Lord Keeper Somers stood beside him, while, at a little distance behind appeared Keppel, Lord Albemarle, and before him, a tall, fine-looking man, somewhat past the middle age, slight, but dignified in his person, and with an air of ease and grace in his whole position and demeanour, which bespoke long familiarity with courts. William gazed at him with a smile, and heard him speak evidently with pleasure.

"Well, my lord," he said, "I am very glad of the news you give me. With the assistance of yourself, and my Lord Keeper here, together with that of our good friend the Duke of Shrewsbury, I doubt not now my affairs will go well. I am happy to see your health so well restored, my lord; for you know my friendship for you well enough, to be aware, that I was seriously afflicted at your illness, for your own sake, as well as because it deprived me of the counsel and assistance of one, who, as I thought he would, has proved himself the only person sufficiently loved by all men, to reconcile the breaches between some of my best friends."

"Most grateful I am, sir," replied the Earl of Sunbury, to this unusually long speech, "that Heaven has made me an instrument for that purpose, and I can never sufficiently express my gratitude, for your not being angry at my long absence from your majesty's service. The arrangements thus being made, sire, I will humbly take my leave, begging your majesty not to forget the interests of my young friend, according to your gracious promise."

"I will not forget, I will not forget," replied the King. "When do you publicly announce your return, my lord?"

"I think it would be better not, sire," replied the Earl, "till after we have notified the arrangements to the three gentlemen who retire."

The King smiled. "That can be done to-morrow, my lord," he said; "and I cannot but say, that the sooner it is done the better, for my service has already suffered."

"That disagreeable task will of course fall on my Lord Keeper," said Lord Sunbury, looking to Somers with a smile.

"I shall do it without ceremony, my lord," replied Lord Somers. "It will be a mere matter of form; and if we could have found a position suitable to my Lord Wharton, I should say that we have constructed the most harmonious administration that I have seen since the glorious Revolution."

The King's brow grew somewhat dark at the name of Lord Wharton; and the Earl of Sunbury making a sign to the Lord Keeper to avoid that topic, took his leave of the King, saying, "I think I have your majesty's permission to retire through your private apartments."

As he was opening a door, a little to the King's right hand, however, he was met by the Earl of Portland, who greeted him with a well-pleased smile, and then passed on towards the King, of whom Lord Somers was taking leave at the same moment.

"May it please your majesty," said the Earl of Portland, as soon as the Lords Sunbury and Somers had departed, "the young gentleman whom you were once pleased to see concerning the Duke of Berwick's coming to England, is now here, together with another gentleman calling himself Green, whom your majesty also, I understand--"

"Yes, yes," said the King, "I will see him. I promised to see him."

"You told me also, sire," replied Lord Portland, "if ever this other gentleman applied, you would also see him. Mr. Wilton Brown, I mean."

"I will see him too," said the King. "I will see them together. Let them be called, Bentinck."

Lord Portland went to the door, and gave the necessary orders, and in a moment or two after, Wilton and his companion stood in the presence of the King.

As they entered, Lord Albemarle said a few words to William, in a low tone, to which William replied, "No, no, I will tell you if it be necessary.--Now, gentlemen," he said, "I understood, from the note received this morning by my Lord of Albemarle, that you requested an audience together, which as I had promised to each separately, I have given. Is your business the same or different?"

"It is the same, sire," replied Green at once. "But I will beg this young gentleman to urge what he has to say in the first place."

The King nodded his head to Wilton to proceed; adding, "I have little time this morning, and you may be brief; for if your business be what I think, it has been opened to me by a friend of yours, and you will hear more from me or him on Tuesday."

"If your majesty refers to the Duke of Shrewsbury," said Wilton, "I have not the honour of his acquaintance; but he promised, I know, to urge upon your majesty's clemency the case of the Duke of Gaveston, in regard to which I have now ventured to approach you."

"We are mistaking each other," said the King. "I thought you meant something else. What about the Duke?"

"When your majesty was last pleased to receive me," replied Wilton, "I had the honour of recounting to you how I had been employed by his grace to set free his daughter who had been carried away by Sir John Fenwick and other Jacobites. I explained to your majesty at that time that this daring act had been committed by those Jacobites in consequence of a quarrel between the Duke and Sir John Fenwick, which quarrel was occasioned by the Duke indignantly refusing to take part in the infamous conspiracy against your majesty. Since then, Sir John Fenwick has been arrested, and has charged the Duke with being a party to that conspiracy. He has done this entirely and evidently out of revenge, and as far as my testimony goes, I can distinctly show your majesty, that after his daughter was carried away, the Duke had no opportunity whatsoever of revealing what he knew of the conspiracy without endangering her safety till after the whole was discovered, for on the morning of her return to town, after being set free, the warrants against the conspirators were already issued."

"You told me all this before, I think," said the King, with somewhat of a heavy brow and impatient air. "Where is the Duke now?"

"He is in the Tower, sire," replied Wilton, "a prisoner of state, upon this charge of Sir John Fenwick's, and I am bold to approach your majesty to beseech you to take his case into consideration."

The King's brow had by this time grown very dark, and turning to Lord Portland, he said, "This is another, you see, Bentinck."

"I beseech your majesty," continued Wilton, as soon as the King paused, "I beseech you to hear my petition, and to grant it. It is a case in which I am deeply interested. You were pleased to say that I had conducted myself well, you were pleased to promise me your gracious favour, and I beseech you now to extend it to me so far, as at my petition to show clemency to a nobleman who, perhaps, may have acted foolishly in suffering his ears to be guilty of hearing some evil designs against you, but who testified throughout the most indignant horror at the purposes of these conspirators, who has been punished severely already by the temporary loss of his child, by the most terrible anxiety about her, and by long imprisonment in the Tower, where he now lies, withering under a sense of your majesty's displeasure. Let me entreat your majesty to grant me this petition," and advancing a step, Wilton knelt at the King's feet.

"Why, I thought, young gentleman," replied William, "that before this time you were married to the pretty heiress."

"Oh no, sire," replied Wilton, with a sad smile, "that is entirely out of the question. Such a report got abroad in the world, but I have neither station, fortune, rank, nor any other advantage to entitle me to such a hope."

"And you, Colonel," said the King, turning towards Green, "is this the object of your coming also?"

"It is, sire," answered Green, advancing. "But first of all permit me to do an act that I have never done before, and kissing your majesty's hand, to acknowledge that I feel you are and will be King of England. May I add more, that you are worthy of being so."

The King was evidently pleased and struck. "I am glad to see," he answered, holding out his hand to Green, "that we have reclaimed one Jacobite."

"Sire," answered Green, kissing the King's hand, but without rising, "my affections are not easily changed, and may remain with another house; but it were folly to deny any longer your sovereignty, and," he added, the moment after, "it would be treachery henceforth to do anything against it.--And now, sire," he continued, "let me urge most earnestly this young gentleman's petition, and let it be at my suit that the Duke's liberation is granted. Wilton here may have many petitions yet to present to your majesty on his own account. I shall never have any; and as your majesty told me to claim a boon at your hands, and promised to grant me anything that was not unreasonable, I beseech you to grant me, as not an unreasonable request, the full pardon and liberation of a man who this young gentleman, and I, and Sir John Fenwick, and I think your majesty too, well know would as soon have attempted anything against your majesty's life as he would have sacrificed his own. This is the boon I crave, this is the petition I have to present, and I hope and trust that you will grant my request."

"And have you nothing else, Colonel, to demand on your own account?" said the King, gravely.

"Nothing, sire," replied Green: "I make this my only request."

"What!" said the King, after giving a glance as playful, perhaps, as any glance could be upon the countenance of William III. "Is this the only request? I have seen in English history, since it became my duty to study it, a number of precedents of general pardons, granted under the great seal, by monarchs my predecessors, to certain of their subjects who have done some good service, for all crimes, misdemeanours, felonies, et cetera, committed in times previous. Now, sir, from a few things I have heard, it has struck me that such a patent would be not at all inexpedient in your own case, and I expected you to ask it."

"I have not, and I do not ask it, sire," replied Green, in the same grave tone with which he had previously spoken. "I may have done many things that are wrong, sire, but I have neither injured, insulted, nor offended any one whom I knew to be a true subject of the Prince I considered my lawful King. Possessing still his commission, I believed myself at liberty to levy upon those who were avowedly his enemies, the rents of that property whereof they had deprived me fighting in his cause.--Sire, I may have been wrong in my view, and I believe I have been so. I speak not in my own justification, therefore. My head is at your feet if you choose to take it: death has no terrors for me; life has no charms. I stay as long as God wills it: when he calls me hence, it matters little what way I take my departure. My request, sire, is for the liberation of the Duke, who, believe me, is perfectly innocent; and I earnestly entreat your majesty not to keep him longer within the walls of a prison, which to the heart of an Englishman is worse than death itself."

"I am sufficiently an Englishman to feel that," replied the King.-- "Your own free pardon for all offences up to this time we give, or rather promise you, should it be needed, without your asking it. Mark the King's words, gentlemen. In regard to the liberation of the Duke, demanded of us, as you have demanded it; that is, as the only request of a person who has rendered us most important service, and to whom we have pledged our word to concede some boon, we would grant it also, but--"

"Oh, sire!" exclaimed Green, "let your clemency blot out that but."

"Hear me, hear me," said the King, relapsing into his usual tone; "I would willingly grant you the Duke's liberation as the boon which you require, and which I promised; but that I granted the order for his liberation some four days ago, not even demanding bail for his appearance, but perfectly satisfied of his innocence. I ordered also such steps to be taken, that a *nolle prosequi* might be entered, so as to put his mind fully at rest. I told the Earl of Byerdale the day before yesterday, that I had done this at the request of the Duke of Shrewsbury, and I bade him take the warrant, which, signed by myself, and countersigned by Mr. Secretary Trumbull, was then lying in the hands of the clerk. It is either in the clerk's hands still, or in those of Lord Byerdale. But that lord has committed a most grievous offence in suffering any of my subjects to remain in a prison when the order was signed for their liberation."

"May it please your majesty," said Keppel, stepping forward, "I questioned the clerk this morning, as I passed, knowing what your majesty had done, and hearing, to my surprise, from my Lord Pembroke, that the Duke was still in prison. The clerk tells me that he had still the warrant, Lord Byerdale seeming to have forgotten it entirely."

"He has forgotten too many things," said the King, "and yet his memory is good when he pleases. Fetch me the warrant, Arnold. Colonel, I grant this warrant, you see, not to you. You must think of some other boon at another time. Young gentleman, I have been requested; by a true friend of yours and mine, to hear your petition upon various points, and to do something for you. I can hear no more petitions to-day, however, but perhaps you may find a kinder ear to listen to you; and as to doing anything for you," he continued, as he saw Keppel return with a paper in his hand--"as to doing anything for you, the best thing I can do is to send you to the Tower. There, take the warrant, and either get into a boat or on your horse', back, and bear the good tidings to the Duke yourself."

As he spoke, the King gave the paper into Wilton's hand, and turned partly round to the Earl of Portland with a smile; then looked round again calmly, and, by a grave inclination of the head, signified to Wilton and his companion that their audience was at an end.

As soon as they were in the lobby, Green grasped his young friend's hand eagerly in his own, demanding, "Now, Wilton, are you happy?"

"Most miserable!" replied Wilton. "This paper is indeed the greatest relief to me, because it puts me beyond all chance of dishonour. No one can impute to me now that I have done wrong, or violated my word, even by a breath; but still I am most unhappy, and the very act that I am going to do seals my unhappiness."

"Such things may well be," replied Green, "I know it from bitter experience. But how it can be so, Wilton, in your case, I cannot tell."

Wilton shook his head sorrowfully. "I cannot stay to explain all now," he said, "for I must hasten to the Duke, and not leave his mind in doubt and fear for a moment. But in going thither, I go to see her I love for the last time. The metropolis will henceforth be hateful to me, and I shall fly from it as speedily as possible. I feel that I cannot live in it after that hope is at an end. I shall apply for a commission in the army, and seek what fate may send me in some more active life; but before I go, probably this very night, if you will give me shelter, I will seek you and the Lady Helen, to both of whom I have much, very much to say. I shall find you at Lord Sherbrooke's cottage, where I last saw you? There I will explain everything. And now farewell."

Thus saying, he shook Green's hand, mounted his horse, and at a very rapid pace spurred on towards London by all the shortest roads that he could discover.

CHAPTER XLV.

The Duke's dinner in the Tower was over. He had been much agitated all day, and Laura had been agitated also, but she had concealed her emotions, in order not to increase those of her father. It was, as we have said, Sunday, and the service of the church had occupied some part of that long day's passing; but the rest had gone by very slowly, especially as the only two events which occurred to break or diversify the time told that there were other persons busy without, in matters regarding which neither Laura nor her father could take the slightest part, but which affected the future fate of both in the highest degree. Those two incidents were the arrival of Wilton's note, which we have already mentioned, and a visit from the chaplain of the Tower, to tell the Duke and Lady Laura that he had received directions and the proper authorization (few of those things were needed, indeed, in those days) to perform the ceremony of marriage between her and Wilton at any hour that she chose to name. A considerable time passed after this visit, and yet Wilton did not appear. The Duke began to look towards Laura with anxious eyes, and once he said, "I hope, Laura, you neither did nor said anything yesterday to make Wilton act coldly or unwillingly in this business?"

"Indeed, my dear father, I did not," replied Lady Laura, "and he promised me firmly to do everything in his power. Something has detained him; but depend upon it there is no cause either to fear or to doubt."

Such assurances, for a time, seemed to soothe the Duke, and put his mind more at ease; but as time passed, and still Wilton did not appear, his anxiety returned again; he would walk up and down the room; he would gaze out of the window; he would east himself into a chair with a deep sigh; and though he said nothing more, Laura, was bitterly grieved on his account, and began to share his anxiety for the result. At length a distant door was heard to open, then came the sound of the well-known step in the ante-room, making Laura's heart beat, and the Duke smile; but there was nothing joyful in the tread of that step: it was slow and thoughtful; and after the hand was placed upon the lock of the door, there was still a pause, which, though in reality very brief, seemed long to the prisoner and his daughter. At length, however, the door opened, and Wilton himself entered the room. There came a smile, too, upon his lip, but Laura could not but see that smile was a very sad one.

"We have been waiting for you most anxiously, my dear Wilton," said the Duke: "we have fancied all manner of things, all sorts of difficulties and obstacles; for I well knew that nothing but matters of absolute necessity would keep you from the side of your dear bride at this moment."

"But you still look sad, Wilton," said Lady Laura, holding out her hand to him. "Let us hear, Wilton, let us hear all at once, dear Wilton. Has anything happened to derange our plans, or prevent my father's escape?"

Wilton kissed her hand affectionately, replying, "Fear not on that account, dear Laura; fear not on that account. Your father is no longer a prisoner.--My lord duke, there is the warrant for your liberation, signed by the King's own hand, and properly countersigned."

The Duke clasped his hands together, and looked up to heaven with eyes full of thankfulness, and Laura's joy also burst forth in tears. But she saw that Wilton remained sad and cold; and mistaking the cause, she turned quickly to her father, saying, "Oh, my dear father, in this moment of joy, make him who has given us so much happiness happy also. Tell him, tell him, my dear father, that you will not, that you cannot think of refusing him your child after all that he has done for us."

"No, no, Laura," cried the Duke: "you shall be his--"

But Wilton interrupted him; and throwing his arms round Lady Laura, pressed her for a moment to his heart, took one long ardent kiss, and then turning to the Duke, said, "Pardon me, my lord duke!--It is the last! Nay, do not interrupt me, for I have a task to perform which requires all the firmness I can find to accomplish it. On seeing Lord Byerdale yesterday, he told me of the whole arrangements which he had made with you, and of the plan for your escape he showed me that, according to the note which he had written to the governor of the Tower, concerning the marriage between your daughter and myself, your escape could not be effected till the ceremony had taken place, as it was assigned as the cause for our leaving the Tower so late at night. He made me pledge myself not to disclose his part in the scheme to any one; and he then said that he would tell me the secret of my birth, if I would plight my honour not to reveal it till after your safety was secure. I pledged myself, and he told me all. I now found, my lord, that you and I had both been most shamefully deceived--deceived for the purpose, I do believe, of revenging on you and Lady Laura her former rejection of Lord Sherbrooke by driving her to marry a person altogether inferior to herself in station. You will see that he had placed me in the most difficult of all positions. If I carried out his plan of escape, I knowingly made use of his deceit to gain for myself the greatest earthly happiness. If I revealed to you what he told me, I broke my pledged word, and at the same time gave you no choice, but either unwillingly to give me your daughter's hand, or to remain, and risk the chance of longer imprisonment and trial. If I held off and disappointed you in your escape, I again broke my word to Lady Laura. You may conceive the agony of my mind during last night. There was but one hope of my being able to escape dishonour, though it was a very slight one. I determined to go to the King himself. I engaged a gentleman to go with me, who has some influence; and this morning we presented ourselves at Hampton Court, His Majesty was graciously pleased to receive us: he treated me with all kindness, and gave me the warrant for your liberation to bring hither. That warrant was already signed; for the Duke of Shrewsbury had kept his word with me, and applied for it earnestly and successfully. The Earl of Byerdale knew that it was prepared, so that he was quite safe in permitting your escape. I have now nothing further to do, my lord, than to wish you joy of your liberation, and to bid you adieu for ever."

"Stay, stay!" said the Duke, much moved. "Let me hear more, Wilton."

But Wilton had already turned to Lady Laura and taken her hand.

"Oh, Laura," he said, "if I have been deceived into making you unhappy as well as myself, forgive me. You know, you well know, that I would give every earthly good to obtain this dear hand; that I would sacrifice anything on earth for that object, but honour, truth, and integrity. Laura, I feel you can never be mine; try to forget what has been; while I seek in distant lands, not forgetfulness, if it come not accompanied by death, but the occupation of the battlefield, and the hope of a speedy and not inglorious termination to suffering. Farewell--once more, farewell!"

"Stay, stay!" said the Duke--"stay, Wilton! What was it the Earl told you? He said that you had as good blood in your veins as his own. He said you were even related to himself. What did he tell you?"

The blood mounted into Wilton's cheek. "He told me, my lord," he said, "that I was the natural son of his cousin."

And feeling that he could bear no more, he turned abruptly and quitted the apartment.

As he did so, Lady Laura sank at her father's feet, and clasped his knees. "Oh, my father," she said, "do not, do not make me miserable for ever. Think of your child's happiness before any considerations of pride; think of the noble conduct of him who has just left us; and ask yourself if I can cease to love him while I have life."

"Never, Laura, never!" said the Duke, sternly. "Had it been anything else but that, I might have yielded; but it cannot be! Never, my child, never!--So urge me not!--I would rather see you in your grave!"

Those rash and shameful words, which the basest and most unholy pride has too often in this world wrung from a parent's lips towards a child, had been scarcely uttered by the Duke, when he felt his daughter's arms relax their hold of his knees, her weight press heavily upon him, and the next instant she lay senseless on the ground.

For an instant, the consciousness of the unchristian words he had uttered smote his heart with fear; fear lest the retributive hand of Heaven should have punished his pride, even in the moment of offence, by taking away the child whose happiness he was preparing to sacrifice, and of whose death he had made light.

He called loudly for help, and his servant and Lady Laura's maid were soon in the room. They raised her head with cushions; they brought water; they called for farther assistance; and though it soon became evident that Laura had only fainted, it was long before the slightest symptom of returning consciousness appeared. The Duke, the servants, and some attendants of the governor of the Tower, were still gathered round her, and her eyes were just opening and looking faintly up, when another person was suddenly added to the group, and a mild, fine-toned voice said, in the ear of the Duke,--

"Good God! my lord duke, what has happened? Had you not better send for

Millington or Garth?"

"She is better, she is better," said the Duke, rising; "she is coming to herself again.--Good Heaven! my Lord of Sunbury, is it you? This is an unexpected pleasure."

"I cannot say," replied Lord Sunbury, "that it is an unexpected pleasure to me, my lord; for though I would rather see your grace in any other place, and heard this morning at Hampton Court that the order for your liberation was signed, yet I heard just now that you were still in the Tower; and, to say the truth, I expected to find my young friend Wilton with you. Let us attend to the lady, however," he added, seeing that his allusion to Wilton made the Duke turn a little red, and divining, perhaps, that Lady Laura's illness was in some way connected with the absence of his young friend, "she is growing better."

And kindly kneeling down beside her, he took her hand in his, saying in a tender and paternal tone, "I hope you are better, my dear young lady. Nay, nay," he added, in a lower voice, "be comforted; all will go well, depend upon it:--you are better now; you are better, I see." And then perceiving that only having seen him once before, Lady Laura did not recollect him, he added his own name, saying, "Lord Sunbury, my dear, the father, by love and by adoption, of a dear friend of yours."

The allusion to Wilton immediately produced its effect upon Lady Laura, and she burst into tears; but seeing Lord Sunbury about to rise, she clung to his hand, saying, "Do not leave me--do not leave me. I shall be better in a minute. I will send him a message by you."

"I will not, indeed, leave you," replied Lord Sunbury; "but I think we do not need all these people present just now. Your father and I and your woman will be enough."

According to his suggestion, the room was cleared, the windows were all thrown open, and in about half an hour Lady Laura had sufficiently recovered herself to sit up and speak with ease. Lord Sunbury had avoided returning to the subject of Wilton, till he fancied that she could bear it, knowing that it might be more painful to her, even to hear him conversing with her father upon such a topic, than to take part in the discussion herself. At length, however, he said,--

"Now this fair lady is tolerably well again, let me ask your grace where I can find my young friend, Wilton Brown. I was told at his lodgings that he had come on with all speed to the Tower, merely getting a fresh horse as he passed."

"He was here not long ago, my lord," replied the Duke, coldly. "He was kind enough to bring me from Hampton Court the warrant for my enlargement. He went away in some haste and in some sorrow, not from anything I said, my lord, but from what his own good sense showed him must be the consequence of some discoveries which he had made regarding his own birth. I must say he has in the business behaved most honourably, and, at the same time, most sensibly; and any-thing on earth that I can reasonably do to testify my gratitude to him for all the services he has rendered me and mine, I will willingly do it, should it cost me one half of my estates."

Lady Laura had covered her eyes with her hands, but the tears trickled through her fingers in spite of all she could do to restrain them. Lord Sunbury, too, was a good deal agitated, and showed it more than might have been expected in a man so calm and deliberate as himself. He even rose from his chair, and walked twice across the room, before he replied.

"My lord duke," he said, at length, "from what you say, I fear that both Wilton and your grace have acted hastily; and I am pained at it the more, because I believe that I myself am in some degree the cause of all the misery that he now feels, and of all the grief which I can clearly see is in the breast of this dear young lady. I have done Wilton wrong, my lord, by a want of proper precaution and care--most unin-tentionally and unknowingly; but still I have done him wrong, which I fear may be irreparable. I must see, and endeavour, as far as it is in my power, to remedy what has gone amiss; but whether I can, or whether I cannot do so, I have determined to atone for my fault in the only way that it is possible. The last heir in my family entail is lately dead: my estates are at my own disposal. I have notified to the King this day, that I have adopted Wilton Brown as my son and heir; and his Majesty has been graciously pleased to promise that a patent shall pass under the great seal, conveying to him my titles and honours at my death. This is all that I know with certainty can be done at present; but there may be more done hereafter, in regard to which I will not enter at present; and oh! my lord," he continued, seeing the Duke cast down his eyes in cold silence, "for my sake, for Wilton's sake, for this young lady's sake, at all events suspend your decision till we can see farther in this matter."

The Duke raised his eyes to his daughter's face, and yielded, though but in a faint degree, to her imploring look.

"I will suspend my decision, my lord, at your request," he replied, "if it will give you any pleasure. But Laura knows my opinion, and--"

"Nay, nay," said the Earl, "we will say no more upon the subject then, at present, my lord: But as your grace has the order for your liberation, and there can be no great pleasure in staying in this place, perhaps your grace and Lady Laura will get into my carriage, which is now in the court; and while your servants clear your apartments, and proceed to make preparations at Beaufort House, I trust you will take your supper at my poor dwelling. There I may have an opportunity, my lord," he added, turning with a graceful bow to the Duke, "of telling you, who are a politician, some great political changes that are taking place, though I fear, that as I expect no guests of any kind, and have hitherto preserved a strict incognito, I shall have no way of entertaining this fair lady for the evening."

Laura shook her head with a melancholy air, but made no reply. The Duke, however, was taken with the bait of political news, and accepted the invitation, merely saying, "I take it for granted, my lord, that Mr. Brown is not at your house."

"As far as I know," replied Lord Sunbury, "he is not aware of my being in England. I came to seek him here, wishing to tell him various matters; but up to this time, I have neither written to him, nor heard from him, since I have been in this country. And now, my lord," he continued, taking up the warrant from the table, "you had better let me go and speak with the Governor's deputy here, concerning this paper, and in five minutes I will be back, to conduct you, at liberty, to my house."

Thus saying, he left them; and Lady Laura, certainly calmed and comforted by his kindly manner, and the hopeful tone in which he spoke, prepared with pleasure to go with him. Her father mentioned Wilton's name no more; but gave some orders to his servant and, by the time that they were ready to go, Lord Sunbury had returned with the Lieutenant of the Governor, announcing that the gates of the Tower were open to the Duke. The Earl then offered his hand to the fair girl, and led her down to his carriage, saying in a low tone as they went, "Fear not, my dear young lady; we shall find means to soften your father in time."

After a long and tedious drive through the dull streets of London, the carriage of the Earl of Sunbury stopped at the door of his house in St. James's Square. None of his servants appeared yet in livery, and the man who opened the door was his own valet. He seemed not a little astonished at the sight of a lady and gentleman with his master; and the Earl was as much surprised to hear loud voices from the large dining-room on his left hand.

The Duke and Lady Laura, however, entered, and were passing on; but the valet, as soon as he had closed the door, advanced and whispered a few words to the Earl.

The Earl questioned him again in the same tone, put his hand for a moment to his forehead, and then said, addressing the Duke, "There are some persons up stairs, my lord duke, that we would rather you did not see at this moment. I will speak to them for an instant, and be down with you directly, if you will go into the dining-room. You will there, I understand, find Lord Byerdale and his son, the latter of whom, it seems, has come hither for my support and advice, and has been followed by his father."

"But, my lord, my lord," said the Duke, "after Lord Byerdale's conduct to myself--"

"Enter into no dispute with him till I come, my dear duke," said the Earl--"I will be with you in one minute; and his lordship of Byerdale will have quite sufficient to settle with me, to give occupation to his thoughts for the rest of the evening. You may chance to see triumphant villany rebuked--I wanted to have escaped the matter; but since he has presumed to come into my house, I must take the task upon myself."

The tone in which he spoke, and the expectation of what was to follow, fixed the Duke's determination at once; and drawing the arm of Lady Laura within his own, he followed the servant, who now threw open the door to which Lord Sunbury pointed, and entered the dining-room, while the Earl himself ascended the stairs.

CHAPTER XLVI.

A scene curious but yet painful presented itself to the eyes of Lady Laura and her father on entering the dining-room of Lord Sunbury's house. On the side of the room opposite to the door stood Lord Sherbrooke, with his arms folded on his chest, his brow contracted, his teeth firmly shut, his lips drawn close, and every feature but the bright and flashing eye betokening a strong and vigorous struggle to command the passions which were busy in his bosom. Seated at the table, on which the young nobleman had laid down his sword, was his beautiful wife, with her eyes buried in her hands, and no part of her face to be seen but a portion of the cheek as pale as ashes, and the small delicate ear glowing like fire. The sun was far to the westward, and streaming in across the open space of the square, poured through the window upon her beautiful form, which, even under the pressure of deep grief, fell naturally into lines of the most perfect grace.

But the same evening light poured across also, and streamed full upon the face and form of the Earl of Byerdale, who seemed to have totally forgotten, in excess of rage, the calm command over himself which he usually exercised even in moments of the greatest excitement. His lip was quivering, his brow was contracted, his eye was rolling with strong passion, his hand was clenched; and at the moment that Laura and the Duke went round the table from the door towards the side of the room on which were Lord Sherbrooke and his wife, the Earl was shaking his clenched hand at his son, accompanying by that gesture of wrath the most terrible denunciations upon his head.

"Yes, sir, yes!" he exclaimed. "I tell you my curse is upon you! I divorce myself from your mother's memory! I cast you off, and abandon you for ever! Think not that I will have pity upon you, when I see your open-mouthed creditors swallowing you up living, and dooming you to a prison for life. May an eternal curse fall upon me, if ever I relieve you with a shilling even to buy you bread! See if the man in whose house you have sought shelter--see if this Earl of Sunbury, with whom, doubtless, you have been plotting your father's destruction--see if this undermining politician, this diplomatic mole, will give you means to pay your debts, or furnish you with bread to feed yourself and your pretty companion there! No, sir, no! Lead forth, to the beggary to which you have brought her, the beggarly offspring of that runagate Jacobite! Lead her forth, and with a train of babies at your heels, sing French ballads in the streets to gain yourself subsistence.--You thought that I had no clue to your proceedings. I fancied she was your mistress, and that mattered little, for it is the only thing fitted for the beggarly exile's daughter. But since she is your wife, look to it to provide for her yourself!"

He must have heard somebody enter the room, but he turned not the least in that direction, carried away by the awful whirlwind of his fury. He was even still going on, without looking round; but it was a woman's voice, the voice of a gentle, but noble-hearted woman that stopped him. Lady Laura, the moment she entered the room, recognised in the bending form of her who sat weeping and trembling at the table, one who had been kind to her in danger and in terror, and the first impulse was to go to her support. But when she heard the insulting and gross words of the Earl of Byerdale, her spirit rose, her heart swelled with indignation, and with courage, which she might not have possessed in her own case, she turned full upon him, exclaiming,--

"For shame, Earl of Byerdale!--for shame! This to a woman in a woman's presence! If you have forgotten that you are a gentleman, have you forgotten that you are a man?" And going quickly forward, she threw her arm round the neck of the weeping girl, exclaiming, "Look up, dear Caroline: look up, sweet lady! You are not without support! A friend is near you!"

Lady Sherbrooke looked up, saw who it was, and instantly cast herself upon her bosom.

The Earl of Byerdale turned his eyes from Laura to the Duke, evidently confounded and surprised, and put his hand upon his brow, as if to collect his thoughts. The next minute, however, he said, with a sneering air, "Ha, pretty lady, is that you? Ha, my lord duke, have you escaped from the Tower? You are somewhat early in your proceedings! Why, it wants half an hour of night! But doubtless the impatient bridegroom was eager to have all complete, and I have now to congratulate my Lady Laura Brown upon her father's sudden enfranchisement, and her marriage with my dear cousin's natural child. Ma'am, I am your most obedient, humble servant. Duke, I congratulate you upon the noble alliance you have formed. You come well, you come happily, to witness me curse that base and degenerate boy. But it is a pity you did not bring the happy bridegroom, Mr. Brown, that we might have two fine specimens of noble alliances in one room."

"You are mistaken, sir," said the Duke furiously; "you are mistaken, sir. Your villany is discovered; your base treachery has been told by a man who was too honourable to take advantage of it, even for his own happiness."

"Then, my lord duke," replied the Earl of Byerdale, "he is as great a liar in this instance as you have proved yourself a fool in every one; for he plighted me his word not to reveal anything till your safety was secure."

"It is you, sir, are the liar!" replied the Duke, forgetting everything in his anger, which was now raised to the highest pitch. "It is you, sir, who are the liar, as you have been the knave throughout, and may now prove to be the fool too!"

"Hush, hush!" exclaimed the voice of Lord Sherbrooke, raised to a loud tone. "Remember, my lord duke, that he is still my father!"

"Sir!" exclaimed the Earl, turning first upon his son, "I am your father no longer! For you, duke, I see how the matter has gone with this vile and treacherous knave whom I have fostered! But as sure as I am Earl of Byerdale--"

"You are so no longer!" said a voice beside him, and at the same moment a strong muscular hand was laid upon his shoulder, with a grasp that he could not shake off:

The Earl turned fiercely round, and laid his hand upon his sword; but his eyes lighted instantly on the fine stern countenance of Colonel Green, who keeping his grasp firmly upon the shoulder of the other, bent his dark eyes full upon his face.

The whole countenance and appearance of him whom we have called the Earl of Byerdale became like a withered flower. The colour forsook his cheeks and his lips; he grew pale, he grew livid; his proud head sunk, his knees bent, he trembled in every limb; and when Green, at length, pushed him from him, saying in a loud tone and with a stern brow, "Get thee from me, Harry Sherbrooke!" he sank into a chair, unable to speak, or move, or support himself.

In the meantime, his son had cast his eyes upon the ground, and remained looking downwards with a look of pain, but not surprise; while treading close upon the steps of Colonel Green appeared Wilton Brown with the Lady Helen Oswald clinging to rather than leaning on his arm, and the Earl of Sunbury on her right hand.

Those who were most surprised in the room were certainly the Duke and Lady Laura, for they had been suddenly made witnesses to a strange scene without having any key to the feelings, the motives, or the actions of the performers therein; and the Duke gazed with quite sufficient wonder upon all he saw, to drown and overcome all feelings of anger at beholding Wilton so unexpectedly in the house of the Earl of Sunbury.

For a moment or two after the stern gesture of Green, there was silence, as if every one else were too much afraid or too much surprised to speak; and he also continued for a short space gazing sternly upon the man before him, as if his mind laboured with all that he had to say. It was not, however, to the person whom his presence seemed entirely to have blasted, that he next addressed himself.

"My Lord of Sunbury," he said, "you see this man before me, and you also mark bow terrible to him is this sudden meeting with one whom he has deemed long dead. When last we met, I left him on the shores of Ireland after the battle of the Boyne, in which I took part and he did not. The ship in which I was supposed to have sailed was wrecked at sea, and every soul therein perished. But I had marked this man's eagerness to make me quit my native land, in which I had great duties to perform, and I never went to the vessel, in which if I had gone, I should have met a watery grave. During the time that has since passed, he has enjoyed wealth that belonged not to him, a title to which he had no claim. He has raised himself to power and to station, and he has abused his power and disgraced his station, till his King is weary of him, and his country can endure him no longer. In the meanwhile, I have waited my time; I have watched all his movements; I have heard of all the inquiries he has set on foot to prove my death, and all the investigations he instituted, when he found that the boy who was with me had been set on shore again. I have given him full scope and licence to act as he chose; but I have come at length, to wrest from him that which is not his, and to strip him of a rank to which he has no claim.-

-Have you anything to say, Harry Sherbrooke?" he continued, fixing his eye upon him. "Have you anything to say against that which I advance?"

While he had been speaking, the other had evidently been making a struggle to resume his composure and command over himself, and he now gazed upon him with a fierce and vindictive look, but without attempting to rise.

"I will not deny, Lennard Sherbrooke," he replied, "that I know you; I will not even deny that I know you to be Earl of Byerdale. But I know you also to be a proclaimed traitor and outlaw, having borne arms against the lawful sovereign of these realms, subjected by just decree to forfeiture and attainder; and I call upon every one here present to aid me in arresting you, and you to surrender yourself, to take your trial according to law!" "Weak man, give over!" replied the Colonel. "All your schemes are frustrated, all your base designs are vain. You writhe under my heel, like a crushed adder, but, serpent, I tell you, you bite upon a file. First, for myself, I am not a proclaimed traitor; but, pleading the King's full pardon for everything in which I may have offended, I claim all that is mine own, my rights, my privileges, my long forgotten name, even to the small pittance of inheritance, which, in your vast accessions of property, you did not even scruple to grasp at, and which has certainly mightily recovered itself under your careful and parsimonious hand. But, nevertheless, though I claim all that is my own, I claim neither the title nor the estates of Byerdale. Wilton, my boy, stand forward, and let any one who ever saw or knew your gallant and noble father, and your mother, who is now a saint in heaven, say if they do not see in you a blended image of the two."

"He was his natural child! he was his natural child!" cried Henry Sherbrooke, starting up from his seat. "I ascertained it beyond a doubt! I have proof! I have proof!"

"Again, false man?--Again?" said Lennard Sherbrooke.

"Cannot shame keep you silent? You have no proof! You can have no proof!--You found no proof of the marriage--granted; because care was taken that you should not. But I have proof sufficient, sir. This lady, whom I must call in this land Mistress Helen Oswald, though the late King bestowed upon her father and herself a rank higher than that to which she now lays claim, was present at the private marriage of her sister to my brother, by a Protestant clergyman, before Sir Harry Oswald ever quitted England. There is also the woman servant, who was present likewise, still living and ready to be produced; and if more be wanting, here is the certificate of the clergyman himself, signed in due form, together with my brother's solemn attestation of his marriage, given before he went to the fatal battle in which he fell. To possess yourself of these papers, of the existence of which you yourself must have entertained some suspicions, you used unjustifiable arts towards this noble Earl of Sunbury, which were specious enough even to deceive his wisdom; but I obtained information of the facts, and frustrated your devices."

"Ay," said Harry Sherbrooke, "through my worthy son, doubtless, through my worthy son, who, beyond all question, used his leisure hours in reading, privately, his father's letters and despatches, for the great purpose of making that father a beggar!"

"I call Heaven to witness!" exclaimed the young gentleman, clasping his hands together eagerly. But Lord Sunbury interposed.

"No, sir," he said, "your son needed no such arts to learn that fact, at least; for even before I sent over the papers to you which you demanded, I wrote to your son, telling him the facts, in order to guard against their misapplication. Unfortunate circumstances prevented his receiving my letter in time to answer me, which would have stopped me from sending them. He communicated the fact, however, to Colonel Sherbrooke, and the result has been their preservation."

The unfortunate man was about to speak again; but Lord Sunbury waved his hand mildly, saying, "Indeed, my good sir, it would be better to utter no more of such words as we have already heard from you. Should you be inclined to contest rights and claims which do not admit of a doubt, it must be in another place and not here. You will remember, however, that were you even to succeed in shaking the legitimacy of my young friend, the Earl of Byerdale here present, which cannot by any possibility be done, you would but convey the title and estates to his uncle, Colonel Sherbrooke, to whose consummate prudence, in favour of his nephew, it is now owing that these estates, having been suffered to rest for so many years in your hands, no forfeiture has taken place, which must have been the case if he had claimed them for his nephew before this period. Whatever be the result, you lose them altogether. But I am happy that it is in my power," he added, advancing towards him whom we have hitherto called Lord Sherbrooke, "to say that this reverse will not sink your family in point of fortune so much as might, be imagined. That, sir, is spared to you, by your son's marriage with this young lady."

Caroline started up eagerly from the table, gazing with wild and joyful eyes in the face of Lord Sunbury, and exclaiming, "Have you, have you accomplished it?"

"Yes, my dear young lady, I have," replied Lord Sunbury.

"The King, in consideration of the old friendship which subsisted between your father and himself, in youthful days, before political strifes divided them, has granted that the estate yet unappropriated shall be restored to you, on two conditions, one of which is already fulfilled--your marriage with an English Protestant gentleman, and the other, which doubtless you will fulfil, residence in this country, and obedience to the laws. He told me to inform you that he was not a man to strip the orphan. You will thus have competence, happy, liberal competence."

Her husband pressed Caroline to his bosom for a moment. But he then walked round the table, approached his father, and kissed his hand, saying, in a low voice, "My lord, let a repentant son be at least happy in sharing all with his father."

For once in his life his father was overcome, and bending down his head upon son's neck, he wept.

Lord Sunbury gazed around him for a moment; but then turning to Lady Helen Oswald, he said, "I have much to say to you, but it must be in private. Nevertheless, even now, let me say that your motives have been explained to me; that I understand them; that she who could sacrifice her heart's best affections to a parent in exile, in poverty, in sickness, and in sorrow, has a greater claim than ever upon the heart of every noble man. You have, of old, deeper claims on mine, and by the ring upon this finger, by the state of solitude in which my life has been passed, you may judge that those claims have not been forgotten--Helen?" he added, taking her hand in his.

The Lady Helen turned her head away, with a cheek that was glowing deeply; but her hand was not withdrawn, and the fingers clasped upon those of Lord Sunbury.

The Earl smiled brightly. "And now, my lord duke," he said, "I besought your lordship about an hour ago to suspend your decision upon a point of great importance. Did I do right?"

"My lord," answered the Duke, gaily, "I hope I am not too quick this time; but my decision is already made. Wilton, my dear boy, take her--take her--I give her to you with my whole heart!"

The Codes Of Hammurabi And Moses
W. W. Davies

QTY

The discovery of the Hammurabi Code is one of the greatest achievements of archaeology, and is of paramount interest, not only to the student of the Bible, but also to all those interested in ancient history...

Religion   **ISBN:** *1-59462-338-4*   **Pages:132**
MSRP $12.95

The Theory of Moral Sentiments
Adam Smith

QTY

This work from 1749. contains original theories of conscience amd moral judgment and it is the foundation for systemof morals.

Philosophy **ISBN:** *1-59462-777-0*   **Pages:536**
MSRP $19.95

Jessica's First Prayer
Hesba Stretton

QTY

In a screened and secluded corner of one of the many railway-bridges which span the streets of London there could be seen a few years ago, from five o'clock every morning until half past eight, a tidily set-out coffee-stall, consisting of a trestle and board, upon which stood two large tin cans, with a small fire of charcoal burning under each so as to keep the coffee boiling during the early hours of the morning when the work-people were thronging into the city on their way to their daily toil...

Pages:84

Childrens   **ISBN:** *1-59462-373-2*   *MSRP $9.95*

My Life and Work
Henry Ford

QTY

Henry Ford revolutionized the world with his implementation of mass production for the Model T automobile. Gain valuable business insight into his life and work with his own auto-biography... "We have only started on our development of our country we have not as yet, with all our talk of wonderful progress, done more than scratch the surface. The progress has been wonderful enough but..."

Pages:300

Biographies/   **ISBN:** *1-59462-198-5*   *MSRP $21.95*

The Art of Cross-Examination
Francis Wellman

QTY

I presume it is the experience of every author, after his first book is published upon an important subject, to be almost overwhelmed with a wealth of ideas and illustrations which could readily have been included in his book, and which to his own mind, at least, seem to make a second edition inevitable. Such certainly was the case with me; and when the first edition had reached its sixth impression in five months, I rejoiced to learn that it seemed to my publishers that the book had met with a sufficiently favorable reception to justify a second and considerably enlarged edition. ..

Pages:412

Reference   **ISBN: *1-59462-647-2***   *MSRP $19.95*

On the Duty of Civil Disobedience
Henry David Thoreau

QTY

Thoreau wrote his famous essay, On the Duty of Civil Disobedience, as a protest against an unjust but popular war and the immoral but popular institution of slave-owning. He did more than write—he declined to pay his taxes, and was hauled off to gaol in consequence. Who can say how much this refusal of his hastened the end of the war and of slavery ?

Law   **ISBN: *1-59462-747-9***   **Pages:48**

MSRP $7.45

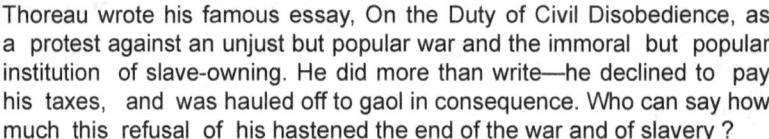

Dream Psychology Psychoanalysis for Beginners
Sigmund Freud

QTY

Sigmund Freud, born Sigismund Schlomo Freud (May 6, 1856 - September 23, 1939), was a Jewish-Austrian neurologist and psychiatrist who co-founded the psychoanalytic school of psychology. Freud is best known for his theories of the unconscious mind, especially involving the mechanism of repression; his redefinition of sexual desire as mobile and directed towards a wide variety of objects; and his therapeutic techniques, especially his understanding of transference in the therapeutic relationship and the presumed value of dreams as sources of insight into unconscious desires.

Pages:196

Psychology   **ISBN: *1-59462-905-6***   *MSRP $15.45*

The Miracle of Right Thought
Orison Swett Marden

QTY

Believe with all of your heart that you will do what you were made to do. When the mind has once formed the habit of holding cheerful, happy, prosperous pictures, it will not be easy to form the opposite habit. It does not matter how improbable or how far away this realization may see, or how dark the prospects may be, if we visualize them as best we can, as vividly as possible, hold tenaciously to them and vigorously struggle to attain them, they will gradually become actualized, realized in the life. But a desire, a longing without endeavor, a yearning abandoned or held indifferently will vanish without realization.

Pages:360

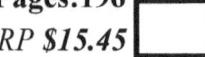

Self Help   **ISBN: *1-59462-644-8***   *MSRP $25.45*

www.bookjungle.com *email: sales@bookjungle.com fax: 630-214-0564 mail: Book Jungle PO Box 2226 Champaign, IL 61825*

QTY

The Rosicrucian Cosmo-Conception Mystic Christianity by *Max Heindel*   ISBN: *1-59462-188-8*   **$38.95**
The Rosicrucian Cosmo-conception is not dogmatic, neither does it appeal to any other authority than the reason of the student. It is: not controversial, but is: sent forth in the, hope that it may help to clear...   *New Age/Religion Pages 646*

Abandonment To Divine Providence by *Jean-Pierre de Caussade*   ISBN: *1-59462-228-0*   **$25.95**
"The Rev. Jean Pierre de Caussade was one of the most remarkable spiritual writers of the Society of Jesus in France in the 18th Century. His death took place at Toulouse in 1751. His works have gone through many editions and have been republished...   *Inspirational/Religion Pages 400*

Mental Chemistry by *Charles Haanel*   ISBN: *1-59462-192-6*   **$23.95**
Mental Chemistry allows the change of material conditions by combining and appropriately utilizing the power of the mind. Much like applied chemistry creates something new and unique out of careful combinations of chemicals the mastery of mental chemistry...   *New Age Pages 354*

The Letters of Robert Browning and Elizabeth Barret Barrett 1845-1846 vol II   ISBN: *1-59462-193-4*   **$35.95**
by *Robert Browning* and *Elizabeth Barrett*   *Biographies Pages 596*

Gleanings In Genesis (volume I) by *Arthur W. Pink*   ISBN: *1-59462-130-6*   **$27.45**
Appropriately has Genesis been termed "the seed plot of the Bible" for in it we have, in germ form, almost all of the great doctrines which are afterwards fully developed in the books of Scripture which follow...   *Religion/Inspirational Pages 420*

The Master Key by *L. W. de Laurence*   ISBN: *1-59462-001-6*   **$30.95**
In no branch of human knowledge has there been a more lively increase of the spirit of research during the past few years than in the study of Psychology, Concentration and Mental Discipline. The requests for authentic lessons in Thought Control, Mental Discipline and...   *New Age/Business Pages 422*

The Lesser Key Of Solomon Goetia by *L. W. de Laurence*   ISBN: *1-59462-092-X*   **$9.95**
This translation of the first book of the "Lernegton" which is now for the first time made accessible to students of Talismanic Magic was done, after careful collation and edition, from numerous Ancient Manuscripts in Hebrew, Latin, and French...   *New Age/Occult Pages 92*

Rubaiyat Of Omar Khayyam by *Edward Fitzgerald*   ISBN:*1-59462-332-5*   **$13.95**
Edward Fitzgerald, whom the world has already learned, in spite of his own efforts to remain within the shadow of anonymity, to look upon as one of the rarest poets of the century, was born at Bredfield, in Suffolk, on the 31st of March, 1809. He was the third son of John Purcell...   *Music Pages 172*

Ancient Law by *Henry Maine*   ISBN: *1-59462-128-4*   **$29.95**
The chief object of the following pages is to indicate some of the earliest ideas of mankind, as they are reflected in Ancient Law, and to point out the relation of those ideas to modern thought.   *Religion/History Pages 452*

Far-Away Stories by *William J. Locke*   ISBN: *1-59462-129-2*   **$19.45**
"Good wine needs no bush, but a collection of mixed vintages does. And this book is just such a collection. Some of the stories I do not want to remain buried for ever in the museum files of dead magazine-numbers an author's not unpardonable vanity..."   *Fiction Pages 272*

Life of David Crockett by *David Crockett*   ISBN: *1-59462-250-7*   **$27.45**
"Colonel David Crockett was one of the most remarkable men of the times in which he lived. Born in humble life, but gifted with a strong will, an indomitable courage, and unremitting perseverance...   *Biographies/New Age Pages 424*

Lip-Reading by *Edward Nitchie*   ISBN: *1-59462-206-X*   **$25.95**
Edward B. Nitchie, founder of the New York School for the Hard of Hearing, now the Nitchie School of Lip-Reading, Inc, wrote "LIP-READING Principles and Practice". The development and perfecting of this meritorious work on lip-reading was an undertaking...   *How-to Pages 400*

A Handbook of Suggestive Therapeutics, Applied Hypnotism, Psychic Science   ISBN: *1-59462-214-0*   **$24.95**
by *Henry Munro*   *Health/New Age/Health/Self-help Pages 376*

A Doll's House: and Two Other Plays by *Henrik Ibsen*   ISBN: *1-59462-112-8*   **$19.95**
Henrik Ibsen created this classic when in revolutionary 1848 Rome. Introducing some striking concepts in playwriting for the realist genre, this play has been studied the world over.   *Fiction/Classics/Plays 308*

The Light of Asia by *sir Edwin Arnold*   ISBN: *1-59462-204-3*   **$13.95**
In this poetic masterpiece, Edwin Arnold describes the life and teachings of Buddha. The man who was to become known as Buddha to the world was born as Prince Gautama of India but he rejected the worldly riches and abandoned the reigns of power when...   *Religion/History/Biographies Pages 170*

The Complete Works of Guy de Maupassant by *Guy de Maupassant*   ISBN: *1-59462-157-8*   **$16.95**
"For days and days, nights and nights, I had dreamed of that first kiss which was to consecrate our engagement, and I knew not on what spot I should put my lips..."   *Fiction/Classics Pages 240*

The Art of Cross-Examination by *Francis L. Wellman*   ISBN: *1-59462-309-0*   **$26.95**
Written by a renowned trial lawyer, Wellman imparts his experience and uses case studies to explain how to use psychology to extract desired information through questioning.   *How-to/Science/Reference Pages 408*

Answered or Unanswered? by *Louisa Vaughan*   ISBN: *1-59462-248-5*   **$10.95**
Miracles of Faith in China   *Religion Pages 112*

The Edinburgh Lectures on Mental Science (1909) by *Thomas*   ISBN: *1-59462-008-3*   **$11.95**
This book contains the substance of a course of lectures recently given by the writer in the Queen Street Hall, Edinburgh. Its purpose is to indicate the Natural Principles governing the relation between Mental Action and Material Conditions...   *New Age Psychology Pages 148*

Ayesha by *H. Rider Haggard*   ISBN: *1-59462-301-5*   **$24.95**
Verily and indeed it is the unexpected that happens! Probably if there was one person upon the earth from whom the Editor of this, and of a certain previous history, did not expect to hear again...   *Classics Pages 380*

Ayala's Angel by *Anthony Trollope*   ISBN: *1-59462-352-X*   **$29.95**
The two girls were both pretty, but Lucy who was twenty-one who supposed to be simple and comparatively unattractive, whereas Ayala was credited, as her Bombwhat romantic name might show, with poetic charm and a taste for romance. Ayala when her father died was nineteen...   *Fiction Pages 484*

The American Commonwealth by *James Bryce*   ISBN: *1-59462-286-8*   **$34.45**
An interpretation of American democratic political theory. It examines political mechanics and society from the perspective of Scotsman James Bryce   *Politics Pages 572*

Stories of the Pilgrims by *Margaret P. Pumphrey*   ISBN: *1-59462-116-0*   **$17.95**
This book explores pilgrims religious oppression in England as well as their escape to Holland and eventual crossing to America on the Mayflower, and their early days in New England...   *History Pages 268*

www.bookjungle.com *email: sales@bookjungle.com fax: 630-214-0564 mail: Book Jungle PO Box 2226 Champaign, IL 61825*

QTY

The Fasting Cure by *Sinclair Upton* ISBN: *1-59462-222-1* **$13.95**

In the Cosmopolitan Magazine for May, 1910, and in the Contemporary Review (London) for April, 1910, I published an article dealing with my experiences in fasting. I have written a great many magazine articles, but never one which attracted so much attention... New Age/Self Help/Health Pages 164

Hebrew Astrology by *Sepharial* ISBN: *1-59462-308-2* **$13.45**

In these days of advanced thinking it is a matter of common observation that we have left many of the old landmarks behind and that we are now pressing forward to greater heights and to a wider horizon than that which represented the mind-content of our progenitors... Astrology Pages 144

Thought Vibration or The Law of Attraction in the Thought World ISBN: *1-59462-127-6* **$12.95**

by *William Walker Atkinson* *Psychology/Religion Pages 144*

Optimism by *Helen Keller* ISBN: *1-59462-108-X* **$15.95**

Helen Keller was blind, deaf, and mute since 19 months old, yet famously learned how to overcome these handicaps, communicate with the world, and spread her lectures promoting optimism. An inspiring read for everyone... Biographies/Inspirational Pages 84

Sara Crewe by *Frances Burnett* ISBN: *1-59462-360-0* **$9.45**

In the first place, Miss Minchin lived in London. Her home was a large, dull, tall one, in a large, dull square, where all the houses were alike, and all the sparrows were alike, and where all the door-knockers made the same heavy sound... Childrens/Classic Pages 88

The Autobiography of Benjamin Franklin by *Benjamin Franklin* ISBN: *1-59462-135-7* **$24.95**

The Autobiography of Benjamin Franklin has probably been more extensively read than any other American historical work, and no other book of its kind has had such ups and downs of fortune. Franklin lived for many years in England, where he was agent... Biographies/History Pages 332

Name	
Email	
Telephone	
Address	
City, State ZIP	

☐ **Credit Card** ☐ **Check / Money Order**

Credit Card Number	
Expiration Date	
Signature	

Please Mail to: Book Jungle
PO Box 2226
Champaign, IL 61825
or Fax to: 630-214-0564

ORDERING INFORMATION

web*: www.bookjungle.com*
email*: sales@bookjungle.com*
fax*: 630-214-0564*
mail*: Book Jungle PO Box 2226 Champaign, IL 61825*
or PayPal *to sales@bookjungle.com*

Please contact us for bulk discounts

DIRECT-ORDER TERMS

**20% Discount if You Order
Two or More Books**
Free Domestic Shipping!
Accepted: Master Card, Visa,
Discover, American Express

www.ingramcontent.com/pod-product-compliance
Lightning Source LLC
Chambersburg PA
CBHW081140020726

47504CB00009B/1931